NAMING THE BONES

NAMING THE BONES

Louise Welsh

WINDSOR
PARAGON

First published 2010
by Canongate Books
This Large Print edition published 2010
by BBC Audiobooks Ltd
by arrangement with
Canongate Books Ltd

Hardcover ISBN: 978 1 408 48717 4
Softcover   ISBN: 978 1 408 48718 1

British Library Cataloguing in Publication Data available

Printed and bound in Great Britain by
CPI Antony Rowe, Chippenham and Eastbourne

For Clare Connelly and Lauchlin Bell

That one should leave The Green Wood
suddenly
    In the good comrade-time of youth
    And clothed in the first coat of truth
Set out on an uncharted sea

Who'll ever know what star
    Summoned him, what mysterious shell
    Locked in his ear that music and that spell
And what grave ship was waiting for him there?

The greenwood empties soon of leaf and song.
    Truth turns to pain. Our coats grow sere.
    Barren the comings and goings on this shore.
He anchors off The Island of the Young.

'In Memoriam I.K.',
George Mackay Brown

Part One

Edinburgh & Glasgow

Chapter One

Murray Watson slit the seal on the cardboard box in front of him and started to sort through the remnants of a life. He lifted a handful of papers and carefully splayed them across the desk. Pages of foolscap, blue-tinted writing paper, leaves torn from school jotters, stationery printed with the address of a London hotel. Some of it was covered in close-packed handwriting, like a convict's letters home. Others were bare save for a few words or phrases.

James Laing stepped out into an ordinary day.

Nothing could have prepared James for the . . .

James Laing was an ordinary man who inhabited a . . .

The creature stared down on James with its one ghastly fish eye. It winked.

Murray laughed, a sudden bark in the empty room. Christ, it had better get more interesting than this or he was in trouble. He reached into the pile and slid out a page at random. It was a picture, a naïve drawing done in green felt-tip of a woman with a triangular dress for a body. Her stick arms were long and snaking. They waved up into a sky strewn with sharp-angled stars; the left corner presided over by a pipe-smoking crescent moon, the right by a broadly smiling sun. No signature. It was crap, the kind of doodle that deserved to be crumpled into a ball and fired into the bin. But if it had been deliberately kept, it was a moment, a clue to a life.

He reached back into the box and pulled out another bundle of papers, looking for notebooks, something substantial, not wanting to save the best till last, though he had time to be patient.

Pages of figures and subtractions, money owed, rent due, monies promised. A trio of Tarot cards; the Fool poised jauntily on the edge of a precipice, Death triumphant on horseback, skull face grinning behind his visor, the Moon a pale beauty dressed in white leading a two-headed hound on a silver leash. A napkin from a café, printed pink on white *Aida's,* a faint stain slopped across its edge— frothy coffee served in a glass cup. A newspaper cutting of a smiling yet serious man running a comb through his side parting; the same man, billiard-ball smooth and miserable on his hirsute double's left side. *Are you worried about hair loss?* The solution to baldness carelessly cut through and on the other side a listing for a happening in the Grassmarket. No photograph, just the names, date and time. *Archie Lunan, Bobby Robb and Christie Graves, 7.30pm on Sunday 25th September at The Last Drop.*

Then Murray struck gold, an old red corduroy address book held together by a withered elastic band and cramped with script. A diary would have been better, but Archie wasn't the diary-keeping kind. Murray opened the book and flicked through its pages. Initials, nicknames, first names or surnames, no one was awarded both.

Danny

4

Denny
Bobby Boy
Ruby!
I thought I saw you walking by the shore

Lists of names with the odd phrase scribbled underneath. There was no attempt at alphabetisation. He was getting glimpses already, a shambles of a life, but it had produced more than most of the men that went sober to their desks at nine every morning.

Ramie
Moon
Jessa * *
Diana the huntress, Persephone hidden,
names can bless or curse unbidden.

Murray would have liked photographs. He'd seen some already, of course. The orange-tinted close-up of Archie that showed him thin and bestraggled, something like an unhinged Jesus, his hands knuckled threateningly around his features, as if preparing to tear the face from his head. It was all art and shadows. The other snaps came from a *Glasgow Herald* feature on Professor James's group that Murray had managed to pull from the newspaper's archive. Archie always in the background caught in a laugh, squinting against the sky; Archie cupping a cigarette to his mouth, the wind blowing his fringe across his eyes. It would be good to have one of him as a boy, when his features were still fine.

Murray pulled himself up. He was in danger of falling into an amateur's trap, looking for what he

5

wished for rather than what was there. He hadn't slept much the night before. His mind had got into one of those loops that occasionally infected him, information bouncing around in his brain, like the crazy lines on his computer screensaver. He'd made a cup of tea in the early hours of the morning and drunk it at the fold-down shelf that served as a table in the galley kitchen of his small flat, trying to empty his brain and think of nothing but the plain white cup cradled in his hand.

He would divide the contents of the box into three piles—interesting, possible and dross—cataloguing as he went. Once he'd done that he could get caught up in details, pick at the minutiae that might unravel the tangled knot of Archie's life.

Murray had handled originals many times. Valuable documents that you had to sign for then glove up to protect them from the oils and acids that lived in the whorls of your fingertips, but he'd never been the first on the scene before, the explorer cracking open the wall to the tomb. He lifted an unsent letter from the box, black ballpoint on white paper.

> *Bobby*
> *For God's sake, find me some of the old!*
> *We'll wait for you at Achnacroish pier on*
> *Saturday.*
> *Yours, closer than an eye,*
> *Archie*

No date, no location, but gold. Murray put it in the important pile, then took out his laptop, fired it up and started listing exactly what he had. He picked

6

up a discarded bus ticket to Oban, for some reason remembering a hymn they'd sung at Sunday school.

> *God sees the little sparrow fall,*
> *it meets His tender view;*

Even this simple ticket might have the power to reveal something, but he put it in the dross pile all the same.

*   *   *

Murray's interest in Archie Lunan had started at the age of sixteen with a slim paperback. He could still remember the moment he saw it jutting out from a box of unsorted stock on the floor of a second-hand bookshop. It was the cover that drew him, a tangerine-tinted studio shot of a thin man with shadows for eyes. Murray had known nothing about Lunan's poetry or his ill-starred life, but he had to have the book.

'Looks like a baby-killer, doesn't he?' The man behind the counter had said when Murray handed over his fifty pence. 'Still, that was the seventies for you, a lot of it about.'

Once he owned the book Murray had been strangely indifferent to its contents, almost as if he were afraid they might be a let-down. He'd propped it on the chest of drawers in the bedroom he shared with his brother until eleven-year-old Jack had complained to their dad that the man's non-existent eyes were staring at him and Murray had been ordered to put it somewhere where it wouldn't give people nightmares.

7

He'd rediscovered the book the following year, when he was packing to go to university, and thrown it in his rucksack, almost on a whim. The paperback had languished on the under-stocked bookshelf in his bed-sit through freshers' week and into most of the following year. It was exam time, a long night into studying, when he'd found himself reaching for the poems. Murray supposed, when he bothered to think about it, that he was looking for a distraction. If so, he'd found one. He'd sat at his desk reading and re-reading Archie Lunan's first and only poetry collection until morning. It was an enchantment which had quietly shadowed Dr Murray Watson in his toil through academe, and now at last he was free to steep himself in it.

*   *   *

It was after six when Murray stepped out from the National Library. Somewhere a piper was hoiching out a tune for the tourists. The screech of the bagpipes cut in and out of the traffic sounds; the grumble of car engines, the low diesel growl of taxis and unoiled shriek of bus brakes. The noise and August brightness were an assault after the gloom of the small back room. He took his sunglasses from their case and swapped them for his everyday pair. A seagull careened into the middle of the road, diving towards a discarded poke of chips. Murray admired the bird's near-vertical take-off as it swooped up into the air narrowly missing a bus, its prize clamped firmly in its beak.

It dawned on him that he was hungry. He hadn't eaten since the Twix he'd had for breakfast on the Glasgow to Edinburgh Express early that morning. He crossed the street, pausing to buy a *Big Issue* from a neat-pressed vendor who readjusted his baseball cap when Murray declined his change. There was a faint scent of salt in the breeze blowing through the city from the Firth of Forth. It suited Murray's mood. His mind still half on the island where Archie had been born, Murray began to walk briskly towards the city centre. The Edinburgh Fringe was well under way. The town had taken on the atmosphere of a medieval fête and it was hard negotiating a path through the crush of tourists, rival ghost-tour operators, performers and temporary street stalls that swamped the High Street. He sidestepped the spit-spattled Heart of Midlothian, at the same time avoiding a masked Death, cowled in unseasonably warm black velvet. On other days the crush and stretched smiles of performers trumpeting their shows might have irritated Murray, but today their edge of cheerful hysteria seemed to echo his own optimism. He turned into Cockburn Street, his feet unconsciously stepping to the rhythm of a busking drum troupe, each stride on the beat, precise as a policeman on duty at an Orange Walk. Murray accepted leaflets shoved at him for shows he had no intention of seeing, still thinking about the papers in the box, and keeping his eyes peeled for a chippy.

In the end he settled for pie and beans washed down by a pint of 80/- in the Doric. He ate at one of the high stools by the bar, his eyes fixed on the television mounted on the wall above the gantry, watching the newsreader relaying headlines he couldn't hear. The screen flashed to soldiers in

9

desert fatigues on patrol then to a crease-eyed correspondent packed into a flak jacket, the background behind him half sand, half blue sky, like a child's what-I-did-on-my-holiday drawing.

Murray slid his hand into his rucksack, brought out his notebook and read again the names he had copied from the red corduroy address book, wishing to God it had been a diary.

> *Tamsker*
> *Saffron*
> *Ray—will you be my sunshine?*

It was a misnomer to call it an address book. It had contained no addresses, no telephone numbers, simply lists of unfamiliar names occasionally accompanied by phrases of nonsense. If he knew the identity of even one of them he'd have something to work with, but he was clueless, the knot still pulled tight. Murray folded the words back into his pocket, feeling the pleasure of possession, the secret thrill of a man on the brink of a discovery that might yet elude him.

His plate was cleared, his pint nearly done. He tipped it back and placed the empty glass on the bar, shaking his head when the barman asked him if he'd like another. It was time to go and do his duty.

Chapter Two

There was already a crush of people beyond the glass front of the Fruitmarket Gallery. Murray eyed them as he made his way towards the entrance. He couldn't see the exhibits from here, but the bar was busy. He paused and took in the exhibition poster, the name JACK WATSON shining out at him from the trio of artists. He lingered outside, savouring the rightness of it all, suddenly wishing he'd bought a camera so he could record the event for posterity. When he looked up he noticed a young woman wearing an orange dress gathered in curious origami folds gazing at him from beyond the glass. Murray half returned her smile then quick-glanced away. He ran a hand through his hair and fumbled in his pocket for the ticket Lyn had sent him, getting a sudden vision of it tucked inside last month's *New York Review of Books* somewhere midway down in the pile of papers that had colonised his couch. He hesitated for a moment then stepped from the damp coolness of the bridge-shadowed street into the warm hubbub of bodies and chatter, steeling himself for the embarrassment of getting Lyn or Jack to vouch for him. But no one challenged his right to be there. Murray wondered, as he helped himself to a glass of red and a leaflet explaining the artists' intentions, how many people were here to view the art and how many had been drawn in by the vision of a free bar.

He was scanning the paper for Jack's name as he turned, glass in hand. His rucksack jarred and a little wine slopped onto his cuff. 'God, I'm sorry.'

The woman he had jolted glanced down at the clever folds of her dress.

'You're fine, no harm done.'

'Are you sure?' Her arms were bare and freckled, her nails painted the same tangy colour as the fabric. Murray realised that he was staring at the point in her midriff where the folds met and felt his face flush. 'I wouldn't want to spoil your dress, it looks expensive.'

She laughed. There was a small scar in the centre of her upper lip where long ago an operation had left its mark.

'It was that.' She had a Northern Irish accent, the kind that sometimes drew comparisons between harsh politics and harsh brogues. It sounded cool and amused. 'You're here to see Jack.'

Murray realised he was still wearing his sunglasses and took them off. The world blended into smudged brightness and the girl's face slipped out of focus. He fumbled for his other pair, trying not to squint.

'I guess that's why we're all here.' He found his specs and slid them on. Everything sharpened. He held out his hand. 'I'm Jack's brother, Murray.'

'I know.' She took his hand and shook it. 'Cressida. You don't remember me, do you?'

Not for the first time Murray wished his brain were as efficient as his computer. How could he retain a minutia of dates, form and verse but dispense with the memory of a good-looking woman? He tried to sound sincere.

'I remember your face, but not when we met.'

Cressida laughed again.

'You're a terrible liar. Jack's up the stairs, his pictures are amazing. Have you seen them yet?'

'No.' He recalled something Lyn had said and repeated it. 'I find openings aren't the best time to see the exhibition. I just pay my respects then come back when it's quieter and I can explore

12

what's on show properly.'

To his own ears the spiel sounded as stilted as one of his students tripping out a half-understood argument they'd read in a book, but Cressida nodded.

'I see your point. But all the same, you must be keen to get a glimpse of them, especially with the subject matter and all.' She'd gone serious, but now she rewarded him with another smile. 'You know what might help?'

'What?'

'Do you mind?' She reached up and took his specs from his nose, placing him back in a landscape of lights and smearing colour. He heard the quick exhalation as she misted his lenses with her breath then caught the orange flare of her dress as she rubbed them against its hem. 'Now you can really see what's going on.'

She returned them and the world slid back into focus just as a man in artfully distressed jeans and a blue and white striped shirt that for all its lack of red put Murray in mind of the Union Jack emerged from the press of people and wrapped an arm around Cressida.

'Steven.' She lifted her face to him and he kissed her on each cheek, his lips making contact with her skin, his arms pressing her into a clinch that made one of her feet leave the ground.

'You clever girl. It's amazing, by far the best thing you've done.'

Murray took the bundle of leaflets from his pocket, cursing his own ignorance and giving the couple the chance to escape. The exhibition guide was sandwiched between an advert for *Richard the Turd*, an adaptation of Shakespeare's classic set in a toilet, and a flyer for the *Ladyboys of Bangkok*, the name *Cressida Reeves* printed just above Jack's. Why hadn't it occurred to him that this woman in her spectacular dress might be one of the trio on show?

Cressida extricated herself from the hug.

'Steven Hastings, this is Murray Watson, Jack Watson's brother.'

'Jack?'

Steven rolled the name in his mouth, as if tasting it for the first time and unsure of the flavour. Cressida met his vagueness with a stab of irritation.

'You know Jack. He's one of my fellow exhibitors, we were at college together.'

'Ah yes, *Jack*. The flayed corpse.'

Murray winced at the memory of Jack's degree show, but he could remember Cressida now. Her hair had been shorter then, her thrift-shop-chic outfit tighter and darker than what she was wearing today. Jack had been impressed and maybe a little jealous. She'd won a prize, a big one, though Murray couldn't remember what. He steadied his gaze at Steven.

'He's moved on since then.'

'Glad to hear it.'

Murray felt an urgent need to knock Steven Hastings' head from the high collar of his jaunty shirt. But he stifled the impulse and instead gave an awkward stiff bow that he couldn't remember ever performing before.

'I'm looking forward to seeing your work, Cressida.'

He turned towards the bar as Steven put an arm around the woman's shoulders, guiding her towards the exhibition space and commanding, 'Now, you're going to explain everything to me in minute detail.'

Cressida rolled her eyes, but she allowed herself to be led away, giving Murray a last smile. He raised his hand in goodbye, then swapped his empty glass for a fresh red and went to look for his brother.

*   *   *

The paintings at the front depicted massive, candy-coloured Manga cartoon characters collaged into pornographic poses. Murray sipped his drink, taking in a doe-eyed schoolgirl in congress with an equally wide-eyed black and white spotty dog. The image was imposed onto a background of a devastated landscape, Nagasaki after the H-bomb. Murray checked the artist's name, relieved to find it wasn't Cressida or Jack, then headed towards the staircase. It was busy here too, the traffic going in both directions, people clutching their drinks as if they were vital accessories. He didn't see Lyn until she was in front of him.

'Hey.' She stopped on the step above his so that their faces were almost level. Murray kissed her, smelling wine, cigarettes and fabric softener.

'How's the wee man?'

'The wee man.' She shook her head. 'The wee man, as you call him, is doing very well, considering he's been working till three in the morning practically every day for the last month and only finished hanging ten minutes before the doors were due to open.'

Murray grinned.

15

'He should have given me a shout. I would have held the ladder for him.'

'Rather you than me.'

Lyn was smiling, but there was an unaccustomed flatness in her tone that made Murray wonder if she and Jack had argued.

He asked, 'And how are you doing? You're looking well.'

His brother's girlfriend had pale freckly skin that couldn't endure sunlight. Maybe it was the contrast between her fairness and the unfamiliar red lipstick she was wearing, but Murray thought she looked a shade whiter than usual.

'I'm doing great. Glad this has come round at last.' She smiled hello to a couple going up the staircase then turned back to Murray. 'You get yourself up there. Jack'll want to see you.'

'Jack will have a lot of people to talk to. I just came to show my support, I'll not stick around getting in the way.'

Lyn raised her eyebrows comically.

'And you've got a lot of work to be getting on with.'

'A fair bit, aye.'

'Well, you'd better go and pay your respects then.' She slid past him. 'I was about to get some wine before it's all sooked up. Do you want a refill?'

Murray looked at his glass, surprised to see that it was almost empty.

'Why not?'

'Give it here then.' She hesitated. 'Murray, Jack talked to you about the show, didn't he?'

He knocked back the last dreg of wine and handed his empty glass to her.

'I think so, maybe a while ago.'

Lyn pushed a stray curl away from her eyes.

'You've no idea, have you?'

He grinned, embarrassed at being caught out.

'Maybe not.'

'You might find it . . .' She hesitated, searching for the right word. '. . . challenging.'

Murray laughed.

'Aye, well, that won't be a first.'

Lyn gave a weak smile.

'Just remember it was done with love.'

'No blood this time?'

'No blood, but it was still painful for him, so be kind.'

'When am I not?'

'Never.'

She touched his arm gently as she descended the stairs to the bar.

*   *   *

Jack was at the centre of a small knot of people, but he saw Murray and broke away, flinging an arm around his brother's shoulder. Murray wondered where it came from, this physicality. He couldn't remember them ever touching as boys except when they were fighting.

'Hiya.'

'Hi, Jack.' He put his arm round his brother, feeling the heat of his body through the fabric of his suit. 'Congratulations.'

Jack's face was shiny, his forehead beaded with sweat and his eyes bright. Murray could hear his brother's voice coming from somewhere else too, a voiceover on a video installation he guessed. The

17

words were indistinct, but Jack's soft tones were cut through with another wilder, higher voice. The Jack in front of him looked anxious. He squeezed Murray's shoulder and said, 'I was keeping an eye out for you. Have you been round everything already?'

'No, I just got here. All I've seen are those Japanese cartoon-collage things.'

Jack gave a quick scan of the room then whispered, 'Pile of pish, eh?'

Murray laughed.

'I don't know about art, but I do know a pile of pish when I see it.'

'Don't let them put you off. Anyway, don't congratulate me till you've seen my stuff. You might not like it.'

'I'd better go and have a butcher's then.'

The walls behind him were lined with photos. They looked more muted than Jack's usual sharp-focused colours, but they were too far away for Murray to take in their detail.

'Wait a moment.' Jack took his sleeve as if worried that his brother would escape. 'Murray, it's all about Dad.'

Murray pulled himself gently from his brother's grip. He nodded, not trusting himself to speak, and walked into the heart of the exhibition.

*   *   *

Their father looked pretty much as he had when Murray had last seen him. He was propped up in the high-backed chair, wearing a pair of brown paisley-patterned pyjamas. His hands clutched the armrests. His head was thrown back, his old face

18

lost in the crazy smile of another man. Jack's camera had caught him mid-word, his mouth open, the wetness of saliva coating his lips. His eyes dazzled.

Murray shut his own eyes then opened them again, the vision of his father remained in front of him, exposed to the wine-drinkers. He could hear his father's voice now, chatting to Jack. He walked to the curtained darkroom in the corner of the gallery, ignoring the display cases and trying to blinker himself to the other photographs. The two long benches inside the blacked-out cubicle were full, so he stood at the end of the row of people leaning against the back wall. The close-up of his father's face was six foot high. Jack's voice came from somewhere off-camera asking, 'Mr Watson, can you tell me if you've got any children, please?'

Their father grinned.

'I've got two boys, terrific wee fellas. Six and eleven, they are.'

'Great ages, and what are they up to the now?'

The old man's face fogged with confusion.

'I don't know. I've no seen them in a long while.' He was getting distressed, his pitch rising. 'They telt me they were fine, but how do they know? Have you seen them, son?'

'I've seen them, they're absolutely fine.'

'Are you sure now?'

'I know for certain.'

'Aye, well, that's good. On their holidays, aren't they?'

'That's right. Away with the BBs.' The old man on screen nodded, quickly comforted, and Jack asked him, 'Do you remember who I am?'

The mischief was back in his father's face.

19

'If you don't know, I doubt that I can help you out.'

The old man and Jack laughed together.

'No idea at all?'

Their father stared at the Jack-off-screen intently. He stared at Murray too, his broken veins scoured and red. There was a patch of grey stubble on his chin that whoever had shaved him had missed.

'I don't think I know you, son.' He hesitated and a ghost of something that might have been recognition flitted across his face, bringing a smile in its wake. 'Are you yon boy that reads the news?'

'Poor auld soul.' The woman standing next to Murray whispered to her friend. 'He doesnae ken if it's New York or New Year.'

Jack-on-screen told the old stranger who had taken up residence in his father's body, 'You've rumbled me.' And the old man slapped his knee in glee.

Murray pushed through the black curtains and out into the brightness of the white-painted gallery. Jack was standing where he had left him. Murray shook his head and jogged quickly down the stairs. Lyn was coming towards him, chatting to another girl, both of them clutching brimming wine glasses. She said his name, 'Murray', but he continued down onto the street, then further down still, towards Waverley Station and the train that would take him home.

Chapter Three

Murray looked at the neat piles of papers he'd assembled, then surveyed the list that he had made.

Jotters	*– 3*
Address Book	*– 1*
Loose Papers	*– 325*
Newspaper Cuttings	*– 9*
Bus Tickets	*– 13*
Train Tickets	*– 8*
Drawings/Doodles	*– 11*
Tarot Cards	*– 3*
Letters	*– 6*
Photograph	*– 1*

The jotters and address book were his biggest prizes, but the photograph pleased him more. Archie and Christie sitting on a rock laughing together, their hair caught in a bluster of wind, eyes screwed tight against the weather. Archie was wearing an old Harris tweed jacket that looked too broad for his thin frame. His hair was long and stringy, his laugh topped by an unkempt moustache. Christie's blonde hair was long too, parted carelessly in the centre. Her wide-lapelled coat looked Edwardian, but it had been a period of retro and revivals, and maybe it had been the latest fashion. She'd stuffed her hands into her pockets, pushing them together through the fabric so it looked like she was hugging herself. Archie had one hand on his knee. His other hand was hidden.

Clasped around Christie's waist or lost in the closeness of the pose? It was difficult to tell. Archie's face was half-obscured by his hair and moustache, but he looked alive in a way that none of the other photographs had shown him. Murray wondered when it had been taken. That last summer up on Lismore? The look was right, the seventies hair and careless clothes, the treeless scrub of heather in the background. He would take a copy with him when he went to meet Christie Graves. Perhaps she would remember the moment it was taken, and maybe that memory would prompt others.

He pulled the jotters towards him. They were similar to those he recalled using in primary school, with boxed-in lines on the front cover for the owner's name, subject and class, which Archie had left blank. He lifted one in the air and shook it gently. A couple of dried leaves slid from between the pages. Murray laid them carefully to one side and added them to his list.

Leaves   – 2

The words looked stupid. He scored them out then took one of the leaves between his thumb and index finger and held it up to the light, seeing the veins still branching beneath the crisp surface. There was no secret message scratched on its desiccated flesh. He placed it gently back on the desk and opened the notebook. A list of words ran close to the margin on the left-hand side of the page, vocabulary or notes for a poem cramped in Archie's now-familiar script.

Dune
Dawn
Dream
Dome
Diadem

He could see no connection between the words and any of the poems in *Moontide*. Murray leaned back in his chair and started to read, making notes in his own Moleskine notebook as he went along. He was a third of a way through the jotter when he came across the entry made in another hand.

I love you and she will love you too.

Beneath, Archie had added:

She loves me! But how can she be so sure that my new love will be a she?

Murray made a note of the exchange, wondering if it offered some kind of insight or was simply a joke. He'd assumed Archie's sexuality was confirmedly heterosexual, but then the seventies had been a time of challenged boundaries, even in Scotland, and Archie's love affair with the drink had frequently placed him between berths. Maybe he'd occasionally flopped into men's beds in the way that he had so frequently flopped (Murray imagined that the word was often appropriate) into women's. It was worth considering. At this stage almost anything was worth considering.

Murray had propped the photo against the desk lamp. He looked at it again, the grinning face and flying hair. How long after it had been taken had

Archie drowned?

*   *   *

He worked until two, then decided to take some
requests for reference books to the front desk. He
supposed he should eat something. He'd woken
with a sore head and mild nausea, remnants of the
wine he'd drunk at the opening and of the semi-
sleepless night that had followed. He should phone
Jack, tell him . . . tell him what?

Murray filled in his request form neatly and
went out into the corridor, closing the door gently
behind him. He heard Mr Moffat's jovial tones just
before the man himself hove into view. The senior
librarian was wearing his customary politician's
suit and tie. His sparse, white hair was cropped
short in a style that might have looked thuggish
on a less amiable countenance, but which lent
Mr Moffat a jolly, monkish cast. He was walking
fast, talking animatedly to an older, thinner man
dressed in khaki trousers, a checked shirt and
saggy cardigan.

Murray would have been content to let the pair
pass with a friendly nod of the head, but the
librarian hailed him warmly, his round face a
testament to the pleasures of books and extended
lunch breaks.

'Good afternoon, Dr Watson.' He shook
Murray's hand. 'Everything working out okay?'

Murray's voice felt rusty. He'd been in
conversation with the remnants of Archie Lunan
all morning, but this was the first time today that
he'd opened his mouth to speak to the living.

'Good, yes. I'm not sure what I've got yet, but it

24

looks promising.'

'Wonderful.' Mr Moffat turned to his companion. 'George, this is Dr Watson, through from Glasgow for a look at some Archie Lunan ephemera we didn't know we had.'

'Oh, aye.'

The older man looked unimpressed, but he held his right hand out anyway. Mr Moffat stood over them while they shook. For a bizarre moment Murray thought he was about to clasp their two hands together like a minister at a marriage ceremony, but the librarian confined himself to his usual easy grin.

'George Meikle is our head bookfinder.'

Murray wanted to tell the bookfinder to call him by his first name, but the action seemed too awkward. Instead he indicated the request forms in his hand.

'I was just heading in your direction.'

Meikle's face remained dour.

'I'll take you along to the desk then.'

George's surliness was at odds with his offer and Murray wondered if he was grabbing the opportunity to escape the weight of Mr Moffat's cheerfulness.

'Excellent.' The librarian couldn't have looked happier had he introduced Lord Byron to Percy Shelley. 'Still, it's a pity we don't have more for you, Dr Watson. I often wish some poets had been more assiduous with their legacy.'

Meikle made a harrumphing noise that might have been a laugh or impatience.

'Some of them are over-assiduous.'

'George has a point.' Mr Moffat lowered his voice as if he were about to tell a risqué joke.

25

'We've been gifted signed notes to the milkman, but your man . . . one slim volume and a cardboard box of papers. Tragic. It's going to make your job pretty difficult.'

'There's more than you might think, references in other texts, letters and the like, and I'm hoping more will turn up once I start talking to people who knew him.'

'I'm a great believer in optimism.' Mr Moffat was already turning away. 'And there's always George. He'll help you out where he can.'

Murray groped for some way of saying he didn't need any help beyond the room already provided. But he was already looking at the broad back of Mr Moffat's blue suit as he headed away from him, along the corridor to his office.

George snorted with the same mixture of amusement and impatience he'd shown earlier.

'This way.'

He started down the hallway in the other direction and Murray followed him, too polite to let on that he already knew his way around. He couldn't think of anything to say. It was like this sometimes when he had been deep in work, as if his mind stayed trapped in the wrong mode, the best part of him caught in the pages he was carrying.

Lunan had been trying to write a sci-fi novel. Murray smiled at the irony. He'd been hoping to uncover lost verses by a neglected poet and instead had chanced upon notes for a pot-boiler. Maybe Lunan had been bored, or perhaps he'd decided to fight penury with pulp fiction. The notes for the book had been sketchy, but the beginnings of the plot were unoriginal, a small colony of people

26

trying to pick their way through a post-apocalyptic landscape. Murray supposed the setting might have been inspired by the isolation of Archie's last home.

George broke the silence, jerking Murray back into the moment and the empty corridor that smelled of books and learning.

'So have all the big boys been covered then?'

It was a question he'd been asked before, most notably by Fergus Baine, Murray's head of department when he'd submitted his request for a sabbatical. He'd pulled out the stops then, explaining his perspective on the poet's neglected place in the canon, how his story crossed boundaries not simply of literary style but of a country divided by geography, industry and class. He'd dampened his love of Lunan's poetry from his voice and presented an argument based on scholarship and fact. Murray had been as passionate as a commission-only salesman about his product, believing every word of his own spiel, but the hours spent in the small room with Archie's slim legacy had left him dispirited. As if the salesman had opened his sample case in the privacy of a hotel room and been confronted with the flaws in his merchandise. He felt a sudden stab of anger. Who was this guy, anyway? Stalwart of the stacks, a glorified janitor with his old man's cardigan and wilted features.

'I don't get you.'

'Archie Lunan. I'd have thought you'd have better folk than him to spend your time on.'

'I still don't get you.'

George turned his face towards Murray, his expression unreadable.

'He wasn't much of anything, was he? Not much of a poet and not much of a man, as far as I could tell.'

'And you'd be the one to judge?'

'I'm not a professor of English literature.'

Murray doubted his promotion had been an accident and didn't bother to correct it. He remembered his joke of the night before.

'But you know pishy poetry when you see it?'

'I know a big poser when I see one.'

The words could have been directed towards Murray, Lunan or both. The corridor stretched ahead of them. He didn't need the guidance of this misery. He knew where he wanted to go, could put on some speed, step quickly ahead and leave the old bastard to ferment in his ignorance. Instead he kept his voice cold and asked, 'So did you see a lot of Lunan?'

'You could see Archie Lunan propping up the wall of an Edinburgh pub any night of the week in the seventies.'

'And you were out in the street with your nose pressed to the Christian side of the window when you saw him, I suppose?'

George Meikle's laugh was harsh.

'No, I wasn't. But it's not me we're talking about, is it?

Murray felt weary with the weight of defending Lunan, a man who he suspected was probably as big an arsehole as George was implying. But it wasn't the man he needed to defend. He said, 'Archie Lunan may not have been Scotland's favourite son, but he produced one of the most remarkable and most neglected collections of poetry ever to come out of this country.'

They had reached the foyer now. George turned to face him.

'And you're going to right that?'

'I'm going to try.'

The older man's voice was sweet with sarcasm.

'A big thick book about a wee, skinny poet and his one, even skinnier volume?'

'If I can.'

George shook his head.

'And the greater part of it about how he went.'

'It'll be a part of it, but not the main part. I'm writing for the Edinburgh University Press, not the *News of the World.*'

'Aye, that's what Mr Moffat said.' George hesitated, as if making his mind up about something. 'You asked where I was when I spied Lunan in the pub. Half the time I was sitting opposite him, the other half I was sitting on the bench beside him.'

'You were friends?'

'Drinking pals, for a while.' Meikle took a deep breath. 'Why do you think Tuffet was bringing me along to meet you? You could find your own way to the request desk fine. He thought I might be able to fill in some gaps.'

'And can you?'

'I doubt it. All we ever did was hang about pubs talking pishy poetry. The kind of thing you no doubt get paid good money for.'

Murray grinned against the unfairness of George Meikle's first-hand contact with Lunan.

'I'd like to hear your memories of Archie, they could be a big help. Maybe you'd let me buy you a drink?'

'I don't drink.'

He wondered if anyone had conducted a study into the link between being teetotal and being a depressing bastard. But then the old man gave his first genuine smile.

'You can stand me a coffee in the Elephant House when I knock off.'

*   *   *

Murray bought a ham and tomato sandwich from the newsagents opposite the library and ate it standing in the street. The bread was soggy, the tomato slick against the silvered meat. He forced half down then consigned the remainder and its plastic box to a bin. He'd turned his mobile off when he'd entered the library that morning, now he switched it on and checked for messages. There were two. He pressed the menu button and brought up Calls Missed. Jack had rung once, Lyn twice. He killed the phone and went back into the library. He had a lot of work to do before he met George Meikle.

*   *   *

The Elephant House was jam-packed, but Meikle had managed to bag the same seat that an insecure Mafia don would have chosen, near the back corner of the second, larger room commanding a good view of the café and ready access to the fire escape. Murray eased his way through the tables to greet Meikle and check on his order, then retraced an apologetic route back, past the glass cabinets stuffed with elephant ornaments to the front counter and the long queue to get served. When his turn came he asked for an Americano, a café latte and two elephant-shaped shortbreads, then negotiated his way back to the corner table, holding the tray carefully, praying he wouldn't upset it, and if he did that it wouldn't be over an occupant of one of the three-wheeled buggies that were making his journey so perilous.

Meikle folded the *Evening News* he'd been reading into a baton and slid it into the pocket of the anorak hanging on the back of his chair. Murray lowered the tray onto the table then unloaded the cups, slopping a little of the black coffee onto its saucer.

'Sorry that was so long, there's a big queue.'

Meikle gave the shortbread a stern look. 'If one of those is for me, you've wasted your money.'

'Watching your figure?'

'Diabetes. Diagnosed three years ago.'

A vision of his father flashed into Murray's head. He wrapped the shortbread in a paper serviette and slid it into the pocket of his jacket.

'That's not much fun.'

'Eat your bloody biscuit.' Impatience made George's voice loud. One of the yummy mummies turned a hard stare on them, but he ignored her. 'Biscuits I can stand. It's the booze I find hard to watch folk with, and I've been off that twenty years.'

'Since Archie went.'

Meikle shook his head.

'You've got the bit between your teeth, right enough.' He leaned forward. 'An unhealthy obsession with your subject may be an advantage in your line, but remember Lunan only touched a small portion of my life. I'm sixty-five now, due for

31

retirement at the end of the year. I've not seen Archie since we were nigh-on twenty-six. My quitting the drink had nothing to do with him. It was necessary, that's all.'

Murray held up his hands in surrender.

'Like you say, it's a bit of an obsession.' He took his tape recorder from his rucksack and set it on the table. 'Do you have any objection to me recording our chat?'

'Do what you have to.'

Murray hit *Record* and beyond the window of the small machine cogs began to roll, scrolling their voices onto the miniature tape.

'So what was he like?'

George's face froze in a frown, like an Edwardian gentleman waiting on the flash of a camera.

'When I knew him he was a great guy.'

Murray rewound the tape and pressed *Play*. George's voice repeated against the backdrop of café noise, *When I knew him he was a great guy*.

'Jesus, I hope you're not going to do that every time I say something.'

The young mother gave George another look. This time he held her gaze until she glanced away. He muttered, 'You'd think no one ever had a fucking bairn before.'

Murray bit the head off one of the elephants and pressed *Record* again.

'So what made him a great guy?'

Meikle answered with a question of his own.

'What do you know about Archie?'

'The work. Basic stuff, where he was born, his death of course, and a few things in-between. I've been interested in him since I was sixteen, but I'm

32

only starting serious research into his life now.'

'Have you talked to Christie?'

'I've corresponded with her. She's promised to meet me.'

'And do you think she will?'

'I hope so.'

George nodded his head.

'Fair enough.' He hesitated. 'I'm not sure what it is you want to know.'

'Whatever you want to tell me. First impressions. You said he was a great guy, what was so great about him? Did he consider himself a poet when you knew him?'

George raised the mug slowly to his mouth, as if it wasn't the drink he wanted so much as the thinking time. He cradled the cup in his hands for a moment, then set it down, running a finger thoughtfully along the rim, rubbing away a thin brown stain of coffee.

'When I first met Archie he didn't know what he was. I mean I think he knew that he wanted to be a poet when he was in his pram. He was always straight about that, but he still wasn't sure about who he was. He was a west-coaster like yourself, but he was living here in Edinburgh and he'd spent his early years on one of the islands, so his accent would scoot about north, east and west.'

'Everywhere except the south.'

Meikle laughed.

'That's one thing that hasn't changed. You don't find many Scotsmen aspiring to come from the south, not the ones who stay, anyway. But what I meant was his voice reflected the way he was, unsettled, always trying out new personas. '

'So would you say his personality was split?'

'Jekyll and Hyde? That would be convenient for your book, wouldn't it? No, nothing as dramatic as that, not when I knew him anyway.' He paused and took another sip of coffee, more thinking time. 'But you could say that Archie had two sides to him, the Glaswegian who wasn't going to take any shit and the mystical islander. Neither of them was a perfect fit.'

Murray scribbled in his notebook.

2 personas, hard v mystical, but not J & H

'I'm not sure what else to say. We were just two young blokes who liked a drink and a craic.'

'At a risk of sounding like Julie Andrews, start at the very beginning. How did you and Archie meet?'

Meikle shook his head. His expression was still stern, but Murray thought he could detect the hint of a smile behind the straight-set lips.

'That was typical Archie. I had a room up in Newington at the time, not so far from where we are now, student digs, a bed, a Baby Belling, an excuse of a sink and a shared lavvy in the stair. I was coming home along Nicholson Street one night. It was late, but not quite pub chucking-out time. That road's not so different now than it was then, unlike the rest of Edinburgh, that's turned into a bloody theme park.' Meikle took another sip of coffee and gave Murray a half-apologetic glance, as if he hated these tangents as much as his listener. 'Aye, well, as I was saying, it was typical Archie, but I wasn't to know that then.'

George grinned, getting into his stride, and Murray realised that this was a story he had told before. He wrote in his notebook, *Well-established anecdote.*

'I turned off into Rankeillor Street. It was a rare night, cold but clear, with a full moon. I could see the outline of Salisbury Crags beyond the end of the street. I remember that distinctly because it was a Friday night and I'd been thinking about taking a climb up there in the morning. Maybe it was the full moon, they say that does funny things to you, but suddenly I felt like I had the energy for the climb right then. I was half-wondering if I should go ahead or if it was the drink that was doing my thinking for me and whether I might end up falling face-first off some cliff or catching my death from hypothermia. Maybe I was aware of the group of lads at the other end of the street, but I wasn't really paying any attention, I was imagining what it would be like at the top of the hill in the dark with only the moon and the sheep for company. I'd more or less decided to go for it when I heard shouting. It was Archie, though I didn't know that at the time. I couldn't make out what he was saying, but what I could see was that the other three lads were laying into him. I've never been much of a fighter, but it was three-to-one, and even from that distance and in the dark I could tell that Archie had a body more suited to wielding a pen than a pair of boxing gloves. So one minute I'm in quiet contemplation, the next I'm running towards the four of them, yelling my head off. They had your man on the ground by this time and they were beginning to put the boot in. I don't know why my appearance on the scene should have made any difference. It still wouldn't have been even odds, not with Archie on the ground the

35

way he was. Maybe they'd finished with him, or maybe they didn't have the stomach for more, because the lads kind of jogged off, not running, but moving at a faster-than-walking pace. They shouted some abuse, but I wasn't going to let that bother me. Truth be told, once I stopped running and yelling, I started to get the shakes. Still, I think I was pretty pleased with myself, a bit smug, you know? Archie was still on the pavement. I leaned down to give him a hand up and that's when it happened. He landed me a good one square in the face.' George laughed and shook his head as if he still couldn't believe it. 'Before I knew it, the two of us were scrapping in the street. Then came the blue light. I guess someone in the tenements must have called the police when the first fight was kicking off. They charged the pair of us with drunk and disorderly and shoved us in separate cells for the night. My one and only arrest.'

Meikle laughed and shook his head again.

'It doesn't sound like a very promising basis for a friendship.'

'No, it doesn't, does it? But someone in the station must have slipped up because we were booked out at the same time the next morning. I wanted nothing to do with him, of course. I mean one minute there I am thinking about moonlit climbs and the next I'm in a cell in St Leonard's police station.'

'So how did you and Archie end up pals?'

'Oh, Archie was a charmer. He made a gracious apology and before I knew it we were in a café swapping our life stories over bacon rolls and coffee. Then it was pub opening time. We went on from there.'

36

'So thumping people one minute and charming them the next, but not a Jekyll and Hyde character?'

'You're keen on that one, aren't you?' Meikle's belligerence had vanished in the story. 'He was full of life and sometimes his energy spilled over into something else.'

Murray glanced at the recorder still spooling their words onto tape and wondered how far he should push the older man.

'He sounds like a violent alcoholic.'

Meikle winced, but his voice remained low and calm.

'The alcoholic bit I don't know about. He liked a drink, true enough, but he was young, it could have gone either way. Personally I think a lot of that's to do with whether you've got an addictive personality or not. I do, my father did too, but I don't make assumptions about other folk, especially the dead. The violence part? Aye, well, he got into fights, like a lot of young lads, but I don't think Archie was violent per se. I used to, but I've had a bit of time to consider. I reckon that when he drank all his insecurities were given a free rein. Archie would hit you, right enough, but then he'd drop his guard and let you give him a proper doing. I got a fair few blows in that night before the police pulled me off him. That was part of the reason I went for a drink with him the next day. I couldn't believe the mess I'd made of his face.'

Meikle ran a hand over his thinning hair. Murray reached forward and turned off the tape recorder. Their cups were empty, the elephant reduced to crumbs. He asked, 'Would you like another coffee?'

'Make it a Diet Coke.' The older man gave him a tired smile. 'There's only so much coffee you can drink.'

Meikle was on his mobile phone when Murray returned. He looked away, as if to guard his privacy, but his telephone voice was as loud as his cursing voice.

'Aye, about half an hour or so. No, don't worry. I can fix myself something when I get in. Yes, okay, love. You too.' He cut the connection and looked at Murray. 'I'll need to be heading off soon.'

'You've already been generous with your time. You said you and Archie talked a lot of poetry.'

'I was bumming myself up a bit there. He talked and I listened. I was more into the politics. I tried to turn Archie onto it.' Meikle snorted. 'That was the way we talked then, you didn't get someone interested in something, you "turned them onto it".'

'Quite a sexual turn of phrase.'

'Aye, it was all sex then, except it wasn't. Maybe down in London, but not up here sadly. Archie maintained that poetry had nothing to do with politics. We used to argue about that. They were happy times—you could even say the best of times—but when you ask me what we did, it's all of a same. Keith Richards isn't the only one that can't remember the seventies. I mean, how well do you remember your student days?'

'Pretty well.'

Meikle laughed.

'That figures. No offence, but look at you. You were probably bent over your books half the time and in lectures the other half.'

'More or less.'

38

'Aye, well, we weren't. What I remember is the odd rumpus, the occasional one-night stand, a lot of parties, a lot of laughs, a good time. For me, Archie was just a part of all that. What they call a wasted youth.'

'Except it wasn't.'

Meikle gave him a sad smile.

'No, I don't think it was. It was what came later that was the waste.'

Chapter Four

He'd missed the main thrust of the rush hour, but most of the seats on the Edinburgh to Glasgow Express were taken. Murray squeezed himself into a spare place at a table for four, smiling his apology at the businessman opposite as he felt the softness of one of the man's smart shoes beneath his own scuffed trainer. The man winced but nodded his acceptance without raising his eyes from the spreadsheets in front of him. Murray glanced down the carriage at the tired eyes and limp collars, the half-read novels and glowing laptops. This was what people called the real world, he supposed, a mortgage, kids and a commute that added a day to every working week. It wouldn't be so bad. He would make it reading time and fuck the spreadsheets.

A recorded message trailed through the scheduled stops as the train slid out of the station. Murray leaned back in his seat, keeping his knees bent to avoid contact with his opposite neighbour.

Meikle had looked tired by the time they'd

finished. Murray had offered to get the bookfinder a taxi, but he'd produced his bus pass from his wallet with an ironic flourish.

'No need. I've got this, a licence to ride.'

'Brilliant.'

The older man's surliness had returned.

'Aye, great compensation for fuck-all of a pension. Take my advice, if you've got any money spend it now while you're still young enough to enjoy it. Don't get conned into saving it for bankers to piss up the wall, the way we were. Old age is no fun when you're skint.'

Murray almost told him that old age had let him in on its dubious charms early and it was no fun full-stop, but there was no point. Instead he smiled to show he agreed and cut the sympathy from his voice because the older man would dislike it.

'Better than the alternative.'

Meikle gave Murray a tough look, and then granted him a grin.

'Mibbe so, mibbe no. I guess we'll all find out eventually.'

He'd headed towards his bus stop, wherever it was, raising his hand in a wordless goodbye as he turned away.

Murray felt infected with Meikle's weariness. He could see the glowing squares of house windows as they passed Broomhouse. It made him think of when he and Jack were boys. The kitchen window steaming with condensation as their dad cooked the dinner, Jack watching *Vision On* or *Blue Peter* while Murray did his homework at the table in the corner of the living room. Eventually there had been the second-hand paraffin heater in

40

their shared bedroom so Murray could study in heady fumes and privacy.

The woman sitting next to him was reading a gossip magazine, flicking through photographs of celebrities shopping on sunlit streets, large black shades and pained expressions. He glanced at her, half-expecting a cut-price version of the girls in the pictures, but she was in her forties, neat rather than fashionable, her clothes carefully chosen. Did she wish herself young and in LA? God knows he did, though the idea had never occurred before. Maybe he could go there, become a movie star. That would show them. It would indeed.

The woman gave him a sharp glare and pointedly turned the page. He looked away. They were out of the city now and there was nothing but darkness in the beyond. He could see his own face reflected in the window; the shine of his glasses against the pits and bumps on the lunar landscape of his skin. Maybe he should shelve the idea of a movie career.

Murray unzipped his rucksack and slid out the manila folder containing the letter from Christie's agent.

Dear Dr Watson
I have passed on your letter to Ms Graves, who has asked me to let you know that she will give your request for an interview serious consideration. To help her in her decision, she invites you to forward through me a copy of your CV, a list of previous publications and a synopsis of your proposed biography of Archibald Lunan.
Regards

He wondered why he had lied to George Meikle about Christie having already granted him an interview. He'd sent the requested documents six weeks ago. They would confirm his credentials, the scholarly nature of his interest. Would that be enough?

Murray's phone chimed with news of a new text. He drew it from his pocket and watched the tiny electronic envelope twirl and open, half-anticipating a self-justifying missive from his brother.

Where are you?

There were people standing further down the carriage. To get up would mean losing his seat, so he dialled where he sat. He expected her voicemail, but Rachel picked up on the third ring. He said, 'Hi, it's me.'

'I wondered if you'd get my message. I'd like to see you.'

'I'd like to see you too.'

'Good.' Her voice was all business. 'Where are you?'

'I don't like to say.'

'I don't have much time, Murray, Fergus has got his big deal of a dinner party later.'

'I'm on the train.'

'Heading where?'

'Home.'

'Can we meet at your office?'

He hated meeting her there, disliked the risk, the clash of associations.

'Okay, when?'

'When can you make it?'

Murray glanced at the display above the carriage door. They were approaching Croy.

'I'll jump in a cab at Queen Street and be with you in thirty minutes.'

'Good.'

She cut the connection without saying goodbye. Outside, the train window started to speck with rain.

Chapter Five

Murray's tiny office was almost, but not quite, dark. Enough light shone in from the streetlamp beyond the trees for him to see Rachel Houghton's features soften. A blast of hail shot against the window and Rachel's pupils widened, edging nearer, but still too self-aware to be there yet. Murray matched his rhythm to the shadows cutting across the room, blessing whatever procurer of office furniture had managed to issue him with a desk of exactly the right height. He clasped Rachel's naked rump, her arms tightened around him and he lifted her from the desk. She gasped and raised her lips to his. Her nipples rubbed against his chest, smooth and hard, sweat-slick. Rachel groaned. Her body stiffened, pelvis pressed down into his. Murray felt the soft leather of her shoes, the spike of their stilettos as they spurred him on.

'No,' he said, 'don't or . . .'

Her ankles gripped him tighter. Murray felt a draught touch his exposed rear and a thin slice of

43

light cut into the room, illuminating Rachel's face, her eyes slitting against the sudden brightness, looking beyond him to the opening door. Murray felt her hands pushing him away. He followed her gaze, unsure of what was happening, and saw the intruder standing in the doorway, face shadowed in the gloom of the room. Murray heard him release a soft shuddering sigh akin to the groan that had escaped his own lips only a moment before.

'Fuck!' Murray's curse acted like a sniper's near-miss. The figure darted swiftly away. Murray extricated himself and stumbled into the hallway, almost catching the door before it closed. He shouted something as he ran, some bark of protest, his unfastened shirt flapping open, the air of the darkened corridor cold against his chest. But whoever it was had vanished, lost in the murky hallways that made up the old buildings. The only comfort Murray had was that he'd remembered to hold onto his trousers instead of letting them ambush him by the ankles and send him sprawling, like the comedy lover he so obviously was.

*   *   *

'I've no idea who it was. Probably a porter doing his rounds.' Rachel stepped behind the desk and began to pull on her abandoned tights. 'More frightened of us than we were of him.'

A few years ago they would have had the surety of a cigarette to smooth the post-coital awkwardness. But these days smoking in university buildings was grounds for dismissal. Fortunately, fucking didn't set off the sprinkler system. Murray

44

fumbled his belt buckle into place and sank into the chair usually designated for visiting students. He lifted a first-year essay that only seconds ago had rustled beneath Rachel's bottom and tried to smooth out the creases in its paper.

. . . he succeeded against the odds. Though his lifestyle was deemed unacceptable by mainstream society his . . .

The page bounced stubbornly back. Murray replaced it on the desk, weighting the bent corner with a mug. A little cold coffee slopped onto the neatly printed words.

'Fuck.' He blotted the stain with the front page of the *Guardian*. 'Was he wearing a porter's uniform?' Murray peeled the newspaper back. A dark shadow of newsprint remained, stamped across the dutifully prepared argument. 'Shit.'

'I told you, I didn't get a good look at him. It was dark and I was . . . slightly distracted.'

Murray wondered if he should have carried on chasing the intruder. He had been breathing in the distinctive reek of recalcitrant students, frustrated scholars and books since he was a seventeen-year-old undergraduate. The corridors' twists and turns were mapped on his mind. He knew all the cubbyholes and suicide steps. The lecture halls racked with seating, the illogical staircases that tricked the uninitiated but led eventually to the out-of-bounds attics from where a man could lose himself and emerge on the opposite side of the old campus. The chances of catching whoever it was were radically slimmer than the odds of looking like an out-of-breath idiot. But the part of him that imagined grabbing the peeping Tom's collar and administering his boot to the seat of their breeks wished he'd given it a shot.

Rachel tugged the hem of her skirt down. Usually she wore trousers. She had, he realised, very good legs.

'You look nice.'

Rachel flashed him the same bright smile that she gave to shop assistants, students, fellow lecturers, porters, her husband, anyone who crossed her path when her mind was elsewhere. He watched as she took a small mirror from her handbag. Her lipstick was hardly smudged, but she perched on the edge of his desk and reapplied it anyway. Murray was reminded of an early author photograph of Christie Graves, long legs, sharp angles and red lips. It was a good look.

The memory of the opening door, the light shifting across Rachel's face, returned and spoiled the knowledge that she'd dressed up for him. He measured the trajectory between their clinch and the door with his thumb and forefinger.

'You don't think it was someone from the department?'

Rachel's smile grew tight. She dropped the mirror back into her bag and zipped it shut.

'It's Friday evening. No one else would be in their office at this time. Most of them have something that passes for a life. Don't worry, I imagine we made his night. No doubt he's crouched in the gatehouse right now, reliving the memory.'

'Of my white arse? I bloody hope not.'

'Irresistible. Your white arse will have a starring role in that little bit of ciné film that plays behind his eyes when he goes home and rogers his tired, but pleasantly surprised, old wife for the first time

46

in months.'

Rachel was on his side of the desk now. Her skirt was made of some kind of shiny, silver-grey fabric, stretched taut across her hips. Murray ran a finger down her leg, feeling the satin slide of the material. She placed a hand on his, stopping its progress, and he leaned back in his chair.

'So what's the occasion?' He wanted to keep her there a while, or maybe be with her somewhere else. Somewhere with subdued lighting, candles, soft music. What a cliché. It was Friday night and most people had a life. 'Fergus taking you somewhere nice?'

'Fergus doesn't take me places. We go together.'

Murray put his foot against the desk. If he were a cowboy, he'd have tipped his hat forward. She hadn't dressed for him after all. He tried for playful and failed.

'We could go together better.'

Rachel bent towards him. He felt her breath, warm and sweet, with a faint scent of peppermint. She'd started smoking again.

'One of the things I've always appreciated about Fergus, he's never boring.'

'He bored me rigid at the last faculty meeting.' Murray reached into his desk drawer and fished out the bottle of malt he'd bought weeks ago in the hope of tempting Rachel to stay longer than the time it took to straighten her clothes. 'I think I need a drink. Do you want to join me?' He hesitated. 'Or we could go somewhere, if you'd prefer a glass of wine?'

Rachel glanced at the clock above the office door. Murray wondered if she'd been keeping an eye on it during their lovemaking.

'I told you. I can't stay long. We're having people round for dinner. Fergus is making his famous shepherd's pie.'

'Proletarian heartiness the latest smart thing?'

'I hope so. It's certainly more economical than some of his other enthusiasms. Here,' She reached into her bag and drew out a bottle of Blackwood's. 'I'll have a splash of this. My alibi.'

Alibi. The word irritated him.

'How long will it excuse you for?'

'Long enough. Fergus was determined to have Shetland gin for aperitifs. They don't sell it everywhere. Why?' She had a pointed face, like a sly little fox. Sometimes, when she smiled, she looked a short leap away from a bite. 'Are you scared he might hunt me down?'

Murray got up and washed his coffee cup. The light stretching across the room was snagged in his mind. Fergus was around twenty years older than Rachel, somewhere towards his sixties, but he'd run the 10K last year. Could he have covered the stretch of the corridor in the time it had taken Murray to get to the door? But why would Fergus run? He had the power to fell Murray without lifting a fist. He ignored Rachel's question, taking the gin from her and pouring a little into the clean mug.

'Sorry about the crockery, not very suave.'

'Not being very suave is part of your charm.'

'Then you won't be surprised to hear I can't offer you ice and lemon.'

'A little water will be fine.'

It was part of what he'd liked about her, this posh gameness. In another era she would have

48

made a great lady explorer. He could imagine her cajoling a team of native carriers through the jungle, taking one of them to her tent at night then ordering him to pick up and carry her bundles the next morning.

Murray went to the sink. Usually he drank the bottled stuff, convinced he could taste the liquorice taint of lead in the university tap water, but there was only a small dreg left in the plastic bottle of Strathmore in his rucksack. He let the cold run for a moment then added a dash to her cup.

'Thanks.'

Rachel smiled, holding it against her chest while he poured himself a nip of the whisky. He was going to clink his cup against hers, but she took a sip of the gin, grimacing then coughing against its burn.

Murray laughed.

'A hardy people, these Shetlanders.' He tasted his own drink. 'Doesn't it bother you? Our visitor?'

'You shielded me.'

He toasted her with his mug.

'Instinctive chivalry.'

'Of course it bothers me.' She glanced at the clock again. 'But what's the point in torturing ourselves? A rumour will start or a rumour won't start. We'll worry about it if it does. The thing we have to make sure of is that it doesn't happen again.'

'You're right. It was stupid, doing it here.'

'That wasn't what I meant.' She saw the expression on his face and smiled. 'We both know it can't go on.'

He couldn't trust his voice. He hadn't known,

didn't know.

'And you're going to be on sabbatical for a year.' She brightened, like a children's nurse who had applied Dettol to a skint knee and was now about to use a sweet to distract attention from the sting. 'You won't have time for all this.'

He tried to keep his words light.

'There's only so much time you can spend on research. I'm sure I could have squeezed you in.'

She looked away. For a moment he thought she might relent, but then she turned her bright eyes on him.

'We agreed it would only ever be a bit of fun. Anyway, term's almost over, Fergus and I are going to Umbria for two months, and you're starting your sabbatical. It makes sense.'

'If we hadn't been interrupted?'

'What does it matter?' She leant forward and kissed him gently on the lips. 'We had fun. We like each other. Let's keep it that way.'

His voice was steady. He'd read about well-integrated autistics, they had to think about every gesture, *smile, make eye contact*. He formed his mouth into a grin.

'You're right. It was fun while it lasted.'

Rachel touched his arm.

Don't flinch, don't argue, don't push her away.

'It'll be a great book. You're always saying how underrated Lunan is. This is your big chance to put him on the map.'

'I hope so.'

'I know so. Fergus does too.'

The pair of them discussing him. Where? Over dinner? In bed? Did he ever feature in the little bit of ciné film she ran behind her eyes while Fergus

50

fucked her?

He said, 'Rachel, Fergus can't stand me.'

She took her coat from the hook on the back of his office door.

'Don't be so paranoid, Murray. You know Fergus. If he didn't think you were a valuable member of the department, you wouldn't be enjoying a year's sabbatical, you'd be looking for a new post.'

*   *   *

Murray stood at his office window. It was still wild outside. The wind caught at Rachel's hair, blowing it across her face. She struggled for a moment with the car door, then she was in, headlamps on, reversed out and away, her only backward glance at the road behind though the rear-view mirror. It was the last time. He wondered if it was the peeping Tom or his own invitation to go for a drink that had pushed Rachel away. Maybe she had always intended to it end like this. Murray stood at the window, watching the trees fingering the sky the same way they would if he weren't there. On his way out he stopped by the gatehouse and handed the almost-full bottle of malt to the porter, who received it with grateful, bland surprise.

Chapter Six

The reasons Murray Watson usually avoided Fowlers were clustered around their customary corner table, looking like a eugenicist's nightmare. The pub wasn't busy, but it was warming up with the overspill of office workers and students from more popular establishments so he was halfway to the bar before he spotted Vic Costello, Lyle Joff and Phyllida McWilliams and remembered that this was where they congregated late on Friday afternoons, playing at being the Algonquin club and staving off the wretchedness of the weekend.

Maybe the need to suffer that misery so often brings in its wake would have led him into their company anyway, or maybe he would have settled for a lone pint and a nod in their direction, but then he felt a hand on his elbow and turned to see Rab Purvis's face, shiny with sweat and bonhomie.

'I'll get this, Moira.' It was typical of Rab to be on first-name terms with the manageress; typical too of him to add Murray's drink to the round and a tip on top of the price. Mrs Noon nodded her thanks and Rab gave Murray's elbow a squeeze that told him his friend was at least three pints to the good. 'Come away into the body of the kirk.'

It had drifted beyond the time where even late diners could pretend to be having a pre-prandial and the department's dwindling stock of alcoholics welcomed Murray with hearty relief. He was the fresh blood, the bringer of new topics, the excuse to get another round in and postpone the moment when the pub door swung home and they each stepped out alone.

'Hello, stranger.' Phyllida McWilliams's voice had lost its usual edge and now held the full throaty promise of a pack of unfiltered Camels. She leaned over and gave Murray a kiss. 'Why do we never see you?'

52

Murray didn't bother to mention that she'd passed him in the corridor three days ago, her head bowed, looking like Miss Marple's hungover younger sister.

'You know how it is, Phyllida. I'm a busy little bee.'

Phyllida picked a blonde hair from Murray's lapel and raised her eyebrows.

'He's a *B*, all right,' said Vic Costello. 'Leave him alone, Phyl, you don't know where he's been.'

The woman let the hair fall from her fingers onto the barroom floor. She nodded. 'Many a true word.'

'He flits from flower to flower.'

Rab conducted a little minuet in the air with his hand.

Phyllida laughed her barmaid's laugh and started to recite,

'Where the bee sucks, there suck I:
In a cowslip's bell I lie;
There I couch when owls do cry.
On the bat's back I do fly . . .'

It was worse than he'd thought. They must have been there for hours. Murray wondered if they suspected about Rachel. He should go home, make himself something to eat, think things through.

Lyle Joff began an anecdote about a conference he'd attended in Toronto. Phyllida clamped an interested expression onto her face and Vic Costello rolled the beer around in his glass, staring sadly into space. Over by the bar Mrs Noon turned up the music and Willie Nelson cranked into

53

'Whisky River'. Vic Costello placed his hand on top of Phyllida McWilliams's and she let him keep it there for a moment before drawing hers away. Murray wondered if Vic's divorce was finalised and if he had moved out of the family home yet, or if he was still camping in the space that had once been his study.

Phyllida leaned against Murray and asked, 'Seriously, where have you been?'

She took his hand in hers and started to stroke his fingers.

'Around.' Murray tried to return her flirt, but he could see Vic Costello's slumped features on Phyllida's other side and, despite the rips in its fabric, the banquette they were sharing was reminiscent enough of a bed to invite unwelcome thoughts of ménage à trois. 'I was at the National Library today, working though what's left of Archie's papers.'

'Oh.' Phyllida's fascination was a thin veneer over boredom. 'Find any fabulous new poems?'

'No, but I did find notes for a sci-fi novel.'

'Poor Murray, out to restore and revive, and all you get is half-boiled genre fiction.'

Murray laughed with her, though the barb hurt. He took out his notebook and flipped it open at the pages where he'd copied down the contents of Archie's jotter.

'I found this, a catalogue of names.'

Phyllida glanced at the scribbled page.

'Obviously trying to work out what to call his characters, and doing rather badly, poor sod.'

Murray wondered why he hadn't realised it earlier. The disappointment sounded in his voice.

'You think so?'

She gave his hand a sympathetic squeeze. 'Undoubtedly.'

'Shit, I thought it might have been something.' He snapped his notebook shut.

Murray's curse seemed to wake Vic Costello from his trance. He necked the last three inches of his beer.

'It's my shout.'

'Not for me, thanks.' Lyle Joff raised his glass to his lips and the last of his heavy slid smoothly down. 'It's past my curfew.' He gave Murray a complicit look. 'Bedtime-story duty. *Winnie the Pooh*—a marvellous antidote to a hard day at the coalface.'

As preposterous as the image of chubby Joff at a coalface was, it seemed more feasible than the picture of him sitting at the bedside of freshly washed, pyjama-clad toddlers reading about a bear of little brain. Murray had been introduced to Joff's wife at a faculty party once; she was prettier than he'd expected. He wondered how they'd met and why Joff was so often in the early-evening company of people for whom the only alternative to the pub was the empty flat, the armchair tortured with cigarette burns and the book collection that was only so much comfort.

Vic Costello looked at his watch.

'It's gone half-nine. They'll be safe in the land of Nod by now surely, long past breathing in your boozy breath, Lyle.'

Lyle Joff looked at his own watch as if astonished to see that the hands had moved round. He hesitated, then looked at his glass as if equally amazed to find it empty.

'You'll get me shot, Costello.' He grinned. 'Just

one more for the road then.'

Vic raised his empty glass in the air until he caught the attention of Mrs Noon. He held five fingers up and the manageress gave a curt dip of her head to show she'd oblige, but only for the moment.

Phyllida leaned over and whispered, 'You're a cunt, Vic. You won't be happy until that boy's marriage has gone the same way as yours and you've got a full-time drinking companion.'

'Why would I need that when I've got you, Phyl?'

Costello gave her a hug. Phyllida pushed him away.

'You forget yourself sometimes.'

Drink took the sting from the scold, but there was a seed of bitterness in her voice that would blossom with more watering, and when Vic Costello tried for a second squeeze her shove was impatient.

The tray of drinks arrived and Lyle Joff helped himself to a fresh pint. He took a sip and wiped the foam from his top lip.

'There's nothing wrong with my marriage.'

'I'm sure it's rock solid.' Rab patted Lyle's arm and asked Murray, 'Have you met Lyle's wife? A beautiful girl, classical profile, a touch of the Venus de Milo about her.'

He winked and Murray wearily took his cue.

'Armless?'

'Wouldn't hurt a fly.'

Phyllida laughed and Lyle said, 'Built on strong foundations. Love, affection, shared values.'

He looked into the middle distance as if trying to recall other reasons his marriage would endure.

'Children,' Phyllida said. 'Children are a blessing.' Vic Costello excused himself to go to the gents.

Keeping his voice uncharacteristically low, Rab turned to face Murray, cutting the pair of them off from the rest of the company.

'I'm glad you dropped by.' The phrase sounded old-fashioned, as if Murray had accepted an invitation to afternoon tea. 'I owe you an apology, for coming on too strong when I saw you last. Just because I'm not getting any doesn't give me a right to become one of the moral majority.' Rab's face set into a stern inquisitiveness, eyebrows raised almost to the ridges of his brow. It was only acting. The look he gave nervous students to encourage them to speak up. He held out his hand. 'Shake?'

*   *   *

Murray had let slip about Rachel a month into the affair. The two men had eaten dinner with a visiting speaker then gone for a drink on their own to discuss the lecture free of its author. Maybe it was the combination of wine and beer or maybe it was the rose-tinted evening. Maybe he was boasting or maybe, just for that instant, Murray had thought his friend might be able to help. Whatever it was, as they'd left the pub, skirting the exiled smokers loitering on the pavement outside and stepping into the gloaming of a pink sunset, Murray had found himself saying, 'I'm having a bit of a thing with Rachel Houghton.'

Rab Purvis had been more forthright than a casual listener might expect a professor of chivalric romance to be.

57

'She's a ballbreaker. I wouldn't touch her with a bargepole.'

Murray had glanced at his friend's tubby abdomen and tried to imagine Rachel propositioning Rab as she had him, shutting the door of his office on sports afternoon Wednesday, pushing the essays he'd been trawling through to one side, sitting on the edge of his desk, so close he'd wondered, then guiding his hand under her sweater so that the quality of his wonder had shifted and magnified.

'It wasn't a bargepole that I was thinking of.'

'Any kind of pole. Leave well alone, if you know what's good for you.'

'What if it's my one last chance of true love?'

'Then run for the hills. Rachel Houghton isn't looking for love, Murray. She's happy with Fergus. She simply likes spicing things up by screwing around.'

'And what's wrong with that?'

'Nothing, if shagging your head of department's wife doesn't bother you.'

'Why should it?'

'Would you like me to give you a list?'

'Not really.'

But his friend had gone on to recite a long, frequently crude but eminently sensible catalogue of reasons why Murray Watson should steer clear of Rachel Houghton. It hadn't made one iota of difference. The affair remained acknowledged but unmentioned again, until now.

*   *   *

Murray took Rab's proffered hand and shook it.

58

'She just dumped me.'

'Ah.' Rab sucked another inch off his pint. 'In that case I take back my apology. You're better off out of it. You know what the department's like. A busy little hive with bees swarming all over each other and Fergus at the centre, gobbling up the golden globules of honey we lay at his feet.'

'Pollen.'

'What?'

'Pollen. The bees bring the queen pollen and she makes it into honey.'

'Pollen, honey—it's all the same.' Rab abandoned the analogy. 'The place is a poisonous rumour mill. Look,' his voice took on the fatherly tone that indicated advice was about to be proffered. 'It's not easy working where we do. Bad as being a diabetic in a candy shop, all those delectable sweet things passing through your hands every day and you not even allowed the tiniest little lick.' He laughed. 'That was slightly filthier than I intended.'

'It's okay, I get your drift.'

'You don't have to tell me how frustrating it can be. When I started it was different but . . .' Rab drifted off for a moment to the happy land where lecturers and students were still compatible. 'But times change.' He sighed, staring into the middle distance. 'I was having a nice drink until you came in looking like Banquo's ghost and reminded me how everything has gone to shit. You had a good time and now it's over, just thank whatever ancient gods it is you worship that you didn't get caught.'

'We did. Someone saw us.'

'Ah,' Rab sighed. 'I suppose that would put a different complexion on things.' He took another sip of his pint. 'Come on then, don't leave me in suspense. Who?'

'I don't know. Someone. A porter maybe. I had my back to them.'

'Spare me the gory details,' Rab grunted. 'I hope to God it wasn't a porter. They'll tell the cleaners, who'll let slip to the women in the canteen, and once it gets to them you're lost. Might as well take out a full-page ad in the *Glasgow Herald*, except there'd be no need.' He shook his head. 'If you don't know who it was, you can't be sure there's a problem.'

'They didn't see us standing too close in the coffee lounge or exchanging notes in the quads, they saw me rogering her on the desk of my office.'

'Rogering?'

'"Making the beast with two backs", "putting the horns on old Fergus", or whatever you Romantics call it.'

'Shagging.'

'What do you think I should do?'

'What can you do?' Rab patted his arm. 'Get a round in.'

*   *   *

Fowlers had quenched thirsts for at least a hundred years. Its high ceiling was iced with intricate cornicing, its windows frosted with etchings advertising whiskies and beers, which let light filter into the bar, but allowed privacy from passers-by to priests, poets, skivers, fathers on errands or men seeing about dogs, idle students and lovers budgeting towards leaving their spouses. Mrs Noon kept things tight and it was

60

rare to wait too long to be served or to see a fight that got beyond the third punch. Fowlers should have been a nice place for a drink, but it was a dump, a prime contender for a brewery theme-pub revamp. There were no ashtrays on the table, but the ceiling retained its nicotine hue and the smell of unwashed old men, stale beer and the cheap bleach used to sluice down the toilets was no longer masked by cigarette smoke. The bar stools, which harboured men who remembered the city when it was all soot and horseshit, were as scuffed and unsteady on their pins as their occupants. The patterned orange and blue carpet, once loud enough to drown out the Saturday night crowd, had sunk to sludge. Murray tipped back his fifth pint of the evening and decided this was where he belonged.

Phyllida McWilliams and Vic Costello had left an hour or so ago, taking their quarrel to one of the West End restaurants where they were known and dreaded. Phyllida had had trouble getting her arm into the sleeve of her jacket and Murray had guided her hand into the armhole while Vic strode to the door with the single-minded purpose of the practised inebriate.

'You're a lovely man, Murray. Take my advice.' She gathered her bags of shopping; ingredients for another Friday night dinner she was destined not to cook. 'Never get involved with someone who isn't available.'

'What made you say that, Phyllida?'

She shrugged and gave him a silly grin. 'I have been drinking, you know.'

Now there were three of them left. Lyle Joff, quieter after his phone call, Rab and Murray. They

61

were still at the corner table, but in the hours they had sat there the pub had transformed from a peaceful place where men could swap confidences into a red-faced rammy. The bar was three-deep, the staff quick-pouring wine and pressing more glasses to optics than they had earlier in the evening, but it was still pints that ruled; a shining spectrum of gold, yellows, browns and liquorice black. Not that anyone stopped to admire their drink. People were knocking them back faster than it was possible to serve and from time to time a barmaid would squeeze into the throng and return with a tall column of tumblers, as if gathering ammunition for a siege.

Two thoughts were pinballing around Murray's brain. The first was his need for another drink, the magic one that would make everything click into place. The second was that he'd drunk too much and should get home before he shipwrecked himself.

Maybe it was the bell that made him think of shipwrecks. It was loud and clanging and spoke to him of treacherous rocks and shattered hulks. What was it like to drown?

'Pushing the boat out tonight?'

That's what they were doing, setting out into perilous waters, and none of them in possession of their sea legs. Murray raised his head. Mrs Noon was holding a tin tray loaded with empty tumblers, their rims edged with tides of dead froth. He wasn't sure he'd ever seen the woman out from behind the bar before.

'I didn't know you had legs, Mrs Noon.' He grinned. 'I thought you were a mermaid. Great singers, mermaids. They lure poor sailors to their deaths, just for the fun of it. Beautiful creatures, beautiful and cruel.'

'You wouldn't want to hear me sing.' The manageress placed his half-full glass in amongst the empties on her tray. 'That really would be a cruelty.' She watched Rab neck the dregs of his pint then took his glass from him. 'Time to head home, gentlemen.'

She was right. They should have left hours ago. Now here he was, drunk and sober at the same time. Each half of him disgusted at the other.

Someone had propped the doors open. The crowd was thinning, people sinking the last of their drinks, reaching for their jackets, all the heat and chatter drifting out into the night. He stretched an arm towards his beer, but Mrs Noon sailed the tray up and away, beyond his reach.

'What happened to drinking-up time?'

It came out too loud. He caught the barman throwing Mrs Noon a questioning look and the woman's answering shake of the head.

'You heard the bell, that's drinking-up time over. Do you want to get me into trouble?'

He was a lecturer in English literature at a distinguished and ancient university. He straightened himself in his chair and summoned forth the spirit of Oscar Wilde.

'Don't you think you may be a little old for me to get you into trouble, Mrs Noon?'

'No need for that now.' Rab was pulling on his jacket. 'You'll have to excuse my colleague. He is the recipient of bad news.'

Murray lumbered to his feet. The battle was lost, there was no more drink to be had, no possibility of reaching the required state here. The landlady disregarded Rab's apologies and turned her practised smile on Murray: ice and glass. She'd once told him she had a daughter at the uni.

'I was just thinking the same thing of the pair of you. You're both too old to be getting into trouble. Go home, gentlemen.'

*   *   *

Outside black cabs and private hires edged along the road accompanied by the bass beat and infrabright lights of sober boys in souped-up cars. It was another kind of rush hour, Friday night chucking-out time, louder, younger and messier than the into-work-and-home-again crowds. Here came the smashed windows, spilled noodles, lost shoes and sicked-up drinks, the pigeon breakfasts and trailing bloodstains.

Two teenage girls perched on the windowsill of the late-night Spar passing a bottle between them while a yard away their friend snogged a youth in a tracksuit, their joined mouths sealed vacuum-tight. The boy's hand slid up the girl's crop top. One of the drinkers tipped back a swig from the bottle, arching her body, her short skirt riding up her thighs. For an instant she looked like an advert for the elixir of youth. Then she lost her balance and bumped against her companion. Both girls giggled and the one who had nearly fallen shouted, 'Fucking jump him if you're gonnae or we'll miss the bus.'

The boy broke the clinch, grinning at his audience, then pulled the girl back to him, whispering something that made her laugh, then push herself free, staggering slightly on her high

64

heels as she tottered towards her friends.

'Virgin,' the teenagers taunted, passing her the bottle.

Lyle Joff gave them a stern look. 'I should bloody hope so.' The girls sniggered, nudging each other, and Lyle took refuge in his kebab. He didn't speak again until they had passed the group.

'If I caught Sarah or Emma behaving like that, I'd lock them up until they were thirty. Fuck it, thirty-five. I'd lock them up till they were thirty-five and even then I'd still want some guarantees.'

Murray looked back at the girls. They were at the bus stop now. One of them—he wasn't sure if it was the one who'd been doing the kissing— pushed the boy. The youth stepped into a half trot, shouting something. The girls roared back, united now as they rushed at him, their high heels clattering against the pavement, laughing, full of victory as the boy ran off down the street.

Murray joined in the laughter. Some people had more talent for life.

'*Brief Encounter.*'

Lyle said, 'It's not funny, Murray. Boys like that take advantage of young girls.'

Rab asked, 'What age are Sarah or Emma now? Five and seven? You don't need to worry about that for a few years.'

'Three and six. Remind me to look up convent schools in the Yellow Pages in the morning. Here, hold this a minute.'

Lyle thrust his half-eaten kebab into Murray's hand and nipped up a lane. Murray lifted the swaddled meat and salad to his mouth, crunching into vinegar, spices and heat. When had he last eaten? There had been a packet of crisps in the pub, but before that? Some sauce escaped the wrap and ran down his chin.

'Hey.' Lyle emerged from the alleyway. 'I said hold it, not eat it.'

'Sorry.' Murray wiped his face. He took a second bite then handed it back. 'I don't know how you can stomach that stuff.'

Lyle fed the end of the kebab into his mouth and started picking at the shreds of salad and onion left in the paper. 'I used to live on these before Marcella got her claws into me.'

His expression looked like it might crumple and he tore at the kebab with his teeth again, as if seeking solace.

They were passing the queue for The Viper Club now. Murray recognised a girl from his third-year tutorial group. She'd caught her long, straight hair back in an Alice band. Her dress was short, her white boots high. She made him think of the test-card girl, all grown up and gone kinky.

'Hello, Dr Watson.'

He nodded, trying not to stagger. Ah, what the fuck? He was allowed a private life, wasn't he?

Rab echoed his thoughts.

'Sometimes you need to cut loose, connect with the elemental, remind yourself of the beauty of your own existence.'

Lyle scrunched the kebab's wrapping into a ball and tossed it into a bin already brimming with rubbish.

'For tomorrow we may die.'

The paper trembled on the peak of the pile, and then tumbled to the ground. Rab bent over, picked up the wrapping and stuffed it carefully back into the bucket. A look of satisfaction at a job well done settled on his face.

'Right, what den of iniquity are we headed to next?'

*   *   *

The thin man with the long hair and the bandanna wanted a pound before he would let them in. Rab dropped three coins into the old ice-cream tub that acted as a till and they went up the stairs and into the electric brightness of the pool hall.

'I should head back.' It had been Lyle Joff's mantra since he'd phoned his wife two hours ago, but he joined the queue for the bar with the others and accepted his pint. 'Just the one, thanks. I'll need to be thinking about getting home.'

The room was busy with the quiet clack of billiard balls and the low murmur of conversation. They were in the first wave of pub exiles and serious pool players still outnumbered those for whom the hall was just another stop on the night's drunken highway. It was about a year since Murray had been here, a night on the town with his brother Jack, but it was as if he'd just stepped out to take a piss. There were the same faces, the same closed looks and poker expressions. The same mix of scruff and cowboy-cool, the lavvy-brush beards, arse-hugging jeans, Cuban heels and tight-fitting waistcoats. Fuck, you'd have to be hard to wear that gear in Glasgow.

Rab lowered himself behind a free table.

'Welcome to Indian country. What time does this place stay open till?'

'Three.'

Rab's sigh was contented, nothing to worry

67

about for two hours.

Lyle stared silently at his pint, as if it might hold the possibility of enlightenment. Slowly his head sank onto his chest and his eyes closed.

A woman bent across the baize, lining up her options. Murray found himself following the seams of her jeans, up the inside of her raised thigh to the point where they met in a cross. He looked away. Would the tyranny of sex never stop?

He nodded towards Lyle.

'Is he all right?'

The woman telescoped her cue back towards their table and Rab shifted his drink beyond its reach.

'He's fine, he'll wake up in a moment.' Rab indicated a pair of women sitting near the back of the room. 'Why don't you go over there and ask them if they want a drink?'

The women might have been sisters, or maybe it was simply that their style was the same. Strappy tops and short feathery hair whose copper highlights glinted under the bright lights. They were grown-up versions of the girls he'd gone to school with. They'd never have looked at him then, but now?

It was stupid. He didn't fancy either of them, and besides, he wasn't up to the aggressive dance of tease and semi-insults that constituted a chat-up.

'They've got drinks.'

'Well, get up, pretend you're going to the gents' and offer them another one en route.'

'Is that how James Bond does it? Hello, ladies, I was on my way for a pish and wondered if I could bring you anything back? Ever wondered why it's going to say "confirmed bachelor" on your obituary?'

'It must be better than mooning over Ms Houghton.'

Lyle Joff awakened slowly, like an ugly toy twitching into life in a deserted nursery. The flesh beneath his eyes trembled and then the eyes themselves opened. He blinked and turned his fuzzy gaze on Murray.

'Rachel Houghton.' He smiled dreamily. 'Good arse. Good everything else too.'

'Lyle.' Rab's voice was warning. 'We're talking about a colleague.'

Lyle's brief sleep seemed to have refreshed him. He wiped away the glue of saliva that had formed at the corners of his mouth and took a sip of his pint. 'Listen to Professor PC. '

Rab said, 'Shut up, Lyle, you're drunk.'

A couple of the pool players looked over. Murray raised his beer to his lips. It tasted of nothing.

'We're all drunk. Say what you were going to say, Lyle.'

'Lyle, I'm warning you.'

Rab's tone was low and commanding, but Lyle was too far gone to notice. He patted Rab's shoulder.

'Murray's one of us, the three mouseketeers.' He giggled. 'It's top secret. Rab said Fergus would have his balls strung up and made into an executive toy for his desk if he found out.'

'The three musketeers, great swordsmen.' Murray turned to Rab. 'What's the big secret?'

'Nothing, Lyle's just being provocative, aren't you, Lyle?'

'Not as provocative as Rachel.' Lyle put an arm around Rab. 'I wouldn't have thought you had it in you.'

Rab lifted the arm from his shoulder. His eyes met Murray's and all of the ruined adventure was in them. There was no need to ask what had happened, but Murray said, 'Tell me.'

Lyle looked from one to the other, wary as a barroom dog whose master is on his fourth drink.

Rab sighed wearily.

'What's the point? She's a free spirit, Murray, a generous woman.'

'I want to know.'

A little beer had slopped onto the table. Rab dipped his finger in it and drew a damp circle on the Formica. He looked his age.

'A one-off mercy fuck, that's all there is to it.'

'When?'

'The end of last term. You remember all that hoo-ha about my introduction to the new Scottish poetry anthology?'

Murray did. Rab had been forthright in his assessment that a new wave of Scottish poets were throwing off the class-consciousness, self-obsession and non-poetic subject matter of the previous generation and ushering in a golden age. The new wave had leapt to the defence of their predecessors while balking at Rab's description of them as non-political. The elder statesmen had been vitriolic in their assessment of academics in general, and Rab in particular. It must have been a week when war and disaster had slipped from the news because the row had hit the broadsheets. Rab had been derided by academics and pundits north of the border and a source of amusement to those south of it.

'It all blew up in my face a bit. Some people thrive on controversy, Fergus for example, but I don't. It got me down. Rachel dropped into my office one afternoon to commiserate and we went for a few drinks, quite a few drinks. Then when the pub closed I remembered that there was another bottle at my place. There's always another bottle at my place.' He gave a sad smile. 'I didn't expect her to come and then when she did I didn't expect anything more than a drink. I was going to tell you.' He laughed almost shyly. 'But a gentleman doesn't talk about these things.'

'You bloody talked about it to Lyle.'

'Oh, come on, Murray. I'm an overweight fifty-five-year-old poetry lecturer and Rachel's a thirty-five-year-old dolly bird. I had to tell someone. Anyway, I'd been drinking.'

'You've generally been drinking.'

'That's a prime example of why I didn't tell you. You can be such a fucking puritan, I thought you wouldn't approve.' He gave a low laugh. 'And then you told me that you and she . . . Well, I was jealous, I admit, but not jealous enough to throw it back in your face.' Rab raised his pint to his lips and then wiped his mouth on the back of his hand. His tone slipped from apologetic to defensive. 'I don't see what you're getting so hot under the collar for, anyway. She's another man's wife. She doesn't belong to you, me or anyone else in the department she might have fucked, except maybe Fergus, and if so I'd say he's doing a very poor job of holding onto his property.'

It was the female player's turn again. Rab moved his drink as she pulled the cue back then fired a white ball across the baize. Murray watched it sail into the depths of a corner pocket, sure as death.

He imagined taking the pool cue from her hand and smashing it into Rab Purvis's beer-shined face. Teeth first, then nose. He'd leave the eyes alone. He'd always been squeamish about that kind of thing.

Lyle said, 'Are you okay, Murray?'

He didn't answer, just got to his feet and left before any more damage could be done.

*   *   *

Murray had been walking for a long time. Once a police car slowed and took a look at him, he ignored them and they drove on past, but their interest seemed to be the signal for his feet to start a winding route home. He left the main road and wandered uphill into the confluence of wide lonely streets that made up Park Circus, the jewel in the crown of Glasgow's West End. Sometime after parlour maids and footmen decided they'd rather risk their health in munitions factories or the battlefield, the smart residences had been converted into hotels and offices. Now they'd been deserted for city centre lets and were slowly being reclaimed by speculative builders. Murray drifted past the weathered To Let signs, half-seeing the sycamore shoots sprouting from neglected guttering, the broken railings and chipped steps that might tumble the unsuspecting into the dank courtyards of window-barred basements. The plague-town atmosphere of the shuttered houses and empty streets matched his mood.

72

He took his mobile from his pocket and accessed the number he'd taken from a list in the front office and stupidly promised himself he'd never use. The night was starting to turn. He'd reached the top gate of Kelvingrove Park. Down below in the parkland's green valley, birds were beginning to sing to each other. Murray pressed *Call* and waited while his signal bounced around satellites stationed in the firmament above, or whatever it did in that pause before the connection was made. He let it ring until an automated voice told him the person he was looking for was unavailable, then hung up and pressed Redial. This time the other end picked up and Professor Fergus Baine's voice demanded, 'Do you know what time it is?'

Murray cut the call. He sat on a wall and listened to the birds celebrating the return of the sun, then after a minute or two his phone vibrated into the stupid jingle he'd never bothered to change. He took it out, glanced at the caller display and saw the unfamiliar number flashing on the screen.

'Hello?' His voice was slurred.

'Is that you, Murray?' Fergus sounded wide-awake. Did he never sleep? 'What do you want? Something urgent, I imagine?'

'I wanted to speak to Rachel.'

It was ridiculous, all of it, stupid.

'Rachel is asleep. Perhaps you can call back in the morning?' The professor's politeness was damning.

Somewhere in the recesses of Murray's brain was the knowledge that now was the time to quit, while he still had the slim chance of writing the call

73

off as a drunken indiscretion. But in the morning he would have lost his courage.

'I need to talk to her now.'

'Well, you can't. Call back at a decent hour.'

The line went dead.

Murray stood and soberly surveyed the sunrise. A door in the empty street opened and some party-goers reeled out, their voices high and excited. A young girl drifted over and draped an arm around his shoulder.

'Look, Dr Watson.' She pointed unsteadily across the parkland. 'Isn't it beautiful?'

The sun was fully up now and only a few streaks of pink remained smeared against the blue. The morning light glinted against the River Kelvin and caught in the trees, shifting their leaves all the greens and yellows in the spectrum. The birds had ceased their revels and calm had settled. Even the concrete hulk of hospital buildings in the distance seemed at one with the day. Murray looked at the new-minted morning and agreed that yes, it really was beautiful.

Chapter Seven

Murray woke suddenly, not knowing what it was that had roused him. The blind was only half down, daylight filtering weakly into the room. He glanced at the radio alarm, but its plug had been pulled, the glowing numbers dead. Saturday or not, he'd intended to be at the library in Edinburgh for opening time, but his drunken self had opted for uninterrupted sleep. His clothes were draped carefully over the chair in the bedroom, the way they always were when he'd drunk too much. His watch lay on the top of the chest of drawers, amongst the kind of small change a man on a spree accumulates. Five past twelve. He felt like Dr Jekyll, his scholarly intentions ruined by a fiend of his own fabric. Murray slid from under the duvet, found his boxer shorts and pulled them on. Then he paused on the edge of the bed and listened.

Somewhere in the distance a road drill rumbled, but otherwise it was quiet. He went barefoot into the hallway and opened the front door, screening his half-nakedness behind it. He'd neglected to lock up the night before, but no keys trembled in the keyhole. Murray shut it gently. The rush of air caught on the hairs on his legs and he realised he was cold. There was a sudden clatter of footsteps in the stairwell outside. He felt ridiculously vulnerable standing there in only his boxers. Murray turned towards the bathroom, but the snap of the letterbox brought him back into the hallway and the letters sprawled on the mat.

He took his dressing gown from the hook on the back of the bathroom door and went into the kitchen. There was no mineral water in the fridge so he filled a mug with water from the tap, drank it quickly and then poured himself a second. Christ, was this what it was like to be an alcoholic? If Archie had felt this way every morning then it was no wonder his published work consisted of a single collection.

Murray didn't want to think about the night before; the row with Rab, the phone call to

75

Rachel, Rab and Rachel. The romance had been a knot in Murray's stomach since it started, but now that it was over—more than over; now that it was ruined—the knot was replaced by a leaden deadness. He realised he'd been sustained by the thought that Rachel—Rachel, to whom he'd have addressed poems if only he could write—Rachel had chosen him. His knuckles tingled where he wished he'd slammed them into Rab's face.

It wasn't Rab's fault. He should send him an email, apologise.

It changed everything; the knowledge that Rachel had slept with him too; Rab's mouth kissing where he had kissed, his hands on her body. The thought disgusted him, even though he'd supposed she still slept with Fergus.

Fergus.

The phone call came back to him, the memory of the professor's voice slick with anger. He groaned out loud. His sabbatical stretched ahead, twelve months for his head of department to nurse his wrath and engineer Murray's successor.

He felt like going back to bed, pulling the sheets over his head and letting temporary death overwhelm the after-drink urge to kill himself. Instead he sat on the couch cradling the cup of water in his hands. A double-decker bus rumbled along the road outside. Murray watched the small ripples disturbing the surface of his drink.

Had there been a moment, a flash of mental clarity in the midst of the storm, when Archie had known he was going to die? He would have been wet already, soaked through by the rain and toppling waves, but the shock of water when the boat upturned must have taken the breath from

76

him. How many times had he gone under before the final descent? How long had it taken? The sea sucking him down then spewing him back to the surface, the frantic struggle to stay afloat, the desperate grab for some purchase met by froth and foam. Or had he been knocked unconscious before he even hit the water? It was possible. The night had been wild, Archie sailing solo. Maybe he had fallen and hit his head against the side or been attacked by the boom. Archie had been careless with his life, sailing into the storm. Perhaps he'd been a careless sailor too. His body had never been found. It left no clues for the coroner. There was no convenient sheaf of newly forged poems slid safe in a waterproof envelope in his jeans pocket, no clues for the biographer either.

Murray wandered through to the kitchen and looked down onto the backcourt. An old man in carpet slippers was scavenging through the bins. He watched him for a while then went into the hallway, picked up the phone and dialled the police. The phone rang for a long time, and then a deep voice said, 'Sandyford police station.'

'Hello, there's an old man out the back of my building going through the rubbish. He's in his slippers and I'm worried he's got dementia or something.'

'Have you spoken to him?'

'I'm not dressed yet.'

The voice at the other end of the phone was weary.

'Do you think he's looking for receipts or anything?'

'Receipts?'

It was like a foreign word. Murray couldn't

77

think what it had to do with the conversation.

'Identity fraud.'

It was in his mind to say that the old man would be welcome to his identity, but he answered, 'No, I don't think he's doing any harm. I just thought he might be confused.'

'Okay,' the policeman sighed again. 'Give me your name and address and we'll send someone round when we can.'

'When will that be?'

The voice contained the full quota of contempt that an early-rising man in uniform could hold for a civilian who had only now crawled out of bed.

'I couldn't say, sir.'

Murray gave his details, hung up and went back to the window. The old man was gone. He stood there for a moment debating whether to call the police again or get dressed and hunt for him amongst the backcourts. In the end he did neither, simply clicked the kettle on and lifted his mail from the table.

A bill from the factors, a leaflet from the local supermarket outlining their offers in colours bright enough to sicken the famished, a bank statement that would show he earned more than his needs, a plain white envelope and a letter stamped with the logo of Christie's agents. He hesitated between the final two, and then tore at the seal of the agent's letter.

Dear Dr Watson

Ms Graves has asked me to advise you that she has given your request serious consideration, but has regretfully decided to decline. Ms Graves has strong views on

*the privacy of artists, and while she wishes
you every success in your critical analysis
of Archie Lunan's poetry, she does not see
what a discussion of their time together
would achieve. She now considers this
correspondence closed and has asked me
to bring to your attention the government's
recent anti-stalking legislation.*

  Yours sincerely
  Foster James
  Niles, James and Worthing

Murray swore and crumpled the letter into a ball.

The airwaves were full of people talking. Child-murderers and drugs casualties, people who had once sat next to someone famous on the bus, even the dead were in on the act, revealing scandals from beyond the grave. Everywhere people were blogging, Twittering and confessing; TV shows ran late into the night detailing private lives that would have been better kept private; but Archie's old love would consider a second approach grounds for prosecution.

He smoothed the letter out and re-read it. The trick would be to bump into Christie casually, at a poetry reading perhaps. Somewhere with wine and easy company where he could lay on the charm, get her talking about old times before he admitted that yes, it was he who was writing Archie's biography.

Some chance.

He smoothed the paper again, knowing it had to become part of his file. Did it tell him anything beyond what was said?

Murray whispered. 'You never left, never got

any distance. That's why you care so much.'

He slit open the second envelope with his thumb, wondering what the penalties for stalking were and if stalkers were still allowed to teach. The green paper inside had been carefully folded in half. The type suggested that the sender had only recently come into possession of a word processor. Fonts battled for prominence, but boldest of all was the heading: *God so loved the world, that he gave his only begotten Son, that whosoever believeth in him should not perish, but have everlasting life.* Service times were detailed beneath.

Murray crumpled the page and balled it into the recycling bag, trying to smile at the thought that—Rachel aside—it was the best offer he'd had in a while.

Chapter Eight

Murray seemed to have been waiting a long time. He decided to count to a hundred then ring the doorbell again. He'd reached eighty-five when a shadow appeared, advancing slowly towards him beyond the thickened safety glass.

'Aye, aye, just a minute.'

Professor James's voice was cracked with age and sharp with irritation. Murray thought of Macbeth's porter, provoked by the knock at the castle door, comic in his anger, the moment of calm before the discovery of horror.

James fumbled with a set of keys and his sigh was audible through the locked door, but it was only when the professor pushed it wide that Murray realised how badly he'd aged. It was almost twenty years since they'd met, but somehow he'd still expected to see the stern-faced lecturer who had approached the lectern like a United Free Church of Scotland minister about to deliver a sermon to a congregation set on damnation. Pipe-smoking, bespectacled and bad-tempered, his stocky body packed into an old tweed jacket, James had been everything that Murray, fresh from a comprehensive school staffed by corduroy-clad progressives, had desired in a university professor.

James shook his hand. 'Come away through.'

The professor had never been handsome, but he'd been a vigorous presence, with the barrel chest and bullet head of a pugilist. Old age had shrunk his body and bent his spine, rendering his face oversized and jutting. The edge of his skull was decorated with a patina of freckles and grave spots. The effect was grotesque, an ancient, nodding toddler with an eager grin.

'This is a rare treat. Two names from the past in one day.'

Murray followed James down a small hallway decorated with photographs of the professor's children and grandchildren. The glass front door had presumably been designed to let in light, but perhaps the house faced the wrong way, or maybe the day was too dull to extract any brightness from, because the hall was dark, the smiles in the pictures cast in shadows.

'Two names?'

'You and Lunan, outstanding students the pair of you.'

81

It was strange, hearing himself coupled with the poet.

'My student years certainly feel a long time past.'

'You'll be part of a million pasts by the time you're finished. Teaching confers its own brand of celebrity. You get hailed by folk you've no memory of. My tip is allow them do the talking and don't let on you've not got a clue who they are.' James led Murray into a burgled-looking sitting room. He lowered himself gently into a high-backed armchair and nodded towards a chintz couch. 'Shift those papers and make yourself comfortable. As you can see, I've reverted to a bachelor state.'

Murray lifted a pile of handwritten notes and placed them on top of a stack of library books.

'Ah, maybe not there. Helen's coming round later to return those for me and if they're hidden she'll miss them.' James scanned the room looking for a suitable berth amongst the books and documents crowding the room. 'Why not put them . . .' He hesitated while Murray hovered uncertainly, papers in hand. 'Why not put them here?' He nodded to the floor in front of him. 'That way if I forget about them they'll trip me up and the problem will be redundant.'

'Are you sure?'

'It would be a suitable ending for an aged academic, tumbled by words.'

Traces of James's dead wife clung to the house. Professor James would surely never have chosen the floral curtains that screened the small window in the hall, nor the sets of figurines gazing unadored from behind the dull glass of the china cabinet, but the tone of the place had shifted from a respectable family home with a feminine bent to an old bachelor's bed-sit.

The kettle was in the sitting room, where it could be easily reached. An open packet of sugar, a cardboard box spilling tea bags and a carton of suspect milk stood next to it. The coffee table was stacked with books, each of the piles tiled together with the precision of a Roman mosaic. A smaller occasional table at James's side held a glass of water, a selection of medication and yet more books. Murray noted a copy of Lunan's *Moontide* on top of the pile, within easy reach of James's right hand.

They parleyed a little about the department, but Murray sensed that the older man's questions were merely form. The part of himself he had given to the university now occupied the books and papers that scattered the room. Murray's presence was a brief distraction, a meeting on the shore before the tide of words dragged him back.

Murray reached into his rucksack, placed his tape recorder on top of one of the piles between them and pressed *Record*. James cleared his throat and his voice slowed to lecture-theatre pace.

'I've only ever kept an appointments diary, so I'm afraid you won't get any great insights from me, but I did look up the year in question and found a reference to a meeting I had with Lunan immediately after he was told his presence on our undergraduate course would no longer be required.' James produced a daily diary stamped 1970, opened it at a bookmarked page and passed it to Murray. It had been a hectic week. James's lectures were marked clearly in black ink, but the rest of the page was scattered with scrawls in several different colours, black battling blue and red, pencilled scribbles and underlinings. 'He was a Tuesday appointment, afternoon of course. I don't think Archibald Lunan was ever a friend of early mornings.'

Murray saw *AL 2.30* jotted in the margin of a busy day. He asked, 'How did Lunan react to being sent down?'

'Sent down?' The tone was mild. 'I wasn't aware we were in Oxford or Cambridge.'

'No.' Murray leaned back in his chair wondering how, for all his preparations, he could have forgotten the pedantry that lay behind James's smile. 'Was he upset?'

'He may have been. But as far as I can recall, he took it like a man.'

'Standard procedure would have been to send Lunan a letter. Why did you feel the need to inform him personally?'

'I asked myself exactly the same thing when I saw the appointment in my diary.'

James's manner shifted and Murray realised he'd hit on a question that interested the old man. He remembered this pattern from his undergraduate tutorials, the professor's initial impatience set aside as he got into the meat of the matter, as if the verbal barbs were self-defence against boredom.

'Let's just say, whatever it was, I wouldn't have trusted Lunan to anyone else in the department at that time. Even I could see we were a bunch of stuffed shirts.' James moved slightly against his cushions as if trying to settle his bones. 'Perhaps it says something about my own prejudices, but Archie looked belligerent. Long hair, cowboy moustache, scruffy clothes . . . there's a particular leather coat that sticks in the memory.' James gave a scholarly chuckle. 'Ten years later teachers and lecturers had adopted the same look, with the exception of a few diehards like myself, the tweed jacket and suede shoes brigade. But back then, in Scotland at any rate, that kind of image still had counterculture connotations. So couple it with Lunan's poor attendance . . . I was possibly worried he might get the stuffing knocked out of him. Despite his posturing, Lunan always struck me as delicate.'

'In what way?'

'He was sensitive, not a prerequisite for poets as you no doubt know. He looked the part, as I said, the leather coat, the ready fists, the all-too-frequently cut lip and black eye, but he wasn't as robust as he made out.'

Murray asked, 'How do you mean?'

James paused and looked at the ceiling as if searching for an explanation in its shadowed corners.

'In those days I had a little group who used to meet once a month and discuss their own verse.' James was being modest. His 'little group' had fostered a school of writers whose reputation had spread far beyond the literary circles of their city. Some of its members had later helped define their nation to the world. 'The first poem Lunan presented was plagiarised. It was badly written enough to be the work of an undergraduate so there's a good possibility I wouldn't have rumbled him, if I hadn't had a poem published in the same back issue of the journal he'd lifted it from.' James shook his head in wonder. 'Amazing.'

'What did you do?'

'My first instinct was to ask him about it in front of the group, but I resisted. I'm not sure why. Maybe I was already aware of Archie's vulnerability. I simply took him aside and told him I knew. I think I expected that would be the last we saw of him, but for all he was weak, Archie was tough too. He came to the following meeting, this time with his own work. I must have been curious because I agreed to read it.' James grimaced. 'The poems he gave me were good. Not perfect, but original.'

Murray nodded towards Lunan's book, perched on top of the pile at the professor's elbow.

'Did any of the poems he showed you appear in *Moontide*?'

'One of them. "Preparation for a Wake". It was revised and tightened up by the time the collection was published, of course, but the concept was there at the start: the raising of the dead man, the play on words between a wake and awake, the horror his drinking companions feel when their dead mate sits up ready to join in the merrymaking. The lyricism of the language wasn't as successful as it was in the published version, but it was still remarkable.'

'What did the rest of the group make of it?'

'I don't recall any particular debate. You have to remember it was a long time ago, and we were privileged to be at the birth of many remarkable pieces.'

James looked Murray in the eye. It was like a door slamming.

'How did Archie get on with the group in general?'

86

'Okay, as far as I remember. But as I said, it was a long time ago.'

Another door shut.

James gave the kind of smile favoured by American presidents on the stocks, but the professor's teeth were yellowed, his gums pink and receding.

'What about your own response to his work?

'My own response?'

The professor made the question sound preposterous.

Murray smiled apologetically.

'What was your initial reaction when you eventually got to see his writing?'

It was a sunny day outside, but the sitting room windows had taken on the smoky taint that glass acquires after a year or two's neglect and the pair were stuck in murk and shadow. The dust that coated the air was formed from James and James's wife, decayed and merged. Murray wanted to brush them from himself, but instead he smiled and waited.

James moved a hand against the arm of his chair, as if trying to make his mind up about something. When he spoke his voice was dangerously gentle.

'Are you asking if I was jealous of Lunan's ability?'

Murray hesitated, surprised by the revelation in the old man's question.

'Your professionalism is beyond reproach.'

James lifted the copy of *Moontide* from the table next to him and looked at Lunan's Rasputin face. Somewhere a clock ticked.

'I was jealous, of course, but I was jealous of

others too. Maybe we were all jealous of each other, beneath the comradeship. I honestly don't think I ever let it affect my dealings with him, and then . . . well . . . how can you be jealous of a dead man?' He put the book back on the table and smiled at Murray. 'But I am, of course, every time I read his poems.' He laughed and gave the chair a slight slap as if rousing himself to business. 'The strange thing was that the filched poem he'd presented was way beneath the standard of what he was capable of creating. That's what I mean about a vulnerable streak. Archie was over-sensitive, lacking in confidence and yet at the same time burdened with an exaggerated ego.'

'Not the most attractive combination.'

'No, but Lunan could be attractive. He had the gift of the gab and a sense of the absurd. When he was in the right frame of mind, he was good company.'

'And when he wasn't?'

'Morose, sarcastic, inclined to drunkenness. I had to ask him to leave the session on two separate occasions. If he'd been anyone else I would have told him not to come back. There were precedents: at least one drunken writer had been barred.'

'But he was too talented to dismiss?'

James leaned back in his chair and gazed at the ceiling again. It was a theatrical gesture, a pause that preceded a point to be underlined.

'Talent's an odd thing, essential of course, but no guarantee of anything. To be perfectly frank I doubted he had the discipline to succeed. I thought he was more in love with the idea of being a writer than with the need to create.'

'What made you think that?'

'Partly, I suppose, because I'd seen it before. We never turned any sober customers away from these get-togethers, you know. We didn't advertise them, of course, it was strictly word of mouth, but from time to time you'd get romantic heroes wafting in. They couldn't play an instrument so they thought they would wield a pen. It's a very powerful image—young Thomas Chatterton, Percy Shelley, Jack Kerouac—the disaffected writer battling the world before dying young and beautiful.' He laughed. 'Well, maybe not so beautiful in Kerouac's case, killing yourself with alcohol tends to be a bit bloating, but you get my drift.' The professor sighed. 'Working with young people for as long as I have, it's inevitable that one is going to encounter untimely deaths, a car crash, an overdose, a climbing accident.' He paused. 'A drowning. It's a cliché to say it's a waste, and yet what else is it? A bloody waste.' There was another pause as if he were silently mourning the young people who had died before their span. 'So, to answer your question, yes I was aware of his talent early on, but I thought it squandered on him. Remember the poems I saw had potential, but they weren't there yet.' He grinned. 'And there was I with my reservoirs of discipline and hard-won knowledge unable to create the magic that he could.' James shook his head. 'My God, I was ripe for some Faustian pact.' His eyes met Murray's. 'But I wasn't the only one.'

The professor laughed and a taint of decay scented the dead air of the darkened room. Murray cleared his throat then asked, 'So how did he take his expulsion?'

'I told you: stoically.' The old man shook his head. 'No, not stoically, casually. Shook my hand and wished me well. I was keen for Lunan to repeat the year, and he said he'd think about it. But I got the impression he was humouring me. It was infuriating. I remember I smelt beer on his breath and thought that if I were his father I'd knock some sense into him.' James gave a second chuckle, though this time it sounded hollow. 'That was the way we thought in those days. But we'd been brought up by men who'd gone to war, and gone to war ourselves.' James sighed. 'Lunan was like a man squandering an inheritance. He had the brains to do well, but he wasted them, the same way he wasted his talent and ultimately his life. He let that slip from him as casually as he idled away his university career.' Professor James looked up at Murray; his too-big head grinning like a Halloween mask. 'I'm glad you're doing this book. Those of us who were left behind could have served his work better. Debts owed to the dead seem to grow heavier with time.'

Murray nodded, though he could think of no debt the old man might owe the dead poet.

The professor's voice took on a lilting cadence and he recited,

> 'My candle burns at both ends;
> It will not last the night;
> But ah, my foes, and oh, my friends—
> It gives a lovely light!'

'Archie despised poems that rhymed, but that describes him perfectly: a fragile light that burned brightly, but all too briefly.'

'So you weren't surprised to hear of his death?'

'Surprised?' James's voice dropped an octave as if some of the shock still lingered on in his memory. 'Of course I was surprised. I still remember discovering that he'd drowned.'

The old man's head hung forward his mouth slightly open, a gleam of saliva wet behind the oxblood lips. The room sank into a long silence. Murray found himself watching the professor's chest. It rested thin and unmoving behind the stains on his woollen pullover. When James eventually spoke his words were slow and measured, as if the old man had conjured up the past and was relaying events as they unfolded before him.

'Valerie and I were going to watch our son Alexander play rugby. It must have been before he got his driving licence, because we were giving him a lift to the grounds. My daughter Helen was heading out on a date and Valerie was determined not to leave before her beau picked her up. She didn't want them left in the house on their own, you see, worried about impropriety.' James paused. Murray got the impression he was hesitating over a revelation, but then the professor continued. 'The young man in question phoned to say he'd be delayed. So we were not a happy home that Sunday morning. There was Helen stewing because her mother didn't trust her, Sandy desperate to get to the game, and Val finding tasks to delay our departure. Are you married?'

The question was unexpected and Murray stuttered slightly.

'No, not yet.'

'I recommend it, if you're lucky like I was and

91

manage to find the right woman, but it's not all sunshine and roses. After a while you get an instinct for when to disappear and that morning was one of them. I made myself a coffee, lifted the *Sunday Times* from the kitchen table and sat in the car where I could read it in peace.' There was a pause as James cleared his throat. 'It was a tiny notice, just a few lines: "Man missing, believed drowned." I'm not sure why it caught my eye. I've never been sailing unless you count rowing Val round Dunsappie Loch when we were courting, and I'm not particularly familiar with the part of the world where Lunan ended up, but for some reason I read it. I saw his name—"Archie Lunan, aged 25"—and knew then and there that he was dead.'

'What made you so sure?'

Professor James hesitated.

'I don't know. I never considered Archie suicidal. Quite the opposite. I still think of him as someone with a keen appreciation of life. His nature poems are full of wonder at the world. Maybe it was just that he wasn't the type for heroics. And the last time I'd seen him he'd been . . .' James paused again, as if searching for a word that would convey Archie's state of being without slandering him. 'He'd been over-elated.'

'Under the influence of drugs?'

'I'm not sure I would have been able to tell back then. But I don't think so. It was more like the kind of rapture you see on the faces of the recently converted. Do you remember the Hare Krishna?'

'Hare, hare, rama, rama?'

'They were all over Edinburgh in those days.

Helen was frightened of them when she was little. Too noisy, I suppose, with all their chanting and bells, but I liked them. They added a bit of colour to what was still a drab city. That's what Archie reminded me of the last time I saw him, a freshly recruited Hare Krishna. One that hadn't yet experienced living through a Scottish winter with a shaved head, wearing not much more than an orange bed sheet. Convention demanded I delivered my speech while Archie hung his head, but it was as if he couldn't sit still. I remember he picked up a photograph of Helen and Sandy when they were toddlers and asked what they were called. I was so surprised, I told him. He nodded his head, as if to say "not too bad", and then enquired how we'd managed to choose these particular names out of all the ones available in the world.'

'Did you tell him to mind his own business?'

'No, it was a poet's question. Suddenly we weren't tutor and student, but two wordsmiths. Maybe I already realised he was master over me in that realm. I told him they were family names. Archie laughed and said that would never be an option for him, but he didn't sound bitter, just happy, as if he was anticipating a future in which he might father children and give them names that would help shape their future in turn.' James's voice faltered and he asked, 'Do you mind if we take a break?'

He wanted to coax the old man on, but Murray closed his notebook.

'Of course. Would you like me to come back some other time?'

'Hadn't you better get it all down before I pop

93

off?'

He looked into the rheumy eyes and lied.

'I'm sure you'll be here for a while yet.'

James snorted.

'I'm eighty-seven. My father died at eighty-six and my grandfather at eighty-two. I switch on the light in the front room at seven-thirty every morning and evening, it's gloomy enough for it to show even in the so-called summer. If my opposite neighbour looks out and all's in darkness, she has instructions to approach with caution.' He sighed. 'Let's have a coffee. My taste buds are shot so, please, make it strong.'

Murray filled the kettle in a kitchen piled with dirty crockery. He noted the microwave, the discarded cardboard sleeves from consumed ready meals and recognised a scene from his own life.

James shouted from the other room, 'Ignore that mess. Irene will be in tomorrow with her mop and brushes to put everything to rights.'

Murray brought the kettle back into the lounge, set it on the dining table and plugged it in, wishing he'd had the foresight to bring along a packet of biscuits.

'Maybe I should get Irene's number.'

'It's a closely guarded secret. It'd be less trouble for you to get married. Not that that would necessarily solve your domestic problems these days, from what I've seen.'

The kettle reached its peak. Murray poured hot water over the instant brown stuff he'd already spooned into their mugs.

'Sadly not.'

'Don't try and ingratiate yourself with misogyny. Times have moved on, and for the

94

better too. Look at your head of department and his wife, top-class academics the pair of them, though Rachel is the better scholar, of course.' The old man looked at him slyly. 'How do you find Fergus Baine as head of department?'

Murray wondered if news of his affair with Rachel had spread as far as here, the self-contained bed-sit in the heart of what used to be a family home. He took a sip of coffee. He'd put in too much of the instant powder and it tasted bitter on his tongue.

'Very efficient.'

'Yes, efficiency has a habit of propelling men to the top.'

Tiredness was slackening the professor's face. If Lunan had been a bright, short-lived flame, James was wax, his features melting with time. Murray turned the tape recorder back on.

'Tell me about Christie Graves. Did you see much of her?'

James sighed, as if disappointed to be abandoning the subject of Murray's head of department.

'Not at first, but pretty soon Christie became part of the package. She was Archie's shadow, or maybe he was hers, who knows? She was very beautiful in a way that was fashionable back then: big eyes, pale skin and that red hair, very pre-Raphaelite. She's always credited as being part of the group and, in a way, I suppose she was. She was certainly there a lot that year, but she never contributed anything, just sat there quietly with a Giaconda-like smile on her face. It irritated the hell out of me.'

'She must have surprised you later.'

'Oh, yes, Christie was a big surprise. Of course, in a way, Lunan's death was the making of her. Maybe that's a resurrection of sorts, though it didn't seem so at the time.' James took a sip of his coffee. The ancient goblin features drooped with the weight of memories. 'There was no funeral. Lunan's body was lost but somebody organised a wake in Mather's, and someone else was mawkish enough to give a reading of "Preparation for a Wake". Needless to say, Archie didn't rise up like some thirsty messiah, ready to join in the drinking. Those that did attend got horribly drunk, myself included. Christie stayed away. I can't say I blamed her. I only saw her once after Lunan drowned, quite soon afterwards in fact, walking down the Bridges. She'd cut her hair. I remember being terribly touched by that. She'd had such beautiful hair, been quite aware of it too. But it was gone, hacked off. I crossed the street to offer my condolences. She saw me, met my eyes and nodded, but she didn't stop. I didn't hear anything of her until a few years later when her book came out.'

'What did you make of it?'

'What could you make of it? It was good. A funny word to apply to a book like that, but it was. Terrible and good.'

'Did you think any of it was based on fact?'

'What does it matter? Would it make it a better book?'

'Not necessarily better, but it's an interesting question, from my perspective.'

James leaned back in his chair and raised his wilting features to the ceiling, showing the full stretch of his tortoise neck.

'Authenticity . . . was it authentic? It existed, I held it in my hands and it impressed me. I think it had something better than authenticity. It had integrity, and that's all the truth that we can ever hope for.'

*   *   *

James accompanied Murray to the front door despite his protestations that he could find the way himself. They shook hands on the doorstep and James asked, 'Are you going to interview her? Christie?'

'Apparently not. My requests have been turned down.'

'A pity. Now that would have been a coup.'

He was halfway down the path when James called him back.

'It's up to you what kind of book you want this to be, but I think you have to find a way of seeing her.'

The older man was a head shorter. Murray looked down into eyes sparked with youth. He remembered James's description of Lunan as an over-elated religious convert and thought it could also be applied to this elderly face brimming with conviction.

'Easier said than done. She's threatened to prosecute me if I try.'

Professor James snorted.

'And you're going to let that stop you?'

He shrugged and the professor shook his head in mock despair.

'Let me tell you something. My father was an engineer at Barr & Strouds, a stalwart of the

97

union, free with his opinions on everything bar sex. He only gave me one piece of advice in that area. A woman you don't have to chase is a woman not worth having.'

Murray softened his voice with the respect due to dead fathers.

'I'm sure he was a clever man, but that particular counsel is as out of date as mass industrialisation. Anyway, I want to interview her about a troubled episode in her past, not marry her.'

'What if she's simply playing hard to get?'

'Why should she?'

'I don't know. Habit? She set herself against talk of Archie for sound reasons, but time has passed and times have changed. Maybe she needs to be reminded of that.' James put his hand on Murray's arm. 'You're a bright lad. I'm sure you'll manage if you set your mind to it.'

Chapter Nine

Murray shoved the carrier bag of books into his rucksack, hefted it onto his shoulder and stepped out of the second-hand bookshop into Edinburgh's West Port. He hadn't found any reference to Lunan in the poetry journals the book dealer had phoned him about, but the bubbled capitals and monochrome type of the adverts for now defunct magazines and readings long past had provided a quick spark of connectivity to the poet's era. Time travel through typeface. The thought made him smile.

He waited at the traffic lights then crossed the road, his mind turning towards lunch; maybe a bowl of soup somewhere in the Grassmarket where he could jot down a couple of points that had occurred to him while browsing the bookshelves. He remembered a quiet café where the service was slow and customers could linger. Perhaps he'd allow himself to continue perusing the journals he'd bought, before returning to the library. He might yet justify the leaden purchase by finding some passing reference to Lunan or his associates. The day was taking shape.

He was trying to remember where the nearest ATM was when he saw his brother's girlfriend turning the corner. Lyn was wearing her work clothes: flat shoes, loose-fitting jeans and a T-shirt topped by a long-sleeved blouse. Murray recalled her joking that she would wear a burka to work if she could get away with it.

'Except the filthy buggers would imagine I was wearing head-to-toe Ann Summers underneath.'

Jack had asked if Ann Summers stocked head-to-toe outfits and she'd given him a wink.

'You'd be amazed.'

Lyn was too intent on talking to the scruffy man in an electric wheelchair who was rolling along beside her to have seen Murray yet. The bookshop was three streets since, the nearest turning a block ahead, but he was almost level with a pub. Murray stepped up his pace and slipped smartly through its door.

His first impression was of darkness and music cut through with the scent of stale beer and something else, a sharp tang that was close to sweat. The couches that lined the room were

99

empty and only a couple of the bar stools were taken. But either the pub's clientele favoured late lunches, or the management were simply optimistic business would pick up, because they had laid on entertainment.

On a stage in the far corner a tall woman in a G-string lazily circled a silver pole. The dancer's face remained blank, but Murray's entrance seemed to be the cue for her to up-tempo. She gripped the pole with both hands and launched herself into a spin that lifted both feet from the air and twirled her into a kaleidoscope of

Breasts
Bottom
Breasts
Bottom
Breasts
Bottom

She hooked a leg around the prop, slowing her progress again and slid into the splits. Murray restrained a polite urge to clap. No one else seemed impressed. The barman glanced at Murray over the newspaper he'd leant against the beer taps, and the men on the bar stools kept their eyes on their pints, all except for a compact man in a grey sweat-suit who turned and looked straight at him.

The dancer resumed her slow gyrations and Murray made his way to the bar, readjusting his rucksack. He'd always liked Lyn. Would meeting her after his defection from Jack's exhibition really be worse than a drink in this dump? But talking to her would mean talking about his brother, and he

100

couldn't face that yet.

The music slid into a series of judders. The dancer ignored it for a moment, then when no one moved to remedy the noise shouted, 'Malky, are you going to fix that CD or do you want me to start fucking breakdancing?'

The barman roused himself from his newspaper, took the disc from the player and wiped it against a bar towel.

'I'd like to see you fucking moonwalking. On the moon.'

His voice was too low to reach the stage, but one of the men laughed and the girl threw the barman a look that promised later suffering.

'You've blotted your copybook there,' the man said.

The barman shrugged his shoulders and slid the disc back in the machine. Sade started singing about a smooth operator and the girl began weaving her hips, keeping her movements close and contained, as if dancing inside an invisible box.

Murray slid his hand into his jeans pocket and found a two-pound coin.

'Coke, please.'

The grey man on the bar stool turned and gave him the smallest of smiles. His voice was low, but Murray had no trouble hearing him over the beat of the music.

'Are you a member, sir?'

Murray took in the uncarpeted floor, the couches draped with cheap cotton throws, the stubbled bartender back in the sports page of his tabloid.

'No, I'm afraid not.'

'No problem. I can sign you in.'

'Cheers.'

He hoped the man wouldn't expect a drink in exchange.

'There's a ten pounds entrance fee for non-members.'

Murray felt his eyes drifting back towards the stage. He forced himself to look at the bouncer.

'I wasn't planning on staying.'

'Fair enough.' The man slid from his stool and put a firm grip on Murray's elbow, but his tone was as courteous as Professor Fergus Baine correcting a departmental rival's slip in literary theory. 'I'll see you to the door.'

'I mean I'm only stopping a minute.'

'In that case it'll be a tenner.'

'The thing is,' Murray gently disengaged himself and leant against the bar, striving for a mateyness he'd long known was outside his repertoire, 'there's a girl I want to avoid.'

The barman raised his eyes from the paper.

'I ken the feeling.'

Murray smiled at him, keen to win an ally.

'So if you'd just let me stop here for a moment, three minutes at the most, you'd be doing me a huge favour. I'm happy to buy a drink.'

He opened his palm, revealing the two-pound coin within. It looked pathetic and he closed his fingers round it again.

'No problem.' The bouncer's voice was slick with the complacency of a school bully extorting dinner money from a swot. 'You can stay for as long or as short a time as you want, but the fee remains the same, ten pounds.' His smile showed surprisingly white teeth. 'We accept all major credit cards.'

Murray wondered if Lyn and her companion had already passed by, but there had been a vintage vinyl shop between them and the pub. The man in the wheelchair had looked the type to linger at its window.

'I'm happy to buy a pint, but you can't really expect me to pay ten quid for one drink?'

The bouncer put his hand back on Murray's elbow.

'Be more like fourteen quid, mate, the drinks aren't free. Anyway, it depends how much you want to avoid her.'

They were approaching the exit now. Murray made one last appeal.

'What harm would it do?'

'Immeasurable, mate.' The man nodded towards the girl on stage. 'Strictly-Cum-Dancing would report me to the boss, and I'd be out on my ear.' He opened the door. 'Nothing personal.' And gave Murray a gentle shove out into the sunshine.

Murray scanned the street. Lyn and her companion were walking away from the pub, their backs towards him. He was safe. He grinned at the bouncer. 'I'll let you get back to the Ritz then.'

The man gave Murray a good-natured smile.

'Is that her there, the skinny piece with Ironside?'

'No.'

Murray started to walk away, just as the bouncer shouted, 'Hey, doll, he's over here.'

Lyn turned. A look of confusion clouded her face, but she raised a hand in greeting. She said something to her companion and started to walk back to where Murray now waited.

The grey man grinned. 'Next time, pay the

103

entrance fee.' He let the door swing behind him, shutting out the darkness and music, leaving Murray to face his brother's girlfriend.

*   *   *

'Hello, stranger.'

Lyn's expression was out of kilter with the jaunty greeting and Murray wondered if she'd noticed what kind of pub he'd been in. Usually when they met they kissed, but neither of them made the first move and the moment was lost.

'Hi.' He readjusted his heavy bag, fighting the urge to take it from his back. 'How are you?'

'Good.' Lyn pushed a strand of loose hair away. The sun was in her face and she narrowed her eyes as she looked up at him. He was reminded of a photograph Jack had taken of her wearing the same expression, battling the light. 'I didn't know you were coming through.'

Her voice was free of reproach, but he felt it anyway.

'I'm here most days at the moment, working up at the library.'

'How's it going?'

'Aye, fine.' He sought for something else to say. 'I'm getting into it.'

Lyn turned towards the man in the chair.

'Frankie, this is my brother-in-law, Murray. Murray, this is Frankie. We were just on our way to the shops.'

Frankie pulled his hat up on his forehead and stared Murray out.

'Any good in there?' He nodded back towards the pub.

Lyn said, 'Frankie.' Half-cajoling, half-warning, and Murray realised that his visit wasn't a secret.

'No.' He tried to keep it light. 'Ten pounds entrance fee and the music was too loud.' He looked at Lyn. 'I went in by mistake.'

She glanced at the A-board outside on the street advertising: *LAP DANCING, FANTASY CABINS, EXECUTIVE BOOTHS, EXOTIC DANCERS, OFFICE DOs AND STAG PARTIES WELCOME.*

'Easy done.'

'No disabled access.' Frankie zizzed the chair into life. 'That's against the law.' He rolled back and forth, letting the tyres hiss his impatience. *Come on, come on, come on, come on.*

A wheel nudged Murray's foot and he took a sharp step back.

'Frankie.' Lyn's voice held an unfamiliar, scolding edge. 'We're only going to Lidl's. It'll still be there if we spare a moment to say hello.'

'But some of those great offers won't be, Lyn.' Frankie glanced up at Murray. Standing, he might have been the taller of the two. 'No offence, man, but you know how it is.'

Murray didn't, but he nodded anyway.

'I wouldn't want to hold you back.'

'Don't worry about it.' Frankie snapped the electric chair around and careered ahead.

'Jesus fuck.' There was a break in Lyn's voice that might have been amusement or despair. 'Watch him go. I'd like to get my hands on the genius that issued him with that thing.'

'They must be cracking offers. Should you go with him?'

'He's a grown man.'

'Difficult customer?'

'Easy customers needn't apply.'

'Aye, I suppose.' He nodded back at the pub. 'I really didn't notice it was a go-go bar before I went in.'

'Go-go bar.' Lyn laughed. 'You've some turn of phrase.' She looked beyond him, following Frankie's progress with her eyes, before turning her attention back to Murray. 'It wouldn't be any of my business if you did.'

'But I didn't.'

'Must have been a shock to the system.'

'A wee bit. I was looking for somewhere to get a bowl of soup.' They laughed together and for the first time he was glad they'd met. Lyn glanced back in the direction Frankie had taken. He was a block ahead now, talking to a *Big Issue* vendor. Frankie reached into his pocket for a pack of cigarettes and the vendor sparked them both up.

'I'd better go after him, our bus is about due. Have you got time to walk to the stop with me?'

It was the opposite direction from the one he'd intended taking, but Murray nodded and they started to follow slowly in Frankie's wake, like parents who had let their child run ahead on a weekend walk.

'So is Frankie your main man at the moment?'

'There's a horrible thought, but now you mention it, I do seem to spend more time with him than I do with anyone else, including Jack.'

'How is Jack?'

'Why don't you ask him yourself?'

'I will, when I have a moment.'

Lyn sighed.

'I'll tell him you were asking after him.'

106

'Thanks.' Murray hesitated. 'Could you tell him that I might . . .'

'Oh, shit.'

'What?'

Lyn started to run.

'That's our bus.'

Ahead of them Frankie stuck out his arm and a maroon double-decker slowed to a halt. Lyn was fast, but she was too short to be a sprinter. Murray shouldered his cursed bag and broke into a dash. The bus's suspension sank until its platform was level with the pavement, and its doors concertinaed open. Frankie raised his arm in farewell to his friend and started to steer himself aboard. Murray shouted, '*Hoi!*'

The vendor saw Murray and put a foot on the bus's platform, holding it there.

'Cheers.' Murray's words were a whisper. He reached into his pocket and his hand closed on the same two-pound coin he'd tried to spend on a Coke. It was too much, but he pressed it into the vendor's palm anyway.

'Nae bother.' The man stepped free of the bus. 'They're not going anywhere.'

He offered him a paper, but Murray shook his head and climbed aboard.

The driver had unlatched the door of his cab and managed to open it a crack, but Frankie had parked his chair against it, blocking his exit. Murray smelt smoke, saw the lit cigarette in Frankie's hand and understood. The driver sank back into his seat, casting an envious glance at Frankie's Mayfair.

'Listen, mate, I'm off shift at five whether I get to the depot or not, but there's folks here got

107

things to do and you're stopping them getting to where they're going and doing them. Why not let them get on their way?'

'You heard the driver.' An elderly woman leaned out from her place halfway down the aisle. 'Get rid of the cigarette or sling your hook.'

Frankie turned his chair to face his audience.

'Do you know the first person to ban tobacco? Adolf Hitler.' Frankie drew forth his pack of Mayfairs and slid another cigarette free. 'Sometimes folks can be too obedient.'

An old man got to his feet. 'I'm betting it was that kind of lip landed you in that chair.' He shifted his shopping bags and seemed about to go down the aisle. But the old women around him broke into choruses of 'Well said, Mr Prentice' and 'You tell him, Jim', and he stayed where he was, chest puffed up beneath his anorak, an elderly pasha surrounded by his well-wrapped-up harem.

'What's going on?'

The run had freed Lyn's hair from its clasp. It burst around her face in a riot of tangles. Her cheeks were flushed, though whether from the exertion or annoyance it was hard to tell.

Murray turned towards her, but it was Frankie who spoke.

'I was holding the bus for you.'

He took the cigarette from his mouth, expertly nipped its lit end and placed it back in the pack.

The driver shut the doors and restarted the engine.

'Fuck's sake, I would have waited if you'd asked.'

'Aye, right.' Frankie backed his chair into the

space by the door, slotting himself next to a toddler in a buggy. The child gave him a baleful look and Frankie nodded back. 'How you doing?'

'Sorry.' Lyn scrabbled in her purse and put the fares in the slot.

'Don't apologise, dear.' The driver issued the tickets, smiling sadly like a man who'd seen it all now. 'You've got my sympathy if you're shackled to that article.'

Murray said, 'She's not . . .'

But the driver's eyes were on the road, the bus gliding from the stop, just as Murray remembered he hadn't intended on travelling anywhere except the library.

*   *   *

In the end he went round the supermarket with them too, listening to Lyn and Frankie discussing the relative merits of the produce on offer. Lyn asked him if he didn't want to get a few things for himself, but he shook his head. He wouldn't know where to start. Frankie, on the other hand, seemed to know exactly what he was doing.

Frankie rolled to a halt by the wine shelves, scanning them with an expert eye. 'I think we'll have a couple of bottles of that cheeky burgundy on special, please, Lyn.'

Murray noticed Frankie checking out Lyn's rear as she reached up to the top shelf to retrieve the wine.

'You enjoy cooking?'

'Beats starving.'

Lyn put the bottles amongst their other groceries and they continued their slow patrol of the shelves.

'Frankie's a bit of a gourmet.'

'Food's one of the few pleasures left to me.'

Lyn snorted. 'Plus the booze, fags and all the rest.'

'All the rest? Are you offering?'

Lyn gave the wheelchair a small push Murray was sure contravened professional guidelines. She looked at Murray.

'So tell me more about how the research is going.'

It occurred to him that she was humouring him the way she'd just humoured Frankie, the way she probably humoured Jack.

'It's dull. You know what I'm like when I get onto that, a train-spotting stamp-collector.'

Murray picked a bottle of oil from a shelf. It had red and black peppercorns suspended in it. He turned the bottle on its side and watched them slide slowly through the yellow viscous, like migrating stars in a steady firmament.

'Come on, you know I like hearing about your mad poet.'

The oil was the same pale yellow as lager. He remembered a night in the pub years ago, Lyn pouring the remains of her pint over Jack in response to something she'd deemed sexist. He remembered the surprise of it, Jack's expression and his own astonished shock of admiration. He remembered laughing then taking a deep draught of his own drink before drenching his brother with the dregs. Their drunken dash to outrun the bartender's curse—*Yous're all barred!*

He put the oil back on the shelf.

'I don't think Archie was mad, not at the start

110

anyway. Sure, he behaved crazily sometimes, but from what I'm hearing he tanked it. I wouldn't be surprised if there weren't drugs somewhere in the mix too.'

'You sound almost hopeful.'

'It's in the past. I can't fix it. All I can do is make sure I get the facts right.'

Lyn's voice was soft.

'Can't you cut your brother's exhibition the same slack?'

The comparison bewildered him.

'As long as I'm around, our dad isn't in the past. I'm surprised Jack doesn't feel the same way.'

'He does, Murray. He just has a different way of expressing it.'

Perhaps Lyn sensed the pressure at the back of his eyes, because she took another tin from the shelf and asked again if he was sure he didn't need anything.

*   *   *

The three of them waited together at the checkout behind an elderly couple. The old man placed his wire shopping basket at the end of the counter and his wife set four tins of dog food, a packet of cornflakes and a bottle of Three Barrels brandy on the conveyor belt. It scrolled forwards and Lyn started to unload Frankie's trolley.

'You had something you wanted me to tell Jack.'

'Did I?'

He didn't want to discuss anything in front of the other man.

'Yes, just before the bus came. It got lost in the

111

commotion.'

'It wasn't important.'

The cashier started to check their stuff through and Lyn and Frankie began bagging it. Murray moved to help, but Frank said, 'You're all right, mate, we've got a system.'

Lyn gave him an apologetic look.

'Weeks of practice. Frankie and I have to get all this back now, but that'll be me finished for the day. Maybe we could grab a coffee, if you've got time?'

He knew that coffee was code for pub. It would be easy to go with her, slip into the comfort of alcohol and company, allow his defences to drift until he was willing to become reconciled to Jack's betrayal of their father's dignity.

'Sorry, I shouldn't even be here. I've masses of work to do and I've got to start my packing.'

'Is that what you were going to tell me?'

'What?'

'That you're going away.'

'For a week or so, to Lismore.'

She laughed.

'For a moment I thought you were going to tell me you were emigrating.'

'No, just a wee trip to fill in some background. It's where Archie ended up.'

'Where he drowned?'

'Yes, I thought I'd take my notes up there, get a feel for the place.'

He meant get a feel for Archie, but it would sound stupid out loud.

The bags were packed. Lyn slung one on the back of the wheelchair. Frankie rolled his wheels to and fro then said, 'Stick another couple on there.'

'I don't want to topple you.'

'Nah, that'll not happen again. I've got the hang of it now.'

Lyn made a face behind his back, but she did as he asked and the three of them made their way slowly out of the supermarket. The sky had clouded over in the time they'd spent shopping and it felt as if it might rain. The promise of the day had gone. Cars edged along on the main road, but the landscape beyond the shop held a concrete bleakness that made it easy to imagine the bombed-out world of Archie's sci-fi novel. Lyn placed a hand gently on the back of Frankie's chair, steadying the bags. She'd restrained her curls, but the wind blowing across the car park threatened to free them again. She pushed a strand of hair from her eyes and gave Murray a smile.

'Are you sure about that coffee?'

'I've got to get back.'

'To your dead poet?'

'He's beckoning through the waves.'

And for a moment it was as if Murray could see Lunan against the dreary expanse, hair floating wild in the water, arms outstretched as he drifted with the current.

'Excuse me, Lyn.' Frankie's voice was weighted with exquisite politeness. 'I'm going to have to use the toilet.'

'No problem.' She was brisk, all business now. 'The staff facilities have good access here. Can you hold on while I get someone to let us in?'

'It's not an emergency.' Beyond the grey of the car park a Burger King sign glowed red. Frankie nodded towards it. 'Why don't we go over there and you can have your coffee.'

'Ach, I don't know, Frank . . .'

'If you grab me an *Evening News*, I can sit on my own and let yous have a catch-up. I don't mind.'

Lyn looked at Murray. He shrugged his shoulders, defeated. It was nigh-on forty years since Archie had drowned, his corpse was long since gone and the best Murray would do was revive his reputation. It could wait an hour or so.

'Why not?'

*   *   *

Murray went into the Burger King with Frankie and the shopping bags, while Lyn went in search of a newsagent's. He followed him awkwardly to the door of the disabled toilets. Frankie halted his chair.

'Do you like to watch?'

'No.'

'So fuck off. I might not be able to piss standing up any more, but I'm still capable of wiping my own arse.'

'One of the few pleasures left to you?'

'Not even close, mate, not even close.' He beckoned Murray towards him and when he got close whispered with breath that smelt of smoke and onions, 'Tell your brother to take better care of her or I'll be in like Flynn.'

Murray's snort of amusement surprised them both.

'I'll pass the message on.'

'Laugh all you want, pal. She's too good for

114

that poofy git. I'm what they call a catch these days.'

'I guess times are tough.'

'Not for me, they're not. I'm getting decent money, I've got my own place and I've knocked the drugs. But do you know what my biggest advantage is?'

'What?'

'I'm a project. Lassies like a project. I'll let her reform me, don't you worry.'

He leered and rounded the chair into the cubicle.

*   *   *

Murray bought three coffees, garnishing his tray with a few sugar sachets and little tubs of whatever substituted for milk. He set it all at a table near the window then got out his mobile. There were no messages. He started to compose a text to Rachel but only got as far as Sorry before he spotted Lyn entering with Frankie's paper. Murray shut the phone down without pressing Send. He couldn't think what he would have said. After all, he could hardly describe himself as a catch.

*   *   *

Frankie sat on the other side of the room, resolute about 'giving them space', though Murray noted he'd chosen a seat with a clear view of their table. Lyn sipped her coffee.

'We'd best not take too long. So what have you been up to?'

'Nothing. The usual, just work.'

115

'Just work. You should take a tip from Frankie's book, get out more.'

'I've been out all day.'

'Visiting strip clubs, browsing round supermarkets. It's some life you literary doctors lead.'

'It's all go.'

Murray drank some of his coffee. It had been a mistake coming here. The sooner he finished it, the sooner he could leave.

'Will you come and see us before you head off?'

It was as if Lyn had read his mind.

'Sure, if there's time.'

She nodded. They both knew that there wouldn't be. Murray felt Frankie's eyes on them. Was it pathetic to feel jealous of a paraplegic? A recently homeless paraplegic, if he was under Lyn's care.

Lyn regarded him over the rim of her paper cup.

'Jack's exhibition has had good reviews.'

'Great.'

His brother's treachery soured the pleasure Murray would normally have felt in his success.

Lyn held his gaze in hers.

'Is that all you're going to say?'

He shrugged, sullen as a recalcitrant first-year presented with a low mark they knew they deserved.

'I met one of the other artists. Cressida something. How's she getting on?'

Lyn raised her cup to her mouth.

'Cressida Reeves? She's more Jack's friend than mine. They were at art college together.'

'So were you.'

'Yes, but they were in the same intake. I didn't appear on the scene until Jack's third year. I'd not seen her for years before this show.' She looked at Murray. 'Did you see her work?'

'No.'

'Maybe you should.' Her voice was dry. 'Cressida puts a lot of herself into it.'

'Preferable to exploiting someone else's weaknesses.'

Lyn sighed. She took another sip of coffee and kept the paper cup cradled in her hands as if trying to thaw them, though the fast-food joint was warm after the chill of outside.

'Jack should have told you what his exhibition was about, but you can't think badly of him for creating it.'

'He didn't create anything, just pointed a camera and took a shot.' Murray folded his hand into the shape of a gun and pulled the trigger. 'Bang, bang, you're dead.'

'Suit yourself.' Lyn's face flushed red. She put her cup down and glanced over at Frankie. 'I'd best get going.'

He wanted to apologise, but instead asked, 'You're supporting disabled people now?'

There was a shine to her eyes, but her voice was steady.

'No, same job, same chronic pay. Frank's an existing client who happens to have become disabled.'

What was wrong with him that he couldn't feel pity for a homeless man in a wheelchair?

'Sleeping on the streets has got to be tough in his condition.'

'He's not on the streets any more. That's why

117

I'm here, supporting his transition from hostel to independent living.'

'So a lucky accident?'

She gave him a look, but didn't rise to the bait.

'It wasn't so much an accident as . . . I'm not sure what you'd call it. A cry for help? A drug-inspired psychotic episode? One day Frankie finds himself walking near the M8, no idea how he got there, just comes to, aware of the lights of the cars going by. It's dark, but it's winter and it's only around five in the afternoon, so it's busy, everyone coming home from work. He sees a motorway bridge, climbs up, and throws himself over the top.'

'Shit.'

'Yes, shit.'

'Did he cause a pile-up?'

'No. Jack says that Frankie's the luckiest suicide artist in the business. He hit the roof of a lorry, bounced off the edge and onto the central reservation. It should have killed him, but instead he ended up in a chair. The funny thing is, we'd tried to re-house Frank before, but it was a disaster. It was too much for him, the responsibility. But ever since he got out of hospital he seems better. I mean, he's still got problems—some days we do this he's three sheets to the wind—but he's trying to help himself. He's cooking—he was a chef when he was in the army—and he's trying to look after the flat. He's not missed an appointment with me. Yeah, he's still a pain sometimes. But it's like Frank's decided to live. Almost as if suicide's been the making of him.'

'He fancies you rotten.'

118

'They all fancy me. I'm the only woman they get to speak to who isn't a barmaid.'

'So the feeling's not mutual?'

'God, Murray, Jack's right about you. You're not of this world.' Lyn glanced at Frankie again. 'I've got to go.'

'I guess you do, the world's waiting.'

Lyn's face flushed. She pushed a curl from her eyes and leaned across the table, so close he felt her words on his face.

'It's my fucking job, Murray, and it's just as important as your book or Jack's bloody art.'

'I know that.'

She looked like she wanted to slap him, but she stretched over and kissed him instead. 'No, you don't.' She squeezed his arm and was gone.

He watched them through the window as they made their way towards the taxi rank. Frankie said something and Lyn laughed, shaking her head as if amused against her will.

Murray poured more sugar into his cold coffee and stirred. Lyn was right, of course, her job was vital, he of all people should know that. But still, he couldn't reconcile the thought that fetching Frankie's messages was as important as uncovering Archie Lunan's life. There were a million drunks in the city; Archie had been one himself. But he had also been a poet, and there were precious few of those in the world.

He took out his Moleskine notebook and looked again at the list of names he'd copied from Archie's jotter:

Danny
Denny

119

Bobby Boy
Ruby!
I thought I saw you walking by the shore
Ramie
Moon
Jessa* * *
Tamsker
Saffron
Ray—will you be my sunshine?

Perhaps Lunan had whiled away the hours composing names for the protagonists of his sci-fi novel, but the jaunty phrases suggested something else. Murray read the list again, and wondered what it could be.

Chapter Ten

There was a voicemail message on Murray's mobile. He checked Missed Calls and saw an unfamiliar Glasgow number. How had he got to the point where an unfamiliar number was a relief? The voice was female and infused with the same assured tones that dominated the university's corridors and lecture halls.

'Hello, I'm phoning with regard to your advert in the *TLS*. My late husband Alan Garrett did some research into Archie Lunan's death.' The woman stalled as if expecting someone to pick up, then continued less confidently, 'Anyway, give me a call if you're interested.' A number and email address followed, succeeded by a click on the line as the widowed Mrs Garrett hung up.

Rachel had suggested the advert to him on one of their early dates. She'd driven them swiftly along the unlit road, the dark nothingness of the reservoir below them, the lights of the city trembling in the beyond. Rachel had guided the car surely round the tricky bends and Murray had tried not to dwell on how well she knew the road. She'd slowed as they got closer to their destination, uncertain at the last moment of their turning, and a stag had started into the full beam of their headlights. Murray caught a glimpse of bright eyes blackly shining, a candelabra of horn, before the creature darted back into the night. He remembered a news report about a driver colliding with a stag, the beast's antlers piercing first the windscreen, then the man's chest, the injured animal tossing its head frantically trying to escape, the ruin of bodies found hours later.

He asked, 'Are you okay?'

Rachel laughed, 'Yes, that was a close one', and pressed down on the accelerator. The turn-off appeared soon after on their left and she bumped the car gently into the pitch-darkness of the car park. 'Here we are.'

He pushed his chair back. Rachel killed the engine and clambered quickly from the driver's seat into his lap. They were kissing, her hands moving thrillingly down to his fly, his fingers unfastening her blouse, tracing the line between the lace of her bra and her not-yet-familiar-breasts, when Murray saw the shadowy form of another car resting mutely in the darkness. He stayed his hand.

'There's someone else here.'

'Mmmm.' Rachel had set him free and was rubbing herself against him. She wasn't wearing any knickers and the thought that she'd driven him there naked beneath her skirt gave him a quick frisson of excitement. But the knowledge of the other car bothered him.

'Do you think they can see us?'

Rachel leaned back and turned on the interior light. Her breasts shone whitely beneath their lace.

'Let's make sure.'

He reached up and quickly clicked it off.

'You spoilsport, Murray.'

'I don't want an audience.'

'Shame.'

She snapped open the front fastening of her bra and let her breasts fall softly against his face. They'd kissed and resumed their play, but the awareness of the car lurking in the opposite bay remained with him, and their coupling was clumsy and hurried.

They'd driven back down from the country park in silence, Rachel taking the turns more slowly this time, only gathering speed when she reached the straight road that bordered the reservoir.

She'd been hitting seventy-five when the headlights of another car shone in from behind, illuminating the dashboard. Murray turned and saw Rachel's face caught in shine and shadows like a black and white photograph, her jaw set somewhere between a smile and a grimace. He realised she would have seen the car's approach in the rear-view mirror and wondered if it, rather than the straightness of the road, had prompted her increase in speed.

The car was a Saab. It started to overtake and Rachel hit the accelerator, staying level with it, racing. Up ahead the road curved into a bend. Murray's right foot pressed on an imaginary brake, the Saab zoomed on and Rachel dropped speed, letting it pull in front. Up ahead the car's brake lights shone red. Rachel tailed it down to the cross, where the Saab made it through the traffic lights. For a second Murray thought Rachel was going to put on a spurt and follow it through, but at the last minute she hit the brakes. Murray jarred forward. The seatbelt's inertia reel held him tight.

'Sorry.' Rachel looked at him. 'Bit of a bumpy ride.'

Murray tried to reconstruct the shadow of the parked car in his mind, but it had only been a shape in the dark. There was nothing except his intuition, or perhaps it was paranoia, to suggest it had been the Saab Rachel had raced.

'You had me worried for a moment.'

'You're always worried, Murray, it's your default setting.'

'That's not fair.'

She put a reassuring hand on his knee.

'Your being old school is part of what I like about you.' Rachel glanced away from the road, letting her eyes meet his for a moment. 'How are you getting on with the elusive Archie?'

'Elusive is the word.' Murray's voice grew warmer. She'd never said that she liked him before. 'I've been on the phone to the National Library. They have a few boxes of bits and pieces they're going to let me have a root aboot in. What I'm really missing is first-hand accounts, contact

123

with people who knew Lunan. It's amazing how many of that generation are no longer with us.'

'That generation.' She laughed. 'He wasn't much older than Fergus, you know. Maybe you should interview him.'

'I doubt they moved in the same circles.'

'You'd be surprised at the circles Fergus has moved in.'

Her archness matched the grudge in his voice.

They drove on in silence, the city taking form for Murray as they began to get closer to the university. He looked again at the clean lines of her profile and wondered why she betrayed Fergus with him, him with Fergus.

They waited at the pedestrian lights on the Great Western Road. He could see the fish fryer in the lit window of the Philadelphia shovelling fresh chips into a vat of hot fat. Maybe he should offer to buy Rachel a fish supper, drive the scent of their sex from the car with deep-fried cod and vinegar. The lights shifted to green and she swung the car round a dawdling pedestrian.

'You should seek them out.'

'Who?'

'Old associates of Archie's.'

'I intend to.'

'It could be fun, like being a detective. Maybe you'll go undercover.'

He put a hand on her knee.

'I'd rather go between the sheets.'

'I prefer you in your natural habitat.'

She changed gear, knocking him away.

'The library?'

'Now there's a thought, between the stacks.'

She hit the emergency flashers and drew into

124

the side of the road, double-parking so he could get out and catch the underground the rest of the way home.

*   *   *

He'd placed the same small classified ad in the *Herald, Scotsman, TLS* and *Scots Magazine* the following day.

> *Doctor Murray Watson of the University of Glasgow's Department of English Literature seeks memories of the poet Archie Lunan from anyone who may have known him.*

It had resulted in nothing, until the phone message. He pressed *Return Call* and listened to the telephone ring out at the other end. He counted to twenty then broke the connection and dialled again. The ring had its own tone, its own rhythm, regular as a heartbeat. It jangled on, until he cut the call.

He thought back again to the drive home, Rachel in the seat beside him, her hand guiding the car down the gears as they descended into the city. Sometimes lately he remembered their moments together as if he were on the outside, a viewer watching a film, or a man behind the wheel of a car in a darkened car park.

Chapter Eleven

Murray wasn't sure what happened to widows in the first three years after their husband's death, but if he'd imagined Audrey Garrett at all, it was as stoical and underweight, a lady depleted if not destroyed.

The woman who buzzed him up to her third-floor tenement flat was well-nourished, with pale skin flushed red, and strawberry-blonde hair tied firmly back in a thick ponytail. Her black jogging pants, white Aertex top and air of no-nonsense vigour reminded him of the members of the Officer Training Corps he sometimes saw loading the university minibuses. Then she smiled, and the impression was dispelled.

They shook hands at the door. Her palm was warm to the touch. Murray was aware of a savour of fresh sweat and realised she was straight from exercising. He'd brought her flowers, a small bunch of yellow roses, conscious of avoiding anything flashy or funereal. He shoved them at her nervously, like an awkward suitor.

'Thank you, but there was no need.' She softened her words with a smile. 'It's a pleasure to share Alan's work with someone who might be able to turn it to some use.' Audrey raised the bouquet to her face, dutifully searching for scent in the cellophane-wrapped blooms, and Murray saw he'd forgotten to peel off the garage's price sticker. 'Come on through.' She led him into a square entrance hall, messy with half-opened cardboard boxes, a jumble of bags and tangle of bikes.

He'd thought she was English, a Londoner perhaps, but now he recognised an antipodean inflection to her accent: Australia or New Zealand? He couldn't tell.

'You'll have to excuse the mess. As you can see we've just moved in. Normally, of course, we're a super-tidy household.'

She turned to check that he had got the joke and Murray met her eyes guiltily, wondering if she had seen his gaze drop reflexively to the tilt of her bottom. He looked away and met another pair of eyes peering at him from behind an open door in the hallway. They belonged to a small, solemn-faced boy with a mass of dark hair. Murray couldn't judge his age: older than five but younger than ten, he guessed.

'Hello, I'm Murray.'

The boy's expression remained grave. He silently pressed the door to.

'You'll have to excuse Lewis. He's shy of new people. My sister-in-law's coming round to take him swimming in a while.' Audrey Garrett glanced at her watch. 'She should be here by now, but as you can see everything's running late—as usual. I meant to be showered and changed before you arrived.'

'I'm grateful you made time to see me at all.'

Murray glanced back towards the boy's bedroom and saw Lewis Garrett's eyes peering out again from the slit in the open door. He wondered if he should play the uncle and slip him a pound. But the boy saw him looking. This time he slammed the door.

Audrey said, 'Lewis, that's not very polite', but

127

didn't stop to argue the point. She led Murray into a large bay-windowed sitting room piled high with boxes, like a fence's secret warehouse.

'Chaos reigns supreme.' She flung herself down on the only piece of furniture in the room, a large right-angled couch that made Murray think of airports and long delays. 'Lewis was only three when his father died. I'm afraid he's a little shy of men, while also being completely fascinated with them, of course. He's currently very taken with Mr Sidique across the landing. His beard is a big part of the attraction—reminiscent of Santa's apparently. He may get his courage up and come through to interrogate you in a while, if Lisa doesn't get her skates on.'

Murray perched on the far promontory of the settee and rubbed his chin.

'No beard.'

'No, that may put you at a bit of a disadvantage.'

He smiled, unsure of whether he should declare himself relieved or disappointed. Instead he said, 'Lewis, after RLS?'

'No, the spelling's different. Choosing names for a child is an unexpected trial. Alan and I made a lengthy list. In the end we chose one we thought original only to spot it a month later, somewhere near the top of the most popular boy's names in Scotland.' She laughed. 'Never mind, it suits him.'

Murray remembered the collection of names he'd found in Archie's effects and wondered if it resembled the list Audrey Garrett and her husband had made. He contemplated showing it to her, but Audrey had moved on. 'I'll make us some tea in a moment. I'm absolutely bushed. I'm

128

usually working when Lewis is at school, but I played hookey this afternoon and went running before I collected him. I'm afraid I overdid it.'

She stretched out a leg. Her feet were bare, their soles dirty, as if she had been sprinting shoeless through the city.

Murray found her friendliness disarming. He wondered if it was typical or if her chatter was a delaying tactic; a means to avoid discussing her husband's work with a stranger.

He leant forward.

'Don't worry about tea. You've enough to do with your boy and all this.'

He waved a hand vaguely in the direction of the boxes.

Audrey Garrett smiled and said, 'You're wondering when I'm going to shut up and let you get on with it.'

'No, not at all.'

'I guess I should tell you. He was in Lismore researching Archie Lunan when he died.'

Just for a second Murray couldn't think which man's death she meant, then it struck him and he said, 'I'm sorry.'

She shrugged, managing to acknowledge his consolation and its uselessness at the same time.

'I thought it might be better to get it out there so you understand if I'm a little . . . well . . .' She smiled. 'Even after this space of time, I'm not always sure how things are going to affect me.'

'No.' He looked away from her towards the piles of brown boxes piled high like a defence, wondering what the correct response would be. 'Perhaps you'd like someone else to join us, your sister-in-law maybe?'

'Lisa?' Audrey Garrett laughed. 'She's worse than me. No, we'll be fine.' The doorbell rang and she got to her feet. 'Speak of the devil and smell smoke. Excuse me a moment.'

He heard a cheerful exchange of women's voices, laughter and a child's high, excited tones. Then the front door shut and there was a pause. He imagined her standing barefoot in the suddenly still hallway, gathering her strength. The new apartment held an atmosphere of brittle bravery. Murray pressed his hands together and sandwiched them between his knees. There would be a point when his own life tipped and the absent outweighed the living.

'Peace, perfect peace.' Audrey flung herself back on the settee, which shifted a little beneath her weight. 'Lisa takes him overnight once a week to give me a bit of a break.'

He unfolded himself and leaned back.

'I'm interrupting your evening off.'

'Don't let it bother you. But you're right, we should get down to business.' She straightened up and turned to face him, brushing a loose strand of hair from her eyes. 'I donated most of Alan's reference books to the department library and some of his colleagues kindly packed up his university office for me a decent-ish interval after the accident.' She gave an ironic smile. 'As you know, space is at a premium up there. Most of what they packed is still in boxes. I kept all of Alan's stuff together when we moved, so you're welcome to work your way through it . . .'

She hesitated and he said, 'But?'

'But inevitably I disposed of some stuff. It's important we start to move on. Not forget, just . . .'

She sought for another phrase and gave up, smiling. 'Just move on.'

'Of course.' He wondered what insights into Archie's life had ended up in the recycling. 'I understand Dr Garrett was a social scientist?'

'Alan did a joint undergraduate degree in psychology and sociology, they both continued to inform his work.'

'And his ongoing research was into artists who die young?'

'Actually, it was more specific than that. Alan was interested in artists who commit suicide.'

There was something shamefaced in the way that she said it. Murray wanted to tell her not to worry, that he had read weirder research proposals, invitations to the psychiatric ward or prison cell. But instead he nodded and asked, 'He believed Archie came into that category?'

'I suppose he must have. We never talked much about that aspect of his work. I found it morbid.'

'I guess I can relate to that, but sometimes when you're doing research,' he paused, searching for a way to explain. 'Things lose their power to disturb. You get fascinated with the minutiae and the subject becomes abstract.'

'Maybe that's part of what bothered me, the desensitisation.' She wiggled her foot, looking at her toes as if she had just noticed them. 'It's sad something that meant so much to him became almost taboo between us. It's one of my regrets. Perhaps if I'd paid more attention to Archie Lunan's death, to the deaths of all the people he studied, I'd understand Alan's more.'

Murray felt the weight of the empty flat around them and wished the child hadn't left. He rolled the pen he'd taken from his pocket between his palms then, when she remained silent, asked, 'What do you mean?'

It was as if the words had been waiting to tumble out.

'When a sober man who's fascinated with suicide slams a car with perfectly good brakes into a tree, you have to ask yourself if it was deliberate.' She looked up. 'I spoke with his doctor and searched his stuff, his effects. But Alan had no secret history of depression, no stash of happy pills he'd suddenly stopped taking. The inquest decided it was death through misadventure. A polite way of saying his own carelessness was to blame. Maybe he was tired, trying to squeeze everything he needed to do into too short a time so he could get home to us—except, of course, that he didn't.' Audrey got to her feet. 'Sorry, that's exactly what I was trying to avoid.' She was all briskness now. 'I've shoved Alan's boxes together and marked each one with an X. I'm not sure if you'll find much. I don't know how long he'd been looking into your mutual friend, but I do know he'd taken some of the relevant notes up there with him. Presumably they were in the car when he crashed. I didn't get them back.'

She paused. Blood and shattered glass were in her silence.

Murray imagined the dead driver slumped against a steering wheel, the unbroken blare of a car horn, precious pages streaming through a smashed window, littering the fields beyond, fluttering down towards the ocean where Archie had drowned.

'I gave his computer to a Malawian appeal. I

guess I should have held onto it, but you know how it is.'

'Yes,' he said. Unsure of whether he did.

'It was wretchedly old-fashioned, anyway. The Malawians were probably appalled when it arrived. I imagine they're hooked up to solar-powered broadband by now, surfing porn like the rest of the world.' She pulled at the hem of her top, straightening creases that bounced back into place. 'Did that sound racist? It wasn't meant to.'

'No, of course not, you just meant we shouldn't lumber charities with our junk.' He realised what he'd said and coloured. 'I didn't mean . . .'

But Audrey laughed and some of the tension lifted.

'No, I know you didn't.' She was still smiling. 'I'll leave you to it. I've got plenty to occupy me. Shout when you're finished.'

*   *   *

There were half a dozen cartons; less than he'd expected. There was always less than he expected, but when Murray started to work through their contents he realised they contained no teaching notes or delayed fragments of admin, no abandoned research proposals or half-written lectures. Everything related to the doctor's suicide studies. The idea that Audrey Garrett had taken time to isolate the right boxes when she had a child, a job and a house full of unpacking touched him. But perhaps it was simply a way of speeding his departure.

She had left the door to the living room ajar and Murray could hear the sound of a shower

133

starting up somewhere beyond the hall. He got up and closed the door, pushing away an uninvited image of bathroom mirrors steaming with condensation and Audrey stepping naked beneath the spray.

He took off his jacket, laid it on the couch, then crouched on the bare floorboards and opened the first box. The topmost folders held tables of statistical analysis that made no sense to him. He set them to one side, pulled out bundles of the *Bulletin of Suicidology* and flicked through a couple of issues. It was like every professional journal or hobbyist magazine he had ever come across: of no interest to anyone outside the group, but manna to the initiated. The abundance of adverts for books, courses and conferences suggested suicide was a booming industry. What would suicidology conferences be like? Rambunctious affairs where the bars roared with laughter, with Russian roulette in the halls and one less for breakfast every morning?

He could understand Audrey's squeamishness. But if Archie had topped himself it might make sense for Murray to read up on theories surrounding suicide. *Topped himself.* It was too flippant. He couldn't remember using the phrase before. Maybe he was reacting to the soberness of the pages in front of him, like a mourner at a funeral suddenly felled by giggles.

Murray extracted a bundle of loose papers and began sorting through them, careful to maintain the order they'd been packed in. A printed list from some website snagged his attention.

Put on his best suit and shot himself.
Gassed herself after bad reviews of her
    recent exhibition.
Overdosed on sleeping pills in Baghdad.
Threw himself on a ceremonial sword, then
    lingered for another 24 hours.
Committed suicide in a psychotic fit, but not
    before killing his family.
Jumped out of a window in Rome.
Overdosed on barbiturates, and left notes
    about how it felt for as long as she could.
Shot himself, then cut his throat.
Hanged himself in the doorway of his
    father's bedroom.

The scant details seemed arbitrary; a method, a location, a reason. Could there ever be a good reason? He imagined how Archie's entry would read.

A poor sailor, he sailed out into the eye of a storm in an ill-equipped boat.

Extreme pain would be a reasonable motive. But then he supposed it would be euthanasia, not suicide. There was a difference. The thought made him stop and stare into nothingness for a moment. Pain that you knew would only get worse. It was just cause.

The room was growing darker; outside the sky was streaked with pink. It had been raining on and off all day, but it was a lovely evening, the turn into night, peace after the storm. Murray got up and clicked on the light switch, but the room stayed in shadows. The light-fitting was empty, the room bereft of lamps.

'Fuck.'

He dragged the box over to the window and continued sorting through it by the urinous glow of the streetlamp.

Alan Garrett had been a biographer of death, every step of the lives he researched travelling towards their final moments, the cocked gun, the knotted rope, the ready pills and waiting cliff. But that was what biography was, a paper facsimile of life hurtling towards death. Murray's book could only end in the freezing waters around Lismore with Archie sucked breathless beneath the waves.

Had it occurred to him that Archie's death might have been deliberate? Garrett's hypothesis wasn't a surprise. But he hadn't considered it so boldly before. It might be good for the book if it were, he supposed. Misery and suicide were more dramatic than self-indulgence and stupidity. Perhaps Murray's could be one of the few academic works that slipped into the mainstream. He caught a quick vision of himself explaining his methodology on *Newsnight Review*, looking like an arse, tongue-tied and over-impressed, trying to avert his gaze from Kirsty Wark's buttoned-down cleavage.

Could Archie have been certain the boat would sink? However great the odds, the fierceness of the storm multiplied by his poor sea legs and simple craft, there was surely a chance that he might escape and sail beyond the squall into clear waters. Was it suicide to consign yourself to the fates? Murray wasn't sure. But there must be a wonderful freedom in not caring.

Murray looked down into the street below and wondered who would miss him if he were to smash his well-educated brains against the pavement.

136

The news would probably work as an aphrodisiac on Rachel. Rab Purvis would organise a piss-up and Jack's grief would no doubt be tempered by the prospect of whole new exhibition: *My Only Brother's Suicide—film, photographs and mixed media.*

He was getting maudlin. Maybe it was the relentless parade of young suicides or perhaps it was that he was on box three and had still found no mention of Archie. He supposed it was possible that all of Garrett's notes on the poet had perished with him.

Archie might be evasive, but he was getting a feel for Garrett. He'd been an organised scholar, thorough and not afraid of the legwork involved in primary research. Murray backed up his own research on a memory stick he guarded as carefully as his wallet. He wondered if he should ask Audrey if she had found anything similar in her husband's effects. Perhaps he could work the conversation round to it by mentioning his own experience of sorting through the detritus the dead left behind.

No, that would be crass and insensitive. He rejected the thought just as there was a knock on the sitting room door and Audrey stuck her head into the room. Her hair was damp and she smelt of something zesty. She'd changed into a scruffy V-neck and a pair of loose cotton trousers. He couldn't imagine Rachel ever dressing like that, but perhaps she sometimes did in the privacy of her home; she and Fergus sharing a bottle of wine and watching a DVD, their bare feet occasionally touching, eyes shining with the prospect of bed.

Audrey smiled.

'I promised you a cup of tea.'

'No, thanks, you're fine.'

'A glass of wine?'

He didn't want it, but smiled and said yes, so she wouldn't have to feel she was drinking alone. Audrey slipped into the darkness of the flat beyond and returned with a large glass of red.

'Can you see okay over there?'

'Aye,' he lied. 'It's fine.'

'The people who sold us the apartment took all the light bulbs with them. They must be rolling in it, the amount I paid. How could they be bothered to be so mean?'

'The rich are different from the rest of us.'

'Yes, they're bastards.' She handed him the glass. 'I won't interrupt you again.'

'I'm making you an exile in your own home.'

'It isn't home yet.' Audrey grinned. 'But it will be.'

She closed the door gently. Murray turned back to her husband's papers and started skimming through a collection of newspaper cuttings.

A promising artist walked out of his studio on the eve of a forthcoming show and was found a fortnight later, hanging from a tree on a nearby country estate. A poet put his affairs in order, travelled to London where he rented a room in a hotel, hung up the *Do not disturb* sign and threw himself through an unopened window onto the street, twelve storeys below. A couple, both performance artists, committed suicide within a week of each other. She went first with a belt-and-braces routine: pills, alcohol, a warm bath and slashed wrists. He dived off the Humber Bridge, ignoring a member of the public's attempts to talk him down. Some performance that must have been.

He wished Garrett had included more of what the artists had produced when they were alive. The cuttings seemed to define each of them by their suicides—as if the only thing they had ever created was their own death, their final audience an unfortunate chambermaid or shocked dog-walker.

He glanced at a transcript of an interview Garrett had conducted with an associate of one of the suicides.

> He was always cheerful, in a depressed sort of way if you know what I mean, cynical, down on everything, but funny with it. I wouldn't have said he was more depressed than anyone else. Everyone's depressed, right? I know I am. Especially since I found him. I can't quite get it out of my head. The smell. I can't remember him talking about suicide. I wish he had. They say the people who talk about it never do it, right?

Murray was willing to bet that was wrong.

He lifted his glass and took a drink. This was getting him nowhere. He put the papers back in the now-empty box and opened the next one. More charts and tables, death graphs and suicide logs. He'd forgotten how scientific social scientists were. There were things that couldn't be measured, of course. Maybe that was part of what had propelled Alan Garrett's car against a tree.

Murray was halfway through the box when he uncovered a bundle of cardboard folders, each labelled with a name. He flipped through them,

139

not recognising anyone until—

'Bingo.'

He slid out a powder-blue file marked *A. LUNAN*. Murray slugged back some more wine, then flipped open the flap and pulled out a few pages of foolscap.

A photocopy of the cover of *Moontide*, a copy of a familiar newspaper cutting noting Archie's disappearance, a brief obituary from a poetry fanzine and a short handwritten list:

Absent father
Mother may have been agoraphobic
Dropped out of university education
Prone to mood swings
Highly creative
Intense relationship with girlfriend?
Uprooting in adulthood that mirrors uprooting
*   as a*
child—catalyst?
Interested in the beyond

He wondered how much Garrett knew of Archie's early life. He was willing to bet that the list had been a summary of long hours of interviews conducted with people Murray was yet to meet— yet to know the existence of. Perhaps he should be glad he wouldn't have to credit a dead man as co-author, but the loss of the sociologist's research sat heavy on him.

Interested in the beyond.

Archie's poetry was balanced between the anarchic joy of sex, heavy drinking and a pantheistic rapture. He wondered if Alan Garrett had been referring to the poet's desire to push the

140

limits of the senses, or if there were something else, a religious twist to the poet's life he was unaware of. Maybe he'd been thinking of Archie's science-fiction habit. Was outer space sometimes described as the beyond?

*   *   *

It was after nine by the time Murray finished going through the rest of the boxes and when he straightened up his legs felt stiff. He re-sealed the tops of the cardboard cartons, and pushed them together the way he'd found them. The hallway was unlit save for a sliver of light leaking from beneath a closed door at the far end. Murray knocked gently.

'Come in.'

The room was more finished than the one he had just left. A rug woven in warm colours lay on the polished floorboards and the far wall was lined with bookcases, already loaded with books. A reading lamp cast a single pool of brightness, spotlighting Audrey, who was sitting on the floor resting her back against an elegant modern chrome and black-leather chaise in the centre of the darkened room. On the floor beside her sat a box of papers, a full binbag and a half-empty glass of wine.

'It would have made more sense to sort these before we moved, but I'm afraid it all got out of hand.' She laughed. 'A bit galling to know I paid a removal firm a fortune to move a lot of crap.'

'I'm sure it's not the first time,' Murray said, and because he didn't know what else to say added, 'Nice room.'

'The biggest in the house and it's all mine.' She raised herself up onto the couch. 'That's not as selfish as it sounds. It's going to be my consulting room.' He must have looked mystified because she added, 'I'm a psychologist. It's the main reason for this move actually, so I can have space to meet with clients and still be around when Lewis gets home from school.' She sipped her drink. 'How did you get on? Find anything useful?'

'I think I might have, yes.'

He handed her the page he'd found.

Audrey drained the last of the wine from her glass.

'Typical Alan, always making lists. Anything you didn't know before?'

'I don't know anything much about Archie's childhood, except that he moved around a bit. But it's the last entry that's intriguing. Archie was working on a science-fiction novel. I wondered if it might refer to that.'

Audrey lowered her eyes to the paper again. A small crease appeared between her eyebrows.

'You mean "to go where no man has gone before"?'

'Something like that.'

'I suppose it could do. But that's not what "the beyond" suggests to me.'

'What do you think?'

'The afterlife.' She made a moue of distaste and handed the list back to Murray. 'You can keep that.'

*　　　*　　　*

The chaos of the move resumed in the kitchen. A

pine table was pushed up against one wall and stacked with brimming boxes. Four chairs balanced precariously on top, their rush seats tilting against the jumble beneath, their feet pointing at the ceiling. The arrangement looked like a neglected fortification on the edge of ruin. The room was lit by small lamps better suited to bedside tables. The piled furniture threw up crazy shadows against their dim glow.

Audrey lifted a strappy sandal from the top of one of the boxes.

'I don't think I've worn these since before Alan died. God only knows where its partner is.' She let it drop. 'When I said put the kettle on, I meant boil a pot. The kettle has yet to resurface.'

Murray laughed.

'Don't worry about me. I've had my tea ration for the day.'

'In that case let's open another bottle of wine.' Audrey reached into a cupboard and pulled out a fresh bottle of red. 'Screw-top. The corkscrew's also missing in action.' She twisted the cap free and fired it into a corner. 'I guess I should have supervised the removal men better. Everything's all over the place.'

'Thanks.' Murray raised his glass to his lips, wondering how much she'd had to drink. 'Can I help?'

She looked squarely at him, as if trying to assess whether his offer was genuine or made for politeness' sake, and he added, 'I'm not doing anything else and there are still a few things I'd like to ask you about your husband's research, if I may.'

'Okay.' Her smile was suddenly wary. 'But I'm

143

not sure there's much more I can tell you.'

*   *   *

Murray set the chairs on the floor and piled the boxes neatly in a line against the far wall while Audrey started to unpack, then together they heaved the table into the centre of the kitchen and set the chairs around it. He straightened the last one and asked, 'What next?'

She was rooting around in a plastic laundry bag and didn't bother to look up.

'I thought you wanted to ask me some questions?'

'Okay.' He leaned against one of the kitchen units, waiting to see what she was looking for. 'A lot of your husband's research seems to have been direct interviews with people who knew the deceased artists.'

'Yes, that was Alan's preferred method.' Audrey pulled out an electric drill and went back to rummaging in the bag. 'He'd completed a historical section, looking into artists of the past—people whose contemporaries and doctors were long gone, but had perhaps left written impressions of the subject's state of mind. Now he was working on modern-day artists. It gave him a lot more scope. His final intention was to do a comparison, see if society's attitudes, artists' attitudes in particular, had altered.' She pulled out a paper bag, 'Aha, gotcha', and poured a selection of drill bits onto the table. 'I shouldn't do that. I'll end up scratching the surface.' She turned and lifted a large carrier bag from behind the door. 'Ask me another.'

144

'Do you know if he interviewed associates of Archie Lunan prior to his trip to Lismore?'

'No.' Her voice was impatient. 'Like I said, I didn't want to know the details of who Alan was interviewing. I can give you an outline of Alan's methodology, beyond that I'm not much good to you.'

'Okay.' Murray injected a false brightness into his voice. 'I'll settle for a summary.'

Audrey shot him a glance.

'The obvious way to begin would be by dividing the subjects into categories.'

'What kind of categories?'

'The classic ones, I imagine.' His face must have looked blank because she started to explain. 'Sociological theory classifies suicide into three main categories, altruistic, egoistic and anomic. The first two are pretty self-explanatory. Killing yourself for the greater good of others. Captain Oates is the classic Western example, "I'm going out now and I may be some time." But it's not unknown in tribal societies for old people to pop off rather than hold back the rest of the clan. I sometimes think our pensioners could learn something from them instead of living on to a hundred bemoaning the state of the NHS while sucking up most of its resources.' She saw Murray's expression and laughed. 'I'm only joking. How are you at heights?'

'Okay, I think.'

'Good, I'm terrible at them.' She pulled a roller blind from the bag. 'How would you feel about putting this up for me?'

He looked up at the top of the window, ten feet or so above their heads.

'Do you have a tall enough ladder?'

'Sure do.' Her eyes shone with the fun of a good dare. 'I'll even hold it for you.'

*   *   *

The ladder turned out to be a little short for the task, so Murray stood on the topmost rung, his feet covering a paper sticker that read, 'Warning! Do not stand on this step.' He waited until he'd drilled the holes for the rawl plugs before asking, 'What defines the other types?'

'Of suicide?'

'Yes.'

Audrey seemed a long way below.

'Well, egoistic is pretty obvious, I guess: an individual feels dislocated from society and decides to take their own life. In a way it's the opposite of altruistic suicide. Most of your artistic suicides get placed in this category, the romantic agony and all that.' The ladder wobbled a little and she asked, 'Are you okay up there?'

'Yes, I think so.'

'Of course, there's an extra investment for artists—the chance that if he or she manages a memorable death, they'll stake a place in posterity.'

'Does falling off a high ladder count?'

'Not unless you've been drinking absinthe and snorting coke cut with your father's ashes. Anyway, it's nonsense. I'd never heard of half the suicides Alan studied.'

Murray finished inserting the rawl plugs and started to screw in the brackets that would hold the blind in place. He risked a look down.

146

'And the final category?'

'Anomic suicide. The result of a big change in someone's life: divorce, death of a loved one, financial collapse. It all becomes too much, and so they end it.'

'Simple as that?'

'No, rarely simple. That's why Alan and his colleagues could theorise endlessly about it.'

One of the screws was refusing to go into its plug. Murray turned the screwdriver round and used its handle to batter it in place, hoping Audrey wouldn't realise what he was doing.

'You said you didn't know much about your husband's research, but that's a pretty impressive summary.'

'I was more involved in the early days. It's the old story, Alan was one of my PhD supervisors. Looking back, I can see it was as his research developed that I started to get a bit squeamish. Maybe it's something to do with having Lewis. Motherhood alters your perspective on some things. I started to find it hard to listen to a catalogue of young lives snuffed out. Too threatening, I suppose, when I had a young life to take care of.'

'Is that the psychologist talking now?'

He pulled the next screw from his pocket and started to twist it home; it went in smooth as butter.

'I wasn't very psychologically aware at the time, I'm afraid. I could get quite vicious about it.'

He was on the final bracket now.

'I find that hard to believe.'

'That's because you don't know me.' She snorted. 'We had a massive row one Sunday

147

morning. It's the climax of the British week, isn't it, Sunday morning? A cooked breakfast, the *Archers* omnibus, Sunday papers—peace perfect peace, or boredom bloody boredom, depending on how you look at it.'

Except for a guarantee of no teaching, Murray's own Sundays didn't particularly differ from the rest of his week, but he said, 'I suppose so.'

'Well, that particular Sunday, the *Observer* carried a front-page story about a young British artist who had committed suicide at the age of forty-one. Walked off into the woods and didn't come back. His body was found a few weeks later. It would be wrong to say the news made Alan happy, he wasn't a complete ghoul, but he was energised by it, abandoned his breakfast and went off into his study to start downloading the artist's work. Not quite whistling, but purposeful. For some reason it incensed me. His cheery, workmanlike mood, while somewhere some mother, wife, or girlfriend was breaking her heart.' She laughed, half-embarrassed. 'I don't know why I'm telling you this.'

'Perhaps because I didn't know Alan.'

'Perhaps.' Her face was turned away from Murray, the red-blonde crown of her head glossy against the streetlamp's glow. 'It's not like it caused a rift between us or anything, but looking back, I think after that row he told me less about his research and I didn't ask.'

She passed the blind up to Murray and he slid it into place, feeling a spurt of achievement. Perhaps he'd feel like this every day if he'd learned a trade instead of going to university.

'How does it look?'

148

'Perfect, thanks. Safe from peeping Toms.'

She held onto the ladder as he descended. He turned, ready to step from it, and glimpsed the hollow between her breasts. He imagined each one snug in its lace cup. Sometimes he wished he could smother his sex drive. It was like a second pulse, forcing his blood, fiercer than his heart.

'Have you eaten?'

'What?'

'Have you had your dinner? Your "tea", as Alan would have said?'

'No, not yet.'

'I was going to order Chinese. Would you like to join me?'

If she hadn't mentioned her dead husband he might have declined, but somehow his presence made it safe. She phoned in their order while he climbed the ladder again and replaced the absent light bulb in the hallway.

*　　　*　　　*

The door to Lewis's room was ajar. Murray clicked on the hall light to check it was working and then pushed the boy's bedroom door wide. Audrey must have started her unpacking here. It was messy, but it was a young boy's normal untidiness rather than the disorder caused by moving.

Posters of fluffy animals and pumped-up superheroes hung on the wall; a small bookcase stacked with books sat next to a comfortable armchair perfect for an adult and child to squash in together and share a story. Lewis's quilt cover was printed with a picture of a wide-eyed cartoon character Murray didn't recognise. On the bedside table, next to the nightlight, was a framed photograph of a man in climbing gear hanging onto a rock face somewhere high above the world. A grin split the man's face, emphasising the deep creases radiating from the corners of his eyes. Alan Garrett looked more alive than anyone Murray could remember seeing.

'Do you have children?'

He hadn't heard her come off the phone and her voice startled him.

'No, not yet.' He turned towards her. The light bulb he'd used was too high a wattage, it stung his eyes and seemed to bleach the colour from her skin. 'I'd have to find a wife first.'

'Very proper of you.'

'I'm a proper kind of guy.'

She was standing close to him now.

He wasn't sure.

Then he was and they were kissing. He slid his hands down the back of her trousers, feeling the smooth roundness of her, slid his fingers up the ridge of her spine, managing for once to undo her bra in one fumbling movement, feeling her gasp. He backed into the room, towards the cartoon-covered bed, holding her close, their lips pressed together.

She pulled away. 'No, not here.' And led him through to the sitting room.

He realised he didn't have a condom, wondered guiltily if she slept around, if she wanted another child, even. They were on the couch now, his hand roaming beneath her top, her fingers pushing under his jumper, below his T-shirt, skin touching skin.

'I don't have anything, protection.'

150

She pulled her top off.

'It's okay, I do.'

Her breasts were almost as he had imagined them, high and rounded; the nipples stiff and proud.

He lowered his head.

'Wait.' She slid from him. 'I'll only be a second.'

Murray watched as she left the room, taking in her smooth back, the faint hint of a tan-line, remnant of some earlier holiday. The door swung gently behind her and he was alone, wondering what the fuck he was doing.

He kicked off his shoes and hauled his jumper and T-shirt over his head in one swift movement, averting his eyes from Alan Garrett's boxes of research and pushing the university code of ethics from his mind. Then she was back, stripped and clutching a packet of condoms. Murray thought he'd never seen a woman who looked so natural, so right, naked. He got rid of the rest of his clothes, pulled her towards him and onto the sofa.

*   *   *

The doorbell rang just as they finished. Murray flinched and Audrey laughed, 'Perfect timing.' She walked naked from the room. There was a second ring and he heard her shout, 'Two secs, just finding my purse.'

He pulled his clothes back on, wondering if the urge to sneak away was social awkwardness or some deeper evolutionary instinct. The aroma of Chinese food wafted into the room, a sweet scent suffused with a hot tang; jasmine and chillies. He hadn't eaten since that morning and was suddenly

151

ravenous. Was this all he was, a creature ruled by appetites?

He found Audrey in the kitchen wrapped in a long cotton robe, taking the fast-food cartons from a carrier bag and setting them on the newly installed kitchen table. She looked like Lewis's mum again. Could she consciously turn her sex appeal on and off, or was it another of nature's tricks? He put his arms awkwardly around her and gave her a squeeze. Her body stiffened and he released her. Audrey screwed up the empty plastic bag the food had came in and flung it towards the piles of boxes.

'I could get used to being a slob.' She peeled back the paper lids from the cartons, stuck a spoon in each of them and handed Murray a plate. 'Mrs Wong's finest. Tuck in.'

The room was too dark for them to see their food properly. Murray noticed two unlit candles on the table. Perhaps the matches were lost too, packed away in the same box as the kettle and the corkscrew. They ate in silence for a moment, then she jumped to her feet and fetched the wine.

'Sorry, I forgot.'

Murray felt her nervousness and knew he should say something to put her at ease. He poked at a piece of pork with the wooden chopsticks the restaurant provided.

'This is great, good food.'

'Thanks.' She smiled as if he had said something amusing. 'Are you going to go to the island?'

'Lismore?'

'Where else?'

'Yes.' He hesitated, looking at the unlit candles.

152

'Sooner or later.'

'And will you meet her?'

'Who?'

'Christie Graves, his old sweetheart.'

'I'd like to, but she doesn't seem too keen on meeting me.'

'I'm surprised. She struck me as a man's woman.' He looked up at Audrey and she said, 'Did I tell you that I met her?'

'No.' He wondered if she knew how important Christie was to Lunan's story. 'What was she like?'

'Creepy. She came to Alan's funeral.'

'Here in Glasgow?'

'I was hardly going to have him buried over there.'

'No, I guess not. Sorry.'

Audrey sighed.

'It should be me that's sorry. I'm such a grinch sometimes.' She forced a cheerless smile. 'I didn't like her.'

'Christie?'

'No.'

'Why not?'

'It's hard to say, exactly. She did all the right stuff, arrived in good time, said lovely things about Alan. She even brought me some photographs of him in his last days there, beautiful photos, much better than I ever took. But I didn't like her. None of it seemed sincere. I felt she was playing the part of a concerned acquaintance. She spoke well, her tone of voice was just as it should be, her face arranged in a sad expression. But I kept on feeling that if I turned my head suddenly, I might catch her smirking. That's a horrid thing to say, isn't it? But it's true. She gave me the creeps.' Audrey

153

paused and they sat in silence for a moment, their food forgotten. 'She asked me if I would like to visit the island, invited me to stay with her.'

'Did you go?'

'Yes, but not to her. My mother came with me and we stayed in a little B&B. I'm afraid I neglected to get in touch with Miss Graves, but of course inevitably we bumped into her one day at the shop. She was charm itself. My mother thought she was delightful, but she made my flesh crawl.' Audrey sighed. 'Perhaps that's inevitable too. You see, Alan was coming back from her house when he crashed.'

'But you don't think it was anything to do with her?'

'No, of course not.' She closed her eyes for a second, as if trying to hold onto herself then said, 'At first I did wonder whether they'd been drinking. Alan would never normally drink and drive, but he was sociable, keen to put people at their ease, especially when he was interviewing them, and you know what it's like on small islands, normal rules don't necessarily apply.'

Murray kept his voice soft, wary of provoking her.

'But he wasn't over the limit?'

'No, apparently not. There were no traces of alcohol, or drugs for that matter, in his bloodstream. It was just one of those things, a bloody unfortunate accident. I guess blaming Christie is easier than blaming Alan, or blaming myself.'

'I know accidents provoke guilt, but it couldn't be your fault, you weren't even there.'

'Ah, but there's the rub. Alan wanted Lewis and

154

me to go with him, to make the trip into a short break, but I refused. I had work to do and I didn't want our holidays to start revolving around his research. Around suicides.'

'You don't know that anything would have turned out differently.'

'He was always extra careful when Lewis was in the car, he would never have put his son, or me, at risk.' Her voice held a fractured edge. She paused again, and softened her tone. 'It would have been the perfect place for a holiday. The island is beautiful, really, really lovely, and everyone was nice to us.' She gave him her sad smile. 'But I won't be going again.'

*   *   *

It was midnight when she saw him to the door. He hesitated in the close, unsure of whether it would be crass to thank her, but she beat him to it.

'Thanks for all your help.' Her voice was a peep above a whisper. 'Lights to see by and blinds to hide behind.'

He kept his own voice low, careful of disturbing her new neighbours.

'I was going to thank you.'

Audrey raised her eyebrows, 'For what?' They both laughed. She held a finger to her lips, 'Shhhsh.'

'For a lovely evening.' He hesitated. 'Can I give you a ring sometime?'

She leaned on the door, half in, half out. Her smile was gentle.

'I think we've covered everything, don't you?'

'I wasn't thinking about work.'

155

'No,' she smiled again. 'I know, neither was I.'

'Ah, I see.'

'Please, don't take it personally. Remember I'm a psychologist. In my professional opinion, I'm not ready for anything serious yet. Sex is easier than all the other stuff. I don't feel disloyal having sex with another man—not that I make a habit of it—but dating . . .' She let the sentence tail away.

'I guess I should feel used.'

'Do you?'

'No.' He hesitated. 'I wasn't thinking about anything heavy, just dinner sometime, a drink if that would be easier, no strings attached.'

Audrey plucked at the door chain. It clinked as it hit the wooden jamb.

'Perhaps.'

Murray reached into his pocket for pen and paper to write down his number, but she stopped him.

'I've got your number already. I called you, remember?' She stifled a yawn with her hand. 'Sorry, it's been a long day. Lewis gets me up at the crack of dawn.'

'I'll let you go then.'

They exchanged a chaste kiss and he jogged down the stairs. He heard the door shut softly behind him before he reached the next landing.

Chapter Twelve

Murray walked swiftly along the empty corridor, his trainers silent against the wooden floor. He'd chosen a quiet time of day, too early for tea breaks or sandwich runs, a mid period when those with classes would be safely ensconced in offices and lecture theatres. The place was studiously silent, no hint remaining of the clatter of students who had milled here fifteen minutes ago and would assault the stillness again soon enough. But behind some of the closed doors his colleagues bowed their heads over books and computers and at any time a sudden thought might send one of them out to the library in search of a remembered text or into the shadows of the quadrangles for a leg-stretch and a smoke.

Murray fished his keys from his pocket and selected the one to his room as he walked, ready to nip in swiftly, safe from fumbles. It felt strange, creeping like a thief towards his own office.

He passed Fergus Baine's door, closed and blessedly silent, then Lyle Joff's, Vic Costello's, Phyllida McWilliams', each shut and graveyard-still. Rab Purvis's door was ajar, a signal that he was in residence and not averse to being interrupted. Murray increased his pace and slipped by, catching a glimpse of Rab's arm resting against his desk, his hand tapping out a smoker's unconscious rhythm as he worked.

Rachel's office lay at the end of the hallway. He looked towards it, willing the door to open and Rachel to step out, half-dazed from reading, brushing the hair from her eyes, forgetting not to smile. The door stood firm, Rachel behind it or elsewhere, beyond him.

There were new posters on the noticeboard by his office, calls for papers, announcements of forthcoming lectures, a Keats/Shelley essay competition he'd once entered when he was a student. He glanced at the dead poets' death masks, side by side above conditions of entry, then turned the key in the lock and went in, closing the door gently behind him.

Everything was as he had left it. The dried stain of coffee still slopped over the essay he should have handed back a week ago, the two mugs drained of whisky and gin set side by side, his chair pushed a little away from his desk.

He ran the mugs under the tap and placed them on the edge of the tiny sink to dry, then glanced at his watch. Eleven-thirty. If he was quick, he might escape before classes changed.

He started to gather the books he'd come for. An anthology of Scottish poetry that didn't feature Lunan, but might be a useful reminder of chronology; a biography of a dead contemporary that mentioned the poet; a seventies literary review citing him as the next big thing.

Murray's copy of *Moontide* was propped face-out on a high shelf. He reached up and tipped it from its perch, the book slipping through his fingers and landing with a slap on the ground. Lunan looked up at him from the front cover. His had once seemed an old face to Murray. Now he could see the youth screened behind the braggadocio of long hair and beard. He picked the book up and slipped it gently into the front pocket of his rucksack.

Christie's books came next. The later ones were of no great concern, but he packed them anyway. As far as he was concerned she'd got stuck in the same weave, horror stories laced with Celtic folklore that sometimes started well, but always descended into a chaos of fantasy and false connections. Critics sneered, but her fans still bought them and so did Murray. He read each one quickly, greedy for a glimpse of Lunan, barely bothering to follow permutations of plots he considered all repetition.

Christie had found her subject in her first novel, *Sacrifice*: a group of young, overreaching outsiders whose lack of respect towards nature invoked their own fall. Murray had written an article on Christie's later novels for one of the more 'out there' literary websites, *Scooby Doo and the Fall: Paradise Fucked Up*. He'd been pleased with the title at the time. Now he hoped that Christie hadn't come across it.

Sacrifice was the final book in his pile. He'd marked a quote on the opening page that he hoped to use in his biography, if he could get permission. He opened the novel and read,

The cottage was six miles from the village,
set back from the road along a rutted path.
We had no visitors in those early days and
when we left the shelter of our tiny cottage
it was usually to go down to the loch side.
Over the summer the path became
overgrown so no one would have known we
were there, except of course that they
already did. We were the topic of
conversation around hearthsides and dinner
tables, in byres and country lanes. The
islanders discussed us as they left church,
hearts shrunken with the conviction of the
saved. They mulled over our vices as they
filled their vans and tractors with petrol at
the one pump station, expanded on them in

159

the mothers' union and the ceilidh house. When we went down into the village to buy what we couldn't make, every detail of what we wore, what we said, what we bought, was stored by those lucky enough to encounter us. Later we gave them something to talk about.

Murray closed the book and slid it beside the rest. The whole operation had taken less than fifteen minutes. If he left now, he might get clear of the building without meeting anyone. He shouldered the weight of his bag and slipped out into the corridor, locking the door on his office.

*　　　*　　　*

Murray was at the top of the spiral stairwell when he heard Fergus Baine's laugh echoing up from the floor below. Loud with a false note of heartiness, the kind of chuckle an inquisitor might give before the final turn of the screw.

'Shit.' Murray hesitated, caught in a stab of shame. He could still make a getaway back to his office or up onto the floor above, but now Fergus was upon him the whole foolishness of hiding became clear. He had to face the professor sometime. He started down the stairs, forcing his feet into a brisk rhythm. If he was lucky Fergus would be in a hurry and they could pass each other with a sober nod of recognition.

'His later work is technically far superior, of course.' Fergus conceded a point to whoever he was talking to. 'But it lacks the fire in the belly of his early stuff.'

'It's not often I hear you extolling passion over technical expertise.'

Fergus laughed again and Murray stopped dead, caught by the last voice, the only voice he wanted to hear.

Rachel was wearing a white silk blouse that buttoned and tied at the neck. There was something provocative about its double-fastening, as if it had been designed to be unpicked. Her grey linen trousers were snug at the hips, flaring down to open-toed sandals. Her toenails were painted pink. All her focus was on her husband. She touched his arm as they turned the corner. It was a simple gesture and Murray wondered if it was his foreknowledge that made it seem a move beyond collegiate.

'Murray.' Fergus's voice lost none of its heartiness, none of its hint of the inquisition. 'I've been hoping to catch up with you.'

Rachel met Murray's eyes. He felt himself colour.

'Fergus, Rachel.' He forced a smile.

Doors were opening in the corridors above and below, noise building as students began to crowd out from classes. Rachel frowned. 'I've got a third-year tutorial group due in sixty seconds.'

For a split moment he despised her. 'Sure, see you later.'

Fergus squeezed her arm, a mirror of the way she'd held him. 'See you at home.' The professor watched Rachel until she reached the landing and when he turned away it was as if he still held her in his eyes, her slim figure disappearing into the black corridor of his pupils. 'On your way out?' Fergus smiled as if there had been no five a.m.

161

phone call. No drunken demand to talk to his wife.

Murray had a ridiculous urge to mention he'd bedded Audrey Garrett. Instead he said, 'I just dropped by to collect some books.'

'Of course, you're abandoning us.'

'Temporarily, I'm sure you'll cope.'

Fergus gave a slow smile.

'Yes, I'm sure we'll manage.' The staircase was crowded, Murray and Fergus a dam in the ascending and descending streams of students. 'Shall we get out of here?'

The professor turned and started to walk down towards the exit without waiting for Murray's reply.

It had rained in the short time he'd been indoors and the air outside was fresh, the flagstones drenched black. The wind tumbled the kinetic sculpture in the courtyard as they crossed the quadrangles together, Fergus setting the pace. It was going to rain again soon. Murray glanced, as he often did, at the wrought-iron bench dedicated to a twenty-one-year-old student he'd never known. It was too delicate to sit on, but it drew the eye.

Fergus asked, 'Book going well?'

'Yes, fine.'

The professor's suit was almost the same cold stone shade as Rachel's linen trousers. Murray wondered if they had bought them together, on their honeymoon in Italy, the Mediterranean sparkling blue on the horizon behind them. He imagined Fergus in a white hat, Rachel in a summer dress, and felt jealousy hot in his stomach.

They cut down an outside staircase, into a smell of damp and ancient mortar roused by the shower,

162

and entered a broad tunnel. Fergus's footsteps sounded hollow against the cobbles. A porter pushed a trolley laden with boxes through a large archway and they stepped aside to let him pass. Fergus nodded, a country squire passing a tenant on the road. The porter returned the greeting, but the professor had already turned his attention back to Murray.

'In a rush?'

'Not really.'

'Good. Walk me to the car and tell me what you've been up to.'

Fergus slowed to a stroll.

'I'm making progress.'

'Excellent. Any thoughts of putting a research student on the trail, see what they might dig up for you?'

'I prefer to do the research myself. It's slower, but at least that way I feel I'm covering all the bases.'

'Yes.' Fergus sighed. 'I suppose those days have passed. Did I ever tell you I knew him?'

'Rachel said you might have.'

The foolishness of the statement rose like bile in his throat. He waited for the professor to ask where they were when she'd mentioned it. But he gave a dry smile and said, 'Good to know she thinks of me when I'm out of sight. Drunk, of course. Archie, that is, absolutely legless. I'm afraid I didn't rate him much. Never managed to get to grips with the poetry either, too fey for my tastes, too Romantic.'

'Where did you meet him?'

'In a pub after some poetry reading or other.' Fergus laughed. 'Where else? To me he

163

epitomised all of the clichés of the working-class poet. Drunken, unwashed, boorish, predatory towards women. At least Dylan Thomas had genius on his side. Lunan? Well . . .' He grinned at Murray. 'Sorry, I never got the hang of revering the dead. I didn't intend to slight your hero.'

'I'm not sure hero is the right word.'

Fergus shrugged. They were almost at the end of the car park now, the bays next to the anatomy building before the path swept down and away from the bounds of the university. He pulled his car keys from his pocket and the lights flashed on a black BMW. 'Let's just say you're keen to give Lunan his place in history.'

It was the same car that Rachel had driven him home in. Murray took in its solid curves, realising he had half- expected Fergus to be driving the Saab which had tailed them down from the reservoir. His voice sounded vague to his own ears. 'I want to bring his poems to a wider audience.'

'And you think biography is the best way to do it? The life rather than the work?'

'The life and the work.'

'Maybe. After all, the life destroyed the work.' Fergus opened the driver's door and leaned against it. 'I know I said I didn't like Lunan's poetry, but I can recognise he had ability. The problem is he pissed it up against the wall.' He levelled his gaze and Murray knew that if this were a lecture, whatever came next would be the key point, a statement to be underlined and regurgitated in the exam. 'It happens sometimes to self-starters. They burn out, as if the effort of pulling themselves up by their boot straps was too much to sustain.' Fergus turned his mouth down at

164

the corners in a parody of a sad smile. 'They do something foolish—sabotage their own hard work—and then, of course, they've got no real support when they get into difficulties, no access to the old-boy network.' He grinned. 'They're on their own, and that can be rather lonely. Whatever one's occupation, it's always important to have allies.' He gave Murray a parting smile, ducked into the BMW and slammed the door. Murray went to turn away as the engine started, but then the window slid down and Fergus spoke again. 'One last thing.'

Murray turned back.

'Yes?'

'Whatever went on between you and my wife, it's over now. Understand?'

'Yes.'

'I knew you would.'

The BMW swung out from its parking space and Murray walked towards the sloping pathway home. Fergus passed him on University Avenue. Neither of them waved goodbye.

Chapter Thirteen

George Meikle had lost none of his gruffness. The bookfinder nodded down at the pavement with the gravity of a funeral director presenting a newly embalmed corpse to its relatives.

'That tells you all you need to know about Edinburgh's road maintenance. Nigh on forty years it's been there.'

Murray could make out the name *Christie*

165

etched roughly into the concrete. He took out his mobile phone, lined up the camera function and snapped. It looked shit, the letters lost in the greyness of the concrete and the damp morning. Done well, it could make a nice image for the book. His brother would know how to capture it. He pushed the thought away.

'Were you here when he did it?'

'I was, yes.'

'And Christie?'

'Christie? No, she wasn't there.'

Meikle turned and started to walk down the street. Murray took another useless shot with his camera-phone, and then followed, jogging a bit of the way before catching up with the bookfinder.

'Archie obviously thought a lot of her.'

'Aye, he did.'

The older man spoke without looking at him, his face set straight ahead. Murray supposed this was what fishing was like, flinging out your line, watching it drop into the deep waters, and then waiting patiently for a pull on the lure.

'So what did he do? Wait till the workies were away, and then fire in with a stick?'

Meikle gave him a curt nod.

'That's about the size of it.'

They walked on in silence, the older man setting the pace. A bus disgorged its passengers onto the street and Murray forced his way through the waiting queue, muttering a mantra of 'Excuse me', 'Sorry', 'Excuse me'. Meikle had drawn further ahead and Murray had to negotiate a squad of draymen unloading a beer lorry, before he drew level.

'Can you spare time for a coffee?'

To his own ears he sounded like a desperate adolescent trying to set up a first date, but Meikle glanced at his watch.

'I've got thirty minutes before I'm due back. There's a place over the way, if you're not fussy about hygiene.'

Meikle stepped into a queue of traffic stalled by a double-parked delivery van. Murray hesitated then hurried after him just as the delivery driver pulled away. The van tooted its horn and Murray raised an open palm in a gesture that was part command, part apology.

Meikle was already climbing the entrance steps to the café. Murray followed him into a broth of hot fat, hamburgers and chips. His bowels shrank, as if giving him due notice of what would happen if he dared eat anything. A motherly waitress in a blue tabard leant against the counter chatting to an old man who sat alone over a cup of rusty-looking tea. 'Naw, hen,' the old man said, 'I'm sweet enough.' They both laughed, and he repeated it, 'Sweet enough', though it wasn't much of a joke the first time. The aisle was almost blocked by a toddler strapped tight in its buggy, like a dangerous criminal under restraint. Its mother sat at a table next to it, reading *Heat*. A milky coffee congealed in front of her, beside a plate of chips smothered in tomato ketchup. She pressed a chip into the redness, with a gesture that suggested a lifetime of stubbed-out cigarettes, and placed it in the child's outstretched hands. The toddler squeezed it into puree and let it drop. The woman muttered, 'For fuck's sake, Liam', and started to pick the mess from his jacket.

Meikle tucked himself into a plastic bucket seat

167

at one of the free tables and set his elbows on its Formica surface.

'Twenty-five to, the clock's ticking.'

Murray shifted a scattering of white sugar with the edge of his hand, a snow plough piling through a fresh fall, and set his tape recorder on the table.

'I wanted to ask you about Christie.'

'I thought it was Archie you were interested in.'

'It is, but Christie's a big part of his story. What did you think of her?'

'I didn't think anything. She was his girlfriend, his bird as we used to call them, that was all. I guess you could say she was the Yoko Ono of the group.'

'She split you up?'

'We were pals, not bloody civil partners.'

The waitress ambled over, leaned her bottom against the opposite table and asked what they wanted. Murray noticed the home-made UDA tattoo on her wrist as she wrote their order on her pad. She gave the table a half-hearted wipe, and sugar grains rained onto Murray's lap. Meikle waited till she had gone and then said, 'Not that I've anything against gays.'

Murray tried to dust himself down, but some of the grains were caught in the trouser-folds around his groin and he gave up.

'Of course not.'

'It's just that I'm not one, so mind you don't put otherwise in your book.'

'Message received and understood.'

The woman with the magazine put a chip into her own mouth and the toddler let out a pterodactyl caw.

Meikle said, 'And don't put any of that "doth

protest too much" stuff in there either. I'm just setting the record straight.'

'Straight as a die, George.'

The older man gave him a stern look that turned to a laugh. The waitress smiled as she set their coffees on the table between them.

'Somebody's happy, anyway.' She took the bill from her pocket and placed it between the cups, asking, 'Whose shout is it today then?' as if they were seasoned regulars.

Murray pulled his wallet from his jacket and handed her a five-pound note.

'Quite right. I bet your dad shelled out enough on you over the years, eh?'

Murray said, 'He's not . . .'

But she had already counted his change onto the table and was making her way to a trio of workmen in fluorescent waistcoats.

'Nosy besom. See she's serving the Diet Coke men quick enough, anyway. No waiting around for them, eh?' Now that his venom had been spent, Meikle softened a little. 'Christie was all right as far as I was concerned. I mean, you wouldn't have expected Archie to go for someone run of the mill. She was a good-looking girl. Didn't say much, but nice to have around. Good wallpaper. I called her Yoko because after she came on the scene Archie and me saw less of each other. That's the way it is with some guys once they hook up. They don't hang out with the lads any more. Maybe it's no bad thing. I spent too much time hanging out with the lads over the years. Look where it got me.'

'I spoke to Professor James. He said Christie never said a word in his writing workshops.'

Meikle's voice was low.

169

'What else did he tell you?'

'That Archie had the potential to make it big, but he wasn't sure he'd have had the discipline.'

'He's changed his tune.'

'Oh?'

Murray stirred his coffee, wary of losing the other man with the wrong question.

'James couldn't stand Archie or his poetry. It was him who made sure Archie was chucked out of uni.'

'Who told you that?'

'Who do you think? It's not like I spent my time hanging around with professors.'

'If he wasn't welcome, why did Archie keep going to the poetry workshops?'

'Why shouldn't he?'

Murray could hear the heat of pub arguments and long-ago resentment in the older man's voice. He levelled his own tones and said, 'No reason, but why go where you're not wanted?'

Meikle sighed. The anger was still there, but now he spoke with resignation.

'They were good at what they did, right?'

Murray nodded.

'Some of them became world-class.'

'The way I read it, Archie wanted to be part of their gang, but for whatever reason they didn't want him. Maybe I can see their point. They were university types—no offence intended—but you know what I mean. Serious guys. And Archie was wild, too wild sometimes.'

'According to James, it wasn't unknown for Archie to turn up drunk and obnoxious. He said that if Archie hadn't been so talented, he would have told him not to come back.'

Meikle sipped his coffee. He gazed beyond Murray and he might have been looking through the café's unwashed window to the busy street outside or into the past. 'That type of thing wasn't unusual, but there was more to it than just drunkenness. Archie had this extra energy. It's hard to explain. Like he had a tincture of quicksilver running through his blood. I think that was part of why he drank so much—to damp his energy down.' Meikle looked at his watch again. 'I'm going to have to head soon. You asked me if I was there when he wrote Christie's name in the concrete.'

'Yes.'

'I didn't show you it to make a good picture for your book. The night he did that was the night Christie introduced him to Bobby Robb.'

*   *   *

They left their cold coffee cups on the table along with the tip and headed back into the street. This time the bookfinder kept Murray close.

'I blamed Bobby for Archie's death much more than I ever blamed Christie. She was only a young lass. Bobby was old enough to know what he was doing.'

The name rang a distant bell, but Murray resisted asking who Robb was for fear of breaking the spell. Meikle continued, 'If I'm honest, I'd been losing patience with Archie for a while.' He glanced at Murray. 'You're too young to remember what the city was like in those days. The phrase "wine bar" hadn't been invented. Men were meant to behave like men, drink as much as they could

171

get down and only greet when their team lost the cup. People were used to blokes with long hair by then, but you'd better bloody act like a man if you knew what was good for you.'

'And Archie didn't?'

'Nowadays, odds are he would be okay. Anything goes, right? But not back then. Archie was too loud. He'd get steamboats and start mouthing off, on sex, religion, politics, poetry—the kind of stuff that gets up people's noses. He attracted aggro and whoever was with him got dragged in. It was beginning to piss me off.'

'And Bobby?'

'Bobby was bad news. I'd heard a bit about him: Edinburgh's a small city and a guy like him doesn't go unnoticed. He was one of those leeches that attach themselves to students—you know the type, that bit older with the kind of contacts some youngsters find impressive.'

'Drugs?'

'Drugs, wideboys, who knows what else. In those days students got decent grants and Bobby Robb was just the boy to help spend them. But even if I hadn't heard of Bobby, I'd have tagged him as trouble as soon as Christie walked into the bar looking up at him like he was Jesus Christ resurrected and ready to turn beer into whisky. There was something Victorian about the whole thing. Like she was a little milkmaid fresh from the country and he was an old villain ready to sucker her in and pimp her out.'

They approached a building under renovation and fell into single file as they entered a tunnel of scaffolding, its supports bandaged at head height with sacking to save careless drinkers from cracking their skulls. On the wooden walkways above men in hardhats hammered into the stonework. Mineral dust powdered the air. Murray held his breath until they emerged on the other side. Meikle picked up the tale.

'Archie favoured working men's pubs. Like I said, there wasn't much else unless you wanted to drink in a hotel. But he went for the rougher end. The bar we were in that night was the kind of place where you'd expect Christie to get a comment or two. The punters stared at her, right enough, when she came in. Then they saw Bobby and concentrated on their pints. It's always struck me as funny that guys with scars get a reputation for being hard. It's the ones that cut them you should be looking out for, right?' Murray nodded and Meikle went on. 'Bobby had a scar running from the corner of his mouth up to his eyelid, looked like he'd been lucky to keep his sight. Side-on, it gave him this horrible, sneering smile, a bit like the Penguin.'

Murray looked at Meikle blankly and he said, 'You know, the baddie in *Batman*.'

'I think you mean the Joker.'

'Shit.' Meikle shook his head. 'That's what my wife calls a senior moment. Sideways, he looked like the Joker, but the funny thing was, he was the kind of ugly git women would be attracted to.'

Murray knew the type, but he asked, 'Why?'

'I don't know. Something about his confidence maybe, the way he carried himself, the fact he looked like a bastard. Some women like that.'

'So you thought Christie might go off with him?'

'There were stars in her eyes when she looked

173

at him right enough, but I got the impression it was Archie he was interested in. Homed right in on him and started to give him the gab.'

'Did Archie reciprocate?'

'Oh, he was taken with him, yes.'

Murray hesitated.

'Are you saying Archie had homosexual tendencies?'

The bookfinder glanced at him.

'If you'd asked me then, about Archie maybe being gay, I would have called you a poof for thinking it. But looking back, I don't know. I don't think so. He never tried anything on with me, but who can say? I guess Archie was the kind of guy that would try anything once, twice if he liked it.'

They were close to the library now. Murray looked at his watch. Five to the hour.

'So, him and Bobby?'

'You're asking the wrong man.'

'But you had your suspicions?'

'No, I had no opportunity for suspicions. I never saw him or Christie again after that night.'

They passed a pub and had to fall into single file again to pass the smokers loitering outside. When they fell back into step, Murray asked, 'What happened?'

Meikle sighed. 'There were a few of us drinking that night. Archie had brought along a student pal that liked slumming it and I was with a couple of mates from the Socialist Workers' Party. They tolerated Archie for my sake, and I put up with his wee snob of a pal for his. It was an uneasy balance, but it was a balance all the same.'

'And Bobby Robb upset it?'

'Big time, as my granddaughter would say.

174

Bobby was all charm, but he wasn't trying to charm me. It was like he was presenting a mask to Archie and Christie, but from where I was sitting I could see the line between where the mask finished and the real Bobby began. And he knew it. He kept turning round and giving me these sly nods and winks. I would have coped with that—after all, it was Archie's business who he hung about with—but then Bobby pulled out a pack of Tarot cards and started laying them out in front of Christie.' George shook his head. 'When it comes to chat-ups, fortune-telling is up there with foot rubs and neck massages.'

Murray had never considered it before, but he could see how the tactic might work.

'I guess it lets you get up close and personal.'

'Exactly. I was a bit pissed off on Archie's behalf, but it was still none of my beeswax and, anyway, something told me Robb was doing it to get Archie's attention, so I let them get on with it.'

'Did Archie join in?'

'Oh, aye, before long he was right in the middle of the hocus-pocus. That made it worse. He was meant to be my mate and here he was giving me a showing-up in front of these serious socialists. Then I heard what Bobby Robb was saying and lost my rag.'

Meikle paused and his face grew tight, as if remembering brought back his anger. Somewhere a car radio cried advance warning of the lunchtime news bulletin and Murray remembered time was against them.

'What was he talking about?'

'Reincarnation.'

'Surely that kind of thing was big back then?'

175

'Oh, aye, it was. Hinduism and all that. Not my bag, but I didn't have a problem with it. No, Bobby Robb was waxing on about how you could gain access to other worlds, other minds, through rituals. According to him, if you hit on the right spell, you'd be able to outlive death. Maybe it was the drugs, or maybe it was the drink, who knows? He'd had a fair few pints by this time, we all had. But according to Robb, the most valuable ingredient was the blood of an innocent, a virgin. You wouldn't necessarily have to kill the girl to get it, Robb said, just cut her. He asked Christie if she'd oblige, and when she told him she didn't qualify, started quizzing her on whether she had any friends who did. I waited for Archie to shut him up and when he didn't, I told Robb he was talking a load of pish. The next thing I know, we're scrapping outside on the pavement.'

'You and Bobby?'

'No.' Meikle gave a bitter laugh. 'Bobby wasn't the kind to fight his own battles. Me and Archie.' They had reached the library doorway now. Somewhere a clock struck one, but the bookfinder made no move to return to his post. 'I went round to his flat the next day, but Archie was either out, or not answering. I reckoned if he wanted to see me, he knew where to look. A month later his book came out. No doubt he launched it on a wave of drink. Eventually I heard Archie and Christie had gone off to one of the islands. Robb was with them.' The bookfinder's voice took on a definite tone, making it clear he was drawing a line under the subject. 'Now you know as much as I do.'

'Except why you blame Bobby Robb for Archie's death.'

176

'It's just my opinion.'

'But you've got a reason. I'd like to hear it, if you're willing to share it with me.'

The older man stood silently, looking down the street in the direction of the crossroads.

'Fuck it.' He took his mobile from his pocket and dialled. 'Fiona? Aye, I'm fine, hen, but I'm going to be a wee bit late back.' He paused while the person on the other end of the line said something, and then answered, 'No, no problem. Just something I've got to deal with. Aye, I remember, I'll be back in time. Thanks, Fiona, I'll do the same for you sometime. Cheers.'

He hung up and Murray said, 'Do you want to go somewhere?'

'No, I can't. I've got a meeting in a few minutes. Let's step away from the door, though. I don't want to chance my luck.' They walked down the bridge a little way and stood looking down onto old Edinburgh. Meikle nodded at the darkened street below. 'From up here, it could be a hundred years ago.' He sighed. 'You're right. Archie was a stupid bastard at times, and I've no evidence Bobby had anything to do with his death. But there were rumours.'

'What kind of rumours?'

'Nothing substantial, only that things got out of hand once they got to the island. Something happened to make Archie do what he did, and Bobby Robb wasn't an innocent party.' He looked Murray square in the face. 'He came back to Edinburgh afterwards, but someone gave him a doing and he moved on.'

'You?'

'What does it matter? It was a long time ago.'

177

In the street below, two old men with open cans of lager in their hands made unsteady progress, arm in arm. 'Classic Edinburgh: up here it's hustle and bustle, down there it's drink and decay. Like lifting a stone.' Down below, the old men lowered themselves onto the kerbside. One of them gestured expansively, elaborating on some point while his companion tipped his beer can to his mouth. Transport them to a gastro-pub and they might be two professors of English literature debating the finer points of theory.

Murray said, 'I still don't see why you blame Bobby rather than Christie.'

Meikle gave Murray a defiant stare.

'Bobby Robb was a walking pharmacy. Archie had no self-control. Put him on an island with someone like that and what happened was almost inevitable.'

'There's more to it than that, isn't there?'

'No.' The bookfinder looked away. 'Except . . .' His phone rang and he took it from his pocket. 'I'm on my way.' He stowed the mobile and turned his attention back to Murray. 'Bobby Robb was a drug-addled opportunist, but even I could see he had some kind of magnetism. And Lunan was looking for a guru. Maybe that was why he palled up with me in the first place. Problem was, I had enough trouble keeping myself straight.'

He turned to walk away.

'George.' Murray put a hand on the other man's arm. 'You've been frank with me. I appreciate it.'

The bookfinder's gruffness had returned. He hesitated an uncomfortable beat, then took Murray's proffered hand and shook it.

178

'I've thought about it nigh-on thirty years, and I believe whatever happened up on Lismore, Bobby Robb was at the bottom of it.'

Murray asked, 'Did you ever see Christie again?'

'Once, I saw her in the street not long after Archie's death.' Meikle shook his head. 'That night in the pub, I remember thinking how beautiful Christie was. She was glowing and her hair . . . well, it was always lovely, but it seemed thicker, shinier.' He paused as if deciding whether to go on, then continued, 'The last time I saw her, it was as if she'd aged. She'd lost weight. It made her features look sharper, witchy. Suddenly I felt that I would have as soon talked to the Devil. I crossed the road to avoid her.'

They started to walk together, back in the direction of the library. George Meilke asked, 'So what next?'

'It's all baby steps at the moment. I'm planning on heading to Lismore, see if I can get Christie to give me her account. And I guess I'll have to try and track down Bobby Robb.' He gave Meikle an apologetic glance. 'Even if he turns out to still be as bad as he was when you met him, I need to hear his account.'

Meikle nodded. They walked on in silence for a while. The lunchtime rush was over, but these days the city was never quiet and there was still a slow crawl of cars edging along George IV Bridge towards the lights.

Meikle gave a tired grin. 'I know where he drinks.'

Murray looked at the older man, wondering if he had intended to keep this last piece of information to himself.

The bookfinder misinterpreted his expression.

'Don't worry. I've not fallen off the wagon. I saw him in the High Street a couple of years back.'

'And recognised him? After all that time?'

'You never forget an ugly mug like that. I'd thought about Bobby Robb from time to time, always regretting I didn't somehow call his bluff that night. But when I saw him again . . .' the older man shook his head. 'It was like I was glad to see him, even though I can honestly say I hate Robb for what he did to Archie. It was around about Christmas time. I remember that because I was going to look in some of those fancy shops they have up there for a nice scarf or something for the wife. But when I caught sight of Bobby I didn't hesitate, just reeled round and followed him, like he was the bloody Pied Piper of Hamelin. I had a hard time keeping up. He's probably got a good ten years on me, but he's fast on his pins, I'll give him that. He went down Cockburn Street and into Geordie's. Do you know it?'

'I've had a drink there.'

'In that case you've maybe even seen him and not kent it.'

'So what did you do?'

'Nothing. Ordered myself a Coke and stood drinking it at the bar, watching Bobby in the mirror. It was him, right enough. I've dropped by a couple of times since, to check he's still around. He always is. Sat in the same seat, no newspaper, no book, no company, just a pint stuck in front of him.'

Something in the older man's voice made Murray ask, 'George, you're not planning on doing

180

anything, trying to get revenge for Archie?'

Meikle gave a bitter laugh.

'No, son, I've got a lot going for me these days: a nice wife, a family that's doing well. I just like to see him occasionally, sitting there all alone over his pint, like he does night after night, that creepy scar of his grinning away on one side, while his mouth droops on the other. That's the best revenge I can think of.'

Chapter Fourteen

A man cowled in a brown blanket sat at the top of the stairway, holding a Starbucks cup in his outstretched hand. Murray dropped some loose change in it, and then loped down into the darkness. Fleshmarket Close was caught between the tourist throng of the Old Town and the Tannoy announcements of Waverley Station, but down here in the piss-fragrant gloom it was as if all that commotion belonged to another city. The bar was set into the basement wall of the high tenements that shadowed the dark wynd. He stepped through its door and back forty years.

Maybe the tartan carpet and framed portraits of clan chiefs had been intended to attract the tourists. But it seemed the Americans and Scandinavians who busied the rest of the city preferred brighter watering holes because the grim faces in the pictures girned down on empty tables.

Murray stationed himself at the small bar. Up in the far corner a mute television played out highlights from the racing at Goodwood. He watched the horses thundering silently towards the finishing line in races already lost and won.

After a while a barmaid appeared from the backroom with a paperback in her hand. Murray ordered a pint of lager. The girl set her book on the counter, took a glass from beneath the bar and went wordlessly to the pumps.

A barefoot man was caught on the paperback's cover, frozen in the act of climbing a steep street with a box on his back. His expression was resigned, as if he knew this was all life held for him and was reconciled to the endless trek. Large block letters, heavy as stone, declared *The Myth of Sisyphus*.

'Great book. Enjoying it?'

The girl placed his pint in front of him.

'I'm not sure what the point is.'

'No, I know what you mean.'

Murray told her to take one for herself, like detectives did in the movies when they were trawling for information.

'Thanks, I'll have a half of lager when I knock off.'

She put a pound in the tips jar, took her book and disappeared again. It wasn't how things were meant to go.

Somebody had left the previous day's *Evening News* behind. Murray spread it across the counter and took a sip of his drink.

A man had pleaded guilty to stabbing his wife of thirty-five years, though all he could remember was his seventh pint. A teenager had hung himself in his bedroom after a flurry of threatening texts from classmates. A ten-year-old cancer sufferer, who the newspaper had been collecting money for,

182

had died before she could go on her dream trip to Disneyland Paris. Murray looked at the photograph of a little girl in a floral baseball cap, her face split in a broad grin, and wondered why life was so shit.

He was almost halfway down his glass when an old man came in, leaning heavily on a walking stick.

'Afternoon.' He took his bunnet off, gave it a shake and bent it into the pocket of his overcoat. 'She in the back?'

Murray folded the newspaper away.

'Aye, I think I scared her off.'

'Always got her nose in a book.' The old man rapped on the counter with his stick. 'I keep telling her this is a pub, not Boots Lending Library, but she doesn't listen.'

The barmaid reappeared and he ordered a half and half. Murray wondered about offering to pay, but hesitated, worried the pensioner would be offended, and the moment passed. He needn't have bothered. He hadn't finished describing Bobby Robb's scar before the old man interrupted him.

'So that was his name, eh? Bobby Robb. We called him Crippen.' He put a hand over his mouth. 'You're not a relative, are you, son?'

Murray hesitated.

'His nephew.'

The pensioner held out his hand.

'In that case I'm sorry for your loss. I'm Wee Johnny.' They shook and the old one gave a smile that showed the full length of his dentures. 'I hope you didn't take offence at what I said there. We like a wee laugh and a joke in here. Don't we,

183

Lauren?'

The barmaid nodded. 'Aye, Johnny, laugh a minute in here.'

She slipped back to her sanctuary, leaving them alone in the empty bar.

Murray knew the answer, but he asked, 'Are you saying Bobby Robb's dead?'

'Christ, I'm no the one to break it to you, son, am I?'

The dentures disappeared behind a frown.

'Don't worry. We weren't close.'

He felt bereaved. Another chance of reaching out to Archie gone.

'That's something, anyway.' Johnny stared at him. 'Aye, now that I get a better look, I can see the resemblance. You've not got the scar, but you're like him round the eyes.'

'People always say that.'

Murray took an inch off his pint. There was no longer any point in hanging around.

'Three days earlier and you would have caught him.' Wee Johnny nodded towards a corner table. 'Could have sat there all night, except Lauren noticed he was still on his first pint when he should have been on his third and went to check on him. She's a good lassie at heart. Some reader, though.' He shouted through to the back room, 'I bet you'd have liked to get your hands on some of Crippen's books, eh, Lauren?' No reply came, and it seemed the old man didn't expect any because he continued, 'He had a whale of stuff, your uncle. A whale of stuff—the books—gee whiz.'

He shook his head in wonder at the size of Bobby Robb's library and sank the dregs of his half pint.

Murray put a hand in his pocket.

'Could you manage another?'

'That's good of you. I'll take a pint.' Johnny knocked back his whisky. 'And a wee malt of the month to chase it down, if it's no trouble.'

He rapped the counter with his stick and Lauren emerged wearily into the bar. Murray gave their order then asked Johnny, 'So how do you know about his book collection?'

It was Lauren who answered.

'Mr Robb rented a flat from my Uncle Arthur that manages this place. He told us about it.' She poured two pints of lager. 'I'm sorry for your loss.'

'Thanks.' Murray took his beer from her. 'So have you any idea what happened to his books?'

Lauren avoided his eyes.

'Uncle Arthur burned them. It took him all afternoon.'

'Aye, well, he agrees with me.' Wee Johnny beamed, enjoying the conversation. 'There's a time and a place for books.'

'He's a Nazi. One minute he's saying I can go through them and have my pick, the next he's splashing petrol all over the place. The neighbours weren't too happy when they saw the state he'd made of the drying green.' She reached up to the gantry and poured a measure of malt into a glass. 'He got a red face when Mr Robb's ex-wife turned up looking to collect his effects, though. I guess that'd be your aunty.'

'Ex-aunty.' Johnny took his nip from Lauren. 'He didn't even know the old boy was dead.'

Lauren's eyes widened.

'You do know your uncle's funeral's this afternoon?' She turned to Wee Johnny. 'You did

185

tell him?'

The old man put a hand protectively around his drinks, as if afraid they might be confiscated.

'I never thought.'

Lauren glanced at the five-minutes-fast clock above the bar.

'Seafield Crematorium. If you get a cab, you might just make it.'

Murray shoved some money on the bar and headed for the door. Behind him Wee Johnny said, 'Haud on while I finish these, son, and I'll hitch a ride with you.'

But Murray let the door swing shut. He headed back out into the murk of the alley, then down towards the station taxi rank, hoping to be in time to see Bobby Robb make the big fire.

Chapter Fifteen

Murray felt the taxi driver taking in his scuffed trainers and worn jeans and attempted a joke. 'My mother always said I'd be late for my own funeral.' He handed over a tenner. 'Keep the change.'

The driver rattled some coins onto the little tray set in the grille dividing them.

'There are times when it doesn't hurt to show some respect.'

He waited until Murray shut the door, then spun the cab round and away, a look of disgust pasted to his face. Murray pocketed his change. As insults went, 'keep your money' was a good one. But it lacked sting when the sum involved was fifty pence.

186

The crematorium looked like a solid place to transform flesh into dust. It had been built sometime in the 1930s, when white facades and art deco symmetry were in vogue. Five frosted glass windows flanked a door wide enough for a coffin and pall-bearers; a giant mouth bounded by milky eyes. There was something grimly cinematic about the whole arrangement; a sombre invitation to a show you might not want to see. Virginia creeper covered the building's front, a shaggy hairdo at odds with otherwise dignified features. The ivy seemed in bad taste to Murray, a graveyard escape reaching out its tendrils to the living, who had only come to bid goodbye.

A few mourners had gathered a short distance from the front door, waiting on the next event. The dark suits, black ties and cupped cigarettes made the men look like members of a pale-faced Mafia family. The women's mourning clothes were less assured, combinations of grey, navy and black, outfits pieced together with emphasis on colour rather than style, as if the occasion was unexpected and they had been forced to rifle their wardrobes for something suitable at the last moment, which Murray supposed they probably had.

The name *Robb* was on a little sign outside the chapel. He shouldered his rucksack, took a deep breath and climbed the entrance steps, feeling the waiting mourners' disinterested eyes on his back.

Inside it was strangely bright after the grey of the cemetery. He slipped quietly into the back row, his trainers silent against the polished oak floor. The minister was reciting a prayer, but the two pints he had sunk with Wee Johnny seemed suddenly to be working on him and Murray couldn't make out the words. He bowed his head, clasped his hands and focused on his interlocked fingers.

Here's the church, here's the steeple, look inside and there's all the people.

No one else had come to see Bobby Robb off. Murray glanced down the chapel, past the empty regiment of seats, to where the coffin still waited. Bobby was inside it, his scar grinning on into death, his secrets destined to be consigned to the fire with him.

It was too warm and there was a bad taste in his mouth. Murray was almost sure he could feel the grit of burnt cinders beneath the savour of stale malts. He wondered if the crematorium powered their heating from the bodies. It would make good sense, though he guessed it was an ecological triumph they might not want to advertise. The minister's words were familiar now.

> *Yea, though I walk through the valley of the*
> *   shadow of death,*
> *I will fear no evil: for thou art with me;*
> *Thy rod and thy staff they comfort me.*

Murray's head began to nod. He dug his knuckles into his forehead and blinked his eyes open.

> *Thou preparest a table before me in the*
> *   presence of mine enemies;*
> *Thou anointest my head with oil; my cup*
> *   runneth over.*

How much credence did he give to George

Meikle's theory? The bookfinder was sincere, but that didn't make him right. His story was based on a bad feeling he'd had under the influence forty years ago and a few unsubstantiated rumours. Odds were Bobby Robb was just another waster who'd grown into a lonely old man. There were enough of those in the city.

> *Surely goodness and mercy shall follow me all*
>   *the days of my life:*
> *And I will dwell in the house of the Lord*
>   *forever.*

The minister was asking him to rise now. Murray unclasped his hands as the organ croaked into a suitably sombre tune. Murray felt a weight of self-pity in his chest. Was this his 'Ghost of Christmas yet to come', a foretaste of his own funeral, the empty chairs and uninterested minister?

He stood up as the tasselled velvet curtain drew magically across the coffin, veiling it from view. A decision forced itself on him.

It was stupid to waste time on quarrels. He would phone Jack.

Down in the front row a short figure he hadn't noticed also got to her feet. Murray slipped from his place and silently left the chapel as the boxed remains of Bobby Robb slid into the furnace.

*   *   *

The waiting mourners' number had expanded while he'd been inside. Murray crossed the pathway and stood a little away from the main body of the group, distant enough not to be

189

accused of gate-crashing, but close enough to be mistaken for one of their number.

He'd only caught a glimpse of the back of the woman's head as she rose from her chair. If Bobby Robb was as bad as Meikle painted him, then odds were the lone mourner was some unfortunate soul Bobby had leeched onto, to look after him in his final years. But a scintilla of excitement had slid into his chest at the sight of her.

An elderly man in the waiting crowd gave Murray a quizzical look, as if trying to place him. Murray straightened his jacket, wishing he didn't look so scruffily conspicuous, then pulled his phone from his pocket and put it to his ear, the ideal alibi.

He called Jack on speed dial, but a robotic female voice primly told him the number was unavailable and cut the call without giving him the opportunity to leave a message. The woman emerged from the chapel and limped painfully down the stairs, resting her weight on a walking stick. She was shorter than he'd imagined. He supposed her height, combined with the chapel's high-backed chairs, had conspired to hide her from him. It certainly wasn't the sobriety of her outfit.

Bobby Robb's only mourner was dressed in a pale lilac trouser suit, with a pink scarf tied loosely at her neck. The colours should have clashed with her hair, but the ice-cream pallet cleverly set off its russet tones. It would only take a posy of flowers to make her look like a tastefully dressed, mature bride. Murray overheard an elderly female mourner whisper, in tones that seemed to hold an equal share of admiration and disapproval, 'The merry widow.'

He would have been inclined to agree, were it not for her tilting gait and grim expression; the kind of look a mother might adopt as she determined to switch off a suffering child's life-support.

Murray took his phone, lined it up as best he could without being obvious, and snapped a picture, hoping the result would fare better than his earlier attempts. His quarry laboured towards the car park, her right shoulder dipping a little with the strain of her limp. He followed her at a distance, hoping for another shot, wary of being spotted, but unsure why. After all, if his instinct about the mourner's identity was right, this might be the perfect opportunity to present himself. He could invite her for coffee somewhere smart—high tea at the George Hotel—and explain his project in full.

The woman stopped, adjusted her scarf and then turned to look back at the chapel, as if searching the sky for evidence that the deed was done. Now was his chance. Murray stepped purposefully forward, his feet crunching on the gravel.

Green eyes flecked with amber flickered towards him. Murray meant to continue on, extend his hand and offer his condolences, but he stalled. The woman's eyes glanced him up and down, then dismissed him. She turned, walked to a red Cherokee and got in, slamming the door.

Murray breathed out. He felt like a mouse that had frozen in the beam of a night owl's reconnaissance flight, only to be inexplicably spared. He watched as the woman he was almost sure was Christie Graves drove down towards the gates of the crematorium and away.

Chapter Sixteen

Somewhere above him Murray's father was smiling as he told Jack all about his two wee boys. Murray quickly surveyed the Fruitmarket Gallery's café and bookshop, and then asked a young attendant if Jack Watson was around.

'Jack who?'

The boy was heroin-chic pale, dressed in shrink-tight black jeans and a too-big studded belt. He glanced Murray up and down, then looked away, as if he had seen enough.

'Watson, he's one of your exhibitors.'

The boy pulled a leaflet wearily from the plastic holder on the wall beside him and flicked it open.

'Six o'clock.'

It had been a long day, punctuated by disappointment and cremation. Murray marshalled his patience.

'What happens at six o'clock?'

All the weary weight of time was in the boy's voice.

'Jack Watson's artist's talk.'

Murray wondered if the date of the talk had been stored somewhere in his unconscious, the better part of him making moves towards reconciliation his sour consciousness couldn't concede.

He glanced at his watch. There was an hour before Jack was due to speak. He wouldn't stay to hear him talk about how their father's illness had inspired his art—the very thought of it invoked a burr of impatience—but if he could catch him beforehand perhaps they could grab a pint together and patch things up.

'If you see him, will you tell him his brother's here, please?'

The boy leaned against the wall, his eyes trained on something beyond Murray's view.

'Sure.'

He made the prospect sound as likely as world peace.

*   *   *

The same Manga cartoons he and Jack had made fun of the last time they'd met still dominated the first room of the ground-floor gallery. The colours were still bubblegum bright, the bug-eyed girl still surprised by the spotty dog's attentions. But now their devastated backgrounds seemed to dominate the image. He felt a sudden kinship with the citizens of Nagasaki who had crawled from the matchstick remains of their homes to find their city gone. Did they wake believing themselves dead? And when they realised the truth, how many committed suicide and regained blessed oblivion?

He had been wrong to laugh. Murray wasn't sure if the artist was suggesting the H-bomb had led to a coarsening of culture, or that cartoons and pornography were destructive forces on society, but he was sure they viewed the world as a lost cause.

'A cesspool.'

The words came out in a whisper, but he

193

glanced round guiltily as he made his way to Cressida Reeves' exhibition space, relieved there had been no one there to overhear him.

Perhaps it was the dust of Seafield cemetery still clinging to his soles that made the dim-lit room seem like a tomb. Or maybe it was the hundreds of faces staring from the walls, like supplications for healing from a saint who needed to be reminded what the sufferer looked like before intervening.

Murray began at what he assumed was the beginning: a cluster of baby photographs, children with cleft palates smiling delightedly for the camera. Some had clearly been taken in hospital, clinical assessments prior to operations, he supposed. But most were the usual bare-bum-on-fluffy-rug style of baby portrait. The distorted grins shone cheerfully beneath bright, fun-filled eyes. Murray felt ashamed by his own quick stab of revulsion at the warped lips and wet gums.

The next grouping was composed of children's birthday parties. There was no sign of the cleft palates now. Murray wondered if they were the same subjects post-surgery, but other visitors entered the gallery and he resisted the temptation to scrutinise the beaming faces too closely.

The sets of photos continued through children's calendar days: the opening of Christmas presents, first day of school, teenage friends. The samples were becoming smaller, some of the faces beginning to repeat. Murray returned to the information board he'd snubbed on the way in.

Cressida Reeves' work is concerned with anonymity, identity and rites of passage. In her installation, *Now You See Me*, commissioned by the Fruitmarket Gallery, Reeves begins by inserting a baby photograph of herself into an anonymous sample of one hundred children also born with a cleft palate or 'hare lip'. The condition is absent from succeeding groupings, reflecting the ease with which it is corrected. Each subsequent set relates a shared experience; birthday parties, Christmas mornings, first day at school, teenage discos, first love, college etc. Reeves includes increasing numbers of images of her friends and family in each set, until she is no longer an anonymous disfigured child surrounded by other equally anonymous infants, but an adult surrounded by people she has chosen to know.

He went back to the birthday photos, wondering if he could identify Cressida in amongst the excited children. The images were simple, snaps executed with no great skill, meaningless beyond their family group. But they might be amongst the first possessions people grabbed if their house were burning, the belongings they mourned most in a flood.

The sitting room wallpaper in his childhood home had been bold and brown, like the wallpaper on the photo he was looking at now. He remembered some of the toys the children were playing with too. A Christmas morning shot showed a little boy stripping the wrapping from a Transformer Jack had coveted. A toddler in kung-fu pyjamas posed military-style with a light sabre.

Murray remembered him and Jack jumping around their shared bedroom, swinging the glowing, plastic sticks, battling for the right to be Han Solo. He would remind Jack of the light sabres later. And maybe sometime much later they would sort through some photos together. It was time.

Murray skipped the first days at school, and the school-uniformed shots that followed, and went directly to the teenage years. Now he could spot Cressida amongst the crowding faces. The ribbons coiled in her long hair, and the black fedora that topped the arrangement, declared her a fan of Boy George. That made her younger than Murray, but only by a few years.

He could see the tiny scar, faintly visible beneath the thick make-up. It had very likely tormented her through her teens, but it was already adding character to features that might otherwise have been too sweet for substance. How would it feel to kiss her there, on the slight pucker above her top lip? He walked swiftly to the college shots that comprised the next section, feeling ashamed of the sudden spark of desire that had transferred itself from grown-up Cressida to her teenage counterpart.

The art school crowd that she'd hung around with later looked edgier and more fashion-conscious than he supposed he and his university friends had, but Murray could still relate to the camaraderie in the images. He was searching for his brother's face too now, and found him, beer bottle tilted to his mouth, hair gelled into a DA, the collar of his leather jacket turned up.

Murray smiled, recalling his father's outrage

when Jack had borrowed his car and driven it over the squeaky new leather jacket to scuff it up. It had looked good when he'd finished, though, a montage of monkeys, skulls and roses painted in red and black over the grazed surface.

They hadn't seen much of each other in those days, each forging their own way, occasionally meeting back at their dad's, going for a beer when their paths crossed, but no more than that. The closeness had returned later.

Jack appeared again, looking very young, in a group shot with others from his class. A youth with a green Mohican who Murray vaguely remembered stood on Jack's right side, Cressida on his other, her arm around his waist, hugging him close. She too looked much younger, her hair back-combed into a massive halo, her black leggings tucked into Doc Marten boots in a style that had always reminded him of Max Wall. She'd looked better on the night of the opening, older but more sophisticated, assured.

He scanned the rest of the set, realising that though the fashions in the photographs might vary, these records of college experience were as similar to each other as the childhood parties had been; as if the beer-drinking, lamppost-climbing, face-pulling and kissing had also been organised with tradition in mind.

He checked his watch. Five-thirty. Maybe he should step out and see if Jack had arrived. Murray turned to go, but something snagged on the edge of his vision and he returned to the display. It would have been easy to miss, and yet he wondered how he could ever have overlooked it: a black and white photo-booth strip. The one-after-the-other shots managed to both capture and animate the moment when his brother and Cressida turned towards each other laughing, touched lips, tongues, and then broke away, still laughing.

*   *   *

He paused for a moment in the next room, letting his eyes rest on Nagasaki. He wondered if Lyn had seen the photos, remembered her strained look on the exhibition's opening night, her curtness in the Burger King when he asked if she knew Cressida. Exploiting a memory that should have been kept private was exactly what he had accused Jack of doing. He wondered if his brother minded, and realised that he hoped he did.

*   *   *

Murray was almost in the street before he become conscious that the young gallery attendant had said something as he passed. He retraced his steps and the boy repeated it.

'Your brother's in the café.'

'Cheers.'

His voice was harsh with ill-use and the strains of the day, but it seemed he'd unintentionally hit on the right note because the young man's belligerence was replaced by solicitude.

'I tried to tell Jack you were here, but he and his girlfriend went past before I could catch them.'

Murray had an urge to enquire if his arse was superglued to the seat, but he ignored it and hurried through to the café, relieved to have the opportunity to see Lyn as well before Jack's show got on the road.

*   *   *

The café was busy. Murray scanned the room, unable to spot Jack and Lyn amongst the close-packed tables. Then suddenly it was as if the photo-booth pictures had come to life.

Jack and Cressida were at a corner table by the window, kissing.

'Jesus.'

Murray stepped forward unsure of what he was going to say.

There was nothing he could say.

A waitress approached, menu in hand, and he turned to leave, desperate to escape before they saw him. He felt his rucksack hit the counter, heard the waitress's gasp and the echoing shatter of glass against concrete, loud as sudden gunshot. Water flashed across the floor as a massive arrangement of Stargazer lilies hit the deck.

Cressida and Jack broke their clinch, principals in a brilliantly choreographed move that had every head turning in perfect unison towards the smash. Murray saw his brother get to his feet, heard the hum of conversation build from the silent instant that had followed. He turned and walked from the building, leaving a trail of wet footprints behind him, like a pathway to disaster.

*   *   *

'Murray, wait.'

His brother's boots sounded loud on the

pavement. Who the fuck wore segs in their shoes? It was another affectation, part of the all-surface-no-substance shit that defined Jack these days.

'Wait.'

'Get to fuck.'

Murray caught the curious stares of the schoolchildren waiting to enter the Edinburgh Dungeons. The bored-looking ghost at the door said, 'Mind your language or it's the bloody stocks for you.' And the queue giggled beneath their teacher's disapproving gaze.

Murray felt a hand on his shoulder and turned, his fists balled.

'Piss off, Jack.'

'Wait a second, will you?'

Jack's shirt had escaped his trousers. He was breathing heavily and there was a smudge of Cressida's lipstick on his upper lip. One of the waiting children opened a bag of sweets and passed out an allotted ration to his friends, ready to enjoy the show.

Murray turned the corner down onto Waverley Bridge, towards Princes Street.

'Why? Are you going to tell me things aren't what they seem?'

Jack caught his arm, holding him there. He looked Murray in the eyes, no longer as young as he'd been in Cressida's photographs, but just as handsome. More handsome, perhaps. The thought surprised Murray: he had never thought of his brother as good-looking before.

'No, things are exactly as they seem.'

It was almost as much of a shock as seeing them together. The anger left him for a moment and he asked, 'Does Lyn know?'

'Not yet.'

Jack wiped a hand across his face. He saw the red lipstick on his fingers, took a hanky from his pocket and rubbed at his mouth.

'What a fucking mess.'

He looked at the red stains again, then at Murray, and it wasn't clear whether he meant his lipstick-smeared face, or the state of his love life.

'Are you going to tell her?'

'Yes.'

'For Christ's sake, Jack.'

'I'm in love with Cressida.'

'Just like that? After twelve years, you've suddenly found someone else?'

'We knew each other before.'

'So I saw, but time's moved on.'

Murray pulled free from his brother's grip. Jack raised his hand as if to snare him again, and then let it fall.

'Life's too short not to live it, Murray. You should know that.'

A group of youths passed them on the pavement. One of them shouted, 'Why don't you kiss and make up?' and his companions laughed. Murray felt the urge to lay into them with his fists, land a good few punches before they beat him senseless. Instead he kept his voice low and asked, 'What about Lyn?'

'I'll make sure Lyn's okay. She'll get over it. She's a survivor.'

Murray shook his head.

'You're a prick, Jack.'

He turned his back on his brother and walked away. This time no one followed him.

Part Two

The Island of Lismore

Chapter Seventeen

It was a while since Murray had driven. The winding road round Loch Lomond was testing and he arrived in Oban with a sense of relief. The car windscreen started to spot with rain as he drove down into the town. There was a glimpse of sunlight behind the wind-harried clouds moving above the sea, but he knew from experience that it was no guarantee blue skies would follow.

Murray followed the signs for the ferry terminus, then found the Lismore dock and parked at the end of the short queue of waiting vehicles on the quayside. The boat was due in fifteen minutes, but there was no sign of it on the grey waters beyond. He turned off the engine, closed his eyes and tried to empty his mind.

He was woken by the lorry in front rumbling into life. The small ferry had docked and the traffic from the island disembarked. Murray turned the key in his ignition, waiting until the lorry driver had reversed the large vehicle laden with building supplies up a tiny ramp and onto the deck. He edged his own car slowly backwards. The ferryman raised his hand in the rear-view mirror and the engine stalled. Murray scrolled the window down as the man came towards him, his face stern.

'There's another sailing at four.'

Murray looked down at the ferry. There were two cars, the building lorry and a post van already sitting on its deck. An empty spot seemed to beckon from beside the van.

'What about the space on the right?'

The ferryman adjusted his cap. 'Four o'clock.' He walked back down the slipway and onto the deck. Murray watched as the ramp was raised and the boat chugged surely out to sea.

An old man standing smoking by the quayside flicked his dout into the sea, strolled over and leaned companionably against the car roof.

'You'd never mistake him for a sunbeam, eh?'

Murray felt his face warm.

'What's his problem?'

'If you're enquiring about his temperament, I'd say an undemonstrative father combined with overexposure to the United Free Church and a lack of serotonin. But if you're asking why he didn't let you board, my guess would be the building lorry brought them up to weight. Away over to the ticket office and get booked on the four o'clock. The island's not going anywhere.'

The stranger slapped the car roof and walked on.

* * *

The booking clerk grinned cheerily when he asked for a ticket to Lismore.

'Tired of life?'

Murray tried to return his smile, but the clerk grew suddenly serious and issued the ticket without further banter.

There were five hours to kill. He phoned the tourist board and booked himself into a B&B on the island, then abandoned the car in the long-term car park and took a walk along the front. All the seagulls hadn't relocated to Glasgow to live off abandoned Chinese carry-outs and dead rats after all. Their country cousins ack-acked machine-gun rattles across the bay as they circled the fishing boats, hovering down from time to time to pick at delicacies the fishermen had eschewed. The scent of brine was sharp in his nostrils and beneath it a bitter smell of decaying seaweed. There was a cold wind blowing in from the sea, carrying a fine spray that might have been rain or spume, as if underlining his ill-preparedness.

Murray went into an outdoors shop and bought a woollen hat, a waterproof jacket, three tartan shirts in a warm, fuzzy fabric, three pairs of heavy socks and a pair of walking boots the salesman claimed would outlive them both. He changed in the shop's tiny dressing room and regarded himself in the mirror. He looked like an older, more leisured version of himself; or maybe a down-and-out, scrubbed up by social services and equipped for a few more months of pavement life.

The season must surely have been drawing to a close, but the streets were busy with tourists drawn to the town from the outlying countryside, fresh fodder for the Clan Kitchen and the Edinburgh Woollen Mill. He passed a middle-aged couple trailing a pair of disconsolate teenage boys. He and Jack had come here with their father years ago, on their way to somewhere else. He couldn't remember much about it.

He went into a café that smelt of cheap air-freshener infused with accents of hot lard and Sarson's vinegar. The room was homely but shabby, as if the proprietor had rejected trade fittings in favour of domestic furnishings not up to the job. The walls were papered with stripes and fleur-de-lis, divided by a floral border, the carpet decorated in a pattern of autumn leaves, not busy enough to camouflage spills and stains. A splotch of something that might have been lentil soup had crusted over the handwritten menu, as if illustrating the quality of the fare on offer. After a while an elderly waitress appeared and Murray ordered fish and chips and a cup of tea.

He was wondering whether his laptop was safe in the boot of the car or if he should nip back and collect it, when his phone rang. Lyn's name flashed on the display.

The waitress placed his cutlery and a plate of bread spread with margarine in front of him.

'Are you not going to answer that?'

Murray wanted to tell her to mind her own business, but anecdotes from students with part-time waiting jobs had taught him never to piss-off someone with access to his food.

'I'll call back later.'

She went over to the counter and returned with his tea.

'Ignoring it won't make things better.'

He took a bite of the tasteless bread, wondering if everyone in Oban considered themselves equipped to advise strangers. The phone burred back into life, Lyn's name flashing again, like a warning signal on its tiny screen.

He sighed and pressed *Talk*.

'Murray?'

'Hi. Everything okay?'

'Yes.' Lyn's voice was wary. 'Why do you ask?'

'You don't normally call me.'

'I guess not.' She didn't sound convinced. 'I was phoning to check if you'd seen Jack.'

He thought about lying, but the truth seemed

easier, up to a point.

'Briefly, before his lecture.'

'So you're talking?'

'Not really.'

'You'll have to make it up sometime.'

'Maybe.'

Silence hung on the line. She said, 'He didn't come home last night.'

Murray internally cursed his brother for being such a bastard, and himself for answering the call.

'He probably ran into some mates and went for a drink. You know Jack.'

'He's a workaholic. He doesn't have any mates.'

Murray had the urge to tell Lyn that she was wrong, his brother had one, very special, old friend. But instead he said, 'Either way, he's a big boy. I'm sure he'll turn up.'

'I'm worried. Your dad's car's gone. It was parked outside when I started shift last night.'

'Ah.' He hadn't meant to frighten her, only to get back at his brother. 'I took it.'

'Well seen you're related, you're as bad as each other. Does Jack know?'

'He will, when you tell him.'

'You tell him.' The relief that had sounded in her voice at the news of the car was hardening into anger. 'I've been up all night at the hostel. I don't think I could manage any more drama. Where are you, anyway?'

'Oban.'

'Of course, the gateway to the islands.'

'Armpit of the universe.'

'Harsh.'

'You're telling me.'

The waitress squeezed his shoulder as she slid

his order in front of him.

Lyn said, 'It sounds noisy there.'

'Just my lunch arriving.' The fish and chips steamed fragrantly on the plate before him, but something in her voice made him say, 'I'm not really hungry, just killing time.'

'You need to eat.'

He wondered why women wanted either to look after him, or fuck him then kick him out the door. There was a time when he could have asked Lyn.

'I wanted to ask you something. Did you ever come across an old guy with an amazing scar at your drop-in centre?'

'Does the Pope shit in the woods?'

It was an old joke and he laughed to show her that nothing had changed, though he suspected they both knew it had.

'I've got a particular one in mind. Bobby Robb. He had a Mr Happy smile carved across one side of his face.'

'Glasgow smiles better.' This time neither of them laughed. 'The name doesn't mean anything to me, but then a lot of them don't go by their given name. I could ask around, if you want.'

'I'd appreciate it.'

'On one condition.'

'What?'

He thought it must be something to do with his brother. The waitress glanced in his direction, as if alerted to potential trouble by the wariness in his voice. Lyn said, 'You remember Frankie?'

Murray smiled, relieved, and saw the waitress resume her conversation with the fish-fryer. He dropped his voice.

210

'Lewis Hamilton in a wheelchair?'

'Yes. Frank's really trying to sort himself out. He's hoping to do an access course at Telford College, then apply for uni.'

'That's beyond my powers.'

'I'm not stupid, Murray.' The impatience was back. 'I'm not asking you to shoo him in, I just meant you could maybe talk to him, tell him how to go about things. Frankie's at a crossroads. He wants to change his life, but it'd still be easier for him to slide back into old ways. If he does, he'll be writing his own death sentence.'

Murray doubted Frankie's educational urges were anything more than a ruse to ease Lyn into his orthopaedic bed, but he put a smile into his voice.

'How can I refuse? Let's make a date when I get back.'

'Thanks, Murray.' Lyn had regained her usual warmth. He wondered if she would ever want to see him again, after Jack had told her his news. She asked, 'So tell me about your mystery man.'

'There's not much to go on. He was an associate of Archie's, which suggests he was around the fringes of the Edinburgh literary scene in the seventies. He left town for quite a while and only came back recently. He might also have been known as Crippen.'

Lyn gave a small snort of amusement.

'Crippens are like Jims and Joes in my business, ten a penny. Do you want to interview him for your book?'

'Yes, but I'm not willing to travel the distance.'

'So you know where he is?'

'Not exactly. He's recently deceased.'

211

'That's not funny, Murray. I've been phoning the hospitals all morning looking for your brother.'

He said, 'You're too good for him.' And meant it, but he promised to get in touch if Jack rang. He reckoned it wasn't a pledge he'd be forced to keep.

Murray hung up and put a chip into his mouth. It was cold and tasted of the cheap fat it had been cooked in. He pushed the plate aside.

He'd emailed Audrey Garrett the photo he'd snapped of Bobby Robb's lone mourner late the previous night; now he found her number and pressed *Call*. The line rang out, and then Audrey's voice said, *Hi, you've reached the answering service of Audrey and Lewis. We're having too much fun to come to the phone right now, but leave a message after the beep and . . .*'Hi!'

She sounded out of breath and Murray wondered if she had been expecting a call. The thought made him awkward and he stuttered slightly as he spoke.

'Hi, Audrey, sorry to interrupt you. It's Murray Watson here.'

'Ah, yes, Murray.' There was no trace of antipodean accent in her telephone voice, but he thought he could detect a note of caution beneath her clear tones.

'I was wondering if you got my email?'

'Hang on.'

He heard the sound of her feet against the bare floorboards and pictured her walking through the chaotic sitting room to the tranquillity of her office. He asked, 'How are you?' but perhaps the phone was away from her ear, because she made no reply. Instead the receiver clunked onto a hard surface and he heard the singsong jingle as the computer came to life.

'Right.' Audrey picked up the phone. 'I've got it in front of me.' She read his message out loud. '"Dear Audrey, this may seem like an odd request, but I have attached a rather poor photograph of a woman I think may be Christie Graves to this message. Would you mind having a look and letting me know if it's her, please? I'm going to be on the road for a while, so will give you a call sometime over the next couple of days. Best wishes, Murray Watson." This is all rather cloak and dagger.'

'I suppose it is.'

There was another pause. In his mind's eye he saw Audrey at her desk, dressed in the same casual clothes she'd worn the evening they met. Then she came back on the line, her voice brisk and the vision was dispelled.

'Well, I don't think David Bailey has anything to worry about.'

'Photography isn't one of my talents.'

It could have been a cue for Audrey to mention what his talents included, but her voice remained businesslike.

'Yes, that's her. Where was it taken?'

'The funeral of one of Archie's old friends.'

'Another funeral? She seems to make a habit of them.'

'I guess people begin to at her age.'

'Perhaps. Why didn't you approach her?'

'I should have, but I wasn't sure if I'd got the right person, and it didn't seem like the ideal moment.'

The excuse sounded lame to his ears, but Audrey said, 'No, I can see that.'

Encouraged, he asked, 'How's Lewis?'

The memory of the small boy's stare had stayed with him. But perhaps Audrey thought he was trying to ingratiate himself, because her response was cool.

'Fine. We were just heading out.'

He wanted to ask where they were going, wanted her to ask him why he was on the road, but instead said, 'I won't keep you then.'

Her goodbye sounded final.

Murray sat for a moment, holding the still-warm mobile phone in his hand, then pulled his plate towards him and splattered it with tomato ketchup. He'd forgotten to shake the bottle and a clear liquid that put him in mind of blood plasma ran onto his food before the red stuff dripped out. He dunked a chip in it anyway and put it in his mouth. The taste of sugar and cold potato made him want to spit. He swallowed it down and pushed the plate aside, just as the waitress placed his bill on the table.

She looked at his uneaten meal.

'What was wrong with it?'

'Nothing, I let it get cold.'

Murray busied himself with his wallet, but perhaps his face betrayed him yet again, because the woman put her hand back on his shoulder and gave it another squeeze.

'Plenty more fish in the sea.' She looked at the untouched battered cod on his plate and laughed, 'It's true. No quota on how many you can catch in your net either'. She caught the eye of the fish-fryer and went lyrical for his benefit. 'It's full of promise for a lad like you. Just you remember that.'

Chapter Eighteen

The women in the tourist board had told him his B&B was about twenty minutes from Achnacroish pier, where the ferry docked. Murray drove slowly along the one-track road that climbed away from the bay, the sea receding in the rear-view mirror as he travelled inland, the mountains ahead in the distance, getting no closer.

The crossing had been smooth, but a faint nausea stirred in the depths of his stomach, as if his own tides had been disturbed. The sky was a palate of grey, iron smudges shifting against gunmetal. The wind was getting up, but there was still a possibility the grey skies might yet blow beyond the island, taking their cargo of rain with them.

Sheep grazed stoically in the fields beyond, their fleeces grey and shit-stained, ruffled by the same wind that bent the tall grasses edging the roadside. He'd left the village behind at the pier, but now and again he would pass a cottage built out of stone as grey and uncompromising as the sky. He slowed to take a corner and saw two children staring at him, hand in hand from the edge of the road, their hair matted, faces bronzed by sun and dirt. They looked like the kind of feral kids that might commune with faeries, and he was almost surprised to notice their stout Wellington boots. Murray raised a hand in hallo and was met with incurious stares.

A few drops of rain smeared the windscreen, but there was no need for the wipers yet. The

215

radio had died, the signal left behind on the mainland. He turned on the CD player and Johnny Cash croaked into 'I've Been Everywhere'.

Murray had a sudden memory of his father singing the song in the kitchen one evening as he dried the dishes, his father's inflections the same as Cash's, but his words slower, his voice leaving the tune behind on his adapted chorus, *I've been to Fraserburgh, Peterburgh, Bridge of Weir, very queer. Dunoon, whit a toon, Aberdeen where folks are mean. I've been everywhere, I've been everywhere.*

Murray turned the music off and, as if on cue, saw the sign for his B&B swinging bleakly at the edge of the road.

*   *   *

He offered to pay in advance, but Mrs Dunn the landlady laughed.

'It's all right, son, I trust you. Anyway, you'd not get far if you tried to do a runner. Peter wouldn't let you on the ferry.'

She was a pensioner of a type he thought HRT and aqua-aerobics had rendered redundant: broad-beamed, big-busted and solid-corseted, dressed in a heather-coloured two-piece too stiff to be comfortable. Her hair looked freshly set, a tinge of blue livening the pewter. He hoped it hadn't been done for his benefit. He felt as morose as Peter, the sullen ferryman, guardian of the island.

Mrs Dunn got him to sign the visitors' book, and then started up the small staircase.

'Your room's up here.'

He followed her to the tiny landing, careful not

to knock his rucksack against the photographs of long-grown-up children lining the walls. The smell of damp reminded him of his father's house towards the end, before he and Jack had agreed a care home was the only option.

'You're on the left. The bathroom's in the middle and I'm on the right.'

He had a vague sense that he should say something to assure her he was no madman come from the mainland with mayhem and pensioner murder on his mind. But the old lady was ahead of him, pushing open the bedroom door as if there was nothing left to be feared in the world.

The little room was suffused with the sickly glow of a Disney sunset, its small twin beds draped in shiny satin spreads that almost, but not quite, matched the princess-pink walls, the rosebud-sprigged carpet and blushing curtains. A portable TV inscribed with a Barbie logo sat in one corner next to a towel rail decked with rosy towels.

'Well?'

It took Murray a second to realise she was awaiting his verdict. He tried to put some warmth into his voice.

'Very nice, thanks.'

Mrs Dunn nodded gravely, as if agreeing with him on an important point of scripture, and then asked, 'What time do you want your dinner?'

The journey still sat uneasily in his stomach.

'Don't go to any trouble, I'll get something in the town.'

The old woman snorted.

'There's no town, son. No café, no pub, come to that. It's my cooking or nothing.'

The small room seemed to do a quick pulse as

the house took an inward breath, closing around him. He drew in the rose-tinted air, silently blessing the impulse that had sent him into an Oban off-licence for a bottle of whisky.

'What about seven?'

'Seven's fine.'

Murray said, 'I'll look forward to it.'

But he mustn't have sounded convincing because Mrs Dunn added, 'Don't worry. It's a while since I poisoned anyone', and shut the door smartly behind her.

Murray sat on the bed nearest the door, wondering again at his talent for alienating every woman he met. Maybe it was losing their mother early that had done it, though Jack had always managed to use the motherless-boy stuff to good effect.

Murray slid his computer from his rucksack and switched it on, vaguely hoping a wireless signal would appear on the screen. It didn't.

No café, no pub.

The pink room took another inward pulse. He'd imagined a tourist brochure cliché, a leather armchair pulled close to a crackling fire, a crystal glass of malt in easy reach as he worked on his opus.

The colour of the room was surely irrelevant. He needed to make progress, to start writing, continue with the research, sure, but move on to the text, begin ordering his thoughts before they spiralled out of reach.

He still knew next to nothing about Archie's childhood, had got ensnared instead in the episodes leading to his death. He could begin with the end, of course; have the poet's head dip beneath the waves, the fronds of his long hair floating free in the water, air bubbles nestling in his beard, lips parting as he welcomed oncoming peace.

Murray took off his shoes and went into the small bathroom on the landing. He had to rid himself of this Hollywood vision. Drowning would be no better than other deaths. Painful and nasty, with shit and vomit clouding the last moments, a desperate clinging to a life already lost.

The smell of damp was more intense here. The shower was hemmed in a tiny, plastic cubicle sealed with a concertina door. He wondered if it leaked, wondered if he would be able to wash in the small space without breaking anything. The thought made him realise he'd forgotten to pack any soap. Maybe there was a local shop where he could buy some (he hoped to God it was licensed), otherwise he'd be forced to lather himself from the same bar that had slid around his host's aged body. The disgust the thought brought with it made him feel guilty and he washed his face in the sink, avoiding his reflection in the mirror.

Back in his room he unpacked the box folder that held his notes. Here were his analyses of Lunan's poems (these, at least, he could be confident of), some notes on suicides he'd managed to glean from Dr Garrett's research, his interviews with Audrey, Meikle and Professor James, each neatly transcribed and assigned its own plastic envelope. He laid them across the spare bed, mourning the bedroom's lack of a desk.

So far his work had amounted to little. Maybe Fergus Baine had been right and he should limit himself to a discussion of the poetry, rather than the man. After all, that was what counted, wasn't it?

He picked James's folder from the pile. In retrospect, he was surprised the professor hadn't raised the same objections as Fergus. Murray remembered James being close to fanatical on the importance of divorcing writers' lives from their work.

Reductive, simplistic, crude and lacking in analysis!

He could still conjure the sound of ripping paper that had shocked the tutorial room as James tore a student's essay concentrating on Milton's blindness to the detriment of his poetry both verbally and physically to shreds. But the projected biography of Lunan had raised no barbed comments. Despite the ready excuses offered by retirement and failing health, James had welcomed Murray, granted him hours from the depleted bank of time reserved for his own researches. The professor might simply have changed his opinion on the significance artists' lives had on their art, or been motivated by a sense of collegiate duty; but holding the folder in his hand, Murray was struck again by a suspicion that the old man hadn't been as forthcoming as he might have.

Maybe he had simply asked the wrong questions. There was no obligation to help those too stupid or lazy to help themselves, and James had always been impatient of anyone whose standards or intelligence didn't match his own. The snowstorm of tattered pages he'd scattered into the bin before the author of the Milton essay's less-than-dry eyes had shown that.

220

Murray slid the transcript from its folder, feeling again a sense of something unspoken. He took his pencil and put a star next to something James had said: *those of us who were left could have served his poetry better.*

Perhaps it was guilt at an unfulfilled obligation to posterity that had made the old man reluctant to explore the intersection of his and Archie's past—especially now he was facing his own death, the prospect of his own un-assured legacy.

Murray drew a squiggle through the star. It was important not to give too much weight to words spoken casually.

You have to remember it was a long time ago, and we were privileged to be at the birth of many remarkable pieces of work.

The professor was realistic. He knew the limitations of individuals against the weight of literature and history. He thought back to James's overstuffed, abortively-feminine room and groaned. The old man's health might be failing, but at least he had space to think and write. Murray lay back on the bed, put the professor's interview over his face and closed his eyes.

He was woken by the landlady's sharpening voice at the door.

'Mr Watson, your dinner's waiting.'

Murray sat up, like Dracula risen from the dead.

He would phone James and ask if he knew Bobby Robb, and perhaps while he was answering that question, the questions unasked would also slip into place.

*   *   *

221

There was no phone signal to be had in his room, or at the melamine dining table where his dinner waited, a slight skin forming over the brown stuff he supposed was gravy. It was a temptation to take his mobile straight out into the evening, but manners prevailed and he managed to work his way through a once-frozen chicken pie, tinned carrots and potatoes followed by half a tin of peaches topped with cream from a can. It was the best meal he'd had in a while, and he said so to Mrs Dunn, before pulling on his new waterproof jacket and stepping out into the bluster of the fading day.

Murray turned his back on the cottage and continued along the road that had brought him there. The bars on his phone remained stubbornly absent. He saw a sign marked *Broch*, and took the right turn its arrow instructed, into a stony road less finished than the last. It felt good to have a destination, even though he wasn't sure what a broch was.

Professor James had known Lunan the man and the poet. He had been there at the birth of his sole collection, and though he'd not been present when the poet died, he had been close enough to go to the wake. If Christie insisted on keeping her silence, James might turn out to be the closest approximation of an eye witness available.

A small house appeared on his right, a square of scrubby grass in front of it, fenced off against the sheep. A toy tractor lay abandoned on its side beside the gate. Murray supposed that if you could stand the weather, this might not be such a bad place to raise a family. He'd assumed Archie and

Christie were after a new centre for poetry and debauch, but perhaps they'd been hoping to put all that behind them, chasing 'the good life' on some hippy self-sufficiency kick. After all, for Lunan it had been some kind of a coming home.

The light was beginning to fade. He glanced at his phone. If he didn't get a signal soon he would walk back to the car, drive down to the pier and try there.

Years ago, when he was working on his PhD, he'd gone out with a girl who studied archaeology. Angela. He'd fallen for her pale skin and red hair, would have been happy to spend all their free time together in bed, but their main recreation had been hill-walking to ancient sites. Angela had wanted to get engaged. He'd considered it, spent hours working out the pros and cons, and then, when the cons had won, broken up with her. He'd not seen Angela for years, hadn't thought about her in a while. She was one of the crossroads in his life, a path he might have taken.

There was some sort of structure up on the rise beyond, or was it an outcrop of rocks? It was hard to be sure. He left the road and began to climb. The wind was mounting now, the ground soft beneath his feet.

As he got closer he could see that the structure was the remnants of a circular drystane dyke. Some sheep sheltering in its lea startled at his approach and rushed away with unwise haste, fat ladies running downhill in high heels. He halted and let them pass, the wind tearing at his face, feared that if he moved on he'd inadvertently round them over some unseen cliff.

Angela had probably told him what a broch was

at some point. A fort, he supposed, or maybe a large tomb. He walked to where the wall had collapsed and peered into its centre, half-expecting to see the usual detritus that clogged lonely shelters: drained half-bottles of spirits, used condoms and dented beer cans. The interior dropped gently down into a slow dip, like a giant cauldron. Nothing except sheep shit sullied it.

Murray could feel the sense of being observed that had always infected him on his walks with Angela. 'City-dwellers' paranoia,' she'd called it. But at least in the city someone would hear you scream. The sight of a few discarded johnnies would have been reassuring, a sign of life.

He looked back the way he had come. Now that he was at the top of the hill, he could see the day had reached the far side of dusk. The light was still with him, but he wasn't sure how long it would last. It might be wiser to turn back while visibility was good, rather than risk a twisted ankle on the way down. Murray took his mobile from his pocket and was rewarded by three bars. He hunkered down in the shelter left by the sheep and found Professor James's number.

He'd expected the phone to ring for a long time, but James answered on the second peal.

'Ah, yes, I meant to ask if you would remember to pick up a packet of those fig biscuits, please, Helen. Iris likes them with her tea and I suspect the ones in the cupboard might be a little soft.'

Murray coughed, 'I'm sorry to interrupt, Professor James . . .'

'Who is this?'

'Murray. Dr Watson.'

He felt like an unsuspecting caller stumbling on

a conversation on the party line, but the professor seemed unfazed.

'I wondered when you would phone. Are you on your way round?'

'No, I'm afraid not.'

'I thought you were my daughter Helen.'

The old man sounder frailer than he had appeared the week before and a vague note that might have been confusion had entered his voice.

'Would you like me to ring back later?'

'No, best to get me while I'm still here.'

Murray knew better than to ask where the professor was going.

'A name has come up. I wondered if it meant anything to you. Bobby Robb. He had a distinctive scar . . .'

'Yes, I knew him.' James's tone became firmer, as if he were on safe ground now the conversation had shifted to the past. 'He wasn't a regular, and when he did attend his work was derivative and confused.'

The professor's manner was dismissive, as if Robb wasn't worth discussing.

'One of Archie Lunan's friends said he blamed Robb for Archie's premature death.'

'I'm afraid that would be beyond my realm of knowledge.'

The statement was like a full-stop at the end of a sentence.

'Was he close to Archie?'

'His work wasn't even in the same stratosphere.'

'I meant emotionally.'

'Dr Watson, are you in the habit of monitoring your students' emotional entanglements?'

225

'No.'

'Then why might you think I would be?'

'Professor James, I got the impression that you expected me to call at some point. Who did you think I was going to ask you about?'

The line went dead and for a moment Murray thought the professor was going to tell him to get back to him when he had completed his research. But then the old man sighed and said, 'Your nemesis, of course. Professor Fergus Baine.'

'My nemesis?'

'I had a feeling you two were at odds.'

The wind blasted at Murray's mobile phone. He wondered if Professor James could hear the sheep calling to each other in the background. They might be stupid, but at least they managed to live together in harmony.

'Not as far as I'm aware.'

'I must have misunderstood. Where are you? It sounds like you're calling from inside the drum of a washing machine.'

'I'm in Lismore. It's a bit blowy, there's not much cover.'

'Have you seen Christie Graves?'

'Not yet.' The wind forced Murray to raise his voice. He already regretted walking up the hill instead of searching for a nice warm telephone box. 'Why did you think I'd want to talk about Fergus?'

'I thought your generation eschewed researchers, Dr Watson? Surely you don't want me to do your job for you?'

Murray wondered if the old man was trying to provoke him away from the subject.

'I've already spoken to Fergus about Lunan. He

226

gave the impression they weren't acquainted, though he did mention they'd met once, at a poetry reading. He said Archie was drunk.'

'I'm afraid Professor Baine may have been rather economical with the truth. He and Lunan were well acquainted. They were both key parts of my little group.'

An ache nagged at his left leg. Murray shifted against the wall, unable to make sense of what James was telling him.

'He never mentioned it.'

'I'm surprised.' James sounded anything but. 'Maybe he chose to forget. Clever men are sometimes reluctant to remember fields in which they didn't shine.'

'Is there something you're not telling me, professor?'

He could hear the old man's smile gleaming across the miles that separated them.

'Many things, Murray.'

It was the first time the professor had used his given name. Was it an invitation to press further, or simply a tease?

'Something to do with Lunan?'

'Why don't you ask Baine? After all, you're colleagues. It was a long time ago and what I heard may have been gossip.'

'What did you hear?'

'The front door, I think it must be Helen.' There was a clunk as the receiver was dropped. Somewhere in the distance James said, 'Did you get any of those biscuits that Iris is fond of?' And more remote still came the indistinct tones of a female voice answering him.

Murray stood up and stretched. Day had

227

slipped into night now and he would have to walk back in the dark. He held the mobile to his ear, hearing the faraway rattle of Professor James's domestic life, distant as the sound of the sea heard through a shell. He was about to hang up when a woman's voice said, 'Hello? This is Helen Trend. With whom am I speaking?'

He hunkered down behind the shelter again, cupping his hand round the phone to protect his words from the wind.

'Dr Murray Watson. I think Professor James may have forgotten he was talking to me.'

Professor James's daughter was briskly cheerful.

'In that case he's been struck with sudden senility since yesterday. I'm afraid my father has just stepped out of the room. Nature calls rather frequently these days. You might be advised to ring back later, unless it's anything I can help you with?'

'I doubt it.'

'So certain.'

Helen Trend's voice assumed an unexpected flirtiness. Murray pictured a well-preserved fifty-year-old with buttery yellow hair. It amazed him that even here, on this inhospitable hillside, his mind could conjure an image worth fucking.

'We were discussing his poetry circle, more specifically Professor Fergus Baine.'

The voice on the other end lowered an octave.

'That's a name I haven't heard in an age. Why on earth were you discussing that rogue?'

'I'm writing a biography of the poet Archie Lunan. According to your father, he and Professor Baine were associates.'

228

The woman laughed.

'I wouldn't pay too much attention to anything my father has to say about Fergus Baine, I'm afraid his name is mud in this house.'

'Do you mind my asking why?'

There was a pause on the line. The sheep had stopped calling to each other, but the hillside was alive with noise. A shrill cry sounded from somewhere in the settling dusk and Murray pulled up the collar of his jacket. He remembered reading of some plan to reintroduce wolves to the Scottish Highlands, wondered if it had ever gone ahead. No, surely the sheep farmers would never allow it.

Helen Trend asked, 'What institution did you say you were associated with?'

They both knew he hadn't associated himself with any institution, but Murray didn't bother to argue the point.

'The University of Glasgow.'

'I see.' Once again there was the slow pause as if she were considering what to say. 'I'd heard Fergus was back teaching there.'

'He's currently head of department.'

'Yes, so my sources tell me. And you and my father were discussing him in relation to a book you're writing about Archie Lunan?'

'Yes.'

'What did my father tell you?'

He had never been much of a card sharp, but instinct told Murray to conceal the fact James had told him nothing.

'I'm not sure that I'm at liberty to discuss that.'

'No?' The flirtiness was gone now. 'Then let me phrase my question in another way. Was it anything that might be construed as libellous?'

Despite the cold and the dread of the downward journey, he was suddenly enjoying himself.

'I'd have to consult a lawyer before I could answer that question.'

'I could recommend the services of my husband or two of my sons, but there might be a clash of interests.'

In Murray's mind the soft, buttery hair shifted into Margaret Thatcher's lacquered helmet. The conversation seemed to be escalating beyond his control.

'Mrs Trend, I get the feeling I've inadvertently offended you. I can only apologise, though I'm not quite sure what I've done.'

'No?' The laugh returned, sharp against the wailing wind. 'Let me make it clear then. If you were to print anything my father told you about Fergus Baine that could even be considered libellous, and therefore detrimental by proxy to my father's reputation, I would have no hesitation in instructing my lawyers to begin a case against you, and remember Dr Watson, I get my legal counsel for free.'

'I've got the deepest respect for your father . . .'

His words were cut short by James's voice on another extension.

'This is a private telephone call, Helen, hang up, please. I'd prefer to talk with Dr Watson alone.'

'I was just telling him that . . .'

'Hang up, Helen. I'll be through shortly.'

Professor James's voice had regained all of its old authority. Murray gave an involuntary cringe at

230

the meekness of his daughter's reply.

'Yes, Dad. Sorry.'

There was a click and a moment that might have been silence, were it not for the wind racing across the hill. Then James said, 'What did she tell you?'

This time Murray told the truth.

'Nothing at all, except that she was concerned I might expose some disagreement you had with Fergus and dent your reputation. She was warning me off.'

'My reputation has nothing to fear from Fergus.' James sighed and Murray got a feeling that an opportunity had been lost. 'How well do you know Professor Fergus Baine?'

'Not well at all. He's only been part of the department for three years. He came here from down south, met and married Rachel in what Mills and Boon would describe as a whirlwind romance.' Murray tried to keep the bitterness from his voice. 'Last year he was appointed head of English literature.'

'Have you read any of his books?'

'I glanced through his last couple.'

'Of course, it's only politic to at least take a glance at your colleagues' work, even if you can't stand them.'

'What makes you think I can't . . .'

'Don't bother to bullshit me, Murray.' The Americanism sounded strange in the professor's mouth. 'You've got as much love for him as I have. Admit it.'

Murray said, 'We've never really seen eye to eye.'

The older man's laugh sounded exasperated.

'I imagine that is as much of an admission as I'm ever going to get. Did you know he published a slim volume of verse years ago?'

'No.'

'No reason why you should. It sank, pretty much without trace. It's out of print now, but I think you'd find it well worth reading. Tell me where you're staying and I'll send you a copy.'

Murray felt like hurling his phone across the expanse of wind and dark. He'd lost control of the interview again, the old man turning it back to poetry, the work, not the life.

'I'm not sure I'll have the time. I need to concentrate my researches on Lunan and his circle.'

'Fergus was part of his circle.' The voice grew softer in his ear, becoming one with the wind and trembling grass. 'Indulge me. Remember, I used to be a professor of English literature, I do know of what I speak.'

'Once a professor, always a professor.'

'They could put that on my gravestone.' James grew serious. 'Remember, Dr Watson. Some people never essentially change. In my opinion, Fergus Baine is one of them. Think of how he is now and that will tell you pretty much how he was back when Lunan and he were friends—and they were friends, whatever smoke Baine has tried to blow in your eyes.'

'Will you tell me what the two of you fell out about?'

'I can't. It affects someone else, someone blameless. What I will say is that Fergus Baine was a prodigy of mine who abused his position. His move down south in 1978 wasn't entirely voluntary. I gave him a reference for a post in England to get him out of the way, but if I had any power he wouldn't be back in Scotland, working at my old university, and certainly not in the capacity he occupies.'

'Where would he be?'

'In Hell.' The old man laughed. 'Or still in the south of England. Tell me where you're staying and I'll ask Iris to send you a copy of his poetry tomorrow by first-class post. I promise you'll find it interesting.'

Murray gave him the address of the B&B, as far as he remembered it, then said, 'It was Bobby Robb that I really wanted to find out about.'

'Bobby Robb was an ignorant fool.'

'What makes you say that? The way he looked? Talked?'

'Certainly not the way he looked, though God knows he looked like an idiot, but then most of them did. Long hair and beards, dressed like Gypsy Rose Lee strung about with bells and cockle shells. No, Bobby Robb was a mess, but he wasn't the worst. It wasn't the way he talked either. Robb wore his working-class roots on his sleeve, but I've met too many intelligent working men and too many idiot toffs to judge a man on his accent. It was Bobby Robb's preoccupations that declared him stupid. He was interested in what has been rechristened as New Age. Occultism, astrology, all that superstitious nonsense the Elizabethans were fascinated with. Excusable in the sixteen hundreds, but astoundingly brainless in the twentieth century.'

'Did Archie engage with it too?'

'Archie could be foolish, but he wasn't dense. I

233

remember him making fun of Robb, calling him the sorcerer's apprentice, but I never paid much attention. Back then a lot of people were fascinated by these things, encouraged by drugs, I suppose. They had amazing sensory and quasi-religious experiences that made them begin to think there were existences apart from this one.'

'You were never tempted to try it for yourself?'

'Try what?'

'LSD, acid. A lot of educationalists got into it—turn on, tune in and drop out.'

'I couldn't drop out. I told you, my father was an engineer at Barr & Strouds, I had a good Presbyterian upbringing and a family to support. No, I was never tempted. I'm what they used to call a square—like you, Dr Watson. Anyway, I find the world we inhabit rather impressive. I also believe it's the only one open to us. Why be in a rush to leave?'

*   *   *

Murray fell twice on the way down the hill, but the going wasn't so bad once he reached the road. The moon was a wisp of itself, veiled by the same clouds that hid the stars. He used the light on his phone as a torch for a while, but then the notion that his progress might be monitored for miles around began to bother him, and so he pocketed it and let his eyes adjust to the gloom. The little house he had noticed on his journey out was in darkness now, the toy tractor still upturned in its garden. The rain came on as Murray had known it would. He kept his head down against the spray and upped his pace, not wanting one of the inhabitants to look out and be frightened by the sight of a stranger walking by so late, on such an inhospitable night.

Helen Trend had been palpably anxious about what her father might say. Her hate for Fergus Baine seemed to outstrip even the professor's. Murray couldn't imagine James taking departmental disputes home to share with his children over the dinner table. He weighed up a list of his academic contacts, hoping to identify someone who might know the manner of Fergus's disgrace, thought about asking Rachel, and rejected the idea almost as it occurred.

The wind seemed to attack him from all sides, the rain swirling around him, blowing into his face, clouding his vision. Murray took his glasses off and wiped them, though he knew it was a useless gesture. He remembered Cressida smiling as she asked if he minded, her orange dress flaring as she'd cleaned his lenses, all the better to view Jack's exhibition.

He thought about the Pictish men, or whoever they were, who had built the broch, imagined them tucked safe within its bounds, huddled together with their dogs and their livestock. They would have had more sense than to trudge through the dark and the wet. He wondered if Lunan had ever walked these paths at night, muddy and drenched to the skin, asking himself what the hell was going on.

Chapter Nineteen

Murray took Christie's first novel, *Sacrifice*, down to the dining room with him. He saw the landlady's eyes on it as she placed his cooked breakfast on the table. Murray set the book aside, making a conscious effort not to rub his hands together with the joy of fried bacon, eggs and sausage materialising before him with no effort from himself.

'That looks great.'

Mrs Dunn acknowledged his thanks with a nod. She went back into the kitchen, stepping neatly round a cat that had stationed itself in front of the electric heater glowing from the centre of the room, and returned with a pot of coffee and a round of toast.

'There's strawberry jam too. I made it myself, with strawberries from the garden.'

Murray was vaguely nervous of home-made produce, but he smiled and said, 'That'll be a treat.' He shifted the book a little to make more space and nodded at the photo on the back cover. 'I understand she's a local.'

'She lives here, yes.'

The woman put the jar of jam on the table and he started to slather his toast with it, hoping she'd kept the cat from the kitchen when she was making it.

'What's she like?'

Mrs Dunn was wearing a serviceable skirt topped by a blue jersey that might have been homemade a long time ago, or recently culled

236

from a jumble sale. Protecting the ensemble was a pinny decorated with a map of the cathedrals of Scotland; Aberdeen and Fort William sanctifying her breasts, Glasgow her crotch. The old lady looked like the BBC drama department's concept of an ideal Scottish housekeeper; Janet to his Dr Finlay. She stared at the book as if she'd never seen it before, her face unreadable.

'She's a little different from her photograph.'

Murray looked at the familiar airbrushed image. A soft, doe-eyed face framed by curtains of long hair, Christie in her twenties. The picture bore no relation to the ravaged woman he'd seen at Robb's funeral.

'I guess it was taken a while ago.'

The landlady laughed.

'Before the flood.'

Murray poured himself a mug of coffee, relieved to see her smiling again

'Are you not having one yourself?'

'No, I'll get mine after, once I've done the dishes.' She must have realised he disliked the idea of her cleaning up after him because she added, 'Don't worry, I've got a machine.'

Murray took a bite of toast and jam. It was good and he said so. The cat blinked at him from its spot in front of the fire, as if letting him know it was onto his game.

'What's the cat called?'

'Archie.' Murray almost choked at the sound of the familiar name, but the landlady didn't notice. She bent over and rubbed behind the beast's ears. It narrowed its eyes and took the salute as its due. 'He's an old soldier, aren't you, love?' She straightened up. 'Do you like cats?'

He had never had much to do with them.

'Very intelligent creatures.'

'They are that.'

The topic of their conversation stretched his hind legs and started to clean his tummy, working meticulously down towards his tail.

Murray stifled the urge to laugh.

'So do you see her around the island much?'

'Mrs Graves?'

He wondered if the title was a courtesy or a slight—a married woman 'promoting' another, all the better to underline her spinsterhood—but Mrs Dunn's features had regained their impassiveness.

'I couldn't tell you the last time I saw Christie Graves.'

'But she still lives here?'

Their moment of communion was gone. Mrs Dunn lifted his empty plate, not bothering to ask if he'd enjoyed his meal.

'I expect so.'

She went back through to the kitchen, leaving him to his book and his coffee. He drank it quickly, aware of the old woman through the wall, waiting on him to leave. She must have heard his chair scrape against the lino as he got up to go to his room, because she returned, tray in hand, ready to clear the table.

'Just one thing, Mr Watson.'

'Yes?'

He gave her the smile he normally bestowed on the departmental secretaries when he had made some administrative screw-up.

'If you're going out walking, would you mind taking off your boots at the front door, please? You trailed mud all through the house when you got back last night.'

He apologised, remembering too late that his smile had never had much effect on the women who ran the English department either.

*   *   *

Murray had intended to spend the morning in his room writing up the previous night's telephone conversation with Professor James, but he had just got started when Mrs Dunn knocked on his door and asked if she could get in to clean. He glanced guiltily at the mud stains on the carpet and told her he would go and explore the island.

This time he took the car and drove to the village shop. Half a dozen vehicles were parked outside, a few men in overalls stationed next to them passing the time of day. They glanced at Murray with enough lack of interest to suggest tourists weren't unusual, or perhaps that they had heard of his presence and already got his measure.

Inside the shop smelt pleasantly of soap flakes. Murray was cheered to see ranks of wine bottles marshalled together on the shelves, next to whisky, vodka and a surprising variety of rum. Three young girls clustered around a computer set in a corner niche, adding something to a Facebook page. Their stares were more assessing, though no less dismissive, than the loitering men's.

Murray browsed the postcard rack looking for one of the broch where he had sheltered the night before, but it was missing from the display. Instead he selected a couple of sea views, unsure who he could send them to. He put the cards on the counter and placed an Ordnance Survey map beside them.

'Can anyone use the Internet?'

The shopkeeper had the kind of doughy look that men with indoor jobs who are confronted by manual workers every day seem to take on. He gave Murray a tense smile wrought from shyness.

'A pound an hour, longest session thirty minutes if there's a queue.' He nodded at the huddle of teenagers. 'They've been on at least an hour and a half. I can ask them to take a break if you'd like to use it now?'

'No, thanks, just checking for future reference.'

The shop man slid Murray's map and cards into a paper bag.

'Over for the walking?'

'Yes.' He wasn't sure why he was lying, except perhaps to make life easier. 'I'm staying with Mrs Dunn.'

'Ah, well, you'll be comfortable enough there.'

The man's smile faltered and Murray sensed another shopper behind him.

'Aye, she's taking good care of me.'

He shoved his purchases into his rucksack and made way for a man dressed in blue overalls with an *Oban Times* in his hand. It seemed that Murray had chosen the time of day when the island folk congregated. He had to press sideways to negotiate his way to the door. It swung wide just as he reached it and Christie Graves lurched awkwardly over the step. Murray stepped back to let her pass, saw her eyes glance over him, and realised he had been half-expecting her all morning.

*　　　*　　　*

240

Murray sat outside in the car with the Ordnance Survey map draped across the steering wheel. Christie nodded to a few of the people outside as she left the shop, a canvas bag in one hand, her stick in the other, but didn't stop to pass the time of day. He raised his eyes from the scant roads and many tracks of Lismore, watching as she got into her red Cherokee, and pulled away. Then he counted to ten, and steered his dad's car out from its space.

Christie drove faster than he dared, but Murray caught flashes of her on the turns and hilly rises of the road ahead. He hit the CD player and Johnny Cash gravelled into life, singing about lonesome prisons and trains that whistled as they went by. It was a song from their childhood. Murray wondered if Jack listened to the CD sometimes, or if it had nested in its tray since before their dad had stopped being able to drive.

The world beyond the car window had a bright, dewy aspect, as if the previous night's storm had refreshed the countryside. The fields had lost their shit-stained look and taken on the cheerful air of a children's storybook. Behind the drystane dykes and high wire fences sheep and cows cropped at grass green and even enough to be plastic. The few cottages he passed seemed shrewdly placed, their stone fronts and sloping roofs the perfect complement to neat gardens cordoned off from nature's wilder reaches by the same artfully built walls that kept the livestock within their bounds. Some small birds swooped in front of his windscreen, their long, black tails wagging. Murray almost hit the brakes, but sped on wondering if the red car had slipped away from him down one of the unmarked lanes that branched off from the road.

The island was small. There would be other opportunities, other ways of discovering where Christie lived, but now that he had begun the pursuit it seemed imperative to press on.

He pushed down on the accelerator, feeling the countryside around him blur and flash, the tarmac whizz into grey, dropping through the gears and speeding into the turn as he rounded yet another rising bend in the road, hoping for the glimpse of red that would tell him Christie was still ahead.

Then suddenly it was all red, the red 4×4 motionless in a passing place, the oncoming post office van in the middle of the road. He cursed and hit the brakes, turning the steering wheel towards the skid that threatened to overwhelm his own small vehicle. There was speed and slowness and an instant when he thought the car would win and pitch him from it, then the wheels obeyed and he drew to a halt a credit-card width from Christie's bumper.

Fuck, fuck, shit, fuck, shit.

Christie's eyes met his in her rear-view mirror.

He held up a hand in apology, then pulled down the sun visor, though the morning's hopeful rays had already been overtaken by cloud.

He had no idea of what he was doing.

Cash sung on about moving the railway station somewhere 'further down the line' and the postie drove by, raising a finger from the wheel in laconic salute.

The red car pulled out.

Murray gripped the wheel tight, trying to

242

banish the trembling that threatened to overtake him and followed on, concentrating on keeping a decent distance from the vehicle in front.

He remembered the sullen ferryman's stare, and Mrs Dunn's joke that he would imprison Murray if he neglected to pay for his board. An island could easily become a jail. He had no doubt that the islanders already knew of his presence and would hear of his foolish near-crash. He wondered if Archie had ever felt claustrophobic, bounded by the sea and the stares of the locals. Perhaps that was why he had taken to sailing, mastering the ability to leave whenever he wished.

Christie's car had disappeared in the twists and turns ahead. He pushed down on the accelerator, dropping gear on the curves, anxious about the unseen hazards that might lurk beyond each bend, sure he had lost her. The road straightened out and just at the last moment he caught a flash of red, dropped gear again, pressed the brake pedal gently, and saw Christie's car turn off the tarmac road into a rough track.

Murray continued on along the main road, still thinking of Christie's red car travelling the twists of the less-finished trail, like poison passing through a vein.

*   *   *

Murray knew that laptops could damage your fertility, but he balanced his on a pillow anyway and set it on his lap as he half-sat, half-lay on the satin counterpane. It was cold in the room. Murray considered stripping the spare bed of its blanket and draping it around himself, but couldn't muster the energy.

He took out his mobile and summoned Rachel's number. He imagined her in a hotel room somewhere in Italy with Fergus, then made himself stop. The whisky was in a carrier bag in the wardrobe. Murray retrieved it, searched the room for a glass and when he didn't find one, took the briefest of nips straight from the bottle. His reflection mimicked his moves in the girlish dressing-table mirror. Murray hadn't bothered to shave that morning and the combination of five o'clock shadow and spirits made him look like one of Lyn's unfortunates.

'Slainte Mhath.'

Murray raised the bottle to his reflection and touched it to his lips.

He felt like another, but stoppered the bottle and put it back in the wardrobe. He didn't want to end up like Alan Garrett, his brains smeared against the windscreen of his car.

*   *   *

There was a phone box by the pier. Murray parked and stationed himself inside, noting the absence of piss and graffiti. There was no phone book either, but he knew the number by heart.

Rab picked up straight away, his voice still the stern side of five p.m.

'Purvis.'

Murray managed to inject some cheeky-chappie cheer into his words.

'Shouldn't that be pervert?'

'Murray?'

Rab sounded relieved and Murray regretted

244

hating him. He forced himself to smile, hoping to tinge his words with a brightness he didn't feel.

'The very same.'

'I heard you'd gone north.'

Murray wondered who had told him.

'You heard right.'

'So what's up? You missing home, or is there something I can do for you?'

Murray could picture his old friend sitting at the desk in his office, the unframed poster announcing a long-ago reading by Edwin Muir tacked to the wall behind him, the small carriage clock that had belonged to his mother marking time on the bookcase by his side. He heard the hurt sharpen Rab's voice and softened his own tone in response.

'Both. Listen, I'm sorry about the other night.'

Purvis's lungs croaked across the land and water separating the two men.

'I never thought I'd be falling out about a woman at my age.' He sighed again. 'Go on then, tell me what you want.'

'How do you know I'm not just calling to say hello?'

'Because you're not.'

The truth of the statement hung in the silence between them, then Murray said, 'You've been in the department a long time, Rab.'

'I remember back to when the term postmodernism was a speck in the eye of the little yellow god and dinosaurs roamed the corridors.'

It was Murray's cue to quip that they were still lumbering around English literature, but he ignored it.

'Did you know Fergus in the old days, before he

245

went to England?'

Rab's voice hardened again.

'Is this something to do with Rachel?'

'No, with Archie. Apparently he and Fergus were friends.'

'And Fergus never said?'

'No mention, even when he was blocking my proposal.'

'Maybe he didn't consider it relevant.'

'Maybe.'

'But you don't think so?'

'Would you? Fergus isn't usually shy about mentioning writers he's associated with, especially if it makes him look like he's got superior knowledge of someone else's research. If anything, it might have strengthened his objections.'

'I take your point, but so what?'

'When I interviewed Professor James he intimated there may have been a reason other than his career that Fergus went to England.' A warning flashed on the payphone's display, letting him know his money was almost done. Murray fired more coins into the slot. 'I think there's something out of kilter. Fergus likes everyone to know how much he knows, but this time he was desperate to put me off the scent.'

Murray could hear a tapping on the other end of the line and pictured Rab's free hand drumming against his desk for want of a cigarette.

'Has it occurred to you that Fergus's reasons for blocking your proposal might have been genuine?'

'He didn't have any reasons, not credible ones anyway.'

Rab coughed and Murray held the phone away

246

from his head. He could see the sea through the thick glass of the telephone box. The waves foaming and peaking, crashing into the deep then resurfacing, shoals of white horses thundering on. He put the headpiece to his ear and Rab asked, 'How far have you got with the book?'

'Not very, but then I've barely started.'

'That's not true, Murray. You've been thinking about it for years. You know as well as I do that you need concrete facts to get anywhere. Without them, all you're doing is speculating. Have you ever considered the possibility Archie Lunan simply wrote a few nice poems, and then slid into the water without much of a splash, never to surface? End of story.'

The payphone flashed its warning again and Murray pushed his last few coins into the slot.

'I'm going to be cut off soon.'

'You'd better get to the point then.'

'James wouldn't tell me why he and Fergus fell out, but whatever it was still rankled. He intimated that he told Fergus to get out of town or he'd blow the lid on some scandal.'

'You make him sound like Dangerous Dan McGrew, pistols at dawn.'

'He was serious, Rab.'

'Listen, Murray, James is an old man. He might have good reasons for wanting to keep what's past in the past.'

'No, he wanted me to find out. He just didn't want to be the one to tell me.' Murray slowed his words. 'If you could ask around, speak to some people you knew in the old days, something might come up.'

'James always was a contrary sod.' The tapping

ceased. 'It's a big ask, Murray. I'm already on Fergus's shit list.'

'Who isn't?'

'True enough, but I'm more expendable than most. Only a few years till I hit a decent pension. It'd save the department a lot of money to ditch me now.'

'Did you know Fergus back then, Rab?'

'You're not going to let this drop, are you?'

He could see the ferry in the distance. The waves had grown rougher, but the boat looked solid, pressing on against the onslaught.

'Probably not.'

'There's not much I can tell you. I was aware of Fergus when he was doing his PhD—he was tipped for the big time even then—but he was on the east coast and I was on the west. Anyway, you know the way he is, superior with a tinge of slime, except for when it comes to the ladies. He's all charm then. I've often wondered why he didn't go into politics.'

'Do you remember anything about the period immediately before he went south?'

This time Rab's sigh was long and harsh. If Murray hadn't known the sensitivity of the university fire sprinklers, he would have assumed the other man had lit up and taken his first, hard drag. Murray smiled. It was the sound of capitulation.

'I'll ask around, discreetly—very discreetly. I'm not losing my pension for you, Watson.'

'Thanks, Rab, I appreciate it.'

'No you don't. You still want to twist my balls off for going with Rachel.'

Murray laughed at the neatly captured truth, and some of his bile seemed to dissolve. He asked,

'Have you seen her lately?'

The payphone's warning message started to flash again.

Rab said, 'I passed her in the corridor the other day. She . . .'

But the pips sounded, and his words were overtaken by the dial tone. Murray stood in the phone box for a while, watching the ferry get closer and hoping that Rab would call him back.

The ship docked and he stepped out into a bluster of wind and spray. A few waiting islanders had got out of their cars to greet some of the disembarking passengers. Their hellos caught in the slipstream and carried across the car park, mingling with the cries of the seagulls; the souls of dead sailors welcoming the travellers home.

Chapter Twenty

'Is it because of the mud?'

'No.' Mrs Dunn lifted a large diary from the telephone table in the hall and held it open for him to see. 'I've got a longstanding booking, a pair of archaeologists from Glasgow University. I've phoned around, but I'm afraid you've chosen the wrong time of year, Mr Watson. The Bruces are away to Canada visiting her sister, Mrs McIver stopped taking paying guests two years ago, and will not be persuaded otherwise, and the Ramseys and the Gilchrists have also promised their rooms to the dig. I would have let you know earlier, but you only booked for the two nights, so I assumed you'd be moving on.'

The landlady's lips narrowed into an expression that was final. Murray said, 'I'll go up and pack.'

Mrs Dunn nodded. She closed the book and stared him in the eye.

'I'd have thought you'd be keen to get back to the city. The only people who come here are walkers and archaeologists, and you're neither, are you, Mr Watson?'

'No.'

It was an effort not to drop his gaze to the carpet, like a guilty schoolboy.

'Are you a journalist?'

'Why would you think that?'

Mrs Dunn held the desk diary to her, like a shield.

'You were asking questions about Mrs Graves yesterday and then there were all those notes in your room, newspaper cuttings and the like.' Her voice took on a defensive tone. 'I couldn't help seeing them when I was making the bed.'

'No.' There was no point in dissembling. Better the truth reach Christie than the island decide he was a tabloid reporter in search of old scandal. Besides, he was heading home. Murray smiled to make himself less threatening. 'I'm not a journalist. I'm a doctor of English literature.'

The photos of children with Purdey haircuts and eighties flicks smiled down on the scene from the stairway above, like well-fed cherubim. The old woman laid the diary back beside the telephone and gave him an offended look.

'You should have stated your title in the visitors' book. I'd be grateful if you could amend your entry before you leave.'

Murray drove to the roughcast path that Christie had disappeared down and parked the car. Mrs Dunn had phoned ahead and booked him on the five o'clock ferry. He'd be back in Glasgow by teatime, would sleep in his own bed that night.

The road looked too jagged for his small vehicle. Murray hesitated, wanting to make progress, but unwilling to risk a burst tyre or, worse still, a broken axle.

He got out and slammed the door, feeling in the pocket of his jacket for his mobile phone. He would have to keep his eye on the time, make sure he left himself space to get back before the sailing.

The cold prickled his skin after the dry air of the overheated car. Murray drew his scarf over his mouth and pulled his hat down over his ears. It had been autumn when he'd started out on his quest in Edinburgh, but already there were intimations of winter. He scented the tang of salt in the wind and wondered what the dark months were like on the small island, set unprotected on the edge of the North Atlantic.

There was no real chance he'd get to speak to Christie this trip. He would have to waste time in Glasgow, then organise himself and come back, rent a cottage or something. He would avoid lodging with Mrs Dunn again. He'd mentioned his research, hoped she might be willing to talk about Lunan's time on the island, but the old woman had grown brisk, reminding him to pack his stuff before his walk.

'I'll need the room clear if I'm to get it ready for Dr Edwards and Dr Grant arriving.'

A slight emphasis on the *Dr*, as if to let him know other academics didn't need to be outed.

Murray silently cursed the archaeology department. He remembered them from his time with Angela; a long-haired, cagoule-clad, unwashed crew, not so different, he suspected, from the ancient tribes they studied, except the ancient ones got more than the occasional drunken shag. He stopped and unlatched the aluminium gate to the next field. There was nothing ahead but stony road, sheep and shit. Wherever Christie lived, it was almost certainly too far to walk to and return from before the ferry sailed. He hoped the archaeologists got mud and Guinness on Mrs Dunn's pink sheets.

He was plucked from his thoughts by the rumble of a diesel engine. Murray turned and saw a small vehicle with outsize wheels, a hybrid tractor-cum-dune buggy, bouncing over the uneven track, pulling a trailer in its wake. He waved a hand, to make sure the driver had seen him, then opened the gate wide, stepping back to allow it room to pass. The vehicle barely slowed as it cleared the opening, but drew to a halt a short distance ahead, waiting while Murray latched the gate. A small Jack Russell regarded his progress from the empty trailer, its tail, nose and ears frozen into inquisitive points.

He was sure the driver was about to turn him back with some warning about bulls or rutting stags, but the man flashed an easy grin.

'Cheers.' He was somewhere in his early thirties, compact and wiry, dressed in orange overalls and mud-spattered Wellingtons. 'Heading for the castle?'

It was the first he had heard of the existence of a castle on the island, but Murray returned the man's smile and said, 'I am if I can get there and back before the ferry sails.'

'Hop in. There's plenty time if I drive you one way.'

The man's accent was English, from somewhere in the Midlands, though Murray couldn't place where.

He gripped one of the bars that composed the open frame of the small cab and hauled himself onboard, unsure of whether he should follow his whim. But the vehicle was already gaining speed, bouncing over the loose stones faster than he would have thought possible. Murray held tight to the crash bar, unable to stop himself jolting with the buggy's movements, feeling the stranger's body hard and unwelcome against his side.

'I saw your car at the top of the road. You'll be the man who almost wiped out Mrs Graves.'

'Did she tell you?'

The weathered creases round the driver's eyes wrinkled in amusement.

'No, I got it from the *Lismore Gazette*.'

'Shit, you're kidding.'

The man laughed. 'Jamie the postman.'

Murray thought he could hear the jolting of the cab in his own laugh. He said, 'I should apologise to her.'

'We're headed in the right general direction, but I wouldn't bother. She doesn't like to be disturbed.'

'Not the sociable type?'

The man slowed the pace and looked back towards the trailer.

'Okay, then, off you go.'

For a second Murray thought his question had offended, but then the terrier jumped from the trailer and started to trot behind.

'Jinx hates the next bit.'

The buggy rounded a bend and the road fell away from them into a precipitous scree-lined descent. Murray tensed his already tight grip and felt a sudden kinship with the dog. The small man's grin grew wider. 'My kids call it Everest.'

His bones were jarring so hard it felt they might soon be loosed from his flesh, but there was something exhilarating in the recklessness of the speed that made Murray dampen the urge to beg the stranger to stop and instead give himself over to the thrill of the plunge. He recalled ten-year-old Jack's spew, candyfloss pink, catching the wind then coating the tough guy birling the waltzers at the Glasgow Green shows, and laughed out loud.

The man laughed with him.

'This hill's the reason I could afford the croft. It makes everything a hundred times harder, but I've got to love it. I wouldn't be here without it.' The terrier had somehow got ahead of them. Its rump flashed white as it ran, tail bobbing, down the rough track, too close to the tractor's front wheels for comfort. The driver didn't bother to slow his pace.

'I'm Pete, by the way.'

'Murray.'

'On holiday?'

'Aye, a bit of a break from Glasgow.' His world seemed far away, here in the plunging gloom, the last greenery of the year still clinging to the leaves of the young trees that lined the sheltered track.

254

Murray realised that the path had been dug into the hill and wondered if it was the small man's doing. He asked, 'Have you lived here long?'

'Three years.'

They were almost at the bottom now. Pete put an extra spurt on the last few yards; the dog anticipated the move and resigned the race, trotting up the verge, where she sat grinning as they passed. The cab listed to the left as it turned the corner, out of the shade of the trees and into the open. Pete slowed to a halt.

'There's the castle.'

But he needn't have spoken. Murray could see the ruined structure perched on top of a plug of rock, silhouetted against the sea. Its walls had been reduced by wind or warfare to crooked columns that pointed towards the sky like a warped crown. Some grazing horses raised their heads at the sound of the tractor and then lowered them back to the grass, reassured it was nothing unusual. Murray tried to envision how the scene must have looked when the castle was whole and occupied by some tribe, but his imagination failed. All he could see was the vista spread before him, like Arcadia restored after the devastation of man.

The dog leapt into the trailer, wagging its tail.

'Decided to trust my driving again, have you, Jinxy?' Pete reached back and rubbed her hard between her ears, then pointed towards a small white-painted cottage, about a mile from the castle.

'That's our place there.'

'And this is your land?'

'Some of it.'

'A beautiful place to live.'

'Yep.' The small man creased his face into a weathered grin. 'You can forget how stunning a landscape is when you see it every day. I do anyway, the wife's more appreciative.'

Murray wondered if Pete had brought him here in the hope of viewing the scene afresh, through another pair of eyes.

'And your children?'

He laughed.

'Desperate for bright lights, big city. The horses are the only thing keeping them here, and them not for long. Meaghan will be off to university next year and I doubt her brother will be far behind.'

Murray scanned the horizon, hoping for sight of a house that might belong to Christie Graves, but apart from the castle and Pete's cottage, there was only land and sea.

Pete started the engine again. 'I'll drop you down at the bottom. You should be able to climb up to the castle and make it back in good time for the ferry. Have you enjoyed your stay?'

'It was too short.'

'That's holidays for you. We threw caution to the wind and took the kids to Corfu last year. I swear I was just off the plane when I was getting back on it again, couldn't understand where I got the tan from.'

'Aye, I would have stayed longer, but I screwed up my booking.'

'Unless someone makes an almighty balls-up, the island will still be here next year. That's what I told myself as we flew away from the sunshine. Mind you, Corfu would be no place for our kind of farming. Dry as beef jerky, no grazing at all.'

'Next year will be too late.'

Pete glanced at him, his face suddenly guarded, and Murray realised he sounded like a man with terminal illness or suicide on his mind.

'My project will have run out of time.'

He told Pete about his research, and the biography he was planning, as they closed the final distance to the ruined castle.

'You screwed up.'

Pete slowed the tractor to a halt and Murray climbed from the cab.

'I did indeed.'

'Ah, well.' The small man grinned. 'It happens. You know where we are now. Next time you visit, don't be a stranger. Drop by and have a dram.'

The Scots word sounded strange married with his flat, Midland vowels.

Murray nodded. 'You're on.'

Jinx perched her front paws on the edge of the trailer watching them. Murray reached out to pat the terrier and her teeth snarled back in a growl.

'No manners, this one.'

Pete shoved the dog gently from its perch and climbed back into his cab. Murray raised a hand in farewell, and then started towards the castle. When he looked back the tractor was bouncing far along the track towards home.

Chapter Twenty-One

Murray climbed up into the grassed-over centre of the castle and stared out to sea, his mind as blank as the white foam frothing on the incoming tide. He would go to Edinburgh tomorrow, seek out the

257

Geordie's landlord and ask why he'd burnt Bobby Robb's library. What kind of books were they that the man had felt compelled to turn them into a bonfire, even though he'd already promised them to his niece?

It was a while before he could find a signal and call a directory service for the Geordie's number. They connected him and he waited, imagining Lauren sitting in the pub's backroom, absorbed in some existential tome while the phone rang out.

Murray killed the call. He looked at the three bars on his phone, wondering how long the battery would last, then found the phone signal again and pressed redial, determined to check whether the man was on shift and break the cycle of disorganisation that would see him expelled from the island. This time a gruff male voice answered on the second ring.

'Yes?'

'Hi, can I speak to the landlord, please?'

'If you make it snappy.'

Murray hadn't thought through what he would say and the words seemed to tumble from him.

'I'm phoning about a recently deceased customer of yours . . .'

'Jesus Christ, let me guess—our dear departed Crippen.'

'How did you know?'

'We might not attract the youth market, but they're still not exactly dropping like flies round here.' The landlord sounded wary. 'What about him?'

This time Murray decided to tell the truth.

'I'm writing a book about someone Mr Robb knew a long time ago. I was hoping to interview him.'

'Aye, well, unless you're planning on following him down into the eternal beer cellar, I'd say you were onto plums.' Someone said something in the background and the landlord muffled the mouthpiece and gave an indistinct reply that sounded impatient. When he returned to the phone his voice was brisk. 'Look, mate, I'm in the middle of a delivery. I didn't really know the guy, just sold him a few beers over the years. I don't think I can help you.'

'I need to ask you a specific question.'

'What?'

'About Bobby's effects.'

There was silence on the line. For a moment Murray thought he'd blown it and the other man was about to hang up, but then he heard a sigh and the landlord said, 'Why don't you drop by later in the day? I'm on until two.'

Murray looked out to where the grey sea met the lighter grey of the sky. The pub would be there tomorrow, but he had the man on the line now. He said, 'You've no idea how good the idea of a pint sounds to me, but . . .'

'But?'

'I'm up north on an island that doesn't have a pub.'

'So you're a long-distance heavy.'

'I'm not a heavy at all. I'm a lecturer in English literature.'

'Christ,' the landlord laughed. 'What are you going to do if I don't cooperate? Make me spell a difficult word?' He snorted. 'This island, did you ken it was dry when you went there?'

'No.'

'Jesus.' He laughed again. 'Did you take anything with you?'

The other man's delight at his predicament decided Murray against mentioning the shop's shelves groaning with spirits.

'A bottle of whisky I'm halfway through.'

There was palpable glee in the other man's voice.

'I'm guessing you're rationing that.'

'I'm down to around an X-ray of a dram every night.'

The landlord's snort sounded down the line.

'This book, is it going to show that old cunt in a good light?'

'I wouldn't think so.'

'And will it have acknowledgements? You know, wee thank-yous to people that helped out in the making of it?'

'More than likely.'

'Right.' The landlord cleared his throat, like a torch singer about to embark on a particularly gruelling number. 'Have you got a pen and paper handy?'

'Aye, hang on a minute.' Murray wedged his mobile between his chin and his shoulder and fumbled in the pocket of his cagoule for a notepad and pen. He found them, put a foot up on a toppled remnant of one of the castle's stone walls and awkwardly rested the book on his knee. 'Okay.'

'Right. My name is John Rathbone. I'll spell it for you, R-a-t-h-b-o-n-e. Got that?'

It was cold and the ballpoint refused to write. Murray scribbled on the damp surface of the paper, but only succeeded in scratching a hole through to the next page.

'Yes.'

'And here's where you can send my copy when it comes out.' Rathbone detailed an address on the south side of Edinburgh, taking care to spell any words he thought Murray might have trouble with. 'On second thoughts, maybe you should send two. I'll give one to my old dear, she's always had a thing about me not staying on at school. It'd give her a kick to see my name in print.'

Murray repeated the address out loud and shoved the useless pen and paper into his pocket, resolving to look the man up and check his details if the book ever made it to publication.

'I'll send you three.'

'Cheers, I'll give one to my bird. No, I'll save it in case I need to impress a new one.'

'Aye, the ladies like a bit of culture.'

'Talking from experience, are you?'

Murray gave what he hoped was a manly chuckle.

'Some.'

'The revenge of the swot?'

'Something like that.'

'Could be my old dear was right about staying on at school then.'

Murray could feel the conversation drifting away from him. He thought of his fading battery and said, 'The main thing I wanted to ask was why did you burn Bobby's books?'

The man's sigh seemed at one with the wind whispering around the fallen fortifications.

'So you heard about that, did you? I'm guessing you dropped by here before you set out for Temperance Island.'

'I never reveal my sources.'

'No need to. My sister's girl Lauren gave me pure grief for it.'

'It's your flat. I'd imagine that, technically speaking, anything abandoned in it's yours to dispose of as you see fit.'

'I wish it was mine to dispose of. A wee place in the centre of Edinburgh? Must be worth a bomb. I would have had that old bum out of it in a shot. Nah, I just manage it for a bloke.'

'So the books?'

'Crippen was always going on about his book collection. When it turned out no one wanted his stuff, I promised them to Lauren. She's a good kid, always got her head in a book. She's saving up to go to uni, and I thought there might be something in there she could use. But they were filth, so I took them out into the back court and burnt them.'

'Pornography?'

'If they'd been porn, I would have kept them for myself, wouldn't I? Nah, it was spooky stuff, books on spells and the like, horrible.'

'He had a big collection of occult books?'

'He had more than that. You should have seen the state of the place. Hang on a wee minute, will you?'

The man put the handset down. Far off Murray could hear him talking to someone. A dark cloud passed across the sky, throwing its shadow over the water. Murray drew his scarf closer, muffling his face against the cold. It was going to rain again. He thought of Hamlet, confronted with the ghost of his father on the castle ramparts at night, and a shiver stiffened the hairs on the back of his neck.

'Well, that's me popular with the bar staff, an

entire delivery offloaded with no help from yours truly.' Rathbone sounded pleased with himself. 'What was I saying?'

'Bobby Robb had more than just a big collection of occult books.'

'Who?'

'Crippen, as you called him.'

'Oh, aye. I had to redecorate before the boss saw the state of the place. You can imagine how delighted I was at that—took me a sander and three coats of varnish to cover up his handiwork.'

'Why?'

'I was meant to do an inspection every six months, make sure the place was ship-shape, but I'd kind of let it slide. It's a good gig, looking after amateur landlords' flats. As long as you've got a wee black book full of reliable tradesmen, it's money for old rope most of the time. But word soon gets round if you slip up.'

'No, I meant what did you have to cover up?'

'I'm getting to that.' Now that he had decided to tell his story, Rathbone's voice was full of relish at the strangeness of it. 'Crippen was lodged in a one-bedroom flat on the High Street, three floors up above the Starbucks. A lot of stairs for an old man, but he looked fit enough. I would have bet he had another ten years in him. Just goes to show.' The landlord paused, giving them both time to take in the impossibility of ever knowing the future, then went on, 'The place wasn't that clean, but I didn't expect it to be. Crippen never had much of an acquaintance with soap and water, so it didn't take a genius to work out he didn't own a pair of Marigolds. It wasn't a problem, my sister's generally happy to earn a few bob cleaning for me, as long as there's nothing too nasty involved. I checked out the kitchen and the sitting room, everything was pretty much as it should be, except for dust and beer stains, but as I said, I expected as much. The shock came when I went into the bedroom. I've found all sorts in my time; bloodstains on top of the mattress, used condoms underneath, mice in the skirting, beetles under the wallpaper. I even had a pair of students who let their kitchen get so fucking beyond them they boarded it up and made it into a no-go zone— needless to say, they didn't get their deposits back. I thought they were the worst I was ever likely to see, but they were just lazy cunts. Crippen's bedroom . . . well, that was something else. Like a scene from a horror movie. To tell you the truth, there was a moment when I thought about calling the police, but I decided it'd be a waste of their time. I mean, if you could be arrested for crimes against decorating, that cunt Lawrence Llewelyn Bowen would be doing a twenty stretch, right?'

'So what had he done?'

'He'd covered the floor in writing.'

'The entire floor?'

'Not all of it, no. The bed was in the centre of the room and he'd made a kind of circle of words around it. When I first saw it, I thought it was going to be some major confession, where he'd hidden the bodies of hundreds of missing schoolgirls or something, but thank Christ it was just a load of crap.'

'Can you remember any of it?'

'I knew you were going to ask that, but no, I couldn't really read it. He'd used some kind of indelible paint and written in this sort of old-fashioned curly script. There were numbers and symbols too, like a lot of algebra in a circle round the bed. Whatever it was it gave me the bloody heebies. I gave it a good hard scrub, tried turps, ammonia, everything I could think of, but it wasn't for budging. In the end I had to hire a sander and take the surface off, then go down to B&Q, for deck varnish and seal it. I had to do the whole bloody floor or else the join would have shown. It was a fucking hellish job, dust everywhere.'

'I don't suppose you took a photo of it on your camera-phone or anything, just to show to your mates?'

'Why would I want to show them sick stuff like that? I wanted it gone before Baine came round and took the job of managing the flat off me.'

Murray started at the familiar name.

'Who?'

'Baine, the guy who owns the place. He's a university bloke like yourself. Oh, Christ.' John Rathbone's voice filled with sudden realisation. 'Don't say you know him.'

'No, I don't think so. What does he look like?'

'I never met him. I just speak to him on the phone and send any paperwork to his uni office over in Glasgow. He talks like he's got a boiled sweet in his mouth, but then a lot of them do.'

'No.' Murray hoped the lie didn't sound in his voice. 'I don't know him.'

'Thank fuck. Not that I'm saying you would have grassed me up.'

'But it would have been a waste of your decorating skills if I had.'

Rathbone gave a bitter laugh.

'That's the funny thing. He phoned up, thanked

me for my help over the years, and asked if I could show the estate agents round. End of story. Told me to take him off my books, he was putting the place on the market. I would have been as well not bothering. I'll tell you something for nothing, though.'

'What?'

'I got the feeling he was relieved to get the place back. I think he'd rented it out to the old boy as a favour, a guy that'd done well helping out an old pal that was down on his uppers—kind of cool, when you think on it. Though why a professor would want to keep up with an old soak is beyond me. Maybe he had fond memories. Crippen told me that him and Baine went way back. I guess they were students together or something. He was an intelligent man, Crippen. Just pissed it up against the wall.' The landlord sounded wistful. 'It happens.'

Chapter Twenty-Two

Murray stood at the top of the castle, gazing out to sea. He remembered Alan Garrett's note, *Interested in the beyond*. Had Lunan had any interest in the occult? Some of his poetry held an atmosphere of the Celtic otherworld, and Christie's novels were generally shelved in the bookshops' horror section; but these were fictions while it seemed Bobby's library had masqueraded as fact. He would need to visit the Geordie's landlord. Buy him a whisky and see if he could remember any of the books' titles. People sometimes recalled more when they had a drink in their hand.

Murray glanced at his watch. He would have to start walking if he were to be sure of catching the ferry home. He hopped down from the crag, thinking now about Fergus's uncharacteristic kindness towards Bobby. Strange that a man's charity should make him suspicious.

He felt his phone vibrate back into life, and then heard its irritating jingle. Murray glanced at the display and cursed as his fingers, clumsy with the cold, struggled to hit the right button to accept the call.

'Murray?'

His stomach swooped at the sound of his name on her lips, but even with that one word he knew something was wrong. Rachel's voice had lost its cool tone, the barrier of mockery she'd managed to preserve between them, even when he was inside her.

He asked, 'Are you okay?' and heard the answering note of concern in his own voice.

'Yes, fine. Listen, have you checked your email?'

'Not recently, no. Should I?'

There was a pause on the line. One of the horses grazing in the shelter of the castle looked at him with mild, brown eyes. He wondered where Rachel was. In the home he had never visited, or in her office, safe from prying ears. He listened for her breath, but couldn't hear it beneath the sound of the wind.

'Rachel?'

'Yes, I'm still here. This is . . .' She paused again and this time he waited, following the curve

267

of the horse's sleek brown back with his eyes, amazed, as he always was when he saw them in the flesh, at how big the creature was.

Rachel came back on the line.

'I wanted to ask if you could do me a favour.'

'Anything.'

He was as obedient as Pete's grinning dog, with none of its bite.

'I think you might have received an email by mistake. You'll be able to spot it, it'll have been sent yesterday by someone you don't know and will have a rather large document attached. Will you delete without opening, please?'

'Is it a virus?'

'Yes.' Relief sounded in her voice. 'A particularly ghastly one. It's designed to leech onto every contact in your address book. Clever, but nasty. Apparently it wipes the hard drive of any computer it's opened on. I'm frantically phoning everyone I can think of.' Her laugh sounded strange. 'It's embarrassing, like chasing ex-partners to let them know you've got VD.'

'Rachel, are you okay?'

'Fine, just . . .' Her voice faltered. 'Just a little overworked.'

'And your computer's wrecked. Did you lose much?'

'I'm pretty good at backing-up, it could be worse.' Her voice wavered again. 'I've got to go. I've an army of people to phone. But please, Murray, delete that email. I wouldn't want you to lose all your research.'

He said, 'I miss you.'

'Don't, there's no point.'

The line went dead.

Murray stood there, the phone warm in his hand, watching the tide's unstoppable shift. He supposed the view should give him a sense of proportion, but all he could think of was Rachel and Fergus, Fergus and Rachel. The wind flapped at his waterproof. He turned even though he knew no one was there. But there was something beyond the rustling noise of his hood. He could hear it. A distant pinprick of sound that rushed to a roar. His chest tightened and the thought, *so this is how it goes*, burst into his head, along with a vision of his father's face. The herd of horses turned together and raced down into the glen, the thud of their hooves absorbed by the almighty surge of sound. Murray felt himself drop to his knees, and then had an abrupt flash of comprehension as he saw the Harrier Jump Jet screaming through the valley. He could have shouted his lungs empty, and no one would have heard. But he simply whispered *fuck, fuck, fuck* under his breath, then got to his feet, wiping the mud from his knees, and started to make his way down.

*   *   *

He hadn't reached Everest when he heard the rumble of Pete's tractor behind him. Murray waited for it to stop, knowing the man had come to offer him something and hoping he was right about what it would be.

Pete climbed from the cab, the terrier at his heels. This time his smile was shyer, as if he was already embarrassed at what he was about to say.

'Were you serious about wanting to stay longer?'

'Aye, deadly serious.'

'I might have somewhere for you then, if you don't mind roughing it.'

Chapter Twenty-Three

Murray sat at the island shop's computer and logged into his email account. It wasn't quite three o'clock yet, but it had started to rain again and the skies outside were already dark. It felt good to be in and warm while the island was washed by wind and rain once more. The lamps had been lit against the gloom and a Calor gas heater hissed in a corner by the counter. Somewhere a radio was tuned to drive time, and he could hear the presenter detailing news of roadworks in the centre of Inverness. The small store, which had been so busy on his last visit, was empty of other customers. The shop man had given him a mug of instant coffee and told him to shout through to the backroom if he needed anything else. Murray took a sip from the steaming cup, relishing the sense of aloneness and study that had been a comfort to him since he was a child.

The number of new messages made him feel helpless for a moment, but there was only one he was interested in reading. He scrolled through the previous day's entries and found it, the sender's address a combination of letters and numbers that looked random, the subject heading *Tis Pity She's a Whore*, the attachment tantalisingly present.

He hadn't believed Rachel's story, but staring at the message with its strange title, remembering

270

the strain in her voice, he wondered if he might be wise to delete it, as he'd promised. Rachel had never asked anything of him before, though God knows he'd wanted her to. He rested his hand on the computer mouse. It was in his nature to investigate, but some knowledge was tainting. Pandora's box, Eve's forbidden fruit, Bluebeard's young wife with the key to her husband's private room. Succumbing to temptation could signal disaster.

He trailed down his inbox, hovering on indecision, deleting junk and outdated messages from the department about meetings he was now exempt from. He scrolled down further, hoping for a message from Rab that might tell him why Professor James had it in for Fergus. There was nothing. But tucked in amongst the list of unsolicited offers and enquiries was a message from Lyn.

Murray leaned back in the chair and gazed at the ceiling of the shop. A couple of yellowing remnants of sticky tape swayed in the rising warmth from the heater. Left over from Christmas decorations, he supposed. He sighed, leaned forward and clicked open Lyn's message.

Dear Murray
    I'm a woman who keeps her promises. I asked around about your smiler, Bobby Robb, Crippen as you called him, Crowley as they called him here. It seems he was one of our regulars until three years or so back, though the word is he was still a slave to the bottle—it's amazing the constitution you need to be a successful addict. I don't have

much for you beyond that except that he was 'a scary shit'. Apparently he was into weirdigan stuff, spells, magic, and wasn't above dropping a curse or two if it looked like someone might cross him. My source also said Bobby was a frightened man who slept with a 'circle of protection' round his bed—whatever that is. A word to the wise. Tempting as it might be for you to leap on this, you should remember that the streets are a hard place to survive. People develop different strategies for keeping themselves safe. If this was Bobby Robb's, it seems like a pretty good one to me. A lot of our clients are daft enough to believe in different dimensions. I wish I could, I'd leave mine in a flash. I'm not sure how much you know about Jack's activities. It's easier for me to assume nothing. It would mean one less person took me for a fool. I can't help wondering, though, that evening you asked me about Cressida Reeves. I thought you were interested in her for yourself, but maybe you knew? Either way, Cressida is off the market. Jack has moved out of our flat and in with her. I wish I could say goodbye to bad rubbish, but we've been together a long time. If you speak to him, please tell him I miss him. He won't take my calls any more. I kept my promise to you, even though your brother broke all the ones he made to me.

    Lyn x

The kiss at the end made Murray's eyes tear. He

blinked, then read the email again, cursing his brother even as he wrote the scant details Lyn had given him into his notebook.

Murray had no stomach for the rest of his messages, but somehow Lyn's words had decided what he would do about the email Rachel had asked him to delete. If love was a game of cheating and deception, then it was better to know what you were up against. He found the anonymous email again and opened it.

Murray tensed, half-expecting the screen to descend into blackness or display some childish victory halloo before fading into computer codes and nothingness, but the body of the email was empty. He moved the cursor to the virtual paperclip, ready to click open the attachment, but then the photographs started to slowly unveil themselves without any help.

He remembered where he was and minimised the screen, glancing behind him to check whether anyone had seen his shame, but the shop was still empty, the proprietor still somewhere in the backroom. Murray half-turned his chair towards the door, the better to hear any new customers entering, and then looked at the image again.

It took him a moment to realise what he was seeing. Then he recognised the room, the familiar desk with its pile of unmarked essays, the uncomfortable chair he reserved for students, shoved to one side. It was the night she dumped him, the night he had rushed into the corridor, chasing after the intruder. He could see his own white arse caught mid-thrust on the screen, Rachel's elegant legs inelegantly spread beneath him.

Murray glanced towards the counter, wondering how good a view someone standing behind it would have of the monitor, realising the computer had been cleverly positioned to allow minimum privacy. He rolled the cursor down the screen anyway, wondering how many snaps the prowler had managed to take. He would phone Rachel afterwards, reassure her that no one could know the woman was her, even if the photo were to be pasted billboard-high in George Square, or more likely distributed amongst a thousand pay-for-view websites.

Jesus, what a mess. But it was a mess they were in together.

He didn't feature in the next image. Instead there was Rachel with a young man Murray thought he might recognise from postgraduate forums. He couldn't be sure. The man's face was turned away and he was naked, Rachel kneeling on the floor between his open legs, her features hidden in his groin. She was naked too, pale and beautiful. Murray felt a sharp surge of jealousy, remembering that they had never completely undressed for each other.

The four remaining images were more of the same, Rachel and sex the only constant. Rachel with a grey-haired man who had kept his watch on. The time was half past three, and she was astride him, her hands fondling her breasts.

Rachel bent over a chair in a hotel bedroom while a hirsute man with a slack belly and balding head held her rear and pointed his erect penis into her.

Rachel on her back, two men with her this time, and the faint blur of other undressed bodies in the background.

Rachel with her legs splayed, the head of some naked stranger pressed between them, her head thrown back, neck exposed so that Murray could see the hollow in her throat he had liked to kiss.

There was a sound behind him. He killed the image and spun round in his chair. Christie Graves was standing at the far end of the aisle, a newspaper and a loaf of bread in her basket. Their eyes met.

The pictures had been so big, so arresting, as loud in his head as the Jump Jet that had brought him to his knees. He couldn't imagine how she could have missed them. Christie held his gaze for a moment, then looked away and went to the counter.

Murray sat staring at the blank monitor, hearing the shop man's cheery greeting and Christie's low replies, feeling a sense of loss that brought back other losses, too sad to even wonder who had sent him the photographs and what he could send them in return. He heard the door swing shut as Christie left the shop, but even then his eyes remained on the black screen of the sleeping machine.

Chapter Twenty-Four

Pete had been apologetic about the state of the bothy, but in the afterglow of the race down Everest, Murray had thought it the perfect solution. Back then Rachel's call had seemed like a spark of hope. She had thought of him, and even though she had hung up when he said he missed her, she'd sounded sad. Sadness had seemed something he might be able to work with. Now he felt that he might drown in it.

In the pale light of the afternoon the small cottage had appeared charmingly simple. Viewing its front room through the beam of his battery torch, Murray thought it embodied a decrepitude that matched his mood. The floor was covered in old cardboard, 'your original underlay' Pete had called it, to keep out the damp in the earth that sat directly beneath the wooden floor the crofter had laid when he and his family had camped there three years ago.

Pete dumped the carton of supplies they'd bought at the shop onto the makeshift table that took up most of the first room and swung the beam of his torch around the stone walls.

'It'll be a bit isolated for you after Glasgow, but we're only a couple of miles down the road and I'll drop by from time to time to see if there's anything you need.' Jinx padded around the room, sniffing into corners with an enthusiasm that hinted at vermin. 'Hi, you. Sit,' Pete commanded, 'or you're going out.' He primed the Calor heater, the blue flames bursting into life on the third press of the ignition. The dog settled herself in front of the fire. Pete scratched her belly roughly. 'That's not for your benefit.' He turned his attention back to Murray. 'There's an extra canister of gas for when this one runs out and there's butane for the Primus stove. I've brought you the wind-up radio we used when we were down here. Do you know how to use an Aladdin lamp?'

Murray said, 'I think so.'

But Pete showed him anyway. The room grew more present, but no more cheerful, in the lamp's yellow glow.

'You're going back to basics. The kids loved it when we lived here, but that was in summer. I made damn sure our cottage was ship-shape well before the winter came.'

'It'll be fine.' Murray opened the door to the cottage's second room and saw the sleeping bag and extra blankets neatly folded on top of the camp bed. An upturned wooden box sat beside it, ready to serve as a bedside table. Something about the Spartan neatness of the arrangement made him wonder if Pete had been in the army. 'I think you've thought of everything.'

'I doubt that,' the crofter grinned. 'It's been a bit of a rush job. But if there's anything missing, you can let me know.' He went out to the trailer and returned with a carton of supplies. 'The plan's always been to eventually turn this place into a summer let, but it's got sidelined over the last couple of years. I'm afraid it's not exactly tourist board standard.' He set a car battery in a corner, then went back out and returned with another, which he placed beside it. 'Okay, that's you got one and one spare. I've another charging at home. I reckon they should last you a week at least, but if they don't, drop round and I'll swap them. I've set up the chemical toilet in the shit box, as Martin liked to call it.' Pete laughed. 'You know what teenage boys are like.'

Murray didn't, but he forced a smile.

'I take it that's the outside lav.'

'Got it in one. There's a rain butt by the door that you can use for washing, and it's okay for

277

drinking if you boil first. Sheila says to come down to the house if you feel like a bath or a hot shower.' He paused. 'Are you sure you're all right with this? I feel a bit guilty charging good money for something so basic.'

Murray wished the small man would go, but he knew that he needed to endure the rigmarole before he would be left in peace. He forced a smile onto his face.

'Don't worry, it's ideal.'

'Good.' The crofter's grin looked relieved. 'I'm hoping the place is still watertight. I put the roof on myself before I moved the family in.' He shone the beam of his torch up into the eaves. 'I had a look this afternoon when I brought the camp bed down, there doesn't seem to be any ingress of water.' Pete clicked the torch off. 'Time will tell.' He reached into one of the boxes he'd brought and pulled out a half-bottle of Famous Grouse. 'A dram to welcome you.' He opened it and poured a little of the whisky onto the floor. 'The old bloke that helped us move made me promise to always do this in a new house. The faeries like a drink too, apparently.' Pete shook his head at his own foolishness. 'It's probably a joke he plays on all the English wankers.' He took two glasses from the top of a box, poured a large measure into each and handed one to Murray. 'Cheers.'

'Good health.'

Murray thought his own toast sounded more like a curse. But Pete smiled and raised the glass to his lips.

'So is your poet well-known in Scotland?'

'No, he's pretty obscure.'

'This glen's going to be proper cultured, what

with you beavering away down here on your biography, and Mrs Graves up on the topside working on her novels.'

Before the blows the photographs had dealt, Murray might have quizzed Pete on the exact location of Christie's cottage. Now he merely asked, 'Do you see much of her?'

'Not really, no. We phone to check on each other in the bad weather, and if the lines go down we drop round—you have to when you're as remote as we are, and her mobility isn't so good these days—but apart from that, we leave each other in peace.'

'Have you read any of her books?'

'Sheila's the reader in our family. She used to be an English teacher before we settled here. She read the first one.'

'*Sacrifice*?'

'I think that was it.' The crofter smiled apologetically. 'It wasn't a great hit, I'm afraid. Sheila usually likes books set on islands.' He took another sip of his drink. 'They remind her of here, I suppose, but she said this one was full of dead folk digging themselves from their graves.'

Murray felt a prickling on the back of his neck and resisted the urge to look towards the cottage's small windows and the night beyond.

'It's about a group of hippies who move to the countryside and start dabbling in things they shouldn't.'

'Raising the dead?'

'Amongst other things. It's a bit silly.'

The wind had got up again. Somewhere a gate was banging, but the crofter didn't seem to notice. He said, 'Maybe I should give it a read.'

Pete met Murray's eyes and his grin was wide enough for madness. Outside the banging became louder, then ceased. Murray wondered who or what had stopped it. He filled the silence with a question.

'What did you do before you moved here?'

'I taught too. Science. I decided to get out before I became the first teacher to do a Columbine and go on the rampage with a shotgun.'

The small man laughed. The lamplight caught the creases in his weathered face and twisted his smile into a grimace. Murray wondered if he had a gun up at the white cottage, and if he drank whisky there at night, alone in the middle of nowhere, with his wife and children asleep in the rooms above.

He rubbed his eyes and said, 'Aye, I sometimes feel that about my students,' though the thought had never occurred. 'I still feel bad about almost bumping into Miss Graves's car, even if she isn't Booker Prize material. Maybe I should call round with a bunch of flowers or something.'

Pete shrugged.

'You'll meet her sooner or later.' He closed one eye and held the half-bottle to his other, regarding the room through a golden whisky filter. 'Mrs Graves is unpredictable. Some days she stops and chats, others it's as if she doesn't see you. Sheila says that a hundred years ago she would have been fuel for a bonfire.' He laughed. 'The way she says it, you'd think it wasn't such a bad idea.'

'Your wife doesn't like her?'

'She doesn't like being snubbed. Me, I don't care. After all, no one moves out here for the company. And it must be hard for Christie. She's got MS. She had a bad episode a while back which more or less paralysed her. We thought that might be it, but she seems to have bounced back. Still, I'm not sure how much longer she'll be able to be independent, let alone live in the back of beyond.' Pete unscrewed the bottle's cap and poured the remains into their glasses. 'We may as well finish this, then I'll leave you to get settled. I promised Sheila we wouldn't go beyond the half-bottle. She doesn't like me driving after I've had a couple, even when there's only sheep to bump into.'

Murray nodded at the unmet Sheila's wisdom, relieved he'd soon be rid of his new landlord. He thought of Alan Garrett and remembered Audrey saying that he wasn't over the limit.

'I heard there was a bad crash on the island a couple of years back.'

Pete's expression grew serious.

'Not long after we arrived. Sheila was really upset by it. Kept saying what if one of the kids had been walking by when it happened? What if he'd hit them instead of the tree? We'd met him too. Seemed like a nice guy, a family man. I heard he left a wife and kiddie.'

'Was he under the influence?'

'Apparently not.' Pete gave him a half-suspicious look. 'You didn't know him, did you? I heard he was a university lecturer.'

'No.' Murray remembered the photograph of Alan Garrett that sat at his son's bedside. 'I heard about it, though. Bad news travels.'

'That's the truth.' Pete clicked his torch on and off, pointing its beam at the edge of the room, as if the sudden shafts of light helped him think. 'I shouldn't do that, I'll waste the battery.' He set it back on the table and looked at Murray. 'If I tell you something, will you promise it'll go no further?'

'Of course.'

The crofter looked Murray in the eye, as if assessing his sincerity. Either he decided to trust him, or the pull of what he wanted to say was strong enough to make Pete disregard any doubts, because he continued, 'I never mentioned it to Sheila—she was upset enough as it was—but I've often wondered if he did it deliberately.'

Murray remembered the piles of journals devoted to suicides, the carefully logged statistics detailing artists' age, gender, sexuality and the means they'd used to end their life. But the notion that Alan Garrett had committed suicide sat badly beside what he knew of his wife and child. He couldn't imagine how the smiling man on the mountainside could have wanted to abandoned them.

'Why?'

Pete shrugged his shoulders. There was something in the gesture that made Murray wonder if there had ever been a time when he'd contemplated smashing his tractor into a tree or convenient wall. He remembered the sickening feeling when his dad's car had slewed towards Christie's, the relief when he'd managed to bring it to a halt, and said, 'I guess you're sincere if you hit something as solid as that at full speed.'

'That's the thing.' The small man's voice was pensive. 'You'll have driven that road a few times yourself now. If you think on it, you'll remember there's not much along there that you could crash into that would have much of an impact. Sure, there are plenty dykes, but they're low. I've dwelt on it more than's healthy. That tree was about the only thing guaranteed to do the job. If he didn't mean it, it was very bad luck.'

'Bad luck anyway.'

Pete nodded and tipped back the last of the whisky in his glass.

'Not a very cheerful subject for your first night.'

'No.' Murray forced a smile. 'So tell me about the sheep.'

The crofter grinned.

'Why? Is there one you've got your eye on?'

They talked farming, then university and education, until the whisky was gone. Murray offered a dram from his own bottle. Pete hesitated, and then turned him down.

'I'd best get back. That's one thing about this life, early to bed, early to rise. It doesn't make you wealthy and wise, but it sure as hell makes you want to avoid hangovers.' He leant into one of the boxes and pulled out an unset mouse trap. 'You'll maybe need one of these. The little buggers like to come in out of the cold at this time of year. Can't blame them, I suppose. I'll lend you one of the cats for a few days if they become a problem.'

'Cheers.'

He must have looked dismayed because Pete laughed.

'Don't worry, they're tiny. Nothing like those big restaurant rats you get in Glasgow, just a bit cheeky. They don't seem to realise we're the superior species.'

He rose and pulled on his jacket. Jinx followed her master to the door, tail wagging. Murray got to

283

his feet too. Standing, the two men seemed to fill the room.

'I almost forgot.' Pete fished the tractor keys from his pocket. 'When I collected your bags, Mrs Dunn said she'd like you to drop by tomorrow afternoon, if you can spare the time. You've not reneged on the rent, have you?'

'No, you can trust me on that score. It might be about her bedroom carpet. I got mud on it.'

The crofter laughed.

'The whole island's mud, and worse. Landladies can't afford to get upset about that kind of thing. Likely she wants to feed you up, doesn't know about all these gourmet tins of sardines and baked beans you hunter-gathered at the shop this afternoon.'

'Aye.' Murray leant down and scratched Jinx between the ears. This time the dog tolerated him. He could feel the warmth of the gas heater still stored in her rough fur. 'That'll be it.'

* * *

Murray stood at the door staring into the cold night, long after the rumble of Pete's tractor had faded. There must have been a host of clouds hidden behind the night's blackness, because the world beyond his door was a trembling mass of dark.

'Starless and bible black.'

He wondered if he would start talking to himself more, now that he was to be so much on his own; found himself envying Pete Jinx's company. He and Jack had campaigned hard for a dog when they were boys, but their dad had been

284

adamant in his refusal. Murray had secretly suspected they would have had their way if their mother had lived. When he was very young there had been a point where the desire for his mother and for a dog had seemed equally strong. The two impossible wishes had merged and he'd imagined her up in heaven, a remote and smiling Isis guarded by a noble canine companion, the lost dog they never had.

Murray closed the door, turned off the heater and took a last glass of malt to bed with him, then lay in the utter dark, unsure of whether the noises he could hear came from the next room or from beyond the cottage's stone walls. Mice or the faerie folk tidying up in return for the dram Pete had gifted them. Either option seemed horrid. He pictured Bobby Robb's bed, shipwrecked in Fergus Baine's grubby tenement flat, and ringed by spells. He wondered if Archie had believed in the occult too—*interested in the beyond*—or if the intelligence which had helped him fashion poems from the rough stuff of words had saved him from that particular delusion.

Murray filled his mind with thoughts of *Moontide*, the perfect ordering of the poems which made the book not simply a collection, but a composition. He pushed away images of Rachel's face, Rachel's body, and started to recite the poems inside his head in the sequence Archie had arranged them.

*   *   *

He woke in the middle of the night from visions of a pink tangle of naked bodies, aware of his own

285

irritating hardness, unable to remember whether his nightmare had been of a holocaust or an orgy. Murray lay muffled under the blankets, waiting for the dawn. He saw the first, grey light creep across the room and watched his breath cloud the cold air. He decided to get up and wash anyway, and then drifted back into a dark and dreamless sleep.

Chapter Twenty-Five

The cottage grew too small for Murray at around eleven the next morning. He pushed aside the notes he couldn't concentrate on and pulled on his rain jacket and woollen hat. It was pelting down outside, but he stepped from the cottage and set out with no thought of a destination.

It seemed that he had lived half his life in the rain. Murray pulled up his hood and kept walking, his face lowered against the wind, the raindrops beating a tattoo on his waterproof. Surely the showers should be softer, more refreshing, in the clear air of the countryside, but it seemed to him that this was the same harsh rain that fell on Glasgow. Without the shelter of tenements and pubs the city offered it was free to sweep across the island and seek him out.

Usually such egotism would have made him smile, but now he just kept his eyes down, concentrating on the grass one plod ahead, trying to put Rachel from his mind. It was impossible. She was in the sickness he felt low down in his stomach. He wondered how many more encounters she'd had with other men, wondered if

Fergus knew.

Fergus.

For all of his suaveness and learning, he was a cuckold many times over. Murray tried to take satisfaction from the thought and failed. He didn't give a fuck about Rachel's husband. It was his own hurt that moved him.

He'd liked her poshness, liked her teases that he was her bit of rough; Murray, the dux of the school. Now he realised she'd considered him gauche, not sophisticated enough to be initiated into her games. She was right, of course. He would have been shocked—was shocked—at the idea of an orgy. His cleverness was of another brand.

It was the sense of specialness he mourned as much as Rachel herself, the belief that she had chosen him above others. His faith had been dented by her marriage to Fergus and her infidelity with Rab, sure. But he had nursed his trust, willing himself to forgive these faults in the knowledge that she had decided to make him her lover. Now he knew she gave her body the way another women might give you a smile, or a touch of her hand; something to be enjoyed, but no assurance of anything. She had made a fool of him.

Had the other men in the photographs treasured her the way he had or had they already known they were one of many? Murray picked up a stick and swiped it through the long grass edging the pathway, letting loose a spray of rainwater.

He wondered how he would ever face her again, and realised that he couldn't. He would have to look for a new job, though he was working in the one place he had wanted to work since he was a boy. Everything was spoiled. The thought

287

was childish in its intensity. There was nothing for him now, no lover, no family and no job. He would pack up and go home, except there was no home, only a carelessly furnished flat where he laid his head. The only home he had known had been handed back to the council when his father went into residential care. At the time he'd taken comfort in the thought that he and Jack were acting in accordance with their father's principles, and some new family would be able to bring up their children in its shelter. Now he wanted nothing more than to turn the key he still had in the lock, climb the stairs to the room he'd shared with Jack and lie face-down on the bed.

Ahead of him was an abandoned cottage, a derelict shell of the same design as the bothy he was renting from Pete. This one was missing its roof and front door. Its windows, free of glass, stared. Who had lived there, alone in the middle of nowhere, and why they had gone? Murray shivered. His waterproof was holding up well, but his trousers were soaked through and splashed with mud. It was stupid, letting himself get drenched like this, an invitation to a cold or worse, but he walked on, unsure of where he was going, seeing other derelict cottages and realising that the place hadn't been the preserve of some lonely crofter or a hermit seeking solitude, but a village.

He looked through one of the vacant doors and saw the grass growing on the floor, the ivy clinging to the walls. How long would it be before the elements toppled these small structures as they had already toppled the broch and the castle? Would future archaeologists dig here, or had records grown so precise every aspect of the recent past would be charted and ready for those who wanted to know? Maybe, soon enough, there would be no one left, no world to chronicle and argue over. All things must end, why not this too? The thought almost had the power to cheer him.

He was still close to the coast, but the track was veering inland now and the sea was out of sight. Murray noticed clumps of plump, dark green shoots in the grass around him. He guessed the ground was boggy and resolved to stick to the path. The sheep who had dotted his route till now were absent here. No birds sang and the sound of the sea, which had beaten a soft accompaniment to the wind when he was on the cliffside, was silenced. He must have descended into the shelter of some glen without noticing, because the gusts of air that had blasted the rest of his walk were gone. All he could hear was the rain drumming against his cagoule and the vegetation around him.

Murray looked at his watch. It was only lunchtime, at least four hours before the dark would come in, but already he thought he could sense the descent of the day. He had a sudden urge to turn back but pressed on, as a not-quite-sober man in a bar might press on into drunkenness.

There were some kind of man-made caves up ahead, small triangular openings in a wall of mortared stone set tight into a high ridge. They looked dark and deep and somehow inviting. Perhaps he could crawl into one of them and die. Murray wondered about braving the boggy ground, but a couple of steps from the path his right boot sunk calf-deep into wetness and sludge, and it took more effort than he would have expected to prise

289

himself free.

'Fuck.'

He was breathing hard. It would be a horrible way to go, sucked into the mud, a living corpse in a soft, enveloping grave. Stupid to die like that, when there were pills and rope, razors and gin-soaked baths for the taking.

Murray stamped his boot, trying to shake some of the mud from him, though he was already wet through. Christ, at this rate he would die of trench foot.

Maybe he should turn around. He had promised to visit Mrs Dunn that afternoon and if he was going to cancel in good time he would have to get back to elevated ground and find a phone signal. He noticed an unpainted wooden fence up ahead, cordoning off a small square of ground. He would walk to that first, though he couldn't think what would need protecting out here, where even the sheep didn't venture.

It appeared to be a depression in the earth, half grown-over with grass. Murray tested the ground beyond the path with his feet. This time it felt firm enough, and he ventured tentatively forth to get a closer look.

'I'd stand back from that, if I were you.' The voice was female, high and cultured. It came from the ridge above him. He looked up and saw a figure dressed in a waterproof of the same dark olive-green as the one he was wearing. She too had drawn her hood up against the weather. What little light there was was behind her, her face lost in the shadows. 'It's a sinkhole. No one knows how deep it is.'

Murray imagined himself aging as he fell

through the fathomless depths, his flesh rotting away, his skeleton still dropping, scream descending.

'Shouldn't it be better marked?'

The person on the ridge may have shrugged, but it was hard to tell through the mist of drizzle and the bulk of rainwear.

'Everyone knows it's there.'

It seemed futile to point out that he hadn't.

'Well, thanks for warning me.'

The figure nodded and turned away. Murray saw the stick, the awkward plunge of the shoulders as it limped from view, and realised that he'd been talking with Christie.

He shrugged his own shoulders. It was all pointless. He had been stupid to think he could write a biography of a man who had died thirty years ago, leaving one slim volume and not much else. The conversation with the Geordie's landlord had been typical of his researches. Tantalising and half-remembered, a dramatic postscript to a drink-addled man careless of his own sanity. It added nothing to Murray's understanding of Lunan. The long, lonely walk had decided him. He would go back to the city, write a tract that stuck entirely to an analysis of Lunan's poetry, and try to think of what to do next.

Fergus had been right. The poetry was the thing, the life an unfortunate distraction from the art. They should delete authors' names from all books and let the works stand or fall on their own merit. Fuck the egotistical, drunken shaggers who by some quirk of the genes were able to forge the stuff he used to think revealed the world to him. As far as he was concerned, they could sharpen their pencils and stick them up their own arseholes.

If Fergus knew about Rachel's 'hobby', then he was a saint. Murray remembered meeting the couple in, the department corridor the day he returned to collect the books he needed. Fergus's hand gently touching his wife's arm. In the professor's place, he would have been tempted to tumble her down the stairs.

It occurred to Murray that his affair with Rachel had coloured his attitude towards the professor. Fergus was gruff and opinionated, there was no denying that, but his actions were consistently on the side of right. He had been outspoken in his opinion that Murray confine his study to Lunan's poetry, going further than he needed in an attempt to stop him wasting his time. And whatever Bobby Robb's faults, it reflected well on the professor that he'd provided an old friend with a home.

It didn't matter any more. Soon they would cease to be colleagues, just as he had ceased to have any relationship with Rachel at all.

There was a shout from the ridge behind him. Murray turned and looked up at the small figure standing precariously at its edge. Christie lifted her hand and waved, though she must have known he had heard her.

'Yes?' Murray walked back to where he could hear her more clearly.

'Can you help me? I seem to have managed to get my car stuck.'

*   *   *

The ridge was too high and slippy to climb. He followed Christie's shouted directions and took the long way round to where the precipice descended, and then walked along the ascent until he found the track and the red 4×4 slumped half-on, half-off the shingled road, one wheel deep in the mud. The walk had taken him thirty minutes and he was sweating beneath his waterproof by the time he got there, despite the chill rain which had blown in his face since he left the shelter of the valley.

Christie must have been keeping watch for him, because she got out of the car as he approached and stood silently waiting as he walked the last few yards.

'I tried putting some cardboard down for purchase, but I just seem to be digging myself in further.'

He might have been a paid mechanic summoned to give roadside assistance, rather than a stranger who had walked a mile or so in a deluge to help her.

Murray squatted down and looked at the back wheel. He could see where it had churned the soft mud. Christie was right; she'd been ploughing deeper into the earth. He got to his feet. It was windier up here, the wetness blowing in all directions. The rain could almost be classed as playful, if it wasn't so fucking unpleasant, the persistence of it. The way it managed to slide beneath his outer layers and onto his flesh.

'I'll try pushing. If you bring the clutch up very slowly, we might be able to get it out. If not, I guess I'll walk back and find someone to give you a tow.'

Christie nodded. She got back into the driver's

293

seat, leaving the car door open. Murray positioned himself behind the Cherokee, waited until she had started the engine and then pushed with what remained of his strength. The 4×4 was huge. He felt his hands slip down its wet surface and knew that it wasn't going to budge. He smelt the petrol fumes and realised what he was doing was dangerous. He might slither beneath the broad wheels and be maimed or even killed. Murray felt a sharp stab of anger at Christie for calling him up here when he should have gone for help in the first place. But he went on forcing himself hard against the tank's boot, walking on the spot as his feet lost their grip and started to slide in the mud, just as he feared they would. He shouted, 'Pull the clutch up gently!' and resolved that when she stalled, he would go for help. But then he felt a small threat of movement, his hands slid again and he pressed them hard against the boot instinctively, knowing that if he let up the game would be over, the vehicle stuck tight. Then it bucked and pulled up onto the track with an audible slurp. Churned mud sprayed the air, a depressed Jackson Pollock abstract splashing his whole length. Murray staggered and would have fallen had he not managed to put a hand out and steady himself against the car's boot, even as it moved onto the shingled pathway.

For a moment he thought she was going to go off without a word. But then Christie stopped the car and leaned out.

'Thanks.'

'No bother.'

He searched his pocket for a hanky, failed to find one and rubbed his glasses against his jeans.

'Where are you headed?'

'Pete Preston's bothy.'

'Jump in and I'll take you to the crossroads, it's only a short way across the field from there.'

Murray looked down at his mud-spattered self.

Christie's voice was impatient. 'Don't worry. This car's seen worse. Besides, I seem to have miscalculated today. I might get stuck again.'

Murray glanced at her as he got into the passenger seat, and thought he could almost detect the hint of a smile.

*   *   *

The landscape looked different from the vehicle's high front seat. Now that he could lift his head and regard it without being battered by the elements, he could see that they were on a wind-blasted moor. The treeless expanse gave a long view of the depthless heavens. Murray felt like it might rain for ever.

'Are you part of the dig?'

He had expected their drive to be conducted in silence, and her question surprised him.

'No, just walking.'

Christie nodded, as if it was perfectly normal to tramp out to this abandoned portion of the island in a storm. She said, 'I don't usually meet anyone out here.' It was unclear whether she was explaining her question or the reason why she'd chosen the lonely spot.

Christie leaned forward and wiped at the condensation misting the windscreen. She'd turned up the hot air and the car felt stifling after the damp chill of outside. Murray had drawn back his hood when he got in; now he unzipped his jacket, pulled his woolly hat from his head and mopped his wet, mud-spotted face with it. He rubbed a hand through his hair. He hadn't had it cut since the summer break and it felt almost long enough to tie back in a ponytail. Perhaps this was how it started. The slow slide, until you became one of those blokes you used to marvel at, marking the time between giros by beating a track between the bookie's and the pub.

He straightened his spine.

'I walked through an abandoned village I don't remember seeing on the map.'

'It used to house the lime-workers.'

For a mad moment he thought of lime trees and imagined an orchard of them tended by cottagers who collected their fruit. Maybe his bewilderment showed because Christie continued, 'You were by the limekilns when I saw you. They employed about fifty men at one time, back in the eighteenth century. It was the extraction of lime that caused the sinkholes. You have to watch out for them, they're unpredictable and not all of them have been mapped.'

A stanza from *The Ballad of Reading Gaol* came into his head.

> And all the while the burning lime
> Eats flesh and bone away,
> It eats the brittle bone by night,
> And the soft flesh by day

He wiped a hand over his face, feeling the roughness of his bristles and said, 'Lime's what they used to use to dispose of dead bodies, wasn't

296

it?'

Her laugh was like a sudden bark.

'You've a morbid turn of mind. It was an essential element in building-mortar. A lot of those fine townhouses and tenements in Edinburgh and Glasgow wouldn't be standing if it weren't for lime made on this little island. What are you doing here?'

The question was abrupt and commanding.

Murray looked at her.

'I came to see you.'

Christie Graves smiled, and for the first time he caught a glimpse of the beauty she'd been.

'You sent me a letter, didn't you?'

He nodded. None of it mattered any more, but he asked, 'How did you know it was me?'

'It didn't really take a master detective. I looked you up when you first sent your request— your photograph's on the university website. I thought you were familiar when I saw you in the shop yesterday, but I couldn't place you. The beard makes quite a difference. But in any case, I would have realised when you said that you'd come here to see me. I'm not exactly inundated with visitors.'

She stopped the car and kept the engine running. Murray started to undo his seatbelt, but she said, 'We're not there yet, I just wanted to show you where I live.'

The heart of Christie's house was a two-roomed cottage of the style Murray now knew was typical of the old island, but it had been extended to form a long bungalow with a picture window at its western end, where it would be pleasant to sit with a drink in your hand, on clear evenings, and

297

watch the sun set. The road away from the cottage was still composed of rough stone, but it was wider and more even than the track they had just travelled, and the sleek black Saab parked outside Christie's fenced garden would have had little trouble driving down it.

'Very nice.'

'Are you afraid of the dark?'

It was sudden and unexpected, like all of Christie's questions so far, and it set off a strange remembrance in Murray. He used to have a recurring dream, of waking to see his mother standing at the door to his and Jack's bedroom, her silhouette shadowy and indistinct, but recognisably her. It was always marvellous at first, this vision of her and the waves of love that wrapped him warm beneath the blankets, but then gradually he would begin to feel her steady jealousy, because he and Jack were alive and cosy in their beds while she lay cold and dead in her grave. The conviction that she had come to take them with her would sweep over him. Sometimes when he woke the bed was wet. For years he had slept with the bedside light on. Jack hadn't seemed to mind. Perhaps he had his own nightmares.

'No, I don't mind the dark.'

'I'll be home tonight. Why don't you walk over after dinner and you can tell me what it's all about?'

Murray felt like the marrow had been sucked from his bones.

'It was about Archie Lunan.'

'I know.'

It was what he had come for, but too late.

'I've reassessed my project. It'll focus on

Archie's work rather than his life.'

They had reached the crossroads now. Christie stopped the car and pulled the handbrake on, but kept the engine running. The wipers continued to sweep the rain from the windscreen. She turned awkwardly towards Murray. Now he could see that some of the lines on her face were from pain, and the tiredness it had brought, but her voice belied any suffering. It was mild and unsurprised, the kind of tone he used when trying to guide a slow student into realising an obvious point.

'Why do you men always give in so easily?' Christie switched off the engine. The wipers stalled mid-swipe and the rain began to melt into sheets, warping the view of grey sky and green scrub. 'You went to the trouble of contacting me and then came over here to hunt me down, even though I said I wouldn't speak to you. Now that I'm willing, you've changed your mind. What happened?'

Murray shrugged.

'I decided it was pointless.'

Christie snorted.

'Everything is, but we have to find some way of passing the time.' She sighed. 'How much do you know about MS?'

He had been ready to open the door and leave. But now that Christie had mentioned her illness, he couldn't muster the strength to be callous.

'It's a slow wasting disease that works on the nerves.'

'That's pretty much it. Except that it works on the sheaths that protect the nerves, and it's not always so slow. If you're lucky, you can get away with years of remission where nothing much happens. If you're not, you can find yourself deteriorating rapidly to the point where you need a wheelchair. Or worse.'

Murray didn't want to know what worse consisted of. He gripped the door handle and said, 'I'm very sorry to hear that. I hope yours stays in remission.'

'It isn't in remission.' Murray looked at Christie and she gave a small nod. 'So if you decide you don't want to talk to me, make sure you're certain. I don't have time to grant second chances.'

He opened the car door and got out.

'Thanks for the lift.'

'I'll leave a light on. Tonight or not at all.'

Murray shut the door. He pulled his hood up and began the walk down towards the bothy. Halfway along the road he looked back, making sure Christie had managed to turn the car without getting bogged down in the mud again. She was gone. All that remained was the rain, beating down on the crossroads.

Chapter Twenty-Six

Murray pushed open the door to the bothy. The last leg of his journey had worn him out, and his teeth had begun to chatter in a way he'd thought only happened in cartoons. He peeled his jacket from him, registering that something was wrong.

The Calor gas heater glowed warmly from the centre of the room, though he had been careful to turn it off before he left. Murray picked up the heavy torch Pete had gifted him and tiptoed

300

towards the cottage's second room just as the door started to creak open.

The intruder took a quick step backwards into the shadows. He raised his left hand to protect his face and his right came forward, knocking the torch away. It tumbled from Murray's grip and skidded across the floor.

'Good God, Murray.' Professor Fergus Baine looked like he had dressed for his very first country house shoot. His Barbour jacket gleamed newly and his tweed cap was set at a rakish angle. He dusted some invisible spot from his lapel, staring at Murray as if unsure of what he was seeing. 'Are you okay?'

Murray pulled a chair out from the table and sat down. He was too tired to do anything except rest his elbows on the table and set his head in his hands.

'What are you doing here?'

'I was in the neighbourhood and thought I'd drop by.'

'There isn't a neighbourhood.'

Murray started to laugh, but the chill had him in its grip now. A shiver that could have doubled as a spasm clutched at him and the laugh turned to a cough. Murray pulled off his hat, dragged his jumper over his head and started to rub his chest dry with his T-shirt. *University of North Alabama.* God, that had been a while ago, back when everything seemed possible.

'So faithful in love, and so dauntless in war, there never was a knight like the young Lochinvar.' Fergus's voice was slick with sarcasm. He lifted the kettle from the Primus stove, felt the weight of water in it and lit the gas. 'You need to wash yourself in warm water.' He went through to the bedroom and returned with a blanket. 'Here, wrap yourself in this while we wait for it to boil.'

Murray draped the blanket round his shoulders, pulled his boots and socks off then stripped away his sodden trousers and underpants. The mud had penetrated his clothing and specks of it clung to his skin. Fergus Baine shook his head.

'What did my wife see in you? You look like Bobby Sands towards the end.' The kettle started to howl. The professor emptied it into a bowl, then filled a cup from the rain butt outside and cooled the boiling water with it. He put the steaming bowl and a cloth on the table in front of Murray. 'Here.'

Murray took the bottle of malt from the table and started to fumble with its cap.

'You don't need that.' Fergus plucked the whisky from Murray's grip. He took the empty kettle, refilled it and set it back on the stove. 'Spirits lower the body's temperature. A hot drink's always better.'

'That's a matter of opinion.'

Murray started to sponge himself. The water turned brackish. He supposed he should freshen it if he really wanted to get clean, but carried on dipping the unfamiliar cloth into the water, wiping himself down the half-hearted way a man might clean an old but necessary piece of equipment that was going to be replaced soon.

Fergus had been rummaging around in the boxes of supplies Pete had set in the corner and found a jar of instant coffee and a tin of powdered milk. He spilled generous measures into two mugs and added water.

'It's none of my business, but why are you camping in this hovel in the middle of nowhere?'

'The archaeology department requisitioned all the good rooms.'

Fergus set a mug of strong coffee on the table and stood cradling his own.

'You do realise that archaeology has much lower RAE scores than us? They're way behind on student numbers too.'

Murray's laugh held an edge of hysteria.

'These things don't count for much out here.' He took the blanket and started to wipe himself dry with it. 'How did you know where to find me?'

'I asked at the shop. Always the hub of island life.'

'No, I meant how did you know I was on the island?'

'Rab Purvis told me.'

'Oh.'

'Don't look so crestfallen, it hardly makes him a quisling. I was coming over to see Christie and had an idea you might be around so I asked Purvis. He didn't know I was going to look you up.'

'Pastoral care?'

'Something like that.'

The two men looked at each other. Murray was the first to break eye contact. He'd wrapped himself back in the damp blanket; now he went through to the other room, found a jumper and a cleanish pair of jeans and put them on. When he returned he said, 'You told me you'd only met Archie once.'

Fergus gave a nod that conceded his lie.

'I suppose I hoped the less fuel on the fire, the sooner it would burn out.'

303

Murray sat back at the table and cradled the coffee mug in his hand, taking comfort from its warmth. He thought about rescuing the whisky from the shelf where Fergus had placed it and found he couldn't be bothered.

'Why are you so against Archie getting his due?'

The older man had taken his cap off, but still wore his heavy jacket. The haggard paleness of his face gave him the air of a distinguished thespian.

'There was something about Lunan, a core of Romanticism perhaps, that's dangerous for your type of approach. Sailing when a storm was coming in was stupid egotism. It was typical of Archie.' Fergus steepled his hands together and rested his forehead on them for a moment as if the strain of memories threatened to loosen his composure. He massaged his temples then looked at Murray. The bright spark of energy that had seemed his defining feature was dulled, but it was still there, a small pilot light in the gleam of his eyes. 'Ultimately I thought you'd reduce a complex life to a simplistic narrative. Naïve but talented young man comes to the city, falls into decadent ways and is punished for his carelessness by an early death. I didn't think it would do either of you justice.'

'You came all this way to say my work's crap and have the balls to tell me it's for my own protection?'

Fergus gave the upside-down smile that meant he knew he had scored a hit.

'I came to see Christie. Her mobility's reduced to the point where living here's no longer feasible. The time has come for her to make a decision about where she wants to go.'

'And you're here to help her decide?'

Fergus bowed his head in a slight nod.

'Sometimes it helps to talk things over with old friends.'

'Was Christie's illness part of the reason you discouraged me from investigating Archie Lunan?'

'No, I told you. I thought it a genuinely poor proposal.'

Murray sipped his coffee. It tasted harsh, but it was hot and he took a second swallow. He shut his eyes for a moment. When he opened them, the professor was still there, staring at him, his expression as alert as an inner-city fox. Murray said, 'I met her this morning, on the ridge above the limekilns.'

Fergus's voice was free of concern.

'I'm surprised she can make it that far.'

'Her car had got stuck in the mud. I helped get it out.'

'She was lucky you came along. Weather like this, who knows how long she might sit there? Something like that could kill her.'

'She wants me to come and see her, to talk about Lunan.'

'When?'

'It doesn't matter. I'm not going.'

The same downturned smile twitched Fergus's lips.

'It's the opportunity you were waiting for.'

It was typical of the man to want to rub his victory home.

Murray kept his voice steady and said, 'I'll be on tomorrow's ferry.'

Fergus picked up his cap and set it on his head at a jaunty angle.

'I think you've made the right decision. Confine yourself to the poems. I'll make sure you get every support from the department.' He slapped the table with his open palm. 'Perhaps I should write an introduction for you? I could include a short reminiscence of Archie. It might help set his work in context of the time.'

The urge to punch him ran through Murray like an electric current.

'I don't know that I'll still be a member of the department.'

Fergus had half risen, now he sat back down and gave Murray his kingly look, a wise old lion giving counsel to a talking ape.

'There will be no awkwardness between us. Rachel and I are going to Italy at the end of next week, but she'll telephone when we're back and you'll come round for dinner. This will be in the past.' He got to his feet. 'If you can get your luggage up to the crossroads, I'll give you a lift to the pier tomorrow afternoon.'

He might have been a father offering to do a favour for a teenage son.

'There's a long way round, slightly more civilised than the route Christie takes in that souped-up jeep of hers, and I brought the Saab over. Its suspension is famous.'

Murray had never been that interested in cars. It had been Jack who'd sat in deep communion with packs of Top Trumps cards, memorising makes and models, comparing maximum speeds and fantasising about what he would drive when he grew up. But Murray should have recognised the black Saab parked outside Christie's cottage. The car was stamped on his memory. The smooth

306

swiftness as it overtook Rachel's BMW by the reservoir on the way home from their country park tryst. He remembered Rachel clambering onto his knee, unbuttoning her blouse, his shock as she flicked on the car's interior light, the brilliant shine of white lace before he clicked it off, the dark shadow of the other car.

He said, 'Don't you mind? Sharing her with strangers?'

The professor's voice was compassionate.

'With strangers, no. It's part of what binds us together.'

Murray nodded, as if he understood.

'Did you email me the photographs?'

Fergus's smile was saintly, a gentle shepherd caring for one of his flock.

'I thought they might help you get over her, and I knew I could rely on your discretion.'

Murray raised his eyes towards the sloped roof. He saw a trickle of water trailing down the stone wall, following the uneven surface of the rock, forging its path along the lines of least resistance. He said, 'I'll get Pete Preston to give me a lift in his tractor.'

'As you wish. Make sure you get back to Glasgow, where you can be safe and dry. The islands can be unhealthy for us city-dwellers.'

'Was Lismore unhealthy for Archie?'

'He died here. I thought you knew that.'

It was a bad joke, all of it. He'd thought all his curiosity was gone, but Murray found himself asking, 'Fergus, what was Archie like when you knew him?'

The older man paused by the door and looked at the room as if wanting to commit its details to memory. He hesitated. For a moment Murray thought he was going to refuse to answer, but then he started to speak and his voice was low and measured.

'Archie was scruffy, with a poor sense of hygiene and a tendency to drunkenness. He was slow to anger when he was sober and fast with his fists when he was in his cups, which, as I said, was much of the time. He liked women, but even after he met Christie he was convinced they didn't like him.' Fergus paused as if considering what he was going to say next, then went on, 'But there was no real edge to Archie Lunan, never any sense of suspicion. If he liked you, he liked you, no judgement attached. He's the only person I ever met to whom I'd apply the phrase, "too good for this world". He would have made a wonderful father, if he'd managed to turn his back on alcohol.' Fergus levelled his gaze to Murray's. 'Do you know what the main problem with Archie was?'

'No, tell me.'

'He thought everyone was as good and as loyal as he was, and of course they weren't.'

He gave his inverted smile again, but this time his face looked old and worn and inclined to tears.

Chapter Twenty-Seven

Mrs Dunn's private sitting room was warm. Murray leaned back in the tasselled easy chair he suspected had once been the preserve of long-dead Mr Dunn and bit into a fruit scone spread with the home-made jam. Archie the cat was basking in front of the electric fire. He peered at Murray through glazed eyes, then lowered his head back onto the carpet and slid into sleep.

'Not impressed?' Murray leaned down and ruffled the creature's furry chest. 'I'll add you to the list.' He sat back, marvelling at the cat's talent for relaxing. Was Archie neutered? Maybe that was the way to be content, sever all desires.

He had meant it when he told Fergus that he was through with the book. Even now, settled in the warmth of Mrs Dunn's front room, waiting to hear her story, he was sure he would never write it. But he had left it too late to cancel his visit and the tea and home-baked spread conferred an obligation. Murray glanced at his mobile resting on the occasional table beside him. Mrs Dunn had allowed him to charge it and the small bars on the display pulsed as the battery filled with energy.

He'd had no idea how hungry he'd been, but the landlady's baking had awakened an appetite in Murray as fathomless as a small boy's at a Sunday School picnic. He realised he was eyeing a plate of pancakes, even as he chewed on what remained of his scone.

Mrs Dunn settled her broad backside into the armchair opposite and freshened their cups with tea from the large pot on the table between them.

'Help yourself, Dr Watson. They'll go to waste otherwise.'

Murray doubted the archaeologists who had taken his berth would let cake go stale, but he filled his plate and asked, 'How did you know I wasn't a walker?'

Mrs Dunn took a bite from a slab of iced

309

gingerbread and brushed the crumbs delicately from the solid shelf of her bosom.

'I'm not sure I would know now. You've turned into a bit of a mountain man. But when you arrived your clothes were too new and you didn't ask any questions about the walking. Even the ones that have been here before want to know what the ground's like or if there are any bulls in the fields.' She looked down at her bulk and picked another fragment of icing from her blouse. 'I don't know why they ask me. It's plain I'm not much of a walker these days.'

'But you used to be?'

'Oh, yes.' Mrs Dunn nodded towards the wedding photograph on the sideboard. 'When I first came here, I could trek with the best of them.'

Murray followed her gaze and saw a thin man in naval uniform arm-in-arm with a slim, young bride.

'You made a lovely couple.'

'I'm not being conceited when I agree with you.' She smiled. Murray searched her face for the girl in the picture, and failed to find her. Maybe Mrs Dunn guessed what he was thinking because she added, 'I sometimes find it hard to believe it was us.'

'Were you married on the island?'

'Along the road at St Mungo's.'

'But you weren't born here?'

'I would have thought that was obvious from my accent. I'm a Glasgow girl, didn't settle here until after we were married in 1970.'

'So you were here when Christie and Archie arrived.'

Mrs Dunn took a sip of her tea.

310

'Yes.'

He waited for her to go on, but she rested her cup on its saucer and began to tell him about a granddaughter studying archaeology in Dundee. Murray worked through the contents of his plate and tried to nod in the right places.

Murray had told the landlady about his biography of Lunan while they drank their first pot, now they were on their second and he was still no wiser. It didn't matter. None of it mattered. He sipped his tea, hoping the caffeine would do its job and keep him awake.

'There's a few of the young ones gone in for it.' Mrs Dunn was well under way. 'They get school visits from the archaeologists when they're here and then there's always a need for free labour on the digs, so they get involved and some of them get hooked, like Kirsty. Of course, there's no guarantee she'll stick with it, but a degree's a degree. She can always do something else.' The old lady beamed. 'We never used to bother about the old monuments much when we were young. It's terrible to think on it now, but there were still crofters who took the boulders from the walls of the broch or the old castle to shore up their own dykes, and more than one who knocked down standing stones to make the ploughing faster. No one thought anything of it.'

Murray thought he could detect a faint, bitter scent of singeing fur, but the cat remained motionless on the rug. He said, 'Things must have changed a lot over the years.'

She turned down the corners of her mouth in a yes-and-no expression.

'The island looks pretty much the way it always

311

did. But in other ways, yes, a lot has gone. We didn't get television on the island until 1979. Before then there was a ceilidh somewhere just about every night of the week.'

The landlady's cheeks were lightly rouged, her lipstick carefully applied. Murray's bristles itched. He wondered at the effort of making up when there was no one to see you. He sat straighter in his chair and asked, 'So you didn't miss the Barralands Ballroom?'

Mrs Dunn laughed, brightening at the slight flirt in his voice.

'The village hall wasn't blessed with a sprung dance floor. But back then a ceilidh wasn't necessarily a dance. More often it was talking and singing, sometimes a wee dram, but not always. Just good company.'

'And were you made to feel at home?'

'People tried. I think they were glad of new blood. But, of course, it was hard at first. I didn't have any Gaelic and there were still some old ones that spoke it. They switched to English out of politeness when I was there, but I knew they'd rather be talking in their own tongue.' Mrs Dunn looked at her wedding photograph again, almost as if she were turning towards her dead husband for support. 'There weren't so many people my age on the island and so a lot of the talk was about the past. Brothers and sisters who had emigrated, old ones who had died.'

Murray could imagine the smoke-laden rooms, the young woman passing round refreshments as the elderly company droned on, correcting each other on the minutiae of events of no importance to anyone outside their circle.

'You wouldn't know who they were talking about.'

'I didn't have a clue half the time, and it took me a while to realise how ancient some of the old ones they spoke of were.'

The nape of his neck tingled.

'What do you mean?'

'Their ancestors were real to them, and they kept their memories alive with words and music. Times were changing, they knew that, but most of them still didn't feel the need to write their stories and songs down. Maybe they thought the power would go out of them if they were put onto a page.'

The cat rolled over, letting his other side get the benefit of the fire. Murray asked, 'And now?'

'Now we have television.' She nodded towards the set in the corner. 'I'm as bad as anyone. When it's dark and cold outside, I turn up the fire and switch on the box. The only chance we have of preserving the past now is by recording it. Kirsty and the archaeologists have helped me realise that. I'm not a gossip, Dr Watson.' The academic title was like savour in her mouth. 'I've kept my counsel for forty years, but you're a scholar. If you think anything I remember will help your book, then I'll tell you what I can, though it isn't much.'

Mrs Dunn eyed his tape recorder with approval. Murray leaned forward and pressed *Record*.

'I know you didn't come to the island until much later, but I wondered if anyone ever mentioned what Archie Lunan was like as a boy, before he left the island.'

'My husband was ages with Lunan, but he didn't remember much of him as a youngster,

313

except that he was clever and the other boys teased him for it.'

'So he was bullied?'

'I suppose he was, but John said Archie gave as good as he got. In fact, that's about as much as John would ever say about him, "He was a bonnie fighter when he was a boy."'

'Strange, on an island where the past meant so much.'

Mrs Dunn nodded.

'Maybe, but my John didn't like gossip, and as for the other islanders . . .' She paused as if grasping for the right phrase. 'I think there was a bit of shame attached to Archie's mother—or maybe not his mother so much as the way she was treated. You see, in a place like this we all have to support each other, whether we get on or not, even more so in those days. But from what I could gather, Archie's mother hadn't really wanted anything much to do with anyone. She'd left as a lass and came back with Archie when he was about three. No one knew who his father was, and she didn't enlighten them, though she styled herself Mrs Lunan. She lived with her father, and when he died she stayed on in the croft for a while. But she was strange and growing stranger. She must have known it, because when Archie was ten or so she left to live with relatives in Glasgow, taking the boy with her. I got the impression that some islanders thought more should have been done for the two of them. They were slow to talk of Archie and his mother in a way they weren't about others who had gone. The croft went to an old uncle of hers. It was a while after he died that Archie came back.'

'Did you meet him?'

'Archie Lunan?'

Murray nodded and Mrs Dunn looked away from him, towards the fireplace where all three bars glowed amber.

'Not straight away. It's easy to stay hidden, even in a small place like this, if you've a mind to.'

'And Archie had a mind to?'

'He must have. I heard reports, of course—they'd gone to the shop and bought provisions, he and Christie had been seen walking along the beach, the odd one with the scar had been spotted driving the old van they shared down to the pier—but I never saw them myself. So I decided to visit.'

Mrs Dunn got up and went to the sideboard. 'I don't normally take a drink, it's not wise if you live on your own, but it can be a help sometimes.'

'Medicinal.'

'That's the word. Will you join me?'

'It would be my pleasure.'

She took out a bottle of malt and two glasses. The cat got to its feet and stalked from the room, tail held high, as if in disapproval at the early-evening drinking. Mrs Dunn followed it through to the kitchen and returned with a small blue water jug. She poured a measure of whisky into her own glass and a larger one into Murray's, then topped her drink up with a little water. She pushed the jug towards him and he did the same. He thought she looked tired. He wondered about the children in the photographs that decorated this room as they had the hallway. Did they visit often? And what would they think if they could see him drinking whisky with their mother in the late afternoon, asking questions that made her go pale beneath her carefully applied make-up?

315

'Are you sure you want to talk about this right now? We could do it tomorrow if you prefer.'

'Some things are better spoken of after dark. I learnt that watching the old people at their ceilidhs. Daylight chases some memories away and the night can bring them on.' Mrs Dunn cleared her throat and began her story. 'I was probably fairly naïve when I married John, but I'd worked in an office and came from Glasgow, so I thought of myself as "with it"—"streetwise", as Kirsty would say. I imagine there's a point early in most marriages when you wonder if you've done the right thing. I think I'd reached that when I went looking for Christie.'

'You wanted to meet Christie rather than Archie?'

'I was desperate for the company of a woman my age, someone to talk to about music and the latest fashions. Even if there was no one to see me wearing them, I was still interested. I wasn't bothered about Archie Lunan. I was wondering if I'd done the right thing settling in the middle of nowhere, but I loved my husband.'

Murray raised his glass of malt and took the smallest of sips. The iodine scent of it stung his eyes and burnt against his chapped lips, but it was smooth and warm on the way down. He set the glass on the table, though he wanted to knock the lot back and then pour himself another. He asked, 'So what did you do?'

Mrs Dunn's voice took on a thoughtful, far-away tone.

'I turned into Little Red Riding Hood. I made a cake, packed it up and went through the forest until I met the wolves. That's something the story got wrong, wolves don't travel solo, they hunt in packs.' She caught his eye and smiled as if laughing at her own fancy. 'Archie's croft wasn't one of the better ones, and his uncle had been gone a while before he claimed it. Have you ever been in one of these old cottages?'

'I'm camping in Pete Preston's bothy.'

'Of course you are. So you know well enough what they're like—barely more than a small barn, no insulation beyond what's offered by the stone walls. But back then people improvised with straw and wood, whatever they could lay their hands on, I suppose.'

'Pete's place is small. It's hard to think of a family living there.'

'Open-plan is nothing new. Everything happened in the one room. By the time I arrived that way of life was more or less gone and there were only a couple of blackhouses left. Like I said, they were basic, but they could be warm and cosy too. When I reached the croft where Christie was staying, I realised they could also be squalid.'

Archie the cat came back into the room, licking his lips as if he had just eaten something particularly choice. He pushed his front paws out in a long stretch that emphasised the length of his spine, then leapt onto Murray's lap.

Mrs Dunn shook her head.

'You're not allergic, are you?'

He stroked a hand across the creature's fur. Archie unsheathed his claws, hooked them through the fabric of Murray's jeans and into his flesh. The cat purred and Murray tried to keep the pain from his face.

'I don't think so.' He wasn't sure.

317

'I can't remember anyone being allergic when we were young.'

He ran his hand over the animal's fur again, fascinated by the way each hair sprang perfectly back into position, the tom's tortoiseshell markings breaking up then reassembling themselves, an ordered universe.

'We've grown softer.'

'I wouldn't say that. But sometimes when you think back it's hard to remember how things were, how you were. It's like looking at someone else. The girl who walked down to that blackhouse was nothing like the old lady sitting in front of you today, and yet they both are—were—me.'

Murray nodded. The man he had felt himself to be had changed since he started his quest for Archie.

Mrs Dunn went on, 'I'm not sure what I expected. Someone a bit like myself, I suppose. A young woman missing the city, but enough in love with her man to shift to an island that didn't even have a café, let alone a cinema or a dance hall.'

The cat had fallen asleep. Murray traced a finger down a black stripe dappled between its ears.

'You were looking for a friend.'

'I think I might have been.' The landlady took a sip of her drink, and when she spoke again her voice was stronger. 'I wasn't certain where the croft was, and back then I didn't drive. But like I said, in those days I could trek with the best of them, five miles was just a warm-up. Anyway, I had nothing better to do. John had gone to the rigs, to try and get a bit of money to help get us started. He'd wanted me to go to my mother's in Glasgow while he was away, but that would have been like going back to being a daughter. I was determined to stay in our wee cottage.'

'But you were lonely?'

'Very. Still, I made my mind up to stick it out and make the best of things. Deciding to visit Christie was part of that.'

'How did you know she would be there?'

'I didn't. Nowadays people don't go anywhere without phoning first, but there were fewer phones around and time wasn't so precious. You called round, and if the person was out, you went away. I simply stuck my cake in my bag and set off.'

'So was she in?'

'No.' Mrs Dunn paused and took another sip of her drink. 'I stopped a short way off from the cottage to tidy myself up. It was a warm day and I regretted not bringing a flask of water with me, but I'd brought what I considered the essentials: a hairbrush, powder and lipstick.' She shook her head, but there was no mirth in her expression. 'What was I thinking? I knew they were hippies, they were hardly going to be impressed by good grooming. Anyway, I was all straightened up and as ready to get acquainted as I ever would be when a man shot out of the cottage like a bullet from a shotgun.' She shook her head again at her young self's folly. 'If he was the bullet, I was the rabbit. I froze and my eyes must have been wide as flying saucers. He tripped over a tussock of grass and landed almost at my feet. If we'd been in a romantic novel, it would have been the start of a great love affair. I certainly behaved like one of those stupid girls in the stories. I gave a silly scream and dropped my bag. The man on the ground started to laugh, and I did too, though whether it was because I thought it was funny or because I'd got a shock, I'm not sure. He got to his feet, graciously returned my bag and asked if I'd like to come in for a cup of tea.'

Murray leaned forward and the cat stiffened in protest, flexing its claws against his leg.

Mrs Dunn went on. 'I think I knew then that the best thing to do would be to go straight home, but I'd spent three long weeks with only elderly visitors for company. I was desperate to meet young folk—young, city folk. Plus I could give myself a genuine excuse. I'd had a long walk without any refreshment and was beginning to feel a little light-headed.'

Murray could see it, the hot day, the girl in her summer frock, the young man looking up at her from his seat on the grass. He asked, 'Was he Archie?'

'I assumed he was, though his accent was posher, a bit more English than I'd expected. I told him I'd dropped round to pay my respects to Christie and was she in? He laughed—he had a nice laugh—and said no, but she would be back soon. I thought, oh well, what's the harm, and went on in, merry as a wee mouse spotting a rind of cheddar in a trap.' Mrs Dunn stopped. Her eyes rested on the tape recorder and she might have been checking to see that its spools were still rolling, or reminding herself why she was telling her story. 'I'd never seen a house like it. It wasn't just the mess. My mother was a hard worker, but there were six of us living in a single end. It was clean, most of the time, but it was no home beautiful. No, it was the strangeness of it all that overwhelmed me.

'The table looked as if no one had washed a dish for days. There was some chemistry equipment in amongst the crockery, a Pyrex flask suspended on a metal stand above a Bunsen burner, with an orange tube dangling from it. The funny thing was it didn't look out of place, even though it was obviously a room where people ate and slept. I could see the bed recess, the bedclothes half-slung on the floor. A woman's dress was hanging all bunched up from a nail on the wall beside it. I remember that distinctly, because I knew it would leave a mark on the fabric. I wanted to go and straighten it, but there was a man's shirt draped on top with its arms tied tight around the dress's waist so it looked like a couple in a clinch. The place stank—a sweet smell, rotting vegetables, unwashed bedclothes and sweat. I could see flies circling in that horrible way that they have, as if they own the place and we're some bit of territory where they might land if they get the notion.

'There were books everywhere, or so it seemed. Piled on the table, the chairs, the floor. When I say piled, I don't mean in neat columns. It was as if there'd been an explosion of books. They were tumbled all over the place, some of them lying open as if they'd been flung away halfway through the reading of them.

'The man who had invited me in said, "We've got a visitor", and the strangest thing happened. A head raised itself from in amongst the mess on the table and looked at me. There was so much chaos I hadn't noticed a man asleep in the middle of it. Like I told you, I'd lived in Glasgow all my life up until then. I'd seen plenty of men with scars on their faces, but this one was a humdinger.'

'A Colgate smile.'

It was as if Mrs Dunn had forgotten he was a doctor of literature. Her voice held a warning note.

'I wouldn't joke about it, son.'

Murray said, 'I went to his funeral the other week,' like it was some kind of reparation for his lapse in taste. 'I'm afraid it wasn't very well-attended.'

Mrs Dunn nodded, taking the empty pews in her stride, and went on with her story.

'I was standing in a block of sunshine by the open door. I could still feel the warmth on my back and hear the birds singing outside, but beyond that small shaft of light, it was a different world. Some of those stories and songs I'd heard at the ceilidhs must have stuck, because I remembered tales of people getting lost in the faery hills. The faeries lay on a fabulous evening of feasting, drinking and dancing, and next morning set their guest on the right path for home. But when they arrive back in the village, the poor soul discovers a hundred years have passed and all their kin are long dead.'

Murray said, 'When seven lang years had come and fled, / when grief was calm, and hope was dead; / when scarce was remembered Kilmeny's name, / late in a gloamin' Kilmeny came hame.'

'You would have fitted in well at the ceilidhs, Dr Watson. I felt like Kilmeny herself, too fascinated to turn for home. The one I'd met first said, "Let's have some of your famous tea, Bobby." And the other one jumped to his feet, though he'd looked half-dead the moment before. Suddenly I

322

realised they were not much more than boys and felt annoyed at myself for being such a teuchter. I think that was one of my great fears, you see, that I would lose my so-called sophistication and end up a wee island wifie.'

The lights shone warmly in the sitting room and it was only when Mrs Dunn rose and drew the curtains that Murray realised the world outside the window had descended into darkness. Archie the cat stood up in Murray's lap, raised his tail and presented an eye-line view of the tiny arsehole set in the centre of his lean rump. He jumped elegantly to the ground. Mrs Dunn opened the living-room door and he slid through, tail as straight as a warning flag.

'As soon as he hears me closing the curtains, that's him out for the night, hunting.'

'I guess the pickings are better after dark.'

'For some things.'

'It was sunny the day you went to visit Christie.'

Mrs Dunn hesitated, as if reluctant to return to her tale.

'Scorching. The man I had met outside introduced himself. It turned out he wasn't Archie at all, but a friend of his . . .'

Murray knew the name was coming, but it was still a shock to hear it on her lips.

'. . . Fergus. The other one, the one with the scar, was Bobby. He came back with the water and said, "It was time for a brew anyway."' Mrs Dunn lifted her glass of whisky, and rested it on the embroidered antimacassar on the arm of her chair, gazing at it as if she could see the scene in its tawny depths. 'I was nervous, sitting there with two men I didn't know, even though they weren't much

323

more than boys. But the door was still open, the daylight still shining in from outside, so I told myself to relax and stop being such a baby. Fergus did most of the talking. I wouldn't have entertained him if I'd been on the mainland. He was the kind of lad me and my pals would have laughed at, a bit of a snob, I suppose. But it was nice to have company of my own age, even if he wasn't talking about the kind of things people our age usually talked about.'

'What did he talk about?'

'Poetry, I think. Remember, I'd got used to being in company where I didn't understand half of what was being said. The other one, Bobby, put the tea in front of me. It was like no tea I'd ever seen before.' Mrs Dunn broke off and looked at Murray. 'You'll be less naïve than I was back then, Dr Watson.' She gave a small laugh. 'I'm less naïve than I was back then, but they were simpler times. I got the cake out of my bag. It seemed a shame not to share it with them. Anyway, I had a feeling I'd need something sweet to help me get that brew down. And I was determined to get it down. It's amazing what folk will do for politeness' sake.' Mrs Dunn straightened herself in her chair and smoothed her skirt beneath her hands, though there was barely a crease in it. 'The two boys held their noses and drank up. I thought, this is funny tea this, but Fergus said, "It's a herbal infusion, extremely efficacious. Christie introduced us to it."' That was the way he talked. But I thought, oh well, if it's good enough for Christie, it's good enough for me, and swallowed the lot.' She took a sip of spirit as if hoping to banish the memory of the awful drink. 'At first it was wonderful. Three

324

children and all these years later, I can still recall the sensation. I never experienced anything else like it. The pair of them ate the cake like they hadn't had a decent meal in days.' She looked him in the eye. 'A bit like the way you ate the cakes I gave you this afternoon. But it seemed so funny the way they wolfed it down. I started to laugh, then found I couldn't stop. It didn't matter, because they were laughing too. I'm not sure how long we sat there, laughing over nothing.' She took another sip of her drink. 'What happened next happened gradually, the way the sea sometimes changes colour. It can be the brightest blue, and then, without you seeing where the change came from, the waters turn to grey. You look at the skies overhead and realise the whole scene has transformed and you could be in a different day from the one you were in, a different world.'

Murray kept his own voice calm, unsure of what he was about to hear.

'That's the way it is in Scotland.'

Mrs Dunn looked away from him, towards the curtained window.

'It crept up on me like that. A feeling of dread. Then suddenly, I was terrified.'

'Of the two men?'

'Of the men, the room, my own hands, the grass outside, the sound of the birds. I'd been fascinated by the books, now I could see bright shadows of them, little diamonds floating in the air, as dazzling as the stained glass in St Mungo's when the sun's behind it. It should have been beautiful, but it was too strange. I'd thought I was going mad, alone without John in the cottage, now I knew that I was. Fergus and Bobby were still talking, but I had no idea of what they were saying. It was as if their sentences were overlapping and repeating. I would hear the same word recurring over and over again, but not the word that came before or the ones that came after.' Her voice rose and fell as she repeated the words in a far-away chant,

> *Sacrifice*   *Pure*
>   *Pure*   *Wisdom*
> *Wisdom*   *Sacrifice*   *Transcend*
>   *Wisdom*   *Sacrifice*   *Pure*
> *Pure*   *Pure*   *Transcend*   *Wisdom*
> *Transcend*   *Wisdom*   *Sacrifice*
>   *Pure*   *Wisdom*   *Transcend*

'I'd thought I was Red Riding Hood, now I was Alice fallen down the white rabbit's burrow. I wanted to ask if it was a poem, but I couldn't because worse than the strange sounds and moving colours was the fear. It paralysed me. I tried closing my eyes, but the shapes were still there, organising themselves into patterns behind my eyes. Did you ever have a kaleidoscope as a child?'

'Yes.'

'I didn't. Maybe they weren't invented, or maybe they were too expensive in those days for the likes of us, but years later my daughter Jennifer got one in a present. I took a wee look through it and felt like I was going to be sick.'

'Because it was like your bad trip?'

'You don't even need me to tell you, do you, son?'

'I've never taken drugs myself.' It was true,

except for the occasional joint, soggy with other tokers' saliva, passed around at parties when he was an undergraduate. 'But I've read about plenty in novels. You had no idea what was happening, or what they gave you?'

'No idea at all.' Her voice softened with the awfulness of the memory. 'I thought I was going mad. On top of the fear and the visions, I had an urge to vomit and yet I wasn't sick until it was all over.'

'Did the others notice you were having a bad time?'

'They must have, because hands—I'm not sure whose they were—took hold of me. I think I struggled. I have a memory of shouting and of hitting out and of something, someone, pinning me down, but then I was drifting, I'm not sure for how long, in a kind of trance, not awake, not asleep. I prayed I wasn't dead, because if I had been I'd have stayed in that state for all eternity.' She stopped speaking and the only sound in the room was the wind tearing down the empty road outside and the hiss of the gas fire. 'That was the wrong thought to have, because then all of eternity seemed to open up in my head and it was terrifying.'

There was a bang at the window and Murray flinched.

'It's okay.' Mrs Dunn gave him a reassuring smile. 'That pane's loose. I'll need to get it seen to.'

Murray asked, 'Why do you think they drugged you?'

Mrs Dunn opened her hands, revealing her empty palms.

'Maybe they thought I would like it. After all, it had no bad effects on them. I suppose they were used to it. Or maybe they wanted to humiliate me.'

The anger was sharp in Murray's voice.

'It was themselves they humiliated.'

'Maybe.' Mrs Dunn gave a sad smile. 'There was one particular thing, though, that's given me the shivers ever since, whenever I think on it.'

She took a sip of her whisky and Murray said, 'Just one thing?'

'No, the whole day has the quality of a nightmare, when I remember it. That long walk in the blazing sunshine, the man falling at my feet laughing, Bobby's scar and worst of all the colours loosening themselves from the books and floating in front of my eyes, no matter if I shut them or not.'

He wanted to ask her to scroll back and tell him the worst part of the memory, but his interruption had distracted her and she was moving on again.

'I'm not sure if I slept, but I came to sometime hours later. I was in total darkness. I sat up and hit my head on the roof of the recess and for a second I thought I'd been mistaken for dead and buried alive. I would have screamed, except that the feeling of dread was still with me, not so intense, but strong enough to make me freeze.'

'You were petrified.'

'Yes.' She gave him a grateful smile. 'That's the word for it, petrified. But I realised that I could hear voices beyond the darkness of what I thought was my coffin and stuck my hand out. It hit wood on one side, but then I found the curtain and drew it back.

'It was still bright outside, but that didn't mean

328

much—it was summer and this far north it can still be daylight nigh-on midnight. Christie and your Archie were sat at the table with the other two. God only knows what I looked like, but they behaved as if it were nothing unusual to see a madwoman appear from nowhere. Maybe it wasn't.

'There was a bottle of spirits on the table. Fergus offered me a drink. It was almost as strange as the trip, the way they looked at me as if nothing had happened. The night was still warm, but Christie had this muckle big coat wrapped around her.' Mrs Dunn shook her head. 'It looked like something you might pick up at Paddy's Market, but she couldn't have been more elegant if she'd been dressed from head to toe in couture. I knew then I'd been foolish ever to imagine the two of us talking about hemlines over tea and cake. Christie was one of those women who make their own style. She glanced me up and down without a flicker of emotion, and then she turned to Fergus and said, "Leave her alone. Can't you tell she's pregnant?"'

Murray wondered why the landlady hadn't mentioned it before and asked, 'How advanced was your pregnancy?'

'So early I didn't know.'

'So how could she?'

Mrs Dunn shrugged as if it was nothing remarkable.

'Some women can tell these things. But of course it gave me a shock when she said it. The one with the scar laughed and said something like, "When did that ever make a difference to him?" But by then I had come to my senses. I just wanted to be away and home.'

'What did Archie do?'

'Nothing. Just sat there as if it had hee-haw to do with him, which I suppose it did, except for that fact that it was his house and his guests.'

'And no one went with you?'

'Fergus got to his feet, but Christie told him to sit down. She said something about him having done enough damage and me knowing the way back myself. Then Bobby got up, and for one dreadful moment I thought he was going to offer to escort me, but she said "And that goes double for you." ' They obeyed her like she was the leader of their gang. I should have been grateful, but for some reason it made me dislike her more. I'd gone all that way, full of hope, and those men had abused me.'

It had been in his mind ever since she mentioned the rough hands and the bed recess.

'Do you think they . . .' Murray paused, searching for the right word and failing, '. . . when you were in your trance?'

'I do remember fighting and shoving, but no. I would have known if anything more had happened. There are ways of knowing.' Mrs Dunn put a full-stop at the end of the sentence, as if to make clear that certain things were not to be discussed outside women's realms. Her voice regained its briskness. 'So that's it. Not much to do with Archie Lunan perhaps, except that was the life he was living and the people he was mixing with, when he was here.'

'And he drowned soon after?'

'A month later. His uncle had left a wee boat, not much more than a rowing boat with a sail stuck on it. Okay for fishing, but not big enough to risk on open water, even if the weather was fine.'

Murray remembered the scant newspaper accounts he had photocopied in the library.

'And it was wild, the night he went out.'

Mrs Dunn nodded.

'A bit like tonight. They reckon he sailed round towards the south-eastern point of the island. There's a reason they put a lighthouse there. A wrecker's paradise, John used to call it.' As if on cue, the rain battered against the window, shaking the loose pane in its frame. 'Archie won't be having a very good night out there.'

Murray caught his breath.

Mrs Dunn met his eyes and said, 'It was my eldest boy that named the cat. I never thought of him as having the same name as poor Lunan before.'

'Why "poor Lunan"?'

'Because he died so young.' She gazed towards the windows and the sound of the storm. 'And because he was with those people. Even in the state I was in, I could see he was out of his depth.' She looked him in the eye. 'Bobby had seemed unhinged to me. And Fergus? Well, Fergus had the kind of recklessness boys usually grow out of, if it doesn't kill them. But Archie . . .' She paused, looking up at the ceiling as if searching for the right words. 'Archie was handsome in a way the other two weren't. He seemed separate from them too. Looking back on it, I'm not sure he knew what was going on. He only had eyes for Christie. I remember he reached across the table and took her hand. She let him, but I don't think she looked at him once.'

'Were you here the night he drowned?'

'Yes, safe in bed like the rest of the island. The

331

alarm wasn't raised until the next day. By then his body had been taken by the currents.'

'Who raised the alarm?'

'I heard that it was the smooth one, Fergus, who came looking for him at the shop. God knows where Christie thought he was, but I suppose that even she didn't think he'd go sailing on a night like that. There was a search, of course, though I think people knew it was a corpse they were looking for. Two days later Fergus and the other one left the island. I hadn't realised it, but there had been talk about strange goings-on for a while.' She gave him a smile. 'The old islanders were maybe unsophisticated by my standards, but they knew a lot more than they let on, a lot more than me when it came to it. The two men were told to leave if they wanted to stay in one piece.'

'And Christie?'

'There were those who would have liked her to go too, but she was a different case. She had ties here, and though there were few that would speak to her at first, that never seemed to bother Christie. I dare say she could have been forced out, but she kept herself to herself, and though there was talk about midnight rambles and the amount of time she spent down by the old limekilns, people grew used to her. There were even a couple that were pleased when she published her first book.'

Murray leaned forward.

'What did you mean when you said she had ties here?'

'Christie's mother came from here. I thought you would have known that? She and Archie Lunan were cousins.' The surprise must have shown in his face because Mrs Dunn smiled. 'It seems strange to us, but I doubt that would have bothered the islanders if Archie and Christie had behaved. They travel far and wide, island folk. It wasn't unusual even back then for men to have crossed the Atlantic and back several times, but there were always some who married not far from their own door.'

'So the cottage where she lives now . . . ?'

'Came to her after Lunan died. I hear she's done a lot to it. I would hope so. But that visit was my first and last.'

She paused and it seemed as if her story might be at a close. Murray said, 'Mrs Dunn, you mentioned that there was something that chilled you even more than the rest of your experience. Will you share it with me?'

She nodded and her voice took on the same clear quality he now recognised as the tone she used whenever she had something difficult to relate.

'It was while I was still in the recess. I was groggy, but I could understand what they were saying. The one with the scar said, "She would do. No fuss, not much blood, a quick stab to the heart, over and out. Painless. All that energy released and the prize of a new dimension in store for her." Fergus laughed, and told him he was talking something-I-won't-repeat. Then he said, "Anyway, you can tell she's not a virgin, and that's what you're always going on about isn't it? Purity?" Christie snapped at them both to shut up. I was grateful to her, but I blamed her too. It might not have been logical, but it was her I had come to see.'

'But she was right about what she said? You were expecting?'

'Yes, I was.' She looked back at the wedding photograph on the table by her side then said, 'I'm afraid we lost that baby. Things just turn out that way sometimes, but I couldn't help associating the miscarriage with what had happened and blaming them, even though I suspected it was nonsense.'

They sat in silence for a moment, then there was the sound of a key in the lock. Mrs Dunn said, 'That'll be my archaeologists. Will you excuse me a moment, please, Dr Watson? They'll be famished.'

'And muddy?'

'As gravediggers on nightshift.' She put the bottle of whisky on the table. 'Help yourself to another dram. You look like you could do with it.'

*   *   *

Murray had no idea of how long he had been asleep. He picked up his phone and checked the time. Seven-fifteen. He must have been out for at least an hour. He shoved the mobile in his pocket. His mouth was dry, the dram where he had left it. He raised the glass to his lips and knocked it back, getting to his feet and banging his leg on the coffee table, almost tumbling it over. Mrs Dunn must have been listening out for him because she opened the sitting-room door.

'I couldn't bring myself to wake you. I kept you a bit of dinner back.'

'That's kind, but I have to be somewhere.'

'You're going to see her, aren't you?'

'I think I have to.' He hesitated. 'Did you ever talk about it with anyone else? A professional?'

334

'Life is for getting on with, Dr Watson.'

'It's for looking back on too.'

'True enough. But if you're wise, you choose your memories. I don't plan to think on this again, now that I've told you.' She smiled. 'You're my sin-eater come to take it away.' Mrs Dunn lifted a padded envelope from the hall table. 'This came for you.'

Murray turned it over and read Professor James's address on the back.

'Thanks. It's a book of poetry someone thought I might enjoy.'

'You say that as if you already know they're wrong.'

He slid the envelope unopened into his pocket. 'I'm afraid I'm not very keen on the author.'

'Oh, well.' Mrs Dunn held the front door open for him. 'You never know, they'll maybe surprise you.'

Murray thanked her and turned to go. He was already on the path when she called him back.

'Dr Watson, Jamie the postie told me you were doing a rare tear the other day. You know, the roads here are good, as they go, but you have to take care. We had a bad crash here a few years back.'

'I heard.'

Mrs Dunn nodded her head, as if everything she needed to say had already been said.

Chapter Twenty-Eight

The wind that had battered against Mrs Dunn's windows was battering against Murray now. It occurred to him that this was the kind of night when ill-prepared walkers drifted from pathways and died of hypothermia. He wondered if he should turn back, but kept trudging forth, head down against the wind, like some gothic rambler compelled to wander the world.

Murray saw the lights of a car blinking from the distant curves and bends of the road ahead as if to emphasise how far he had left to walk. The warmth of Mrs Dunn's living room had blown away in the wind. He started to murmur a song his father used to sing late on sleepless nights when he and Jack were boys. It was a ballad about what it was to be a cowboy; the impossibility of ever finding love and the inevitability of a lonely death. Sometimes, when he was young, it had seemed to Murray that misery was all he had. He would nurse it to himself, not daring to let it go for fear of losing himself. Murray remembered taking the point of his maths compass and twisting it slowly into his palm, digging a homemade stigmata. It was stupid. All of it. Life and what you made of it. Stupid.

He heard the rumble of the vehicle's engine, saw its headlights round the bend and stepped aside into the verge as a large, grey Land-Rover hove into view. The vehicle slowed to a halt beside him and the driver wound down his window.

'Murray Watson?'

'Yes?'

His first thought was that something had happened to Jack and this person had been sent to find him, but the man was smiling beneath his shaggy beard.

'Hop in and I'll give you a lift.'

'I'm going in the opposite direction.'

The man grinned. His teeth shone piratical against the black of his beard and the dark of the night. He said, 'We're on a small island, how far can it be?'

The wind picked up tempo, bringing a hail of rain with it. Murray jogged round to the passenger side, pulled open the door and climbed in. The stranger might be a descendent of Sawney Bean intent on reviving the family business, but if he was offering a lift, Murray was willing to give him the benefit of the doubt. He snapped the seatbelt home.

'Good lad.' The driver was wearing a chunky Shetland knit. His long hair was twisted into two plaits fastened with mismatched elastic bands. 'There's a place down here I can turn.'

Murray thought he could smell the faint taint of marijuana beneath the pine car-freshener scent he always associated with long journeys and travel sickness. He said, 'This is good of you.'

The stranger reversed the Land-Rover into the entrance of a field then looked at Murray.

'You don't remember me, do you?'

Murray stared at his face. Some memory stirred, and then slithered from his reach.

'Maybe it's the beard?'

'You're pretty beardy yourself.' The man laughed. 'I probably wouldn't have clocked you if

337

Mrs Dunn hadn't mentioned you were on the island. She likes her academics, does our landlady.' He stuck out his hand. 'Jem Edwards. You used to go out with Angela Whatsit, didn't you? I was in her year. We went for a drink a few times.'

'God, yes. You were there the night we went to see The Fall.'

'That was a good gig.'

The driver held out a hand and Murray shook it. Jem looked older and broader, but he remembered him now. He's been one of Angela's archaeology crew. Good-natured, hard-drinking, tendency to dress like a Viking. Murray could have hugged him.

'Didn't you used to play the bagpipes?'

'Still do. But not so often at parties these days.' Jem turned the jeep. 'So where are we headed? Tell me you've found a wee shebeen full of beautiful women, good whisky and fearless fiddle-players.'

Murray laughed and realised that the archaeologist's hearty normality might have the power to edge him into hysteria.

'Sadly not. Do you know the crossroads on the marsh above the limekilns?'

'I know the limekilns—they're where our new dig's planned—but as for the rest, you'll have to be my guide. What are you doing here, anyway? You're a historian, aren't you?'

'English lit.' Murray wiped a patch of condensation from the windscreen. 'If you go straight on for now, you'll see a turning on the left, just after the church.' He sank back in his seat and began to tell Jem an edited version of his quest.

They saw no other traffic on the road, but the

338

archaeologist kept his speed low, sailing smoothly over hills and round bends. They passed a cluster of cottages here and there showing a lit window. Then they were into the dark countryside, the full beam of their headlights unveiling drenched hedgerows and waving trees that looked like they might swoop down and snatch the car up into their branches. Something that might have been a weasel or a stoat dashed across their path and into the undergrowth. The solid bulk of St Mungo's Church appeared on their left. The headlights glanced into the graveyard, bending across the crooked headstones and slumbering tombs. Jem slowed the car.

'Left here?'

'Yes, the road deteriorates now.'

'No problem, we're in a tank.' Jem turned the wheels onto the roughcast path and their conversation back to Murray's quest. 'So this woman Christie could be key?'

'She was intimate with Archie at the most interesting period of his life.'

'It must be amazing to be able to speak to someone who actually knew the person you're researching.'

'I guess that's never going to happen to you?'

'Not unless someone invents time travel. It'd end in disaster, anyway. We'd be hailed as gods, given the best of everything for six months then sacrificed to the harvest.'

They had left the church behind now and were climbing towards higher ground. Murray's phone beeped, letting him know he had voicemail.

Jem said, 'You should check that.'

Murray took it from his pocket. The stern

female robot that guarded the exchange told him he had three new messages. He pressed *1* to listen and his brother's voice was suddenly in his ear, *Murray I . . .* He pressed *7* and deleted without listening. The next message was also from Jack. *Murray, you fuckwit . . .* He scrapped that as well, though he guessed his brother meant the insult to be an endearment. The final message was from Rab Purvis.

Murray, I'll keep it brief. I had a drink with Phyllida McWilliams in Fowlers. Apparently she used to be bosom buddies with Professor James's daughter Helen in the old days. She says the reason Fergus was in James's bad books was simple. He got Helen up the duff then did a runner. Not the done thing back then. Poor girl had to get scraped out. According to Phyl, Helen always claimed he forced her, but Phyl was never a hundred per cent convinced. She says Fergus was a charmer, and she would have given him one for free—you know our Phyl. All in all, it sounds like the James family have good reason to bear Fergus a grudge, so maybe you should take what they say with a fistful of salt. Do me a favour and delete this message, and Phyl says don't let on it was . . .

The tone sounded, cutting off Rab's last words. Murray thought back to the telephone call from the broch and something James had said: 'Some people never essentially change. In my opinion, Fergus Baine is one of them. Think of how he is now and that will tell you pretty much how he was back when Lunan and he were friends—and they were friends . . .'

James had been right. The two men had been friends. But James was also wrong. Fergus had surely changed. The reckless hippy who had spiked Mrs Dunn's tea had been replaced by an urbane professor. Then Murray thought of Rachel, the blankness in her face as she'd fucked her way through a host of strangers, and wondered if James had been right after all, and Fergus Baine the same man he was on the night Archie sailed out to meet his death.

Jem said, 'Everything okay?'

'Yes, fine.' Murray saw his own face reflected in the rain-washed windscreen and realised he was scowling. He worked his mouth into a smile. 'Are you digging for anything in particular?'

The archaeologist's teeth shone whitely.

'Ideally a dead body or two.'

'Sounds gruesome.'

'Our lot are just resurrection men at heart. There's a good chance that there was an ancient settlement on the site of the lime-workers' village. Officially we're looking for confirmation that the settlement was there, but where there's folk there's usually bodies buried somewhere about. The peaty ground round there's perfect for preserving *flesh*.' He gave the last word a ghoulish tinge. 'They were big into sacrifice, our ancestors. I'm hoping for a martyred bog man. Or a bog lady, I'm not particular.'

Murray recited, 'Your brain's exposed / and darkening combs / your muscles' webbing / and all your numbered bones.' He pulled himself up and said, 'I'll keep my fingers crossed you come across

341

a murder or a graveyard.'

The wipers swept swiftly to and fro, but the rain was winning the war, water streaming across the glass, warping their view. The crossroads came on them suddenly, its white sign worn free of destinations by long exposure to the elements. Jem hit the brakes. Murray was thrown forwards and felt the seatbelt tighten around him.

'Sorry about that.' The archaeologist's laugh was embarrassed. 'That seemed to appear from nowhere.' He wiped the windscreen with his hand and peered at the blank sign. 'Which way now?'

Murray thought for a moment, reconstructing the direction of his journey with Christie.

'Left.'

'Sure?'

He hesitated for the smallest beat.

'Yes.'

Jem turned the wheel.

'Sinister it is then. Christ, I can hardly see where I'm going.'

'Rotten conditions for your dig.'

Jem lowered his voice to a comic baritone and sang, 'Mud, mud, glorious mud, nothing quite like it for cooling the blood. It'll be like the Somme out there.'

'I'd have thought this was the wrong time of year.'

'You'd have thought right. We're at war with the industrial archaeologists. Word is they want to excavate the limekilns this summer, so we leaned on some contacts and got in first. Forecast was for a dry autumn, but as you can see, the forecast was shit.'

'So will you postpone?'

'Come hell or high water, we'll be out there tomorrow.' Jem's laugh was cheerful. 'We've a dozen students stashed around the island. I've pledged to keep them from drinking the contents of the shop, indiscreet drug-use and orgies, which is hard if I can't tire them out.'

'Does it ever disturb you?'

'No, they're good kids for the most part. We were the same when we were their age.'

'I meant digging up the dead.'

'I wish, but most of the time it's not so dramatic. We turn up bits of crockery, bones from the midden, the odd cooking pot. A skeleton or even a skull is big excitement. But I take your point. These people were buried according to whatever beliefs and rituals they had, and then along we come and disturb their rest. But I manage to comfort myself with one thought.'

'What's that?'

'When you're dead, you're dead. You won't hear the sound of the shovel that's come to dig you up.'

A light shone wanly up ahead.

'I think this might be it.'

Jem slowed the Land-Rover.

'A bit of a derelict spot. I wouldn't fancy it, and I rob graves for a living.' He pulled the handbrake on. 'Do you want me to wait?'

Murray pulled his woollen hat back on and zipped up his waterproof.

'No, thanks. I'm staying not far from here, I can walk back.' The red Cherokee was parked in the drive, but he was relieved to see no sign of Fergus's Saab. Murray patted his pocket and felt Professor James's slim volume stiff in his pocket, still in the unopened envelope it had been sent to Mrs Dunn's in. He thought about dumping it on the seat of the car, but suspected Jem would go out of his way to return it. 'It was kind of you to give me a lift in the first place.'

'No worries. I'm bored out my skull.' The archaeologist's sharp teeth were hidden behind a bearded frown. 'Watch how you go round here. The ground's good for preservation, but it can be a bit dodgy.'

'Sinkholes.'

'Yes.' Jem gave him a grin that only needed a cutlass to complete it. 'Sounds like you know what you're doing.'

Murray returned his smile.

'I wish I had your confidence.'

He jumped out of the Land-Rover, slamming the door behind him, then raised a hand in thanks and jogged through the rain to Christie's front door.

Chapter Twenty-Nine

Murray stood under Christie's porch light and watched as Jem turned the Land-Rover towards the crossroads. The archaeologist gave a friendly toot, and then he was away, driving back to the warmth of Mrs Dunn's pink guest room or maybe off to check his students weren't disgracing the venerable institution now so widely represented on the island.

The Land-Rover's lights glowed distantly then faded from view, and the cottage's front door opened, as he knew it would. Christie was all in black, dressed against the cold in a pair of stretch pants tucked into woollen socks and a chunky polo neck that drowned her slim form. She wore silver sleepers in her ears, but was otherwise free of jewellery. It was the kind of outfit a dancer might adopt after a heavy workout, and it looked both stylish and incongruous matched with her stick.

'You're earlier than I expected.'

There was a slur to her words, the kind of imprecision that might occur after a couple of drinks.

Murray pulled back his hood. The scent of wood smoke mingled with the falling rain and the damp rising from the sodden earth. It was an ancient smell, the same one the earliest islanders who could yet be resting, preserved beneath the peat, had known a millennia or so ago.

'Would you like me to take a walk around the block?'

'Of course not.'

She gave Murray a smile that might have been nervous and ushered him through the small vestibule into a brightly lit lounge. His glasses clouded in the sudden warmth. Murray unfastened his waterproof and rubbed his lenses against his scarf. The exam-day tingles were on him, a cocktail of excitement and dread that fluttered low in his stomach.

The contrast between this room and Mrs Dunn's overstuffed lounge couldn't have been greater. The space was long and open, its oak floors laid with good rugs, the ceiling gabled. One wall was completely taken up by a large wooden bookcase loaded with hardbacks. He scanned their spines, looking for copies of Christie's own novels, but they were absent, or perhaps his eyes simply missed them amongst the mass of other volumes. A large desk was set at right-angles to the shelves, its chair facing into the room to avoid the distraction of the view. A brown couch sat opposite a wood- burning stove, the coffee table in front of it also piled with books.

Everything was simple and well-constructed, a living space composed of clean lines, too practical to be stylish, too cold to be completely comfortable. This was the place where she had lived with Archie. Murray tried to imagine it as it had been, the tumbled bed recess, the squalid table and circling flies, but it had grown too civilised for him to recognise.

Unlike Mrs Dunn, Christie hadn't yet closed her curtains. Two armchairs sat staring out onto the blackness of the moor through the large picture windows. A slim document folder rested on a small table between them. Christie led him towards the chairs and he saw that her limp had grown worse. The right side of her body swung stiffly with each step, her leg rigid, as if muscle and bone would no longer co-operate.

'I thought we could talk here.' Christie settled herself awkwardly into one of the armchairs. Murray took off his wet waterproof, bundled it on the floor beside him and sat. He could see their reflections in the glass. The two of them unsmiling on the high-backed chairs, like an old queen and her younger, more barbarous consort. He wondered how she could stand it, this view of the self imprinted onto dark nothingness, like a glimpse of purgatory. But Christie was looking

346

away from the window, towards him.

'Have you deliberately styled yourself to look like Archie?'

'No.'

Surprise made him sound defensive.

'You gave me a start the day I saw you in the shop. Though now I look closely, I can see you're not like him at all. Archie's features were finer, almost feminine.'

Murray was taken aback by his disappointment.

'Do you have many photographs of him?'

'Some. I might show you a few later.'

'It'd be a privilege.'

'The ones of him as a young boy are charming.'

She was like a cruel child baiting a kitten.

He leaned down and took his tape recorder from his jacket pocket.

'Do you mind if I record our conversation?'

'I'm afraid I do.' He hadn't noticed the smallness of her mouth before. It was the feature that robbed her of beauty. She twisted it as if strangling a smile. 'Before we start, let me ask you a question: what would you like from me?'

Murray leaned forward, opening his palms in an unconscious, ancient gesture designed to show he came unarmed.

'Your memories of Archie, what he was like.' He paused and said, 'What you remember of his final days.'

She nodded. 'Nothing else?'

'You mentioned photographs.' To his own ears Murray's voice sounded as if it had been infused with the oiliness of the life insurance salesmen who had always done so well from his widowed father. 'I'd appreciate the opportunity to go

347

through them, but obviously I'd also be very keen to see any other notes, letters or memorabilia you have relating to Archie.'

'Strange how you call him by his first name, as if you know him.'

'I don't feel I know him at all.'

'But you're in love with him?'

She arched her eyebrows. It was an old-fashioned style he'd encountered in some female academics of her generation, a need to provoke, as if years of being overlooked had left their mark.

'I'm in love with his poems.'

'What would your ultimate prize be?'

Murray looked at his feet.

'To discover a new work, even one new poem.'

Christie smiled. 'Of course.' She leaned back in her chair and stared out into the darkness. 'I think it's only fair to tell you that I've written an account of my time with Archie. It will only be published, even in extract form, after my death. I should also tell you that as far as I'm concerned it's the only statement I'm prepared to make on Archibald Lunan's life and death.'

Murray closed his notebook and slid his pen into its spiral spine. She had brought him here to make clear her refusal to cooperate, nothing more.

'Thank you for being so frank. I've taken up enough of your time.'

Christie's tone was soft and reasonable.

'Dr Watson, you must realise you're here because there's something you can give me.'

He still hadn't reached out for his coat, though it was on the floor at his side.

'All I can offer you is the chance to bring Archie's work to a wider audience, and the possibility of a more secure legacy for him.'

'No.' Christie's gaze was level and serious. 'That's what I can offer you.' Her voice grew brisk. 'Could you go into the top drawer of the desk, please, and pass me the box you find there?'

Murray crossed the room to her desk. He pulled open the drawer and saw a white plastic box. Even before he lifted it, he knew it held medication rather than the papers he'd hoped for. He handed it to her.

'Thank you.' Christie snapped open the lid and Murray glimpsed a bewildering range of pills. She caught his gaze and said, 'One advantage of living miles from a chemist is that I'm issued with more or less as much medication as I need.' She selected four tablets. 'There's some bottled water by the couch. Could you pass it to me, please?' He did as she asked, then stood by the window as Christie swallowed the pills, placing each one singly in her mouth then washing them down. She choked on the last one and he moved to help her, but she waved him away. When she'd regained her breath she asked, 'What would you do to lay your hands on my recollections of Archie Lunan and a final, unpublished collection of his poems?'

Murray turned towards the window so she wouldn't witness his expression. But once again the darkness threw his image onto the glass.

'I don't know.'

The nervous undercurrent he'd noticed before was back in Christie's voice.

'I've done what all the blackmailers do in the movies and provided you with a sample of the goods.'

Murray wanted to look at her, but stayed where

he was, staring out into the blackness, seeing nothing but the room's reflection and the rain streaking in rivulets down the outside of the pane.

'A poem by Archie?'

'No, the poems are elsewhere.' She slid a page from the folder and handed it to Murray. 'You've got three minutes in which to read it. I think that should be more than enough time for a doctor of English literature.'

Murray asked, 'What do you want?'

'Read first, then I'll tell you.'

The paper was in his hand. He lifted it and started to read.

Archibald Lunan and Christina Graves were born three years apart to two very different sisters. Archie's mother Siona Roy left the island of Lismore at the age of sixteen to work as a maid of all work at a hotel in Inverness. The war came as a boon to girls like her and in 1939 she moved to Glasgow, where she became a canary bird in one of the large munitions factory. Archie arrived the year after the war ended. Mrs Lunan, as Siona was now known, was never forthcoming about the circumstances of Archie's birth, but his arrival sent her home, to her father's croft.

Life was to change a lot in Scotland over the next decade, but many crofters still lived very much as their ancestors had. They heated their cottages with peat which they cut from the ground. Lighting came from oil lamps. They grew crops, baked their own bread, and salvaged what they could in the

way of driftwood. Some, like Archie's
mother, collected their cooking and washing
water from streams and wells.

The island, rich in plant and bird life,
was a paradise for a young boy, but for
Siona, fresh from the camaraderie of blitz-
torn Glasgow, it may have seemed like a
prison. Who can blame her for returning to
the city when her father died ten years
later?

Siona's mind may always have been
unsettled, or it might have been the years of
drudgery on her father's croft that disturbed
it. Maybe it was even her move back to the
city and the loneliness that she encountered
there that were the catalysts. Whatever the
origins of her deteriorating mental health,
there's no record of it until after she and her
son returned to Glasgow.

Murray looked up from the single page. Christie
smiled at him. 'Interesting?'

'Yes.' He wondered if his face looked wolfish.
'How much more is there?'

'A lot.'

'And this is as much as you're prepared to show
me?'

'Of his childhood, for the moment.' Christie
slid her hand into the folder, pulled forth a second
page and held it out. 'Here.'

He took it from her and read on.

Edinburgh was still a small city in 1969, but
Archie and I could have passed each other
daily without knowing. I used to look for

351

him on the street; desperate to meet this 'son of an abomination' my mother had warned me about so many times. Eventually I asked around, discovered his local and persuaded a girlfriend to go there with me. Later I got used to places like that, but this was the first time I'd ever been in a working men's pub.

The barroom was lit by a naked one hundred-watt bulb, the floor strewn with sawdust. Even though we'd never met, I knew Archie straight away. He was slouched at the bar, so drunk he seemed to sweat alcohol. Archie was a good-looking young man, but when he drank his features grew slack and lost their air of intelligence. He behaved stupidly too. I watched Archie embrace a man, and then insult him with his arm still clasped around his shoulders. I heard him flirt like a fool with the barmaid and saw him lavish drinks on strangers who laughed in his face. I told my friend I'd made a mistake and left without speaking to him.

A week later he took the seat opposite mine in the university library and started to read Baudelaire's 'Fleurs du Mal'. I couldn't keep my eyes off him. Eventually I plucked up the courage to introduce myself. Later I'd discover Archie was always shy when he was sober. He offered to take me for a drink, but I persuaded him back to my digs instead. We talked all through the night and when the sun came up we went to bed together.

Murray looked up from the page and saw Christie's small mouth widened in a smile.

'You look shocked. We were cousins, not brother and sister.'

'I'm not shocked. But I'd like to know what happened next.'

'After we went to bed?'

'No.' He forced a smile. 'After that.'

'After that, we spent most of our free time together. I soon realised there was no way I was going to be able to keep him sober, so I learned how to drink.'

'If you can't beat them, join them?'

'Drink was his wife, I was just his girlfriend.'

'Was Archie writing a lot when you knew him?'

Christie took on a look he had seen in other interviewees, a far-away stare as if gazing back into the past.

'Apart from drinking, it was all he seemed to do. When we first met, Archie was matriculated at the university, but the only classes I ever knew him attend were poetry lectures. He used the library, of course, but that was for his own reading. He would lie around in the morning in his dressing gown, sipping beer and reading detective fiction or sci-fi. At midday he'd go down to the pub for a pint and a bite to eat. Then he'd either browse the local second-hand bookshops or go back to his room and write. He'd step out again at about nine in the evening.'

'How could he afford it?'

'Archie had been lucky. His mother had died and left him some money.'

'An odd definition of luck.'

'Do you think so? I used to envy him terribly.'

He ignored the playful note of provocation in her voice and asked, 'Were you writing too?'

'I didn't pick up my pen until after Archie's death. Then it was as if a new well had been sunk in me, it all came bubbling out.' She reached into the folder again. 'The final extract.'

He took it from her, noting the page number, 349. Earlier in his quest the completeness of Christie's memoir might have frustrated Murray, but it no longer mattered if his own book was rendered redundant. There were new poems. The thought thrilled him.

Archie might never have returned to the island if I hadn't suggested it, but when I did he leapt at the plan. By that time we were a trio plus one. That extra man was vital to our group; Bobby was Renfield to our Dracula. We thought he was harmless.

Ours was an era of new societies, ideal communities and communes. Property was theft, jealousy bourgeois, and anyone over thirty, suspect. We set out with bags full of acid and hearts full of idealism. But it was soon clear the cottage was too small to house four adults and the sickness which had eventually left me in Glasgow returned with a vengeance.

Archie's sickness followed him too. There was no pub on the island, but he found a ceilidh house where he was very quickly unwelcome. That didn't bother Archie. He'd already made enough contacts to be able to draw on a seemingly endless source of homebrewed spirits. Some mornings he was as sick as I was and the two of us lay groaning together in the bed recess we'd requisitioned as our own.

As if overcrowding, bad trips, drunkenness and sickness weren't enough, the weather descended into a long period of dark skies and relentless rain. Bobby would probably have stayed with us for ever, lost in his muddled world of drugs and spells, but very quickly I realised that Fergus was planning to leave. I couldn't blame him. I had sold the island as an adventure, an opportunity to create, but there was no privacy to be had in the damp cottage, and my hopes of keeping the three of us together until what had to pass had passed were beginning to fade.

Murray read the page twice, and then he set it aside on the table and looked at Christie.

'You were pregnant when Mrs Dunn visited the cottage, weren't you? That's how you knew she was too.'

Christie rolled her eyes. Her voice was impatient.

'She was the kind of woman Fergus always seems to attract—buttoned-up, but desperate for some kind of adventure, some kind of debauch. The trouble is they never realise how far Fergus is willing to go.' Was there a gleam of pride in her eyes? 'He always pushes them beyond their limits.'

Murray thought of Rachel. He asked, 'Like he did with Helen James?'

Christie snorted in amusement.

'I very much doubt little Nelly was raped, but

what could she say when her mummy and daddy found out she was unmarried and with child? It was the wrong time of year for an immaculate conception.'

'She had an abortion.'

'You didn't strike me as a man who would be against a woman's right to choose what she does with her body.'

'I'm not. In fact, I'd go further and say everyone has a right to know what they take into their body. Mrs Dunn lost her baby.'

'That was nothing to do with me.'

'Was the baby Archie's?'

'I think it was Mr Dunn's.'

It took all his effort to keep his voice low and his words polite.

'Was your baby Archie's child?'

'I like to think so.'

'What happened?'

'I delivered her here, in the bed recess.' She nodded towards the far corner. 'Where my desk is now. The first major piece of work I produced there. A perfect little girl.'

It was the same bed where Mrs Dunn had lain drugged. Murray saw it for an instant, the curtain drawn to one side, the soiled bedclothes slung onto the floor. Mrs Dunn had lost her baby. He wiped a hand across his face and asked, 'Where is your daughter now?'

'With Archie's poems, buried down by the limekilns.'

*   *   *

Murray wasn't sure how long he sat staring in

silence at Christie after she had spoken, but eventually he said, 'I think you've miscalculated how much I want to get my hands on Archie's poems, Miss Graves.'

'Nature can be cruel.' Her face tightened. 'It had its way.'

'So you took the child and buried it? Simple as that?'

'More or less.'

'Did Bobby Robb have anything to do with the baby's death?'

Christie's laugh was hard and brittle. She said, 'Bobby Robb was a fool and a fantasist. We'd tolerated him because he could supply us with drugs, but Fergus had grown sick of him and his stupidity. If the weather hadn't been so bad, he would have been gone on the ferry to the mainland and a lot of tragedy would have been avoided.'

'The child would have lived?'

'No, the child was never going to live. It was small and weak and had been born to fools who didn't know or care enough to look after it. Idiots who filled the room with smoke and fed it with water when the stupid girl that was supposed to be its mother let her milk dry up and still drank and got high, and the stupid man that might have been its father drank and smoked, took drugs and talked poetry.' She sighed. 'We'd thought we could manage it ourselves, but the birth was horrendous. Bobby shot me full of something to help with the pain. It knocked me out so hard it's a miracle the child was born at all. She must have clawed her way out.'

'Didn't Archie do anything?'

'Archie had been big on having the child. He

357

was full of fantasies about what it would be like to belong to a real family, but when she arrived, sickly and underweight, Archie did what he always did. He drank. When we discovered she was dead, he was sure it was Bobby's doing. Bobby was always setting his stupid spells, rambling on about purity and sacrifice. Archie jumped to conclusions, even though there wasn't a mark on her body. Maybe he wanted someone to blame. He beat Bobby badly. He might have killed him, if Fergus hadn't managed to force him out of the cottage and bolt the door. I was a little mad too, I suppose. I didn't know what had happened, but I knew that my baby was gone. I held her by the fire and rubbed her body, but it stayed as limp and as cold as she'd been when I found her dead in the bed beside me. Bobby and Fergus finished our supply and I joined them. We didn't think about Archie until the next day. We had no idea he would take the boat out in the storm. It was stupid.'

Murray whispered, 'It was suicide.'

But it was as if Christie didn't hear him.

'She was tiny. I wrapped her in my silk scarf and we put her in a tin box we'd found in the cottage. Fergus placed the poems Archie had been working on beside her and then we buried her and marked the spot with a stone.'

'Why?'

'What else could we do? Archie was missing, presumed drowned, and we were drug-taking hippies in the middle of nowhere. It wasn't like we believed in God. I had neglected her and lost her. Do you know how the judicial system treats neglectful mothers? How the press crucifies them? How they get dealt with in prison? A funeral wasn't going to make any difference and jail wouldn't have made us better people. Archie had paid the ultimate price, people would have thought that I should too. We did what we thought we had to.'

'And now?'

'Tomorrow they're going to start digging where we buried her. It's only a matter of time before they uncover her corpse and Archie's poems. It's the last chance I have to be reunited with her before I die.'

Murray got to his feet. He felt weary in his bones.

'Where's your phone?'

Her voice was wary.

'Why?'

'Because one of us has to call the police. I think it would be better if it was you, but if you won't then I'll do it myself.'

'There are no police on the island.'

'I think they might consider this worth the journey.'

Christie leaned back in her chair, looking old and ill.

'You haven't asked me where Fergus is.'

'I know where he is, up to his neck in shit.'

'He had to go back to Glasgow. Apparently his wife tried to commit suicide. Like I said, he has a penchant for attracting women who want to explore their limits, then pushing them too far.'

The horror of it was hot in Murray's throat.

'Will she be okay?'

The woman made a gesture of impatience.

'I expect so. There's a difference between seeking attention and doing it for real.' She looked him in the eye. 'It takes real courage to kill yourself.'

Christie held Murray's stare, and he remembered a piece of advice his father had given him: 'Always approach a trapped animal with caution. It'll bite you, whether you've come to kill it or set it free.'

He wanted to go now, back to Glasgow to see Rachel and find out how she was, but a suspicion that the woman still had more to reveal held him there.

'Dr Watson, do you think I spent forty years on an island where I'm hated because I'm in love with the landscape? I stayed to be close to my child. She's been on her own for too long. I want us to be buried together. If you help me, I'll give you the original manuscript of my memoir, all the photographs and documents I have relating to Archie, and the poems buried beside our daughter. It's more than you could have hoped for.'

The temptation of it stopped Murray's breath for a moment. He took a gulp of air and plucked his jacket from the floor.

'I reckon it'll be around twenty minutes before I can get a signal. As soon as I do, I'm calling the police. I advise you to ring them first.'

Christie gave a wry smile.

'It won't be the ferry or a police launch that takes me from the island, Dr Watson. I already have what I need to transport me. I think I've proved my staying power, but I've no intention of waiting for the final chapter.'

He took a step towards her.

'There's no certainty you'll go to jail.'

'My mother would have said that my prison had

already been appointed by a higher court—a wheelchair, incontinence, loss of speech, choking to death.'

'You're nowhere near that stage yet.'

'Aren't I? I didn't realise you were a medical doctor as well as a doctor of literature.' She sighed. 'I'm tired of it all. If it's time for me to leave my home, then it's time for me to leave. You said you supported a woman's right to choose. Well, this is my choice. Fergus understands that at least. He brought me the means.' She forced herself to her feet and stood, her face raised, her eyes locked on his. 'All I wanted was for you to help me make a good death, and to bring some peace to Archie and to our daughter.'

It was the words 'good death' that did it. Murray sat back down in his chair and put his head in his hands.

Chapter Thirty

Murray drove slowly, with the headlights off. It was the kind of night that men who wanted to be up to no good craved. The sky was free of moon and stars, the road ahead black, his vision marred by mist and rain. Murray kept his eyes on the darkness before him and asked, 'How will I know where to dig?'

Christie's voice was hushed, as if she were still afraid Murray might change his mind.

'We left a marker. I used to visit every day, but lately it's been too difficult.'

'Is that what you were doing when I met you?'

'The weather was too poor to drive down, but I could see her grave from the ridge.'

The rain battered against the metal roof of the car, a hundred drumming soldiers marching forth to halt the outrage.

Murray said, 'It's worse tonight.'

'It helps. No one will be about and the ground will be soft.'

'Isn't there a chance it might have been dislodged? If it has, we may not be able to find it.'

'Perhaps.' Christie was in the seat beside him, but her words seemed to come from far away. 'Her face was the last thing I covered. I swaddled her in my scarf, as if I was about to take her out for some air, then I tied it around her head. The people of the islands used to believe children who died as infants had been stolen by the faeries and a faery replica left in their place. I can understand why. She looked like my baby, but I knew she wasn't. My child had gone.'

Murray glimpsed Christie's ghost-white face as she turned towards him. Perhaps the fear showed in his expression, because she said, 'It won't be as bad as you're anticipating. Imagine it's simply the poems we're excavating. We wrapped them in polythene. You don't even have to go into the box, I'll take them out for you.'

'What then?'

'You drive me home, collect the papers and photographs I promised you, and leave.'

'And you?'

'Will wait some days, perhaps months. Who knows, maybe remission will return and I'll be spared for years. But I'll have my child's body and the means to make a good death when the time

362

comes. Do you know how important that is?'

Murray stared at the road ahead and thought of the promise he and Jack had made to their father.

'Yes, I know what a good death can mean.'

She reached out and stroked a finger down his cheek. It was a lover's touch and he flinched.

Christie whispered, 'I always half-thought he would come back. Some nights I still do. I sit by the window reading, something catches my eye and I think, *There's Archie, come for me.* It used to frighten me. I'd wonder if he would still be angry, what he would look like after all that time. Do you remember "The Monkey's Paw"?' Murray nodded, but perhaps Christie didn't see him in the darkness, because she continued, 'A husband and wife wish for their dead son to be returned from the grave. No sooner is the wish from their mouths than they hear a hideous banging at the door. When they open it, in place of the hale and hearty boy they dreamt of stands a mangled wreck of a corpse half cut to shreds by the wounds that killed him. Wounds that now have the power of endless torment rather than the power of death.'

She reached out her hand to touch his face again and he said, 'Don't, I need to concentrate on the road.'

'They never found his body. As long as it was missing, there was a chance he was still alive somewhere.' Christie sighed. 'I wouldn't mind if he came back drowned.'

Murray imagined Archie striding towards them through the blackness, his body bloated and bloody, his ragged clothes strung about with seaweed.

He asked, 'Did Fergus do away with Bobby?'

'No.' In all the long evening it was the first time she'd sounded shocked. 'Fergus is an exploiter of women, but he's not a murderer. Bobby was an old man who had a heart attack.'

'He was a drain on resources. Fergus looked after him, gave him a flat and who knows what else.'

Christie was back in this world. She said, 'I'd been sending the old fool money for years. Giving in to bribery doesn't incriminate you in murder. Bobby contacted Fergus after he moved back up to Scotland. There was a piece in the newspaper referring to Professor Baine and Bobby came across it. I can just picture him.' There was something unseemly in her laughter. 'Sitting in some horrid bar, ringing the article with a pen borrowed from the barmaid, ordering a whisky and knowing that his ship had come in.'

'He was scared. He'd made a circle of protection around his bed.'

'He was always scared. The day we arrived on the island he made a circle of protection around the cottage. Much good it did us.'

'Did Archie believe in all that stuff?'

'What stuff?'

'The occult. Spells.'

'Archie didn't believe in anything much, certainly not in himself.'

'He believed in poetry.'

'That's the kind of meaningless statement I'd have thought an academic would avoid.'

Murray stole a glance at Christie. Her head was resting against the rain-streaked window, her expression hidden.

'He believed in you and your child. I found a

364

list of names among his papers in the library. He was trying to decide what to call it, wasn't he?'

Christie's voice was gentle.

'He talked to her. Laid his head on my belly, recited poetry, sang songs and told her his dreams. A jealous woman might have grown bitter, but I understood. Archie had never had anything much to look forward to before. This baby was to be all the Christmases he never had.' She sighed. 'It was more than that. He thought the child would save him. The reality was rather different.'

'And Fergus?'

'He worshipped Fergus.'

'Was he worthy of Archie's faith?'

Christie lifted her head from the glass and straightened her spine against the passenger seat. Her profile looked brittle.

'Neither Fergus nor the child turned out to be Jesus Christ.'

'I'm beginning to think Professor Baine bears more of a resemblance to Judas Iscariot.'

Christie snorted.

'Archie would have hated that kind of melodrama.'

Murray kept his tone mild, though Christie's words had hit their mark.

'If Fergus can supply you with the means to kill yourself, he could do the same for Bobby.'

'That was one of Fergus's few truly altruistic gestures.' Christie's voice was a monotone and it was hard to tell if she was being sincere or sarcastic. 'He went to Switzerland with his mother. He'd promised to make sure she didn't suffer too horribly at the end. I think it was a transformative experience. He came back convinced of the

365

individual's right to die.'

Murray remembered the death of the professor's mother. Fergus had been absent from the university for an appropriate period, but perhaps it was unsurprising that no mention had been made of trips to Swiss clinics. He recalled Baine's stoicism, his dignified receipt of condolence, and the new house that had followed. Rachel had moved in soon after.

'He isn't here with you tonight.'

'Fergus doesn't know about the dig.'

'And you didn't enlighten him?'

'He would exhume her body, but he wouldn't give it to me. The one thing I'm worried about is the possibility he did it years ago, but I don't think so.'

'Why not?'

'Fergus has a talent for forgetting. All sensationalists do. The rest of us sustain ourselves on memories and police ourselves with obligations. Men like Fergus can set these things aside. Oh, he can make a plan and see it through, you only need to look at his career to know that. But Fergus lives largely in the moment. As long as he's getting his own way, he forgets. He doesn't have a conscience to remind him.'

Murray thought about Rachel. His sadness was shot through with guilt. He'd believed hers the guiding hand, but could he have unwittingly exploited her, too dazzled by her zest for sex to interrogate her motives? Had he been like Fergus, unquestioning as long as he was getting his own way? He wondered what she had done to herself, and if Fergus was taking good care of her.

The car heater was on full blast, but the

366

windscreen was fogging. Murray reached forward and wiped it with his palm. The makeshift road seemed to be getting narrower and he suspected that before long they would have to abandon the car and make their way on foot. He asked, 'Do you know where we are?'

'Almost there.' Christie didn't seem to be looking, but her voice was sure. 'We should see the first of the lime-workers' cottages in a moment. Be careful, the ground will be softer here.'

Murray dropped their speed to crawl. They drove on in silence. Soon he saw a shape up ahead, blacker than the darkness that surrounded them. A ruined cottage came into focus, the shadowy forms of the derelict village behind it. He stopped the car, turned off the engine and pulled on the handbrake. 'What now?'

'Can you drive any further?'

Murray opened his door. Outside it sounded the way he supposed a rainforest removed of wildlife might, the steady slap and drip of rain against leaves and puddles, accompanied by the white-noise hiss of the downpour. He looked at the ground in the glow of the interior light. Water was pooling into miniature streams and gullies, the earth turning to sludge.

'I don't think so. We're taking a chance as it is.'

Christie leaned into the glove compartment and handed him a rubberised torch. He felt the weight of it in his hand and thought what a good weapon it would make.

'It won't take long.' He saw her profile in silhouette, the set of her jaw, her half-open lips. 'Just think of the poems and forget everything else.'

She pulled up the hood of her jacket, then opened the door and stepped into the dark. Murray jogged round to the boot of the car and took out the spade they'd stashed there earlier. He had to shout to make himself heard.

'Are you sure you can manage?'

Christie wrestled her walking stick from the car, then linked her free arm through his. 'If I can lean on you.' She pointed her stick straight ahead. 'It's this way.'

Murray clicked on the torch, aiming its beam at the path's greasy surface. Christie skidded and he hauled her to her feet.

'Are you okay?'

'Yes. Let's keep moving.'

But Murray could feel her already flagging. He put his arm around Christie's waist, holding her close. She was so light her bones might have been hollow. But still her body weighed on him. Murray swung the shovel, using it like a staff. Hill-walking had taught him that when weather and conditions conspired against you, the trick was to think of nothing, not the distance that remained, nor what would follow once you reached home, nothing but the next step, then the one after and the one after that.

They were almost in the heart of the tiny hamlet now. The trees had grown denser, but instead of sheltering them from the rain they seemed to add to its force, shedding their own hoarded load as they passed. Murray kept the torch aimed at the treacherous ground beneath their feet, but he could feel the stares of empty windows and gaping doors on either side. Christie tugged his arm and pointed towards one of the houses. She said something that was carried away by the sound of the rain. Murray swung the torch in the direction she'd indicated. An abandoned cottage glared at him.

'There?'

She nodded and they turned their uneasy progress towards it, Murray half-dragging, half-carrying Christie.

'Careful.' She yanked on his arm again. 'Keep to the path.'

He shone the beam across the ground and saw that instead of leading them straight to the cottage, the mud track curved around a patch of green. He corrected his course, swearing softly under his breath, following the trail, thinking they must look like Hansel and Gretel, grown up and evil, visiting old haunts.

The cottage's doorway was clumped about with long grass. He hauled Christie over it and pulled her inside. Like the rest of the abandoned village, the cottage had lost its roof, so there was no real shelter from the rain within its bounds, but the stone walls seemed to deaden the sound a little. Christie propped herself against one of them. Murray thought she looked bad, but didn't pause to ask her how she felt.

'Where is it?'

'There, just outside, to the left of the door. It's shaped like a heart.'

Murray gripped the shovel tighter and went back through the opening. He found the marker easily. He could see what Christie meant. The stone was flat on top, pointed at one end and slightly bifurcated at the other. The whimsy disgusted him.

He passed the torch to Christie. 'Here, aim where I dig.' Then he took the shovel and prised it beneath the marker. He felt the stone shift and slid the shovel further in. The earth's grip slackened again. The stone was loose now, but it had the hidden mass of an iceberg and he couldn't get enough leverage to force it free of its socket. Murray cursed himself and Christie for not having had the foresight to pack a pair of rubber gloves. He squatted down on the ground and wobbled the half-excavated boulder with his bare hands. He could feel the grave-dirt on his flesh, creeping beneath his fingernails. He found a stick and used it to scrape away the mud, probing the ground like an ape hunting for termites. Finally he wedged his hands down the sides of the hollow and wrenched the stone free. The hole started to fill with water.

'Fuck, fuck, fuck, fuck.'

Murray lifted the shovel and began digging. He dug in the same way he would approach a desperate walk, taking it one step, one spade-full, at a time. The trees in the valley creaked and shivered with the weight of the rain and the cramping coldness of the night.

In Murray's mind, he was alone in the small bedroom he shared with Jack. The room was in darkness, save for the light from his desk lamp pooling on the page before him. He felt his eyes droop, then the gentle weight of his father's hand on his shoulder.

'Time to stop now, son. Slow and steady wins the race.'

The shovel struck against something solid.

He took the torch from Christie and shone it into the hole. He could see nothing in its depths except the brown water rising from beneath, turning the mud to sludge. Murray got back down on his hands and knees, and stretched into the swelling pool. Whatever it was was too far down for him to reach.

'Fuck.'

He lay flat on his belly in the mud and tried again. This time he made contact. His fingers were numb and he couldn't tell if they were brushing against stone or metal, but the surface of the object was smooth, whatever it was set too deep for Murray to get a proper grip. He got to his knees and scrabbled around in the dirt again until he could find his stick, then stretched back into the pool and tried to hollow it free. The stick broke. He cursed, got to his feet and set-to with the spade, attacking the sides of the hole, swearing as this new excavation tumbled earth back into the pit. Finally it was wide enough. He put his glasses in his pocket then eased himself down into the grave. The loamy scent that had been in his nostrils all through the digging seemed to slide down into his throat. He prised the shovel beneath the object, hoping to God he'd have enough purchase to haul himself out, knowing that should the walls collapse in on him Christie would be unable to pull him free. Murray felt the box move. He squatted down in the dirt and gripped the smooth square thing with his dead fingers. He grunted and pulled, feeling all the while that the struggle was two-sided and whatever lay below wanted to drag him down there with it. Once, the box slipped from his grasp and he feared it had broken and he would see the child's face staring up at him, squashed and leathered, like the bog folk

Heaney had written about. But then, with a last sucking slurp that threatened to tug him down, the earth relinquished its dubious prize. Murray leant over the box, hands on thighs, gasping for breath.

'Fuck, fuck, fuck, fuck, fuck.'

He gripped the box in both hands, took a deep breath, and heaved it up onto the surface. He then hauled himself over the mud-slathering sides of the hole after it.

It was more of a trunk than a box. Larger than he'd expected, but light for all the trouble it had caused him, and obscene in its ordinariness. Still on his knees, Murray turned to face Christie. His hair was plastered to his head, his hands and body coated in mud too clotted for the rain to wash away. His voice sounded old and rusty.

'Please, don't open it until I get you back to your cottage.'

Christie pursed her lips, like a woman trying not to laugh. She staggered from the doorway and put a hand on his shoulder. For an awful moment he thought she might kiss him, but she merely stood there, staring down at the makeshift coffin.

'Thank you.' The rain was slackening and Murray could hear her breath, harsh and ragged. 'We should go.' She danced the torch beam around the site of the exhumation, searching like a seasoned detective for evidence of their visit. 'Perhaps you should fill that in, so no one wonders what's been going on.'

Murray took his glasses from his pocket and held them under the rain, trying to wash the lenses free of the spangles of mud which decorated them. He replaced them, lifted the spade and started to shovel the earth back into the grave. Their visit

372

would still be evident to anyone who cared to look, but he had lost all will to argue. He had no idea of how long they had been there, but the light was changing, the dawn creeping towards them much sooner than he would have expected. He wiped the mud from his watch—02:54—but even as he checked the time, Murray heard the grumble of an engine and realised that the sweep of light was no premature daybreak. He heard Christie's gasp and saw her sickened expression a moment before he was blinded by the full beam of a car's headlights.

Chapter Thirty-One

Murray threw the shovel to one side and put his hands up in the air. It was a ridiculous gesture born of the American cop shows he and Jack had been addicted to as boys, and he dropped them almost immediately. He shaded his eyes, squinting to see who had interrupted them, but the car's full beams were still aiming at them from the mud track, and he could make out nothing beyond a blur of smur and bright light. The car door slammed.

'You should have gone home, Murray.'

Fergus Baine's voice was full of regret.

'You're right as usual, Fergus.'

'This is between Christie and me. The best thing you can do is walk away and forget it ever happened.'

Christie gripped his elbow. She whispered, 'Don't leave me alone with him.' It was more of an order than a plea, but he could hear the fear in her

373

voice.

'I'll go, but I'm taking her with me.'

'Fine. Did you find it?'

Fergus had stepped in front of the lights. His shadow stretched towards them, tall and thin. He'd abandoned his Barbour jacket for a long raincoat which fell in skirted folds to his ankles, giving him the outline of a Victorian hunter.

Christie's voice was shrill.

'You can't take her from me, Fergus.'

The professor might have been at an overcrowded cocktail party where the hubbub required raised voices. His tones carried sleek and smooth across the grassy divide.

'Don't be silly, Christina.'

Murray shouted, 'What happened to Rachel?'

'Why don't you come and see for yourself? She's in the car.'

He leapt forward, but Christie had him by the arm, her grip tighter than he would have thought possible. She hissed, 'Don't. He's lying.'

Murray shouted, 'Rachel!' But there was no reply. It would have been an easy thing to shake Christie free, but he stalled, hesitating, beside her.

'She's there, I promise you.' Fergus advanced slowly towards them, his arms open, like a TV evangelist ready to embrace the world. 'Let the boy go, Christie. It's nothing to do with him.'

Murray said, 'If you've hurt her, I'll fucking kill you.'

Fergus laughed.

'It's me she loves, Murray, me she married. You were just a diversion. Look at you, crawling around in the mud on an old witch's errand. You're not really Rachel's type.'

374

Christie kept her hand locked on Murray's elbow and hauled herself in front of him.

'She prefers old men who have to watch because they can't manage it themselves any more.'

'Your insults are almost as clichéd as your books.'

Murray heard Christie draw in a deep breath and then another.

'We're old friends, Fergus. Can't we come to some arrangement?'

'Of course.' The professor had taken another slow step forward.

He was like a hunter, right enough, thought Murray. One that wanted to take his prey alive, or maybe simply get close enough to make certain his aim was true.

'Give me the box and I'll make sure she gets a decent burial.'

Her voice was plaintive.

'Why can't I have her?'

'Because you can't be trusted to keep her safe.'

'I'm her mother.'

'And her murderer.'

Christie tightened her grip on Murray's arm and looked up into his eyes.

'He's lying.'

'Come on, Christie.' Fergus's voice was reasonable. 'I don't know what you told young Dr Watson, but I was there, remember? We may be old, but neither of us is senile. You and Bobby used her for your little occult experiment.'

The box was still at Christie's feet. She leaned down and touched it with her fingertips, as if reassuring whatever lay inside of her fidelity.

'You lie.'

'You know I don't.' Fergus was closer now, facing them through a curtain of soft drizzle. 'You didn't just kill her. You killed Archie too.'

'No, he killed himself.'

'Technically I suppose that's true. But we both know he would never have taken that leaky sieve out into a storm if he and I hadn't come back to the island and found a butcher's shop.' Fergus looked at Murray. 'She didn't tell you that did she?'

Murray said, 'She gave me her version of events. Why don't you give me yours?'

Christie spat, 'Do you think he's going to tell you the truth?'

Fergus sounded clear and rational against Christie's passion.

'Lunan and I had got fed up of our country idyll. He'd tried to persuade Christie to come back to the city with us, but she was adamant. The child wasn't due for weeks, so we left her here. I thought she'd come trailing after us as usual. I didn't see how anyone could stomach living alone with Bobby Robb for any length of time. But it seems I underestimated his charms. Lunan couldn't drive, so a fortnight after we'd deserted, he persuaded me to bring him back. His excuse was he'd left his manuscript behind. If he had, it was deliberate.'

Christie started a soft, keening mantra: *'You're lying, you're lying, you're lying, you're lying . . .'*

For the first time Fergus lost his cool.

'I'm not bloody lying, and you know it. Who are you trying to fool? Him?' He pointed at Murray. 'Let's see if he wants to help you after he's heard the truth.'

'You're lying, you're lying, you're lying, you're lying . . .'

Christie continued her chant, and it seemed to Murray that the waving trees and still-falling rain picked up the rhythm of her words and carried it through the glen. Perhaps Fergus thought so too, because he paused for a moment and when he spoke next his voice wavered beneath its calm.

'Archie was a chaotic drunk, but looking back I think he was desperate for that child. Maybe he thought being a father would help put some of his demons to rest. Who knows?' The professor shrugged. 'I had an interest in it too, of course, so I drove and he drank. By the time we reached the ferry, he was insensible. But when we reached the cottage, he'd sobered up enough to take in what had happened. The child had lived its whole life in the time we'd been gone. When you see something like that . . .' His voice trembled. 'It's as if your eyes refuse to let you witness it. We stood on that doorstep staring at Bobby and Christie, sky-clad in the middle of a charnel house. God knows what they'd taken while we'd been in Edinburgh, but all of Bobby Robb's fantasies about purity and sacrifice had been realised. I'm not sure how long we were frozen there, trying to make sense of the scene . . . all that redness . . . Archie understood what had happened first. Suddenly he went wild. I thought he was going to murder them both, me too perhaps. I don't know where I found the strength, but I bundled him out of the cottage. I thought I was preventing another death.' Fergus took a deep breath. 'The rest you know.'

'Why didn't you call the police?'

'Why haven't you?'

It would have taken too long to explain. Murray replied, 'I don't know.'

'I don't know either. Maybe out of pity for Christie. She'd realised what she'd done and was screaming fit to wake the dead. Maybe out of a fear I'd be implicated. After all, it was only my word against theirs that Archie and I were innocent. I knew Bobby Robb well enough to be sure that if he went down, he'd do his best to pull the rest of us into Hell behind him. Whatever the reason, it was a big mistake. I opened myself up to blackmail and nightmares. But I do know I'm damned if I'm going to have the whole thing resurrected.'

Murray could see the fly-blown kitchen, the naked couple leaning over the kitchen table, the baby at its centre. It was too much. He closed his eyes for a moment then asked, 'What did you mean when you said you had an interest in the child as well?'

Fergus was close enough for Murray to see his sad smile.

'Can't you guess?'

Murray nodded.

'I suppose I should have.'

Christie ended her mantra. She shouted, 'If you want her, you're going to have to come and take her.'

Fergus looked at Murray.

'Are you going to stand in my way, Dr Watson?'

'It depends on what you intend to do.'

All this time they had been standing a distance apart, like opposing foes reluctant to fight or flee before they saw each other's weapons. Now Fergus adjusted his cap and started to walk across the grass to parley face-to-face. This was the Fergus Murray recognised: the lecture-theatre showman, darling of the students, despair of the secretaries, the canteen boaster and distinguished scholar, crass enough to pimp his wife, vain enough for a bespoke academic gown.

Murray looked down at his own mud-drenched clothes and knew that whatever the truth of the child's death, and whatever followed next, his career was over. He was too stunned to feel the full impact of the knowledge, but he knew it would come, just as a bereaved man knows his numbness will be replaced by grief. He straightened his back, wanting to walk away and leave them to it, but unwilling to abandon Christie to Fergus's ruthless self-interest.

It was as if his thoughts touched the woman. She stirred and made a noise somewhere between a gasp and a sigh. Murray glanced down at her. Christie's eyes looked huge. She bit her bottom lip, half-smiling. He looked back at the professor making his way across the grass with his usual assurance, not bothering to stick to the beaten path, and suddenly Murray realised what was about to happen. He shoved Christie from him and yelled, 'No, Fergus, stop!' The other man faltered, and for a second Murray thought his warning had been in time. Then the professor fell.

At first it looked as if Fergus had simply lost his footing and skidded backwards onto the mud. But all at once he groaned and began scrabbling for purchase on the slippery ground. The battle was too fast and too desperate for him to cry out again. The only sound was of the wind in the tree-tops and the desperate slap of Fergus's arms and legs flailing in the wet mud as he fought with gravity, like a man showing how it was to drown. Then it was as if something beneath the earth grabbed him tight around his legs and pulled hard, sliding him swiftly and horribly down the unmarked sinkhole and into the below.

Murray started to run forward, but Christie grabbed his ankle and brought him down.

'Do you want to follow him?'

He'd landed beside her and their mud-spattered faces were unbearably close. Murray scrabbled in his pocket and brought out his mobile. She knocked it from his hand.

'He'll be in Hell by now.'

Murray shoved her away. He was beyond speech, beyond thought. He pushed himself up, slipped and cried out in terror of the earth, but it was merely the same mud he had been wallowing in for the last hour. He dropped down onto his hands and knees again and started crawling towards the sinkhole, but he stopped after a few faltering inches, too feared of Fergus's fate to go on.

Murray sat back up onto his hunkers, sobbing as he hadn't in a long while. He saw the glint of his phone, picked it up and hauled himself to his feet. He stood there for a moment. Then he started to stagger away from the cottage, careful to keep to the path.

Christie shouted, 'It was all lies, everything he said, lies.'

Murray set his back to her and followed the curving track to where Fergus's Saab sat, its lights still glaring. He leant in through the car's open door. The vehicle was empty, no sign of Rachel.

Murray turned and looked at Christie. She was lying spot-lit in the mess of mud they had churned up between them, her hands clutching the tin trunk; a savage pietà. There was a rush in his stomach. He bent double and spewed the remnants of Mrs Dunn's cakes onto the ground.

Chapter Thirty-Two

Murray wiped his mouth on the back of his hand. He walked back, helped Christie to her feet as gently as he could manage, and then lifted the long-dead child's coffin onto his shoulder. He carried it silent through the darkness and the sludge, like a doom-laden St Christopher. Christie said nothing beyond a whispered thank-you; merely let herself be gripped around the waist and supported back to her car. The rain had almost stopped, but they were already soaked through and coated in filth. Somewhere a bird hooted. It was a strangely human sound and Murray felt his stomach lurch.

Christie was shivering. He took a tartan travelling rug from the boot, wrapped it around her shoulders and then settled her and his other burden in the back seat. Her hand went to the trunk's hasp and he whispered, 'Please, you promised. Not until you're home.'

Christie nodded and shifted her hand to the lid, where she let it rest.

Murray started the engine. There was no point in questioning whether he was fit to drive. He was fit for nothing. He raised the clutch gently and the car eased forward.

'Thank Christ.'

The dashboard clock glowed 03.45. The whole adventure had lasted less than two hours.

There was no option but to retrace the route they had taken earlier. Murray was shivering too now, his hands so numb he wouldn't have known he was gripping the steering wheel, except for the fact that somehow he was managing to guide the Cherokee round the curves in the road.

The night was still pitch murk. Murray realised he was driving faster than he had on their journey out, but made no effort to cut his speed. Their tyres would leave marks in the mud which, now that the rain had stopped, would not be washed away. There was no helping it. He kept the headlights off, amazed he could still think of his own self-preservation when deep down he cared nothing for it. He glanced at Christie in the rear-view mirror. Her hand was still resting on the box, but her eyes were shut, her skin yellowed, mouth slack.

'Christie?'

She started. 'Where are we?'

'We'll be there soon. Stay with me.'

'Sure.'

The slur in her voice had grown worse, but when he checked her again her eyes were open.

He said, 'You knew Fergus was going to fall down there, didn't you?'

'How could I? The sinkhole wasn't marked.'

'I saw your face. You've lived here for decades. At the very least, you knew there was a danger of it and you didn't warn him.'

There was a shrug to her voice.

382

'He should have kept to the path.'

'Fergus should have kept to the path. Archie should never have gone out in the boat. Men who associate with you seem to become careless.'

Her voice held a challenge.

'In that case perhaps you should be careful.'

'What about Alan Garrett? Should he have been more careful?'

'Obviously. If he had, he wouldn't have smashed himself up against a tree.'

'Did you kill him too?'

'I never killed anyone, except maybe Miranda.'

'Who?'

'My little girl. And that was a sin of omission.'

'Not according to Fergus.'

'He lied.'

'He's not here to contradict you. But even if he did, you appear to be a jinx, a magnet for demisuicides.'

Her tone was scornful.

'A spellbinder.'

'Being called a witch isn't the slander it once was.'

She sighed.

'Dr Garrett was into risk-taking. We talked about it. He was the kind of man who slowed down on the level crossing when the train was coming, who walked to the brink of the cliff in bad weather, the edge of the subway platform during rush hour. Did you know he was a rock-climber?'

'Yes.'

'He'd started climbing freestyle, without ropes. He told me that sometimes he would deliberately take extra risks, go for an unsure hold, let fate have its hand.'

Murray's voice was dry.

'I have been half in love with easeful death, called him soft names in many a mused rhyme.'

'Half in love, half frightened of. Men like that shouldn't get married, but they do. I suppose they want to anchor themselves to something. I met his wife. It amazes me how these sturdy women ally themselves to reckless men.'

'Like you did with Archie?'

'Oh, I was never that robust. If I had been, I would have picked myself up and got on with my life instead of endlessly sorting through the bones.'

It was an unfortunate image, and they both fell silent for a moment. Then Christie said, 'I don't know if he'd ever talked about it before, but it excited him, discussing his obsession with someone who understood. I can picture his death as clearly as if I'd been there. He saw the empty stretch of road, the tree, and put his foot down, giving fate one last chance to let him make the corner or crash.' She snorted. 'It was one chance too many.'

Murray closed his eyes. He felt the urge to press the accelerator to the floor, to test whether she could maintain her glibness as he raced the car onwards into their deaths. But he opened them again, kept his speed level and turned the Cherokee out onto the open track at the edge of the moor.

He could see the windows of Christie's lonely cottage burning brightly in the dark. He supposed it would look beautiful in the summertime, the small white house shining from a midst of green, but tonight it looked like a Halloween lantern, its windows blazing, door glowing like the mouth of Hell. He dropped their speed.

'Christie, did you leave the front door open?'
He heard her rustling upright in the back seat.
'No.'
There was a halo around the building. It rippled gently. Murray glanced at Christie in the mirror again and saw her head silhouetted against the back window, a tuft of hair spiked at a crazy angle.

'Fergus.' Her voice was full of wonder. 'I always knew he'd be the death of me.'

Murray drove on, expecting to hear the sound of sirens, but nothing disturbed the night except the gentle rumble of the Cherokee's engine. He could see the flames now. They had burst beyond the windows and were licking the outside walls of the house. Soon they would begin to consume the roof. They were less than half a mile from the cottage when Christie commanded him to stop.

Murray eased the car to a halt, got out and helped her from the back seat. The interior of the house had seemed full of natural materials—wood, paper and brightly woven rugs—but the fire smelt toxic, as if the whole place had been formed from plastic. Murray started to cough, his eyes teared, but still he stood there, Christie leaning on his arm, both of them watching the flames' progress.

Eventually she said, 'I should have put the photographs and my memoir in the boot of the car.'

He nodded, knowing the answer to his question, but asking it anyway.

'They're all in there?'

'Yes, all your pretty chickens lost at one fell swoop. Fergus always wanted to know if I'd written any of it down. I told him no, but I guess he didn't want to take the chance.'

Her smile was strangely peaceful, as if none of it mattered any more. She turned and lumbered awkwardly towards the car's back seat. Murray moved and helped her in. The mud was beginning to dry on his clothes, stiffening the fabric. He wanted nothing more now than to be gone. He asked, 'What will you do?'

'What I was always going to do.'

It was too much in one night. He looked back towards the burning cottage, expecting to see car headlights racing towards it, half-hoping for the whole sorry mess to be taken from him. But the only brightness came from the flames. They were alone on the dark expanse of moor.

'Why hasn't anyone come?'

'Perhaps they hope I'm inside.'

'Are you really hated that much?'

'Who knows?' She shrugged as if it didn't matter. 'People sleep deeply in the countryside, and I suppose the house isn't overlooked. They would probably come if they knew.'

'You don't have to do this.'

'I want to.'

'It would be better to wait.'

'For what?' She nodded towards the distant house and placed her hand on her daughter's coffin. 'I've lost everything and gained everything. Life seldom achieves such perfect balance.'

'I won't help you.'

'You don't need to. I brought what I needed with me, just in case.'

Murray took a deep breath and walked a few yards into the darkness, wondering if this had always been what she'd intended. He rested his hands on his knees and bent over, fearing that he was going to be sick again. When he returned, she was propped up against the car window with her legs stretched out along the back seat. She'd pulled the blanket up to her neck, and Murray could see that beneath it she was clutching something to her. He was reminded of a woman preserving her privacy with her child's shawl while she breastfed in public.

She gave him a smile that beckoned visions of the girl she'd been, and said, 'I'm sorry. The poems weren't inside Miranda's coffin.'

'Were they ever?'

'I suppose not. It was Fergus who suggested placing them beside her. I thought it was an overly sentimental gesture, but he ran back to the cottage to get them. I guess he didn't follow through.'

Her voice was empty of rancour.

Murray said, 'What really happened?'

She ignored his question.

'There should be a bottle of water in the boot. Will you fetch it for me, please?'

He got it and handed it to her.

'Tell me Fergus made everything up.'

'I already did.'

'Convince me.'

Christie's voice was devoid of emotion.

'Fergus lied. Miranda died of neglect. It's a measure of your own madness that you could even contemplate the possibility I'd make a sacrifice of my own child.'

Murray looked into the dark and then back at the old woman, searching for the truth in her face. Her eyes held the reflection of the burning cottage. Murray said, 'I'm going to go now.'

Christie nodded.

'It's all right. I'm not alone.' She looked up at him. 'Do you think I'll meet them again?'

'Who?'

'All of them. Archie and Bobby.' She hesitated and added, 'Fergus.'

'I don't know. Would you like to?'

'If we could be young again. We had a lot of fun in the early days.' Christie smiled. 'A lot of good times.' She looked at him. 'Maybe you could meet them too.'

'No.'

'I've read all your articles, Dr Watson, everything you ever published. Archie's in every word, even when you're writing of something else, just as he's in your thoughts, even when he's absent. And now you've lost him too.'

'Not completely. There are papers in the library.'

'Who do you think gifted them to the archives? I only gave away worthless doodlings. Enough to tantalise, but too little to tell.' Her voice was soft and comforting. 'Anything of worth went up in flames tonight.' She lifted a hand from beneath the blanket and stroked his mud-smeared fingers. 'Who would miss you? Your wife?'

'No.'

'Family?'

He looked away.

'I thought not.' Christie's voice held the promise of peace. 'I can always tell.'

She took something from her pocket and put it to her lips. Murray made no move to stop her. Christie started to choke. He held the water bottle to her lips. She drank, then raised a vial to her mouth and drank again. The coughing overtook her. He tried clumsily to ease it with more water, but most of it escaped her mouth and ran down her front. Her coughs faded to faint gasps. Murray held her head and pressed the water against her mouth, but Christie had grown limp. He let her sink back against the seat and saw her face flush in the glow of the premature dawn. He stood there for a while gazing at her body, knowing that if he lifted the blanket he might get closer to the truth of the child's death, but unable to bring himself to.

He wasn't sure how long he'd been frozen there when he was roused by the sound of a rook cawing. He turned and saw it treading the edge of the path like an old-world minister on his way to kirk. The crow met his stare and set its beak at a quizzical angle. The bird looked scholarly and demonic, and Murray couldn't chase away the thought that it was Fergus, transformed and returned for his revenge. He rushed at it.

'Go on, away with you.'

The bird flapped its wings and fluttered a yard or two before landing beyond his reach and continuing its perambulations, still fixing him with its dark stare.

Murray slammed the car door, guarding the bodies from the rook's iron beak. He took off his scarf and wiped the handles and steering wheel clean of fingerprints, not sure why he was bothering, except he supposed he didn't want his memory associated with any of it. Then he started to walk across the fields towards Pete's bothy, the rook's caws grating on in his head long after he was out of earshot.

Chapter Thirty-Three

The water bottle was still in his hand when he reached the bothy. Murray looked at it as if unsure how it had got there, and then launched it into a corner. The room was freezing and he fired the Calor heater into life. The flames blazed blue, and then took on an orange glow that made him think again of Christie's cottage. He wondered how long it would burn.

Murray pulled off his jacket and saw the package James had sent him still miraculously jutting from his pocket. He took it out and laid it on the table. One end was scuffed and edged with mud, but otherwise it had weathered the dreadful adventure better than he had. It seemed that paper was more durable than flesh and blood. James had been trying to tell him something, but it didn't matter now. He had got as close to Archie as it was possible to get. All the rest was nothing.

Murray stripped off his clothes and washed outside at the water butt, not bothering about whether he soiled his drinking water. He dried himself in front of the heater, still shivering, then slid his belt from its loops, shoved his filthy clothes in a carrier bag and sealed it. They would tell their own story.

He guessed that Pete would come round at some point to discuss the island's finds. Murray would add to its discoveries. It couldn't be helped. He wondered about writing an account of what had happened, but found he didn't think that he could write; he, who had lived half his life with a pen in his hand.

Murray took the whisky from the shelf where Fergus had placed it and drank a good long swallow straight from the bottle. He started to cough as hard as Christie in her last throes and it was a battle not to splutter the precious spirit across the floor.

Archie had slammed out of the cottage, or maybe he had been slammed from it. Either way the door had crashed in its frame, expelling him from the disaster that lay inside.

Murray remembered the red corduroy notebook he had held in his hands in the National Library all those weeks ago, the list of names:

> *Tamsker*
> *Saffron*
> *Ray—will you be my sunshine?*

What visions had sprung in Archie's mind from Christie's swelling belly? What hopes had he harboured? The poet had been right to let their loss propel him into the waves. Archie had purified himself, accepted his share of blame and escaped the future, the pain, the whole fucking uselessness of living on.

Murray sat naked in front of the fire, his elbows resting on the table, and took another deep draught. He looked up at the hook he had noticed when Pete first showed him the cottage. He supposed it had been used for drying herbs or curing meat.

What had Archie thought of as he walked down to the shore, his hair flying around his face? Had he known death was waiting for him, or had he simply given himself over to the fates in the same way Alan Garrett had? Murray raised the bottle to his mouth again and imagined Archie on the little jetty, freeing the small boat of its moorings then jumping aboard. If his fate had been a throw of the dice between Death and Life-In-Death, surely better that Death should win.

Murray gave the bottle another tilt and slid James's envelope towards him. Fergus's face gazed out in black and white from the book's back cover. He'd been handsome when he was younger, a blond shock of fringe falling across his eyes, every inch the poet. Murray had an idea what lay between the covers, but he let the book fall open and began to read where fate had chosen.

> A moored boat tied tight
> Has more play than you
> Wood and water
> Earth and rope

He worked his way through the rest of the bottle, reading the poems as he went. Each swallow and every word seemed to make him more sober. There were computer programs that could decode vocabulary and syntax to show the truth of his conviction. Perhaps someone would pursue it. Rab Purvis maybe. He took a pen and wrote on the title page: These poems were written by Archie Lunan.

That would be the extent of his biography.

He drank the final dregs in the bottle and sent it across the room. It landed unbroken and rolled until it rested softly against the wall.

If there had been an open fire in the cottage, Murray would have taken his notes and consigned them to the flames. He could have spent an hour ripping them apart instead, then scattered them to the wind, but it would simply be another delay, an empty gesture in a night of weighty deeds.

Instead Murray took his belt from the floor, where he had dropped it. He used the chair as a step and climbed up onto the table, hoping it would take his weight. The belt had been his father's. It was a good one, made from Spanish leather. Originally it had boasted a buckle in the shape of a Native American chief in full headdress. Jack had replaced it with a plain silvered one and given it to Murray. He'd given him the old buckle too, wrapped in an envelope he'd marked *Cowboy Chic*. It was an old joke from when they were teenagers. A long time ago.

Murray slid the belt's tongue through its buckle, not bothering to fasten it. He'd never got round to getting it shortened to fit his waist and he reckoned it would be long enough.

It was better to decide your exit for yourself. You could be a long-legged, wisecracking urban cowboy, good for a laugh or a wise word, and then, quicker than you could credit, an old man unable to recognise the people you held most dear.

The people you had held most dear.

Murray wiped his eyes. He tied the belt around the hook, gripped the collar he'd made and swung on it for a moment. The knot above tightened, the buckle crushed against his hand, a painful flaw in his design.

It would have to do.

Murray stepped back down onto the floor, the cardboard gritty against his bare feet. He dragged the table a little to the left, climbed back up and fitted the makeshift collar around his neck.

It was still dark outside. Somewhere a bird crowed. He thought of the rook pacing the path beside Christie's body, and drew a hand across his face; a moment's courage and then peace.

> Soonest our best men with thee do go,
> Rest of their bones, and soul's delivery.

Murray stepped from the table, seeing Archie's face at the window as he fell. His legs kicked and the noose tightened, belt buckle biting into his neck as he'd known it would. There was a rushing in his ears, an ocean's weight coming towards him, and above it another sound.

Someone—*Archie?*—grabbed his legs and raised him shoulder-high, taking his weight. Murray could feel his assailant's face against his hip, their arms around his knees swinging him back to the table's raft.

'You stupid fucking bastard!'

The voice was loud and frightened and instantly recognisable.

The belt was still around his throat. Murray clawed at his neck, but the noose stayed tight. Jack leapt up on the table beside him and pushed his hands away, trying to ease the buckle loose. Murray could hear him panting and smell the alcohol on his breath. At last he got it free and Murray managed to take one deep whooping lungful of air and then another.

His brother pressed his head against Murray's chest. After a moment Jack pulled away and managed to untie the belt from its hook. He said, 'You better be trying to kill yourself, Minty,

394

because if this is some fucking sex thing, I'll bloody swing for you myself.'

Murray grabbed his brother in a hug. He'd all but lost his voice, but he managed to croak, 'We let him down, Jack. We promised he'd die at home and he didn't. He died on his own in that fucking place.'

'I know he did.' His brother was holding him tight. 'But they'd told us there were days, weeks maybe. Dad knew we were doing our best. He was proud of you, Murray. He loved you. He wouldn't want you to do anything like this. You know that. He'd be fucking furious. Now, come on. Let's get down from here and get you dressed.'

*   *   *

Murray sat at the table, wrapped in his brother's coat. He whispered, 'Are you back with Lyn?'

'No.' Jack went through to the other room and there was a sound of rummaging. He came back and flung a pair of trousers and a jumper at Murray. 'You were right. I was a stupid cunt. Like the song says, you don't miss your water till your well runs dry.' He looked at Murray anxiously as if trying to weigh up his state of mind. 'There's good news, though. You're going to be an uncle.'

'Cressida's pregnant?'

'Christ, I hope not. That's why I came to see you. Lyn's going to have a baby, our baby, and now she won't have anything to do with me.' He raised his brown eyes to Murray's. 'I came to see you because I was fucking depressed.'

Murray thought of the blazing cottage on the moor side, Christie and her child together in the red Cherokee and Fergus's Saab abandoned by the desecrated grave up by the limekilns. He said, 'Jack, I think I might be going to jail.'

Postscript

Glasgow

Chapter Thirty-Four

'I've got two boys, terrific wee fellas. Six and eleven, they are.' Murray was alone in the dark, watching the expression on his father's face switch from eager to anxious. 'I've no seen them in a long while. They telt me they were fine, but how do they know? Have you seen them, son?'

Jack's voice was warm and reassuring.

'I've seen them, they're absolutely fine . . .'

'Aye, well, that's good.' Their dad regained his happy aspect. 'On their holidays, aren't they?'

'That's right.' Murray heard the smile in his brother's voice. 'Away with the BBs.'

Murray leant forward, elbows on knees, chin resting on his clasped hands.

Jack was asking his father if he recognised him and the mischief was back in the old man's face. 'If you don't know, I doubt that I can help you out.'

Up on screen the two men laughed together.

'No idea at all?'

Their father's stare was intense.

'I don't think I know you, son.' He hesitated and a ghost of something that might have been recognition flitted across his face, bringing a smile in its wake. 'Are you yon boy that reads the news?'

Jack said, 'You've rumbled me.' And the old man slapped his knee in glee.

Murray got to his feet. He pushed through the black curtains and out into the brightness of the white-painted gallery. Jack was standing where he had left him, his face anxious.

Murray gave him a sad smile.

'Maybe you can let me have a copy.'

His brother reached into his jacket pocket and pulled out a DVD. Murray took it from him and shook his hand.

*   *   *

Murray wasn't sure how he had got through his first police interview. Jack's roll-neck had covered the marks of the ligature and Murray had blamed the croak in his voice on a cold combined with a night on the batter, but he couldn't imagine that his faltering performance had been convincing. Perhaps it helped that the Oban police were too overwhelmed by the clues they already had to want any more.

The morning had uncovered empty petrol cans in the boot of a distinguished professor's recently abandoned Saab. The professor himself was suspected to be somewhere in the depths of a newly breached sinkhole. There also seemed a probable link between him and the razed cottage no one had seen burn down, and from it to the cottage's owner, dead in her car with a vial of poison at her feet and a baby's disarticulated skeleton beneath the blanket covering her lap.

Murray's story that Christie hadn't answered her door, despite his appointment, appeared to be believed, and his connection with Fergus picked over, but not unkindly. Eventually two detectives from Strathclyde police had called at his Glasgow flat to thank Murray for his cooperation.

If they were surprised by the boxes of Jack's possessions piled in the hallway, or the unmade bed-settee in the sitting room, the officers managed to hide it. The four of them gathered in the small kitchenette. The policemen seemed to occupy twice the space the brothers did, and it was a squeeze. Jack, canny as ever, had stationed himself in the open doorway, leaving the detectives and Murray to squeeze together in the little galley with their backs against the kitchen units.

The officers accepted the offer of a cup of Jack's over-strong coffee. The making and pouring of it proved a palaver, but eventually it was done and they each held a steaming mug in their hands.

The elder of the detectives favoured Murray with a stern smile. 'I've got to say, Dr Watson, your face was in the frame when we found out you and Professor Baine were colleagues, especially once we discovered your relationship with his wife.'

He glanced slyly at Jack, as if checking for his reaction.

Murray said, 'It's all right, I already told my brother.'

'Ah.' the policeman sipped his coffee, grimaced, and set it on the kitchen counter at his back. 'Your brother.' He looked at Jack. 'I gather you were there too?'

Jack gave one of his winning grins.

'My girlfriend had just shown me the door. I was feeling a bit sorry for myself and decided to visit Murray. I ran into a crowd of archaeology students on the boat over, we got talking, had a few drinks together, and then I stumbled down to the But 'n' Ben. The fire at the cottage must have been well under way by then, but sadly my route didn't take me anywhere near it.'

'Aye,' the policeman nodded. 'That's what your statement said.'

The knowledge that their statements had been circulated as far as Glasgow bothered Murray. He asked, 'So what wrapped up the investigation? Or aren't you allowed to say?'

This time it was the younger detective who spoke. His face was impassive, and he might have been talking about a jumped red light or a stolen bicycle.

'DNA samples taken from his house indicate that the baby whose bones Ms Graves was found with were those of a daughter she'd had with Professor Baine.'

'Christ.' Murray wiped a hand across his face. 'So where does that leave things?'

The younger detective shrugged. His tight smile gave away nothing.

'Officially, it's accidental death and suicide. As to what actually happened, your guess is as good as mine.' He levelled his gaze to Murray's. 'Better perhaps.'

The older officer's expression was grim. 'The bottom line is, we're not looking for anyone else in relation to their deaths.'

Murray looked down at his feet, sinking into one of the silences he'd always been prone to, but which seemed to be affecting him more frequently. Jack filled what threatened to become an awkward pause.

'We both appreciate it. Like you say, I guess the whole story will remain a mystery.'

'You never know.' The young detective turned to go. His coffee sat cooling in its cup. 'Cases that have been dead for thirty or forty years can suddenly get resurrected.' He looked at Murray. 'Like old bones.'

The exhibition didn't open until the following day, and they were alone in the small Glasgow gallery except for the curator busy on her laptop at the front desk. The place was less prestigious than the Fruitmarket, but this time it was a solo show, and according to Jack that made it okay.

They walked side by side through the exhibition, their father's face shining from every wall. It was still hard, but Murray found he could look now. The montages devised from photos of their dad when he was young were his favourites; the Glasgow boy superimposed on the American landscapes he'd admired so much. There were even a couple of him with his arms around their mother, the pair of them relocated to a 1950s consumerist utopia. After her death his father had abandoned thoughts of emigration. Strange to think they could have become Americans. Strange too to remember that Jack had never known her, that he didn't even possess the shadowy memories Murray had nurtured.

He asked, 'Did Lyn call you back?'

'Yes.' Jack stared at a line of photographs and he might have been checking they were straight. 'She's going to let me come to the birth. It's a start.'

'The baby isn't due for three months. Maybe things will have moved on by then.'

'Maybe.' Jack didn't look convinced.

'Is she coming tomorrow?'

'I don't think so. Her own opening's at the end of the week, there'll still be things to prepare. It's a

403

while since she's exhibited. She never had time when she was working at that place.' He glanced at Murray. 'Did she send you an invite?'

'I can give it a miss if you like.'

'No, go. Put in a good word for me.'

This was how they were with each other these days—polite, considerate—not like brothers at all, it sometimes seemed. Murray supposed it was a consequence of their sharing his small apartment. There was too much of a danger that in the cramped space their usual banter might descend into acrimony. But it was more than that. They had talked a lot in the weeks after—about their parents, Lyn, Cressida, Murray's strange adventure—and now it seemed there was nothing much left to say. It didn't matter. There was time.

He said, 'Do you fancy a pint?'

'Maybe later, I've still got a few things to do here.' Jack put a hand on Murray's arm and nodded towards the young curator. 'Why don't you ask Aliah? She's big into books and I happened to let slip you're a doctor of English literature.'

'Ach, I don't know, Jack. I'm meeting the university press tomorrow.'

'You don't have to get wellied.'

'All the same, it took a while to set this up.'

Jack shook his head.

'Amazing you can be sure the poems were Lunan's.'

'Surely it's the same with visual art? You can tell who made a work even if they didn't sign it.'

'Nah,' Jack laughed. 'The art world's full of frauds, but most of them take the money and run, unlike your professor. Imagine buying up second-hand editions for all those years, trying to suppress

404

the work in case someone clicked that it belonged to Archie. Does Baine's wife know her husband was a poetry thief?'

'Yes.' Murray looked away. He tried to avoid thinking of Rachel these days.

*   *   *

He'd phoned her at home after his return and been met with the shy English tones of her mother, who'd thanked him for his concern and promised to pass on his condolences. His letter had taken days to write. It said nothing and remained unanswered. It was a Sunday morning in the third week of spring term when Murray noticed that the door to Rachel's office was ajar. He'd hesitated for a beat, then knocked softly and pushed it wide.

For a second he thought the woman filling the cardboard carton with books from the tall shelves that edged the room was Rachel. Then she turned and he saw that although she had the same slight build and gleaming hair, she was a little older, her features different.

'I'm sorry.' There was an apologetic tremor to his voice. 'I thought Dr Houghton might have dropped by.'

The woman glanced towards the gloomy corner where a neglected cheese plant drooped, its wilting leaves blocking the light from the window. Rachel straightened up from behind the desk where she had been crouched, a book destined for the box she was packing still clutched in her hand. She was dressed casually in jeans and a rough-knit sweater that looked several sizes too large. Murray realised it had probably belonged to Fergus.

'Murray.'

Her eyes looked bigger than he remembered. Their lids had a bruised look. The sense of guilt that had shadowed him since the final night on the island took on a darker hue. He stood awkwardly on the threshold, not quite able to bring himself to enter the room.

'I saw your door was open.'

'I'm collecting the last of my stuff.'

The other woman glared at him.

'A car's on its way for us.'

Rachel dropped the book she was holding into a box and said, 'Maybe you could go and check whether it's there, please, Jenny.'

It was more of an order than a request. The older woman paused. For a moment Murray thought she was about to refuse, but then she let out a sigh and pushed past him without a word.

Rachel said, 'You may as well shut the door. Who knows who else might be lurking here on a Sunday morning.'

Murray closed it gently, hearing the soft click of the latch as it sank home.

'Maybe the rest of the department have a life.'

Rachel turned away, lifting more books from the shelf and fitting them neatly into the box.

'Thanks for your letter. I'm sorry I didn't get time to answer it.'

'No one mentioned you were leaving.'

'No, I'm afraid I've been a bit indecisive lately. I only posted my resignation today.'

Murray nodded, not daring to speak for a moment, then asked, 'Where will you go?'

'My sister has a house near Fontainebleau. She and her husband have persuaded me to stay with them for a while.'

Her voice was devoid of inflection. It gave her words a vague, robotic quality.

'Will you come back?'

'To Glasgow?' Her eyes met his for a moment. 'I doubt it.'

He wanted to ask if he could write to her, but instead said, 'How are you?'

'As well as can be expected.'

'I'm sorry.'

'Yes, everyone is. It was a great loss. To me, if not to literature.'

Once again the flatness in her voice rendered everything insincere. He watched as she added more volumes to the box, then said, 'I was on Lismore at the same time as Fergus.'

He waited for Rachel to ask what had happened, unsure of what he would tell her. But she merely nodded.

'I was going to leave him. I told him before he left for the island. The photographs he sent you were the last straw. Well,' she gave a small smile, 'not the photos themselves, the fact that he sent them to you.'

'He never mentioned you were leaving.'

'Why would he?' Rachel slid another stack of books from the shelf and set them in the box at her feet. She turned back to Murray. 'I couldn't help wondering if it had anything to do with what happened.'

He felt stupidly out of his depth, standing by the door, his ears straining for the return of her sister.

'What?'

'The fact that I was going to leave him. You

knew Fergus. He wasn't a clumsy man. He was graceful, cautious despite his recklessness.'

'Fergus was the least suicidal person I can think of.'

'Perhaps. But he was distracted. Maybe, just for a moment, he forgot to be careful.'

'I was told you'd tried to kill yourself.'

'Did you believe it?'

Murray nodded, and for the first time Rachel's voice took on some colour.

'You should have known better. I may occasionally be unwise, but I'm rarely stupid.'

Murray faltered. The door behind him opened and Rachel's sister said, 'Ralph's downstairs, parking the van.'

Murray asked, 'Can I help?'

'No.' Her voice was curt. 'We'll manage, thank you.'

He turned to go, but Rachel called him back.

'Murray, remember—take good care of yourself.'

'You too.' He gave her a last smile and stepped back into the familiar darkness of the department corridor.

*   *   *

Jack said, 'You did what you set out to do. You resurrected Archie Lunan. Two posthumous books in the same year, that's bound to make a splash. Remember you said you'd let me have a look at the sci-fi novel as soon as you'd made a copy.'

'Sure. Shall I photocopy the poems for you too?'

Jack shrugged. 'If you like.'

It was the answer he'd anticipated, and Murray smiled in spite of himself.

Christie had dismissed the science-fiction novel Archie had been writing as worthless, but the poet's apocalyptic vision might yet turn out to be a classic of the genre, with the potential to attract more readers than the poems ever would.

His brother was still talking. 'I guess if this poetry collection's as good as you say, people will take another look at his early stuff.'

Murray shrugged. 'What does it matter who wrote the poems? It's the work that counts, right? The art, not the artist.'

Jack laughed. 'I'm not sure I can agree with you on that one.'

He raised his hand in a wave and walked swiftly towards the reception desk where the curator sat, her long hair falling across her profile like a black satin curtain. 'Aliah, this is my brother Murray, who I was telling you about. He's the clever one in the family.'

The woman looked up from her computer, her brown eyes dubious behind her stylish spectacles.

'Really?'

Murray put a smile on his face and walked towards her. The smile was forced, everything was forced, but for the moment that was just how it had to be.

Acknowledgements

The author would like to thank the Internationales Künstlerhaus, Villa Concordia, Bamberg, and the Civitella Ranieri Foundation for their hospitality and support during the writing of this book.

Lismore is a beautiful island, rich in wildlife and archaeology, situated in Loch Linnhe on the west coast of Scotland. The islanders are friendly, the B&B is well kept and welcoming. For more details, go to www.isleoflismore.com